T0278606

GITA DESAI IS NOT HERE TO SHUT UP

SONIA PATEL

DIAL BOOKS

For survivors

DIAL BOOKS

An imprint of Penguin Random House LLC, New York

First published in the United States of America by Dial Books,
an imprint of Penguin Random House LLC, 2024
Copyright © 2024 by Sonia Patel

Visit us online at PenguinRandomHouse.com.

Library of Congress Cataloging-in-Publication Data is available.

Printed in the United States of America
ISBN 9780593463185 | 1 3 5 7 9 10 8 6 4 2
BVG
Design by Jason Henry | Text set in Calluna

She is still a prisoner of her childhood;
attempting to create a new life,
she reencounters the trauma.

—Judith Herman, MD

PROLOGUE

*L*et's set the scene: Move-in day at Stanford, fall of 1992, and I've just found out that I'm one of the few freshmen to score big-time with a dorm room all to myself! Does the English language even have a word to describe this feeling of beyond ecstatic? (Answer: Probably not—not that I know of, anyway.)

Hauling the black garbage bags and cardboard boxes of my stuff from our car to my single doesn't take long with my parents and older brother, Sai, helping me. We finish lickety-split, and then my family starts unpacking.

"Don't worry about that," I say, gently tugging my medical dictionary and human anatomy book out of Sai's hands and setting them on the desk. "I'll finish putting everything away—I know the donuts aren't going to sell themselves."

Back in 1980, my Gujarati-Indian immigrant parents opened a Donutburg—just one of many Donutburgs dotting the California coastline—in Union City. They kept costs down by operating the entire business themselves, and to this day, it's still all in the family.

Dad immediately lets go of the flaps on the box with my bedding and towels and nods. In a thick Gujju accent, he says, "Unfortunately, that is true, Gita beta. We should be going."

Behind Dad's back, Sai rolls his eyes, then smiles and sticks out his arms. "Bring it in, sis."

I wrap my arms around him and hold on tightly as he gives me a giant bear hug. Meanwhile, Mom squeezes my shoulder, and Dad lays his hand on my back. When we release, I give them each a grateful half smile. "Thanks for everything," I tell them, fully intending to be upbeat, then horrified that I can feel tears in my eyes.

"Oh—one more thing, beta!" Mom says suddenly, and bile rises in my throat. The excitement in her voice shatters the sweet familial moment between us, because I'm certain that she's about to remind me—for the third time since we drove away from our Union City apartment at sunrise—that my arranged marriage dharma isn't expunged, only delayed until I graduate from Stanford. As the daughter of strict Gujarati parents, it's my duty to accept an arranged marriage to a suitable Chha-Gaam—six village—Gujju guy *they* select for *me*. Chee.

Chee: To get the full experience of this Gujarati word that literally means "shit" but colloquially means "gross," say it while drawing your face back in disgust and curling your upper lip, then after, poke your tongue out a little.

Chee, chee, chee. To both the arranged marriage and the hairy dude who'll probably want me barefoot and pregnant in the kitchen, making him dal-bhaat-shaak-rotli. Did I mention I can't cook?

Much to my relief, though, Mom doesn't bring it up again. Instead, she holds out a plastic grocery bag with *India Spice Bazaar* printed on one side. Swallowing, I take the bag and check out the contents.

My mouth starts watering at the sweet and savory packages of Gujarati love—burfi, magas, methi khakhra, and chevdo. I look at Mom, eyes wide. "Thanks."

"Welcome," she says, then grins.

"Share it with the friends you make," Dad chimes in. Then he smiles too.

I stand there, tugging my ear and staring at them as if they've suddenly opened their third eyes all Shiva-like.

My parents never smile. Well, hardly ever that I can remember. Sure, Sai's told me stories otherwise—like the time he and Dad shared laughs after my bhai's first botched attempt at parallel parking. Or when Mom used to grin and stroke Sai's hair while he sipped on the mug of cha she'd make for him every day after school. Or their proud parental smiles when he won the national science fair at age fourteen.

Back in the homeland, Mom and Dad gave away smiles like kaju katri on Diwali. I know because a year ago, I found a box of my parents' old Polaroids in the hall closet. I sat there, clutching the photos against my heart, overcome, as if I'd discovered an ancient, illustrated Hindu book entitled *Raj and Tanu Desai Left Their Best Smiles and Extended Family Behind in India*. I felt my smile bloom as I studied the photos the way I studied flashcards. . . .

A sweaty Dad and his friends taking a break from cricket, sharing grins and beers.

A beaming Mom decked out in a silver, gold, and black channia chori, in full dandiya raas ecstasy with her cousins.

Mom flashing a toothy smile as she and my grandma pick tiny pebbles and other debris out of large stainless steel thalis of split mung beans.

Giddy-faced Dad taking Mom for a ride on the back of his scooter through the crowded, littered streets of Gujarat.

But I didn't get those parents. I got the work-is-always-busy-therefore-no-time-for-smiles parents whose primary form of communication with their two children—mostly me, though—involved muttering, growling, or yelling, "chup-re!"

Chup-re: The Gujarati expression for "be quiet." But depending on the tone, volume, and coinciding facial expression with which it's delivered, it can also sound more like, "SHUT UP!"

Growing up, Sai occasionally tossed a chup-re my way. But when he said it, it wasn't layered in disgust. Quite the opposite—it was playful. Or protective. Come to think of it, the same was true when Pinky Auntie or Neil Uncle said it to me.

4

Pinky Auntie and Neil Uncle left Gujarat and moved in with us for a couple of years when I was six. Like my parents, their plan was to try to make it in America. But even more than the opportunity to work better jobs, save up enough to afford living on their own in the Bay Area, and eventually thrive, the essence of their coming-to-America story was necessity: They'd eloped.

When Sai—who was twelve at the time—told me that, I'd scratched my head. "Sai bhai, what kind of bad crime is 'eloped'?"

"Chup-re." The corners of Sai's lips ticked up and he flicked my arm, a little harder than intended. "It isn't bad or a crime. It means they ran off to get married in secret."

I pouted at Sai and rubbed my arm. Why wasn't Mom and Dad's marriage a secret but Pinky Auntie and Neil Uncle's was? Only later, when I learned that Pinky Auntie and Neil Uncle had met and fallen in love in school, but their families had forbidden them from marrying, did I understand why their "love marriage" had been secret. Mom and Dad, on the other hand, hadn't even known each other before their marriage, because it had been arranged in Gujarati-Chha-Gaam tradition by their parents, and was therefore highly approved of.

None of that mattered though. I loved Pinky Auntie and Neil Uncle: Especially Pinky Auntie, who I thought was the most beautiful, kind, smart woman in the world. With her broad, closed-mouth smile, affectionate gaze, and lovely nose adorned with a small gold nath, she was even more beautiful than that Bollywood star Sai was gaga over—Rekha. And in my eyes,

Pinky Auntie was smarter and kinder than any of the characters Rekha played on the big screen.

Put simply—I worshipped my dear Pinky Auntie.

This one time, after she and I finished playing Candy Land, I tapped her glinting nose ring and asked if I could get one. I'll never forget what she said:

"Of course! Only, wait a little. My nose ring honors Parvati, the goddess of marriage, and she wouldn't want you to get married so young."

I sat up in excitement. "Yes! I'm going to become a doctor first, right, Pinky Auntie?"

Back then, Pinky Auntie was the only one I'd revealed my future career plan to.

It surprised me when she had paused to check over her shoulder before pressing her index finger to her maroon-painted lips. "Shhhh," she whispered. "Don't let your parents find out about that."

My eyes widened. "Why not?"

"Because they want you to marry a doctor, not become one. So chup-re, Gita beta."

I hesitated. An unusual, uncomfortable silence descended around us.

Finally, after a beat: "Okay, Pinky Auntie," I said slowly, nodding. And with that, I sealed my lips, locking away my secret.

CHAPTER 1

*T*his virgin Gujju girl just got her cherry popped—optical cherry, that is. Forget the naked flesh I've seen on the glossy color pages of my human anatomy book or on a twenty-seven-inch Panasonic; I'm talking about a real life, down and dirty, deflowering of my eyes. And while everyone and their mothers are premed at Stanford, I—for one—am suddenly less boring. The next time I meet someone new, I'll be wearing a sly half smile as we shake hands: "Hello, I'm Gita Desai, a frosh premed by day and voyeur by night. How do you do?"

But just as I'm starting to enjoy this little fantasy, my stomach drops. *How could I?*

Reality hits me like Mom's thappada against my cheek—Less than twenty-four hours into attending the university of my dreams, I'm already a Freudian-level case study. Fantastic.

Face-palm and sigh.

How did it come to this?

My thoughts rewind to late this afternoon, in the minutes before the sweeping entrance of the girl now living in the dorm room—also a single—directly across from mine, Jane West.

I'm arranging my CD collection in alphabetical order by artist. When I get to *J* and trace the hard plastic edge of the Jesus Jones CD, I feel a spark against my fingertips, leaving me no choice. I drop the disc into my boom box and skip to "Right Here, Right Now."

The ebullient music bursts out of the speakers. I close my eyes, picturing myself as one of the three hundred Stanforders being led by the Black Student Union from campus to the Palo Alto police station in protest of the Rodney King verdict. I'd read about it in the paper: *Fists and signs raised high—"No Justice in AmeriKKKa for Black People," "People's verdict: LAPD guilty," "Same Shit Different Year," "Down with the Racist Attacks Against Black People"—we're chanting our indignation over the acquittal of the police officers who'd savagely beaten Mr. King . . .*

I open my eyes, sad and angry and ready to change the world.

That's when Jane, the blond-haired beauty in a little black dress, saunters into her room, a cell phone glued to her ear.

First of all, the only people I know who have cell phones are adult-adults—my parents, Sai, and some teachers at Union City High. Not me.

I stop organizing my CDs.

Second of all, I'm starstruck. This girl is Hollywood-level

gorgeous. She probably has more boyfriends than I have A+'s. Why does she even need college?

My stomach pretzels as I realize how eerily similar those thoughts sound to what I overheard my mom say a month ago—albeit in mostly Gujarati—over the phone to her friend Shilpa Auntie: "Shabash! One look at your beautiful Tinu's photo and ten wealthy Gujju men want to marry her. Why does she even need college?" A pause, then: "You know what I told Gita—forget the BS degree! 'BS' for 'bull' and 'shit' if you ask me. . . ."

I'd cringed—I hated Mom's suggestion that college was less important for a girl than marriage. That Mom equated Tinu's worth with being beautiful and wanted by men.

Now I take in Jane with fresh eyes as she plucks a magazine out of her Louis Vuitton purse—*The Economist*—and flips it open, still on her cell phone. "Yes, I read it," she says. "Très intéressant."

Impressive. My imagination skyrockets. Jane is the modern-day Renaissance girl, well-rounded in intelligence, charisma, and beauty. I picture her waving to a cheering throng of her subjects from the top of Stanford's red-domed Hoover Tower at sunset, a gradient of purple-pink sky behind her.

"Je te parler plus tard, chérie," Jane says—smoky yet commanding—then hangs up. She turns to face me, sliding her oversized sunglasses onto her head and looks me up and down. I surreptitiously adjust my MTV T-shirt over my baggy jeans, both dusty from the long day of moving.

Before I can say anything, Jane sashays toward me. "I like your outfit." She nods approvingly at me, then holds out her hand. "I'm Jane. Jane West."

I touch my neck, mesmerized by her name—it sounds like something straight out of a film noir. Three thoughts collide in my brain at once:

First—Jane West's initial impression of me, surprisingly, seems positive.

Second—Jane West is obviously unaware of the existence of insecurity.

And third—I've suddenly become the embodiment of it. I swear I can feel the seed of self-doubt pushing gnarled shoots through my innards.

My words cower like unworthy minions at the back of my throat. That, and with the way she's holding out her hand, I'm not sure if I'm supposed to shake or kiss it.

Deciding on a shake, I wipe my sweaty palm on my jeans before reaching out. "I-I'm Gita, Gita Desai," I stutter. As hard as I try, I can't peel my eyes off Jane. I've never met anyone so, so . . .

Jane lifts an eyebrow.

Crap! Does she think I'm a gawking weirdo? Panic yanks my gaze to the floor. I swallow my lower-class status the way I once swallowed gau jal (a soft drink made from cow urine, of all things, though it didn't actually taste terrible) on a dare from Sai.

"How do you like my nose?" I hear Jane say.

I lift my eyes again, unsure if I've heard her correctly.

Jane stands there, pointing toward the slightly upturned tip in the middle of her face.

". . . Nice?" I reply. It is nice—but even if it wasn't, what else am I supposed to say?

Jane doesn't respond. She adjusts her purse strap dangling from the crook of her elbow, her large blue eyes unblinking.

It's only a few seconds, but it feels like she's been giving me the silent treatment for hours. Did I insult her? A thin layer of sweat seeps out of my pores. Is she waiting for me to sing more praises about her nose? *Your nose is small and straight-edged perfection compared to the tuberous potato in the middle of my face.* Yeah, that could work—poetic and funny. I open my mouth—

Jane smiles, her eyes sparkling like the open ocean. "Thank you, Gita. I just had it done last month."

I shut my mouth, relieved to have said the right thing, and a tiny smile surfaces to my lips.

"Well." Jane throws her thumb over her shoulder toward her room. "Looks like I need to catch up." And with that, Her Highness crosses the hall and over the threshold to her royal chambers, where her mountain of luggage is already waiting.

I stand in my doorway, fidgeting. Is Jane's nose job medical or cosmetic? I'm leaning toward cosmetic because, you know . . . royalty.

After a moment, I whisk around and get back to organizing my CDs.

But not twenty minutes later, her luggage half-unpacked, Jane glides into my room without knocking or waiting to be invited in. "I'm bored," she says, flopping onto my extra-large fuzzy beanbag and lifting my teddy bear, Snuffles. Both gifts from Sai: the beanbag for my graduation, Snuffles for my sixth birthday.

Jane hugs Snuffles the way I used to hug Sai, with Snuffles in the middle. I'd release my brother and then, thrusting Snuffles over my head, run around in circles like a puppy chasing her tail, scream-singing, "SNUFFLES HUG SANDWICHES ARE THE BEST, BETTER THAN THE REST!"

"CHUP-RE!" one of our parents would roar, if they were home.

Jane pats Snuffles's squat body. "How adorable is he?" Then she clears her throat and sets him down beside her. "Gita, do you want to hear a story?" Jane watches me over steepled fingers, French tips tap-tap-tapping.

Still processing the sudden appearance of Jane in my room, I nod slowly and lower myself to the floor in front of her, as if she's the Buddha and I'm her most faithful disciple.

Jane opens her mouth and begins recounting a sophisticated fairy-tale autobiography. She speaks confidently, evenly, in a way that makes it clear she's used to people hanging on to her every word. The CliffsNotes version of her history: She's French and British, born in London but raised in Manhattan since age two—hence the American accent—and fluent in French and

Italian. Her father, a big-time Broadway director and producer, bought her brand-new college gear—a red convertible Jag, a Louis Vuitton trunk full of designer clothes, a fancy bike. She's an econ major with big plans she says she'll "reveal on a rainy day."

How can I not be completely intrigued? Intimidated, even. She's the first immigrant I've met who's blessed with everything: triple-threat power (beauty, brains, charisma) *and* Daddy's wealth.

When Jane's finished, she sits back and nods once as if to say, *You may proceed now with your commoner's tale.*

My eyes drop to my hands, fiddling in my lap. Chup-re tries to gag me, but I manage to pry my lips apart. "Um . . . My parents immigrated from Gujarat . . . that's a state in India," I say, then pause. "My brother—Sai—he and I were born in Union City. First ones to be born in America on both sides of the family. We've lived in Union City our whole lives." Another pause. "My family owns a Donutburg."

Thus ends my short—decidedly *not* sophisticated, nor fantastical—life story.

Not that there isn't anything else to tell. But chup-re seals up all other facts about me and my family into my head's pretend safe-deposit box, the way Mom locks aways our passports and gold and diamond jewelry in a real one at the bank.

I don't tell Jane how much my parents would have preferred I let them arrange a marriage for me right after high school, rather than attend college. I don't tell her that they and Sai share a rusty Toyota to get them between our apartment and Donutburg. I keep my mouth shut about the old bike Sai found and fixed up for me—it gets me from point A to point B and that's what matters. As far as a trunk full of designer clothes, I think my sales-rack outfit speaks for itself.

Still, Jane clasps her hands over her knees and listens attentively to the few details I do give her. I watch her face carefully as I talk, but her countenance remains neutral.

A good sign, I figure.

"Also, I'm pre-mad." I blurt, then cringe. "I mean, premed."

Jane smiles. "You're funny, Gita Desai. I've been missing funny in my life."

I blink. *I am? You have?*

She looks to her left, staring at my CDs for a second. Then she stands, saying, "I'll let you finish unpacking," before flouncing back to her room.

Thus begins our next round of room prep, both of us keeping our doors open. At some point, I look up from folding my clothes: Jane has finished organizing her room and is running her fingers over the spines of her own CDs. A few seconds later, the aggressive, distorted guitar riff at the start of "Zoo Station" from U2's *Achtung Baby* erupts from her boom box.

Goose bumps spangle my body.

I love U2. I have all of their CDs, bought used, like the rest of my collection and half my clothes. Unlike me, U2 isn't afraid to put it all out there, especially about protesting atrocity. "Sunday Bloody Sunday" is my favorite of theirs: In all of its anti-terrorism glory, the song is everything I wish I could be. Defiant. Pissed off. Loud.

So Jane also likes U2—*interesting*. Maybe, I dare to think, freshman year is off to a magnificent start.

Later that night, Jane shows up at my door wearing the expression of a kid about to tear open an exquisitely wrapped present. "There's a Sigma Nu party. Come with."

She *wants* me *to accompany her?*

Jane grabs my hand. "Come on, Gita-the-hilarious, let's have fun!"

I can't believe my ears. For a millisecond, her flattery almost persuades me. . . . Until I remember tomorrow's detailed schedule, which I've already committed to an all-caps list, printed in bloodred ink. Which means it's legally binding, according to Gita-law.

"Sorry, but it's my bedtime." I gently pull my fingers from hers. "Thanks for the invite, though." Then I clasp my hands behind my back and swallow my lips so I don't grab her shoulders, shake her, and shout, "You won't retain any knowledge from your classes tomorrow without a solid eight hours of uninterrupted sleep!"

"Your loss." Jane shrugs, then smiles at me. "See you later, Gita."

I smile too. "See you," I say, waving goodbye before closing my door.

The numbers on my clock blaze a bright red: 9:00 p.m: an ideal bedtime for success the next day. I climb onto the top bunk and curl up all comfy and cozy, like an innocent kitten smiling and purring softly.

Vivid images of my perfect first Stanford day lull me into a blissful slumber. . . .

. . . The elegant welcome of over one hundred towering palms along the iconic Palm Drive. The vast grassy Oval buzzing with sweaty students in the middle of ultimate Frisbee and Hacky Sack. A sun-drenched view of the Quad and Memorial Church, with their red tile roofs and buff sandstone walls. Finding out I nabbed a coveted work-study lab position with the world-renowned plant geneticist Dr. Eleanor Peters. The friendly hellos from dorm neighbors and RAs, and keeping our doors open . . .

Suddenly, REM sleep plucks me off the campus, dropping me smack in the middle of a joyous crowd in Ahmedabad—or is it Surat?—during a colorful Holi celebration. I turn my head, and a thousand firecrackers explode in my face. Cackling people chug bhang and smear me with cow dung instead of the usual powdered colors—

I bolt up, rubbing my eyes open. It takes me a couple of seconds to get my bearings.

I check under the covers, then huff out a sigh of relief: I

haven't pissed myself, the way I used to do as a kid after bad dreams. Luckily for me, my perpetually exhausted parents never found out about those episodes; Pinky Auntie always helped me quietly clean everything up.

A pang in my chest. *My dear, dear Pinky Auntie . . .*

Abruptly, I realize music has been blasting from the hallway this whole time: AC/DC's "You Shook Me All Night Long." Maybe it was the song that woke me up.

I check my clock: midnight. My heart sprints the way it did at the state cross-country championship finish line last fall, when I missed second place by four seconds. Have others on the floor been rudely awakened as well? Should I march out there and demand they turn it down?

What if they tell me to take a hike? What if they laugh in my face? But I've handled awkward situations as high school student body president. This non-presidential matter should be easy.

Plus, I have to be up at 5:00 a.m. for my run so that I can be showered, breakfast-ed, and ready to get ahead on reading by 6:30. Don't these people realize they're ruining my strict schedule?

I need my schedule.

I *need* to be the brightest star in the Stanford universe.

Another AC/DC song blares: "Have a Drink on Me." I groan— is someone drinking? Don't they know that alcohol will mess up however many or few stages of sleep cycle they manage to get tonight? How can some of the smartest kids in the country be so ignorant?

Irritated, I flip onto my belly, then my side. I lay there, staring at the little particles floating in the moonlight.

The song gets louder.

That's it. I kick off the covers, climb down the ladder, and fling my door open, ready to chup-re the hell out of my rowdy neighbors.

I survey the hallway: Gathered by a boom box and an open door are some freshmen nursing beers and chit-chatting. One of the guys is waving around the latest *Vogue* that features the one and only Marisol Walter on the cover. He points at her photo, then proceeds to make out with it.

I shake my head, recalling how, earlier today, some guy in the cafeteria was staring at the same glossy magazine while trying to get a forkful of mac-'n'-cheese into his mouth. To his credit, Marisol was a vision in a body-hugging, long-sleeve silk gown. *Model Marisol Walter, Thai-Black-Peruvian-German Goddess for the Ages!* the headline exclaimed. With his eyes glued to her photo mac-'n'-cheese guy's hand-eye coordination regressed back to infancy: he kept forking his cheek.

Dumbass, I thought, immediately followed by: *Not that I want someone to accidentally mutilate themself over me. But if Marisol is the gold standard, then I might need that arranged marriage after all.*

Back in the hallway, two of the freshmen clink beer bottles together, laughing.

I take a tentative step toward them before laughter from

Jane's room snaps my head back. Her door is open a crack, and a guy's voice drifts out. "Of course you're the only one."

The only one of what? I tiptoe toward her door, reaching for the knob to shut it, when he continues:

"West. The hottest thing I've ever seen."

My hand stops.

"Don't know why I bothered getting dressed," he murmurs.

I tug at the turtleneck collar of my pajama top, convinced that someone has cranked up the heat. The guy's words roll around in my mind as I creep forward, peeking in.

Jane and some curly blond-haired guy wearing a Sigma Nu shirt stand in the middle of her room, drenched in moonlight. Sigma Nu boy flashes her a devious smile, then the two of them start making out. My eyes widen as I realize that besides the smudged mascara and lipstick she's wearing, Jane is completely nude!

Sigma Nu boy takes a quick kissing break to get out of his shirt and shorts. In nothing but his boxer-briefs, he reminds me of Marky Mark in that Calvin Klein underwear ad—glistening washboard abs, a baby face, an incredible smile, the bulge of his package. . . .

Sigma Nu boy grabs a can—beer!—off the desk and takes a swig. Then he burps with his chin tucked and mouth wide open, the same way Neil Uncle used to do when he and his best friend Bhavin drank at our apartment.

Bhavin Uncle isn't actually related to us, but he practically lived with us the two years Neil Uncle and Pinky Auntie did. See, after the engagement for Bhavin Uncle's upcoming arranged marriage fell apart, so did he. At least, that's what Sai and I once overheard our parents say in hushed tones. Mom and Dad apparently took pity on "how lonely" Bhavin Uncle seemed and gave him the spare key he asked for.

Was he lonely? Was that why he sometimes got wasted while Neil Uncle didn't?

Is Sigma Nu boy wasted? Is Jane wasted? What does it feel like to be wasted? I've never touched alcohol, or drugs. Not even cigarettes.

Sigma Nu boy takes off his boxer-briefs.

My eyes dart to the ceiling. I mean, I'm not *trying* to see either of them naked.

"I love this song," Jane whispers.

I can't help it—my ear twists closer to the door. It's Chris Isaak's "Wicked Game." *The perfect soundtrack for this,* I think.

I may be a virgin, but I'm not naive.

I am, however, a solid statue, the way I've been many times before at home. After all, it isn't new for me to witness something forbidden. Like the time Pinky Auntie and Bhav—

My thoughts cut themselves off like patang strings during Uttarayan. Jane starts swaying to the sultry beat.

Sigma Nu boy can't seem to resist the living, breathing, dancing hourglass in front of him. He pounces on her faster than a jungle cat on unsuspecting prey. He pushes Jane against the wall, holding her hands above her head. His lips devour hers.

My lips part slightly, while my mind races. What's wrong with me? Why am I still watching? I should be closing Jane's door.

I reach out again for the knob when Sigma Nu boy pries his mouth off Jane and pants, "Round two."

What does that mean? Have they gone all the way once already?

I've never done any part of any round—not even kissing. Boys never noticed me in high school. Not that I cared: I mean, being single *and* celibate is probably what led to me being top of my class. So why is a sense of inadequacy needling me now? My parents' six-word lecture on the birds and the bees— *hanky-panky is forbidden until after marriage*—echoes in my mind.

My other hand still rests on my turtleneck collar. I slip a finger under the fabric to check my carotid pulse—slightly elevated.

Jane moans as Sigma Nu boy's hands roam over her boobs. With his shirt off, his broad back ripples. Is he a swimmer?

He kisses his way down, down, down. Then his face is in her crotch.

My yoni tingles. My head gets cloudy. I make myself shut my eyes, but they're greedy, fluttering back open.

Watching this is so wrong. Besides not brushing my teeth

before bed once, being too loud a few times according to the grown-ups, and getting into Mom's makeup and nail polish as a kid, I haven't done anything else wrong. I've never stolen or cheated. I've never been cruel to anyone.

Wait! There *was* that summer after eighth grade—when I'd accidentally watched a porno at my neighbor Cindy's house, before she and her family moved to the East Coast.

Her parents hadn't been home, and she'd invited me over to make brownies. We took the brownies out of the oven, setting them on the counter to cool. Then we searched her father's VHS collection of Hollywood blockbusters for something to watch. Hidden in the bottom row of tapes was one labeled *Dirty Western*. Cindy plucked it out, the two of us exchanging inquisitive glances as she popped it into the player.

The brownies cooled.

I couldn't take my eyes off the naked bodies licking, sucking, grinding, and thrusting on the screen. I also couldn't stop eating the brownies—the oh-so-rich-and-moist brownies—once Cindy and I remembered their existence.

Ever since then, whenever I bite into a brownie, the image of Foxy Felicity sexy-saying "fuck me" while riding Bronco Bill gets stuck in my head. . . .

"So good," Jane mumbles now, her eyes closed. A satisfied smile spreads across her face.

Sigma Nu boy looks up at her, sporting a cunning smile. "You like that, huh?" he asks, his voice self-assured, even at a whisper.

With her eyes still shut, Jane bites the corner of her lower lip and nods.

Sigma Nu boy stands up. He totters for a second, the moon shining a spotlight on his muscular, creamy white butt. Then he turns around and walks toward his cargo shorts that lie crumpled on the floor. I catch a glimpse of his stiff junk before he bends down to get something out of one of the pockets.

For a fleeting moment, I hear the *whump* sound of spinning fan blades.

I blink, then mash my lips together to chup-re the gasp of seeing my first real-life dick. I can't help but feel a little sorry for Sigma Nu boy—it must suck to have to walk around with all that ugly dangle between his legs.

Jane catwalks her naked body to him, gives him a seductive half smile, then stretches out on the white sheepskin throw rug in the middle of her room.

I hold my breath, my eyes and ears perked.

The condom package Sigma Nu boy is holding makes a crinkling sound as he tears it open.

At least he won't give Jane HIV, or vice versa, I think. Though I wonder if they know that HIV can also be transmitted in non-sexual ways through blood or certain other bodily fluids. Then I find myself hoping they don't believe any of the false AIDS rumors, like "Only gay people get AIDS" or "The government developed AIDS to kill off people of color and gays. . . ."

Sigma Nu boy unrolls the latex. I swear the moon shifts at

that exact moment, splashing light onto his face. Suddenly, he glances toward the door, his blue-green eyes hitting an unanticipated target—my dilated pupils.

I inhale sharply. Freeze.

A weird grin stretches across his face. No boy, let alone an Adonis, has *ever* smiled at me like that.

My thoughts sputter. My yoni tingles again.

Sigma Nu boy blinks. His eyes change from wild and blazing to cold and calculating. *The jungle cat has cornered another prey.*

He presses his index finger to his lips, the way my parents did when they demanded chup-re, the way Pinky Auntie and Neil Uncle also did, the way—

I become putty.

Putty doesn't move unless other hands make it.

I don't move.

Putty doesn't think for itself.

I go blank.

The next thing I know, Sigma Nu boy is down on the ground and on top of Jane, thrusting.

I get wet. My heart is hammering, trying to break out of my chest. I start sweating as I feel my lips move. "Fuck me," I sexy-whisper in a Foxy Felicity voice.

That's when I catch sight of the clock on Jane's desk: 12:32 a.m., September 1. I turned eighteen thirty-two minutes ago, I realize. The jaunty tune to "Happy Birthday" spins around and around in my head.

CHAPTER 2

Indian instrumental flute music sets a temple mood in my dorm room, as does the agarbatti exhaling wisps of jasmine-scented smoke. The delicate cords of rain streaking the window outside add to the meditative, dreamy atmosphere, and I get lost in a reverie.

Hippocrates, the ancient Greek "father of medicine," is instructing me on wound care. My human biology notebook transforms into one of his treatises. Carefully, I turn the crumbling page inked with precious teachings that are, fortunately, already translated to English. . . .

The brilliant flash of aakash vijali followed by rumbling. I stare out the window. Rain is knocking. . . .

Sigma Nu boy smiled at me fifteen hours ago—the best birthday gift ever!

The right side of my mouth curves up. Then the raindrops start pounding.

Not my fault! They left the door open.

But I kept watching. So it was my fault.

What's wrong with me? How could I do that to Jane?

I touch the agarbatti and, though I waver between atheist and agnostic, a whispered prayer in Gujarati tumbles out of my mouth. "Please, Thakorji, forgive me for being a peeping Gita." I close my eyes and wait for some sort of divine reassurance to wash over me, the way it used to when Pinky Auntie and I prayed to Thakorji, a nickname for the god Krishna.

Nothing.

I open one eye.

Still nothing.

Both eyes open.

I don't feel forgiven.

Lightning forks. Thunder cracks.

I get it, I get it! The smoke of the burning agarbatti isn't enough for Thakorji to bestow his pardon. He wants more dedication than that—Pinky Auntie kind of dedication. She kept her beloved deity's framed photo nestled between small velvet pillows in an ornate shelf-mandir. Her daily worship was a tender ritual of love, as if caring for a child.

I exhale softly.

If only I could ring Pinky Auntie's handheld brass ghanti three times to gently awaken Thakorji. If only I had the tiny bowls of malai, mishri, and mathari with pickles set out for his meal . . . the gold-bordered orange dhoti, a matching turban, and colorful moti ni mala to adorn his framed photo . . . the silver arti plate arranged just so with red and white carnation flower heads, rice, agarbatti, and five cotton wicks dipped in ghee, each one placed in its own earthenware lamp and lit. . . .

When I was a kid, Pinky Auntie used to hold the arti plate with me and lead us in making a slow clockwise air circle with it in front of Thakorji's decorated photo. When the plate was at seven o'clock, we went backward to five o'clock and then clockwise again.

We repeated the air circles like that.

"This is when you can ask forgiveness for things you did that hurt him or others. You can also ask for strength for what lies ahead. You can tell him your secrets. Thakorji loves you no matter what," Pinky Auntie would say.

I nodded, grateful that I could tell Thakorji my secrets—I had a few about the grown-ups, little things I'd seen and heard in the apartment when they didn't notice me. And what a relief that Thakorji would forgive me! But had I hurt him or anyone else? I didn't think so.

After a few more air circles, Pinky Auntie and I would exchange glances. Then she'd smile at me.

My breaths slow and deepen as I mirror my lips in the memory of her smile. Thinking about it now, it was that smile of hers, not Thakorji, that felt like proof that I was forgiven. That *she* loved me no matter what.

My lips fall.

Pinky Auntie's long gone. She and Neil Uncle abruptly moved back to India when I was almost nine, for reasons Sai and I weren't privy to. And, to this day, our parents continue to be chup-re about it with us.

A pang in my chest.

This particular chup-re of theirs was—is—salt on the raw, gaping wound Pinky Auntie left on my heart when she abandoned us. Me.

Why did she and Neil Uncle leave like that? Why weren't Mom and Dad more upset about it? Or were they, just not in front of Sai and me? Why won't they talk to us about any of it?

Mom and Dad, keeping big ol' family secrets.

Flash and boom.

Me, keeping baby-sized family secrets.

Throbbing under my skull.

Me, keeping a new, fully-grown Gita-the-voyeur secret.

I massage my temples, to no avail. My thoughts and heart are Olympic sprinters crossing last night's finish line: *Was that Jane's first time? Was it Sigma Nu boy's first time? What would Jane's parents think if they found out? What would Jane say if she knew I watched? If she knew Sigma Nu boy knew that I watched?*

I grab Snuffles, throwing him over my face and groaning into his furry back. The unanswerable questions, waves of them, continue to pull me under . . .

. . . Until I tell myself to cut it out, just study again already.

Studying always saves me from things I can't figure out or things I don't want to think about—and from things I'd never admit to anyone else.

I frown. Is studying a way I chup-re myself?

I stare at my handwriting in the notebook as if it's a cipher, this morning's riveting Hum Bio lecture replaying in my head. To get us pumped to learn, Professor Kenton had introduced "the good inflammation" that fights infection and speeds up healing. She walked back and forth in front of the lecture hall, scanning the sea of eager yet anxious premed faces, pushing up her black cat-eye glasses every five seconds.

I strategically sat front and center, and I could smell her vanilla perfume. I could tell she was preparing to ask the first question of the year. I leaned forward, my fists clenched and my breath held. I was more than ready to one-up.

One-upping is a lifestyle for me. Everyone who gets into Stanford has a high school 4.0 GPA or higher, near-perfect SAT scores, and valedictorian status. But did all the other freshmen also get into Harvard, Yale, and Princeton like I did? Maybe. Maybe not.

More importantly, rather than caving to parental or societal expectations of achievement, are all these other premedders heeding a call that's been accumulating in their bones, like calcium, since they were six, solidifying one unforgettable morning when they were eight? Doubt it.

That morning, a week after my eighth birthday, I was

sprawled out on the sofa, lost in a *Choose Your Own Adventure* book, while my brother—fourteen at the time—was hunched over the dining table studying the physician's Hippocratic Oath to help him with his science fair project: crafting a "modernized code of ethics for research physicists." He began to slowly read the Hippocratic Oath out loud. I peeled my eyes off my book and lifted them to Sai, noticing the way sunlight spilled like madhu over his thick, black hair.

I listened. When he got to the line *I will keep them from harm and injustice*, my book slipped out of my hand. Not because I fully comprehended the words, but because I felt the weight of them: *Don't hurt people.*

Without trying, I made the words even heavier: *Don't hurt people, heal them.*

I didn't bother picking up my book, preferring instead to whisper the balm-like words to myself a few times so I wouldn't forget.

Don't hurt people, heal them.

I shut my eyes.

Don't hurt people, heal them.

I imagined carving the words inside my skull.

Don't hurt people, heal them.

A second later, a dark shadow cast over the words. . . .

Don't hurt people. . . .

Then it was gone.

When Sai finished reading, he called my name and said,

"Dr. Hippocrates had the best job in the world. What's better than saving a person's life? Maybe *I* should be a physician. Dr. S. Desai . . ." He paused, shaking his head. "No, I'll stick to being a physicist. Helping to save the universe saves everyone."

I nodded, but I was stuck on "what's better than saving a person's life?" All the envy I felt watching the doctors save soldiers on *M*A*S*H*, or the curiosity that bubbled up when I flipped through Sai's copy of *How the Human Body Works*, mutated into resolve—nothing would stop me from becoming a physician.

Back to Professor Kenton. She took her time, slowly smoothing the sleeves of her navy blazer. A scheming smile appeared on her face. She seemed to be enjoying the infliction of this prolonged torture on her overly ambitious students who would surely be gunners if they got into med school.

Finally, she asked, "What happens when inflammation gets cranked up too high? Or lasts too long?"

Before anyone else's lips even parted, I was already delivering a confident response: "The immune system keeps deploying white blood cells and chemical messengers, so that acute inflammation becomes chronic. This can result in an immune attack on healthy tissues and organs. In turn—"

Someone cut me off.

I looked to the left.

It was a white guy sitting two seats away, with wavy brown hair that reminded me of Joey Russo in *Blossom*. His Stadium Polo and crisp khakis reeked of trust funds and country clubs.

31

"There's evidence that chronic inflammation is associated with diseases like arthritis, cancer, diabetes, and heart disease."

In the second it took Professor Kenton to shift her gaze from me to him, he'd already finished smirking at me.

I glared at him.

"That's exactly right," Professor Kenton said, meeting his oh-so-innocent eyes with her own.

Why was she ignoring the fact that he interrupted me?

She smiled at him. "Too much of a good thing can be bad. It's important to distinguish between inflammation that's doing its job and inflammation that's causing problems." Then she turned to face the screen.

The Joey Russo wannabe puckered his lips in my direction and kissed the air.

I sat back, startled a little but mostly disgruntled. All I could do was cast an evil side-eye at him, then at Professor Kenton. *She* was the one who'd let *him* chup-re me.

Thunder claps. The sound brings me home from the mind trip.

I take a deep inhale of jasmine and remind myself that revenge will be mine when I destroy Joey Russo wannabe on the midterm *and* leave Professor Kenton stunned with my perfect score.

An hour later, I'm done with Hum Bio. I stretch my arms over my head and yawn. It's one of those long, slow yawns that ends in a satisfied smile. For a moment, I indulge in a vision of the future, selfless Dr. Desai healing people who've been hurt.

I'll ace the course, not just the midterm. People have no idea how hard I can work when I want something. And I want—need—a spot in med school. Therefore, I will crush Joey Russo wannabe and dazzle Professor Kenton.

My smile fades.

That's selfish, not selfless. But wouldn't Ayn Rand shake my hand and say something like "Gita, if your actions boost your self-interest, then your actions are rational in their selfishness. Remember, it's rationality and reason that allow society to prosper, while emotions, self-sacrifice, and selflessness are its demise."

Yup, I read all thousand plus pages of *Atlas Shrugged* in high school. For the fun of it.

Hold up. Was it *really* "fun"? I gently thump my mouth with my fist, contemplating. I blink rapidly, processing—for the first time—that *Atlas Shrugged* was shocking rather than "fun." That's the real reason it had captivated me.

I make a chee face. Ayn Rand's suggestion that altruism is destructive goes against everything that feels like human nature *and* common sense to me. Sai and Pinky Auntie would definitely agree.

Still, am I Ayn-Rand-selfish? I don't want to be like that, especially because it's hitting me that her self-centered philosophy isn't intelligent. It's immature at best and cruel at worst.

I tap my pencil against my upper lip, reassuring myself that there's nothing Ayn Rand about wanting to be number one in my Hum Bio class since it's a means to my deeply held, well-intentioned, and altruistic goal of helping people.

To seal the deal, I remind myself that perhaps if I wanted to be a doctor only to outsmart classmates, or for the typical reasons Indian immigrant parents seem to push their kids into it—security and prestige—or if I was doing it solely to avoid an arranged marriage . . . then it would be selfish.

I exhale a slow breath, picturing Anna Freud shoving Ayn Rand off a high horse. Touching her pearl necklace, Ms. Freud winks at me and says, "Gita, altruistic surrender will give you more pleasure than fulfillment of your own instinctual desires, and that's not selfish."

The telephone rings—a time-out on the Anna-Ayn cage fight in my head. I grasp the handset. "Hello?"

"Happy birthday, Gita!" It's my parents and Sai on speaker phone.

Oh yeah. "Thanks," I say.

"Jai Shri Krishna, beta," Mom adds.

Before I have a chance to reply to Mom, Sai says, "We're having birthday donuts in your honor."

"Yum." I smile. "Is the shop busy?"

"Not really. So, how does it feel to be an official adult?"

"Uh . . ."

"Beyond official enough for R-rated movies."

I chew on my lip.

"But not official enough to drink," he adds, in a parental voice.

"Very funny," I say. "As if I'd ever break the law."

Wait. Is voyeurism illegal?

"A birthday card from Pinky Auntie arrived today," Mom says in Gujarati.

A sudden chill sweeps through me, the same way it does every year when Sai and I get one of Pinky Auntie's birthday cards. Her beautifully handwritten birthday wishes never include any mention of her life or her contact info, and the envelopes are always sans return address. But since the postage marks are either from Darjeeling or Kalimpong, Sai and I figure she's most likely in West Bengal.

West Bengal. That's about 1,300 miles from Gujarat and 8,000 miles from Cali. Sometimes, I fantasize about hopping on an Air India flight . . . but how would I find her in one of the most populous states in India?

My chin dips slightly. The only ongoing connection I have to my beloved Pinky Auntie are nine birthday cards that I've obsessively read and reread countless times. Nine birthday cards that I left stashed under my mattress in Union City for safekeeping.

Mom says, "I'll mail it to you."

Nine birthday cards, soon to be ten. Better than the nothing-no-contact our parents have gotten from her, I guess.

"Okay, thanks." I hear my voice petering out, muffled and

distant. I bite off a hangnail and don't feel a thing. I'm wondering for the millionth time if Pinky Auntie really misses me.

"But why wait?" Sai jumps in. "I can hand deliver it to you in less than thirty minutes after traffic dies down *and* take you out for a proper birthday dinner!"

His cheerful, expectant voice tempts me.

"Come on, Gita. Of course you should take me up on it," he says, like he's reading my mind. "Seven?"

"Not today," I sigh. "I've got a ton of work to do. Besides, the predawn ice cream cake yesterday was enough celebration."

"Cake for breakfast *was* cool on your Stanford move-in day, but today is your birthday. And we didn't even give you a birthday gift. . . ."

Going to Stanford counts as a gazillion gifts! I open my mouth to say as much but end up blurting, "How about another kind of gift?"

"What?"

"Mom, Dad," I say slowly. Pause. "Please tell me why Pinky Auntie and Neil Uncle moved back to India."

I don't ask about Bhavin Uncle—I never do—even though he moved back to India around the same time.

A sharp, quick pulse in my throat. Then I hold my breath—99 percent of me is sure my parents will refuse. The other one percent is hoping for a birthday miracle.

"Out of the question," Dad says.

"But—" I protest, despite knowing full well it's an exercise in futility.

"Bhus!" Dad snaps.

Sai tries to help me out. "Dad, why do you always—"

"CHUP-RE!" Dad roars.

And there it is. The old broken-record exchange about Pinky Auntie that ends in the same awkward, brittle silence. It bothers me, but what's new?

Yet I don't understand why Dad gets so pissed over it. Doesn't he realize that it just fuels my curiosity? Is Dad angry at Pinky Auntie the way Neil Uncle was before they moved back to India? Or does Dad blame himself for Pinky Auntie leaving? I know it's possible because Dad blames himself for what happened to his first younger sister, Mira, back when they were kids in Gujarat. . . .

Pinky Auntie hadn't been born yet when Dad found two-year-old Mira unconscious on the floor, a bottle of their father's iron pills by her limp hand, a few shiny red capsules strewn around her. The wet monsoon had brought torrential rains and their parents were at the sari shop trying to save rolls of fabric, unaware of Mira's predicament. Dad had no time to inform them as he scooped his little sister up and waded with her in his arms through ankle-deep and rising waters all the way to the hospital. But it was too late.

Every year on the anniversary of Mira's death, Dad recounts

the story, always in Gujarati. I've practically memorized it. But there's one part that sticks out the most:

When Mira died, my soul died. I wanted to die. It was all my fault. But hard work saved me. By the time I was eighteen, I'd turned my parents' money pit into the most lucrative shop in the area. I couldn't save Mira. But I helped my parents accumulate enough savings to be comfortable for the rest of their lives.

Sometimes I wonder if that's why Sai tells me to "give the old man a break" when I complain too much about Dad's refusal to share Pinky Auntie information.

Mom clears her throat.

I blink.

"What are your plans today, beta?" she asks, changing the subject as per usual after a Pinky Auntie squabble.

"Studying."

"The Gita I know won't move from her desk all day," Sai says in a voice meant to flatter. "Don't forget to take a time-out, birthday girl."

"I won't." A quick dinner in the cafeteria and using the bathroom count as breaks, right?

"Are you sure you don't want me to come over?"

Sai sounds so hopeful that my heart aches a little. I picture my twenty-four-year-old brother—6′3″ and 185 pounds of pure muscle with the gentle giant good looks of Sanjay Dutt—waiting for my reply.

"Next time," I say. "I promise."

Though Sai towers over us, I think it's his benevolence that's his greatest strength. Even as kids, there were times Sai would yell at me to leave him alone or push me a little too hard, but he'd never let me fall.

Like this one time when I was six, and we were playing Star Wars:

"I'm the Rebel doctor and you're Luke Skywalker," I said.

Sai smiled and nodded.

"You're hurt, Luke." I tried to make my voice match the deep one of our pediatrician.

Sai winced and clutched his belly. "Vader sliced me open with his lightsaber."

I swiped Mom's new bottle of fire-engine-red nail polish off her dresser and made Sai lie down. Then I dumped the entire contents of the bottle onto his shirt. "Blood," I whispered, trying not to giggle.

Mom walked in. Her eyes quickly surveyed the scene, homing in on the bottle of nail polish in my hand. Even though she was thin and short, rage transformed her into the Hulk's twin sister: "Ahre bopre!" she screamed, larger than life, pressing her hand to her chest. "More work for me! Ungrateful chokro anē chokri! Gita, thu ah kavi rite kari saku?"

Gita, how could you do this?

I was a deer in headlights. Warm susu ran down my leg.

Palms up, Sai blurted, "It's my fault. It was my idea, Mom. I'm sorry. It's only on my clothes, it didn't get anywhere else—"

"Chup-re!" Mom thundered. Her hand rose like a guillotine. Sai flung his body over mine to shield me.

"My drunk father would've punched me in the face for this. I didn't want to be like him with you, but you kids make me!" Mom yelled, landing solid blow after blow on Sai's arched back.

The red nail polish coating the front of his shirt squished onto my white T-shirt and jeans. I started to wail.

I could tell my big brother was trying not to cry when he whispered into my ear, "Chup-re."

This gave me pause: Sai's chup-re wasn't like Mom's. He was just trying to keep Mom's wrath away from me. I was so much younger than Sai, yet he chose to see me as more than his pesky little sister, someone to avoid, to let take the fall. He chose to see me as . . . a human.

He also chose to see our parents not just as parents but as humans. His junior year in high school, a Caltech professor reached out to him regarding his national science fair projects and guaranteed him a full ride if he applied. The path to Sai's dream of becoming a physicist seemed gilded. But when senior year rolled around, Sai didn't apply to Caltech, or any college. Instead, he *chose* to help our parents full-time at Donutburg in order to "ease their burden." He gave up his American dream, and gave our parents their first consistent days off.

What Gujarati-Indian immigrants' first-born-in-America son does that? None that I knew. All those sons were off pursuing medical, engineering, or law degrees. And a full ride to Caltech?

Most Indian sons would rather gouge an eye out than willingly refuse that.

Rendered speechless by Sai's selfless decision, our parents walked around in a daze for days because, unlike for me, "sons should go to college and have careers." Meanwhile, I spent the next week heartbroken and shuddering for my brother, unable to stop imagining what it would be like to give up my own dream of becoming a physician.

In the spring, when I asked our parents for permission to attend Stanford—I chose Stanford over the East Coast Ivys because I hate the cold and I wanted to remain close to Sai—they immediately shut it down.

"No premed mumbo-jumbo, only marriage to a good Chha-Gaam boy," Dad said in English with a thick Indian accent. He held up a finger. "We must arrange it while you're still young. It's our duty as Hindu parents to make sure you don't end up with anyone unsuitable."

Sai and I took deep breaths and prepared ourselves for the racist and casteist remarks we knew our parents were about to let fly.

Frowning and shaking his head, Dad went first: "Sameer's daughter ran off with a Musilman. And Kiran's daughter—a kario! Outrageous. Bringing such shame to their families like that."

Sai and I exchanged horrified glances at their anti-Muslim people and anti-Black people talk.

I opened my mouth. "Dad, there's nothing wrong with—"

"Chup-re." Mom shook her open palm at me. "And just because school's over and you'll have more time to roam around outside, stay out of the sun! A suitable boy will want a fair-skinned beauty, not a kari chokri who could be mistaken for a dirty, sewer-cleaning untouchable." I could feel the chee expression blanketing my face like a shadow. Just because Mom and Dad bought into the socially constructed, degrading caste system, which designates a whole class of people deemed "untouchable" as outside that system, didn't mean Sai and I had to.

"You're so cruel," I mumbled under my breath.

Dad heard me. "No, it's *you* who are cruel for arguing with your loving parents."

"No one is better or worse than anyone else." I took comfort in the fact that, even if I couldn't get them to become more open-minded and tolerant, *I'd* never be so closed-minded and intolerant. Neither would Sai.

"That is naive. Our word is final, Gita. You will get married to who we say. We will not let you struggle," Dad continued.

For a second, I dropped my eyes, capitulating to good-Indian daughterly duty. Then I cringed myself out of it. I wanted to scream, *Pinky Auntie was right! I don't want a nose ring. I don't want to get married young. And I definitely don't want an arranged marriage, ever!*

But I couldn't fight the automatic chup-re in my head. I didn't say a word.

Once again, it was Sai who saved me. He sat our parents

down. In a composed voice, he said, "The shop is fine. No one will struggle long-term. Please let Gita go to Stanford."

Dad shook his head. "Marriage into a wealthy family is better." He rubbed his graying chin stubble. "Also cheaper, even with the dowry."

I cringed again and began to cry. I couldn't believe my ears: *Dowry? How belittling. And wasn't it outlawed—like the caste system—anyway?*

Sai kept his cool. "I gave up my college dream because I wanted to. Please don't force Gita to give up hers. Isn't that why you moved here from India? For the opportunities? To let us all live the American dream?"

My parents froze.

I bit my knuckle, waiting for their reply and, at the same time, wondering if they ever imagined their American dream would include selling donuts to grumpy strangers who sometimes told them to "go back to where they came from."

"Whatever financial aid and scholarships don't cover, I will," Sai said.

That took us all by surprise. My mouth hung open.

I managed to squeak, "Sai, no! That's your hard-earned money."

Sai put his hands up. "It's okay, Gita. I want to."

My parents exchanged glances, then whispers.

Finally, Mom sighed. She drew back her mostly gray, unruly hair and fixed it into a long, tight braid. "Okay," she said, turning to me and wagging her finger. "But you *will* get married right after college." Then she got up to go to bed.

Dad didn't say anything. Which was basically another "okay," as far as Sai and I were concerned.

Later that night, I hugged Sai. "Thank you, bhai." I decided right then and there that I couldn't let his generosity—his sacrifice—go to waste. I would make Sai proud.

And hopefully, one day, our parents too.

"Gita?" Sai's voice through the phone makes me jump. "You still there?"

"I am." I clear my throat. "Well, better get back to the books."

"So much hard work, beta," Dad says, a hint of rarely expressed pride in his voice.

"Always." I smile, feeling better that Dad and I can at least relate when it comes to hard work.

"Dad, are you saying I was right about Gita going to college instead of shaadi?" Sai jokes.

"Not *instead* . . . only before. There will be different hard work after her shaadi." Dad's voice is shrouded in mystery, as if he's one of those akashvani—unseen oracles—in the *Mahabharata* or *Ramayana*.

Hard work . . .

I inhale sharply.

That's it!

I remember about ashrama—the stage of life system—that

I learned from one of those colorful Hindu mythology comic books I used to tear through like homework. I realize that I've been going about this all wrong with the folks. I switch to Gujarati when I ask, "Dad, hard work in my studies is important. But isn't it more than that? According to ashrama, isn't being a dedicated *single* student—a brahmacharya—my individual dharma until I'm twenty-five?"

Dad pauses. "Yes, but—"

"So, technically, I can't get married until after med school. Marriage is for the grihastha stage of life between the ages of twenty-five to forty-eight, right?"

"Suu bhole che, ah chokri?" Mom mutters, then clicks her tongue. "MD banavu che? Master of doubu, huh?"

Doubu basically means "idiot."

Gee, thanks, Mom.

But I let go of Mom's disparaging remark.

Neither of my parents say anything else. And that is a *big* win for me. Because even if they don't agree—even if they eventually try to force me into an unwanted match—I can and will claim strict belief in ashrama.

A celebratory grin bursts onto my face. I just beat my parents at their own game. And I didn't even need Sai to rescue me. I high-five myself for all of it: Once again, studying has saved me!

"Mom and Dad went back to the front." Sai's smirk radiates through the phone. "You rattled their cage, sis."

"Sorry to leave them like that for you." But I laugh.

"They'll forget about it soon enough. We just got busy—I'll call you tomorrow."

"Okay. Later." As I hang up, my eyes land on the framed photo of the four of us at my high school graduation.

I lift the frame, tracing the matte silver edge. Sai and I are in the middle, Mom and Dad on either side. I study Sai's face: For the first time, I notice that his smile is "unfettered" in the same way he said mine was one day when I was six and he was walking me to school.

I remember being impressed by the big, strange first name he had given my smile. What did *unfettered* mean? I thought about it all day at school. But my fledgling pride refused to let me ask my teacher.

Later, at home, I didn't ask Sai either, or consult his well-worn dictionary. I wanted to figure it out myself—so I climbed on the bathroom step stool and studied my smile in the mirror. What I saw made me giggle: My mouth was open wide, the corners of my lips reaching toward my eyes, my upper lip curled in on itself, showing off the full length of my top pearly whites.

But how can Sai be so happy in this photo when he's made the ultimate sacrifice? Even if it was his choice . . .

My eyes start to sting. Blinking back a wave of tears, I inspect Mom's and Dad's faces instead. Their lips are flat, like they're too tired to lift the corners, even for their daughter's big day.

Mom, Dad, and Sai work so hard. Harder than me.

As I prop the frame back on my desk, it strikes me: The three of them were probably just getting home from the shop last night when I watched Adonis have his way with Jane.

He's a jerk!

But she welcomed it. She was enjoying it.

Still, she's too smart—too perfect—for him!

Being smart and perfect didn't keep jerks away from her. And then Adonis with the jungle-cat eyes smile-trapped me— seduced me—too.

But I welcomed it. I enjoyed it.

Did I?

Obviously, if I kept watching. My stomach rolls.

I'm the jerk.

CHAPTER 3

Three days later, I'm sitting at my desk as if I've taken root in my rickety dorm chair, analyzing *Guernica*—the painting that was Picasso's reaction to the Nazi German and Fascist Italian bombing of the namesake Basque town—and preparing to write my first paper for my Integrated Humanities course.

Classical music is playing on the radio. When the next piece begins—Adagio for Strings by Samuel Barber—gruesome images of war flash in my mind. My heart trembles; goose bumps erupt up and down my arms. Since I first heard this music in the movie *Platoon* (a very American take of the conflict in Vietnam), my body always *feels* it as war. And though I'm studying a different war right now, I'm pretty sure they're all horrific.

A knock on my open door. I look over my shoulder to see Jane standing there.

Jane. I haven't talked to her since . . .

I go completely still, trying to reconcile how the royal girl standing there is the same one who was naked with Sigma Nu boy a few nights ago. My voice gets caught in my throat—or is it a self-imposed chup-re?

It makes no difference because Jane doesn't wait for me to say "Come in." With a flip of her long golden hair, she glides toward me, her honeyed Jezebel lips stretching into a smile that melts my heart. An experienced temptress under the guise of a prim and proper lady. Her lips part, casting a spell of seduction that I'm helpless to resist. . . .

Psych!

That was Bronco Bill's audible internal monologue in the porno Cindy and I watched five summers ago. Bronco Bill stared at the naked Foxy Felicity as she slowly walked toward him, her lips curving up into a knowing smile. When she stood in front of him, he stripped off his clothes and snarled, "You're so hot. And that fuck-me-smile? It's your fault that I can't control myself." Then he pushed her onto the bed and forced himself inside her, no condom.

How selfish of Bronco Bill to blame Foxy Felicity for why he funneled his wayward thoughts into aggressive action!

Speaking of selfish: Would Ayn Rand say Bronco Bill's behavior was rational because he took what he wanted from Foxy Felicity, and that Foxy Felicity's smile was an invitation anyway?

But what if Foxy Felicity had said no?

I feel my face contort into chee on steroids. *Why am I only now realizing that Bronco Bill was a terrible person with the mindset of a rapist?*

I freeze for a second.

Was what he did to Foxy Felicity . . . rape?

Maybe if I'd talked to Sai—I couldn't and wouldn't dare talk to our parents about it—he might've helped me to understand things better. But I didn't talk to anyone about the porno. I swallowed and partially digested what I saw, then forgot it . . . until I peeped on Jane and Sigma Nu boy doing the wild thing.

Jane's smile to me now is a regular, friendly smile: nothing more, nothing less. As such, it's powerless against my academic focus. I quickly get a grip and turn my attention back to *Guernica.*

"Why are you studying like it's already finals?" she asks.

"Every day is finals for us pre-*mads.*" My voice is as serious as an aortic aneurysm rupture.

Jane laughs.

I clutch my pencil tighter. I wasn't trying to be funny—I was trying to scare her off with my intensity.

"Full Moon on the Quad is awaiting our presence, Gita dear," Jane announces, laying a hand on my shoulder.

Gita dear? My pencil slides across the page, turning the *r* at the end of *anti-war* into a deep line of division. Only the closest adults in my life—my parents and Pinky Auntie—have ever called me "Gita dear," except in Gujarati: *Gita beta.* The handful of friends I've had over the years didn't call me anything besides Gita.

Does Jane consider us close already? Or is she one of those people who calls everyone "dear"?

Don't overthink it, I tell myself, regripping my pencil. Thesis ideas drift across the vast sky of my mind like clouds on a breezy day. I jot them down, pleased with the brilliance of each one. *Ha,* I think, giddy. *I won't just finish this analysis paper—I'll conquer it.*

I turn my head and cast a cocky, triumphant glance at Jane. But she doesn't notice—her gaze bores into the image of *Guernica* in my textbook. "Have you heard of Jean-Michel Basquiat?" she asks, her voice distant.

I remember reading about him in *Nat Geo.* "The graffiti prodigy?"

Jane nods. "He made graffiti into high art." Her hand slides off my shoulder. She points to the image of *Guernica.* "Jean-Michel's mother took him to see this very Picasso piece at the MoMA when he was younger."

"Lucky kid." I would've loved it if my mom did that. The one time Pinky Auntie took Mom and me to the San Francisco Museum of Modern Art, Mom scoffed and said, "These aren't even pretty. What's the point?"

"Lucky kid indeed." Jane bites her lip, dropping her eyes. "The first time I saw a Basquiat was when my mother took me to see *Untitled* at a gallery. I was eight." She wraps her arms around herself. "I remember Mom and I sat on the bench in front of it. We didn't speak—we didn't have to. I stared at the large, colorful skull that seemed to be alive and staring back at me. But it didn't freak me out. . . . It was calming." She inhales a deep breath and releases it slowly.

"Maybe you should major in art instead of econ."

She lifts her eyes to me, shaking her head. "Econ has a special place in my heart."

I want to ask her why but before I can, she says something else: "When I told my father about *Untitled* later, all he had to say was, 'A waste of time. Child's play compared to a Picasso.'"

I'm watching Jane as she speaks and there's a storm brewing in her ocean eyes.

She groans. "Have you ever been around a person and still feel completely alone?"

I nod. An unsettled feeling is descending upon me, engulfing me like fog around the Golden Gate Bridge. Jane breathes out heavily, inspecting her manicured fingernails. "Sometimes I can't shake that lonely feeling even when I'm around others."

My brain glitches: *Pinky Auntie has been softly snoring on the sofa for an hour. . . . My bedroom door was open but now it's closed. . . . I didn't close it. I never do. . . . I hug Snuffles and make a silent wish that Pinky Auntie will wake up and open my door, or someone else will come home and open it. . . .*

I blink, snap out of it without a second thought, and bring my attention back to Jane.

How—why—is she so honest and vulnerable with me, an almost stranger? I feel for her and I want to say something supportive. Unfortunately, a cat named Chup-re has once again got my tongue. The announcer on my radio introduces the next classical piece in a delicate voice, sounding the way I imagine a feather would speak. Jane blinks, and it's tranquil waters in her eyes again. I go back to scribbling notes.

"But enough about that!" Jane claps. "Tonight, I can't let you miss Full Moon on the Quad. This annual tradition is your opportunity to become a true Stanford woman."

The bull, strong and steadfast, represents the stampede of fascism across Spain. . . .

"Oh Geeeeta," she sings, with a hint of desperation. "Do you know exactly how you can become a true Stanford woman and not just another frosh?"

Still immune, all I do is look at her askance.

She ignores my refusal to play along and kneels on the carpet next to me, balancing her elbows on my chair's armrest and holding her chin in her cupped palms. "Do you?" Her face is radiating childlike wonder, her spicy perfume is wrapping invisible tentacles around me.

I'm stubborn when it comes to studying, yes. But with the effort she's making, it suddenly feels impossible for me to brush her off anymore. And I'll admit that—deep down—I'd much rather hang out with the person who might be my first real friend here. . . .

Staring at Picasso's miserable horse, I pry my lips apart. "Uh, no, how?"

Jane flings an arm around me like we've been best pals since elementary school. The only other person who's ever done this is Sai, and I find myself automatically leaning into her. I can feel a tentative smile nudge itself across my face, like a turtle poking its head out of its shell.

"I'll enlighten you, oh young one. To become a true Stanford woman we must—in the moonlight, on the quad—" she wiggles her eyebrows up and down dramatically. "Steal a kiss from a senior."

Chee!

The hopeful beginning of my unfettered smile tucks itself away, replaced by my tongue poking out in disgust. Contemplating cubism and the devastation of war makes kissing seem ridiculous. And would Leland and Jane Stanford, the founders, really approve of making out with strangers as a worthy tradition? I think not.

Seems to me that Full Moon on the Quad was probably started by pervy, Ayn-Rand-loving, full-of-themselves senior guys a long time ago. If Sigma Nu boy, aka Adonis, is a senior, I bet he's going.

Is he a senior?

Is he even in Sigma Nu? Because wearing the shirt doesn't mean he's in the frat. Or does it? I'm not sure. I peek at my shirt that's got an image of Queen Latifah on the front. *Damn straight I'm not Queen Latifah.*

I'm an eye-slut.

Queen Latifah wouldn't secretly watch her dorm neighbor have sex. No decent person would.

Guilt pushes down on my chest like a CPR compression.

I glance at the Bible on top of the stack of other religion, philosophy, literature, and art history books—all required reading for our Integrated Humanities class—before my eyes shift back to *Guernica.* I stare at the screaming dove between the bull and the horse. It's crying about the threat to peace in Europe . . . but I swear it feels like a few of its invisible tears are for the impending rift between Jane and me. Because eye-sluts don't make for good potential friends.

At least I'm not a straight-up slut.

I startle at the thought. Where did it come from? I go over the definition of slut that was pitched around the hallways of my high school, mostly by boys to shame and shun girls.

Slut: A girl who sleeps with guys for attention.

Jane slept with Sigma Nu boy, but I don't think she did it for attention—and what does "doing it for attention" even mean, anyway? Besides, Jane seemed to be enjoying it. The fact is, she isn't some fragile little flower, begging to be picked. If anything, I bet *she's* the one who does the picking.

Also, if a guy sleeps with a lot of girls, he gets a ton of high fives from his buddies. Isn't that attention? So why is he called a stud instead of a slut? None of it makes sense.

I sneak a peek at Jane, tapping my pencil on my chin. To my relief, her expression is as mild as a spring day. Which means she isn't reading my mind. And doesn't know that three nights ago, I watched her and Sigma Nu boy—

Or does she?

I'm clinging to the hope that he didn't say anything about me standing there. I put my pencil down as I try to convince myself—again—that she doesn't have a clue. For starters, neither of us have stopped each other in the hallway or cafeteria to bring it up. I nibble on the inside of my cheek, wondering if I should confess. It doesn't seem right to keep a secret this big from a friend. I open my mouth, letting the secret dance along the tip of my tongue.

If I rat myself out, will a chee expression burst onto her face? Will she slowly back away from me, then warn everyone on the floor to watch out for that pervert Gita? Will she report me to campus security, get me in trouble?

Maybe, maybe, and maybe. Guess those are risks I'll have to take. But the second I practice telling Jane in my head, I can only picture her image disintegrating and blowing away like sand in a desert storm. All that's left is the echo of her pained voice: *Gita, how could you?*

My heart goes into V-fib. I shut my mouth—I can't do it. I don't want to hurt her.

Chup-re, whispers a voice in my head.

Yes, yes: Chup-re is the answer—the only option—and it'll protect Jane.

I exhale slowly, mostly satisfied at having chosen a course of action that won't jeopardize Jane's feelings, or our budding friendship.

Jane pokes my arm. "Come with me, Gita. Why won't you come with me?" she whines, sounding like a petulant child on the brink of a tantrum.

I stare at her for a second, my eyebrow lifted, before shaking my head. "I can't. I've got—"

"I know, I know. You've got work to do," she cries, throwing her hands up.

I peek at my list of assignments. It appears I've got another secret: I don't have a legitimate excuse to turn her down because I'm done with today's work. *Guernica* is the first thing on *tomorrow's* schedule. But I love how it feels to be ahead, so my lips remain sealed.

My eyes bounce to Jane for an instant.

"Are you mad at me or something?" she asks, turning away.

Sigma Nu boy did *say something!*

I touch her shoulder. "Jane. I'm not mad at you." I decide to test the waters of Sigma Nu boy's chup-re abilities. "Why would I be?" I blink a little too quickly.

With a mollified smile, Jane shrugs.

He didn't say anything. I sigh, relieved.

The silence that follows sweeps over us like seasonal winds carrying away any lingering Sigma Nu boy awkwardness. All without ever mentioning him.

Jane perks up. "Then I don't get it. Why wouldn't you want to be kissed by a Stanford hunk?"

This time I shrug. "I-I'm shy?" But that's only half of it—the rest is that I've never kissed anyone.

I touch my lips; they're hot and prickly for a second, then they're not.

Aren't you supposed to go on a date or something before kissing? The thing is, every time I picture Sigma Nu boy, it feels like his eyes and smile actually *did* kiss me, and my body tingles a little.

Chee to all of it!

My eyes shift to the injured woman on the bottom right of *Guernica.* I see me, bleeding out confusion. I blink, then see Jane, bleeding out disappointment.

Jane's wide eyes search my face. "That's not a good reason to miss out on this once-in-a-lifetime event." She lifts my hand, pulls me to a stand. "We're going."

I don't want to let Jane bleed out. I don't hurt people. Someday, I'll heal them.

Also, what if Jane is testing me? If I pass, then she'll let me be her friend! My heart flits in my chest.

"But I'm not even dressed for it." I fan my Queen Latifah T-shirt, glancing down at the rest of my casual study attire—gray sweats and fuzzy socks. Compared to Jane, who's decked out in full makeup, a plaid miniskirt, white collared shirt, and high socks, all school-girl-sexy style, I'm basically ready for a middle school sleepover.

"You look fine." She pats my arm. "Let's go."

I take a step back. "Did you try asking someone else?" I'm certain that any other girl in the dorm would jump at the chance to hang out with Jane.

Jane shakes her head. "Oh Gita, Gita, Gita." She walks over to my CD collection and plucks out Nine Inch Nails' *Pretty Hate Machine.*

One of the greatest albums of all time, in my humble opinion: The intense synth music and hardcore lyrics—about corrupt people getting what they deserve and about feeling perpetually on the verge of a nervous breakdown—somehow cause an internal eruption of emotions that I swear I otherwise never feel. After I listen I always feel better, even if I wasn't feeling that bad to begin with.

Jane holds out *Pretty Hate Machine.* "Bet you didn't know

that on the first day, I did a quick scan of your CDs to see if you had this one. You did! None of my other friends own it. It's one of my top five of all time. I still can't believe that Trent Reznor is a one-man band."

"Trent is a genius, and this album is the greatest terrible beauty to ever exist."

Jane's face lights up. "See, that right there! You get it. I've never met another person who *gets* it like that. You and I, Gita, are twisted, kindred spirits. Why would I ask anyone else to go with me?"

I'm speechless, no chup-re necessary. Feels like two butterflies are playing tag in my stomach.

Jane drapes her hands on my shoulders, and our eyes meet. Her irises shimmer all the blues that Brahma is said to have used to create nature—sky, ocean, lakes, and rivers. All the blues meant to be worshipped.

I can't look away. I can feel my entire body being pulled into her orbit.

"Besides, what kind of friend would I be if I let you stay here to write one of the hundreds of papers you'll churn out over the next four years? We're going. That's that."

The queen has spoken . . . and she called herself my friend!

Jane smiles a gentle smile now, soothing and warm. I bask in it, picturing the two of us lounging together in her palace sunroom.

Next thing I know, I'm envisioning a new music video for "That's What Friends Are For." Stevie Wonder's harmonica and then Dionne Warwick's alto crooning are the background to a montage of Jane's and my future: *Us dancing wildly in my room to Nine Inch Nails' "Head Like a Hole" as we scream the lyrics. Us laughing as we share an enormous ice cream sundae. Running side by side to The Dish. Sunbathing in the Oval. Studying together at Cecil H. Green library. Munching on popcorn from the same bucket as the theater lights dim and the trailers start. . . .*

"Ready?" Jane asks, smoothing her hair.

I blink myself back to reality. I swallow. I hear myself say, "Fine. But let's head back by midnight."

"Deal, Cinderella."

We make our way to the Main Quadrangle. The breeze, born of the surrounding foothills and wilderness, is cool. The sky is a black velvet sari studded with twinkling gems. I imagine the palm trees as thieves, stretching their long fronds up toward the loot.

Jane reaches into her purse and produces two lollipops in white and green wrappers. "My dad got these on his recent trip to Europe. They freshen your breath. Nothing kills a good kiss—or desire—like bad breath, trust me." She offers one to me. "Want?"

"Thanks," I say, grasping its stem. I unwrap it, trying to recall the last time I had a sucker; I'm more of a chocolate person.

"You're welcome." She winks. Then she rolls her eyes and mutters to herself, "Of course, he left it to his assistant to send me gifts instead of calling me like I'd asked. So trite." She groans. "Forget him."

I stick the lollipop in my mouth. A burst of chilly mint forest in the dead of winter sprouts along my tongue, and I remember I *did* used to have another favorite sweet treat flavor—neither mint nor chocolate.

I was six, and Neil Uncle and Bhavin Uncle were watching a cricket match—India vs. South Africa—in our apartment. They were sipping on frosty bottles of Kingfisher and tossing peanuts into their mouths. Every once in a while, they cheered or yelled at the television.

During a commercial, Neil Uncle went to the bathroom. Bhavin Uncle called Sai and me over. He reached into a small paper bag and pulled out a bouquet of strawberries and cream Chupa Chups lollipops.

I had yawned then, not expecting much. But as soon as I got my first lick, my eyes widened. Then I stuck it in my mouth, and the taste of strawberry milkshake exploded there. I was hooked.

After that, Bhavin Uncle started bringing different flavors for me. . . . But not for Sai. Once, I asked him why—

Jane taps my shoulder. "Do you want another one? They're so small."

"No," I say, certain it would be selfish to ask for seconds. "One was perfect." I finish my lollipop, tossing the stick into a nearby trash can.

The Main Quad's courtyard sprawls before us, thick columns and intricately carved archways forming an open border. Lush islands of palms and other plants dot two rows in the middle. I turn my head left and admire Memorial Church, the rich colors of its Italian-mosaiced facade glowing in the moonlight.

How am I even worthy to walk in this lovely oasis?

Eager Stanford students flutter about, chattering noisily while Van Morrison's "Brown Eyed Girl" blasts from a large speaker. All around us, students are making out. It's not that easy to tell the freshman from the seniors. I wonder if some of them are sophomores and juniors who've crashed the party just to get some action.

Jane and I squeeze through the crowd of gawkers and kissers. With all the shoulder-bumping and elbowing, it's like we're in the beginnings of a mosh pit. Meanwhile, the only thing on my mind is if everyone's kissing everyone else, isn't this just a giant petri dish for mono? Someone really should do the research and get it published. Then maybe this infectious-disease-bordering-on-predatorial-nightmare of a tradition would be deemed a legitimate health hazard and banned.

A few kissing couples block our path. I stand on my tiptoes, searching for another way through. A white girl with a black pixie cut standing next to me leans toward her friend—who has perfectly cut thick chestnut bangs—and asks, "Remind me *why* we're at this lip orgy?"

Perfect bangs girl shakes her head, scoffs. "I don't know. . . . Because even at Stanford, our value lies in being kissable?"

They exchange glances.

Pixie girl says, "Let's ditch this."

They turn around and disappear into the crowd.

Wait for me! I want to cry. But that's when the sea of kissers part. Jane tugs my hand, and we keep moving forward.

Up ahead, there's a tight circle of maybe eight or nine guys. Jane's eyes light up like a thousand Diwalis. She leads me straight to it before letting go of my hand, pushing her way into the circle. The image of her diving in headfirst reminds me of a diagram in my Hum Bio textbook of an X sperm penetrating an egg. I stand on my tiptoes to get a view of the fertilization in action, giggling at the thought.

What I see stops me short. There in the center, Jane is introducing herself to Marisol Walter!

I rub my eyes.

It's still Marisol Walter.

I get seeing one of the hottest models in the world on magazine covers everywhere, but what the heck is she doing here, at one of the most prestigious academic institutions in the world? How does that make sense?

One of the guys in the testosterone circle tosses his chin

toward Jane and Marisol, then points to his crotch and whispers to his friend, "This sausage needs some salt and pepper."

They snicker.

Idiots. I hate these guys, and their comparison of Jane and Marisol to condiments. Still, I can't help but picture myself as the stinky hing in Mom's masala dabba, while Jane is the sweet cardamom and Marisol is the spicy garam masala.

Marisol sends a wave to the guys behind her. "Sorry fellows, I've got to go."

"But you haven't kissed any of us yet," one of them whines.

Marisol quickly checks that the top of her crisp black dress shirt is buttoned up all the way, then blows a few air-kisses at the guys. "There," she says, towing Jane out of the circle.

Chup-re is no match for my joy at seeing the pathetic expressions on all the boys' faces—I laugh out loud.

Marisol steps in front of me, her curls bouncing along as if in a Pantene commercial. "What's so funny?" She cocks her head to one side and fiddles with the wooden beads on a sterling silver rosary around her neck, the nadir of which features a nickel-sized Virgin Mary pendant.

"You and Jane have groupies. Must be nice." I try to make my voice playful.

Marisol's smile emerges like the sun on a cloudy day. Then she throws her chin over her shoulder and practically yells, "Those guys are so full of shit."

A few of the circle jerk boys cringe, their faces crumpling

like wads of paper. I gasp, but my shock quickly dissolves into laughter.

Jane plants herself next to Marisol. "Gita, this is—"

"I know. Marisol Walter." I extend my hand.

"Nice to meet you, Gita." The sincerity in Marisol's voice and double-handed shake throws me off—I guess I was expecting more aloofness from a goddess.

"What are you doing here? At Stanford, I mean."

Marisol tosses back some of her curls. "I'm a freshman too. Didn't want to miss out on tradition, even if I'm not kissing anyone. Joey—my boyfriend—would be pissed."

"I bet," I say, rolling my feet onto the outer edges of my worn red Converse high-tops. I wonder what it would be like to have a boyfriend. Would he be pissed if I kissed someone else for the sake of tradition?

"Turns out we're all in the same dorm," Jane adds.

"I'm one floor up," Marisol says.

"Cool." I have trouble saying much more right now: I'm excited, but also overwhelmed at my first ever run-in with a celebrity.

"You guys free for breakfast in the caf tomorrow at seven? I've got an eight a.m. class," Marisol says, buttoning the cuffs of her long-sleeve shirt.

"Sure," Jane replies.

They look toward me. I'm about to politely decline, because according to the schedule I've set for myself, I need to eat at

6:00 a.m. But then Marisol pokes my shoulder: "Come on, Gita. Don't you want to be breakfast buddies with us?"

I stand there, wondering if I've heard her correctly. At the same time, I feel myself nodding.

Jane wipes pretend sweat from her brow. "Phew! For a second there, I was afraid you'd pick *Guernica* over us. I would've been so sad."

Really? I scan Jane's face for any hint of sarcasm, but come up short. She seems serious. My heart runs hurdles—I can feel chup-re closing in, but I manage to squeeze some words out. "I . . . I'd never want to make you sad, Jane."

Marisol grins. "See, this is why traveling all the time for my job sucks—I've missed hanging out with girlfriends who give a shit. Not like—" She pauses. "Never mind."

"Poor Marisol." Jane tsks. "So many first-class trips and photo shoots at exotic locations . . ."

Her sarcasm is obvious this time, and I laugh. Marisol does too. Then she turns to me, one arm crossed under the other, and taps a finger on her chin. "Jane said she's econ. What's your major?"

"Hum Bio. I'm premed."

Marisol's eyes widen. "That's, like, the hardest."

"Oh, I don't know about that," I say, even though I agree with her. *At least I have one thing over the goddess.* I can feel my ego soar. "Any idea about your major?"

Marisol puts one hand on her hip and gestures with the other when she says, "Math. Then maybe I'll go to business school. I'd really like to set up nonprofit after-school learning centers for underprivileged children."

I feel my jaw drop toward the ground, as if I'm one of the characters on those Saturday morning cartoons I used to watch. "But you're a model," I blurt.

Instantly, I regret saying it: I just reduced Marisol to her looks, the way my mom reduced Shilpa Auntie's daughter to nothing more than a bride with the question *Why does she even need college?*

Marisol twists her rosary. "Modeling is my temporary gig. The money lets me help my parents with their bills and save up for my nonprofit."

Now my jaw wants to completely detach, but I clench it in place, thinking, *Here is the girl version of Sai standing before me.* When I manage to chill, I say, "Wow. Uh, nonprofits. And math. Now *that's* the hardest major." It really would be for me; I think about how much studying and extra help it took for me to excel in all of my high school math classes and math club.

Marisol, the famous model, dutiful daughter, and future Mother Teresa type—a math major. Jane, the modern-day Renaissance girl—econ. Two beautiful, genius people.

The amount of girl power—no, human power—between the two of them leaves me awestruck. Like I'm lying on the grass, dazzled by the Milky Way, when two new constellations suddenly appear.

I get a faraway feeling: *Am I dreaming that these girls want to hang out with me?*

Jane rests her elbow on my shoulder. "Gita, I think it's time to find some seniors to kiss. Time to become true Stanford women."

A slow smile spreads across Marisol's face. She clicks her tongue. "Joey's going to have to understand." Resting her elbow on my other shoulder, she declares, "Ladies! Let's do this."

Even though she's next to me, her words sound galaxies away.

CHAPTER 4

*T*here's a hush in the crowded dorm caf as Jane and Marisol, lunch trays in hand and heads held high, make their way to an empty table at the back. All eyes are on them, including mine.

Jane and Marisol are the strutting stars in En Vogue's "My Lovin' (You're Never Gonna Get It)" video, while I'm hunched over the napkin dispenser feeling like the epitome of Radiohead's "Creep"...

Marisol stops and, without so much as a glance, calls out, "Coming, Gita?"

I grip my tray and stare off into space. It's been two weeks since Full Moon on the Quad, and Jane and Marisol still want me around—I almost can't believe it. I force myself to snap out of it, grab a few napkins, and—as if my new friends might change their minds if I'm not fast enough—dash after them. The sinus tachycardia in my rib cage confirms that this is a do-or-die moment.

As the three of us sit, everyone else awakens from their Jane-and-Marisol trance to resume chatting and stuffing their faces. Marisol takes a bite of her loaded cheeseburger. Chewing, she turns her head to Jane, then swallows and asks, "Want to work on econ together tonight?"

Jane nods, nibbling on a piece of the fried chicken we both got. "Today's problem set seems impossible."

I sink my teeth into a drumstick. The buttermilk crunch followed by tender leg meat is astonishingly delicious. Crispy bits stick to my lips, but I don't bother wiping them off, too busy savoring the simple and satisfying flavors.

Jane checks her watch, then pushes her tray away. She reaches into her purse and plucks out her Nokia that's the size of a candy bar rather than the brick-like cell phone Sai has. "He better not give me the runaround," she mutters, punching in numbers on the keypad. She holds the cell to her ear and drums her fingers on the table as she waits.

"Hello? Dad?" Jane straightens in her chair. "Yes, this'll only take a— But your secretary said—" Frustration quickly splatters across her face. "I know you're— Please, I need Mom's— Why are you mad?" A beat of silence, then Jane pulls the phone from her ear and glares at it.

"He hung up on me." Disbelief coats her voice.

Marisol and I exchange glances. Jane shakes her head, dropping her cell back into her purse. "Why am I surprised?" She slouches down in her chair, a faraway look in her eyes.

I know that look. And when Jane drapes her hand over her heart, I can almost predict the pained sigh that escapes her lips a millisecond later. I can't help but to surmise that her father's disregard is a recurring thing.

I want to pat her hand and commiserate with her: *I'm sorry. I know how you feel. It stings and I release that exact sigh every time my parents refuse to tell me what happened to Pinky Auntie.* But the needle of chup-re has already sewn my lips shut, save for four words: "Wanna talk about it?"

Jane shakes her head. "Not really."

Marisol touches Jane's arm, and Jane sighs again. "I'm just . . . mad at myself. He blows me off every time, and it still catches me off guard. But I'll get over it . . . I always do." She looks like she's about to say something else but then changes her mind and picks up a wing instead. She takes small bites, occasionally blotting her mouth as elegantly as possible with a rough, two-ply cafeteria napkin.

The three of us go back to lunching, in silence this time. Finally, Marisol swallows the last bite of her burger, then kisses her fingertips and tosses them in the air. "Salty, greasy, charred perfection. And my agency wants me to give up this kind of food? Forget it."

I hold up my milk carton. "Cheers to that."

Marisol lifts her chocolate milkshake. "Cheers."

"Cheers—to meal buddies!" Jane raises her glass of iced tea, and the three of us gently bump our beverages together.

After taking a sip, I set my milk carton down and lean forward. "Hey, speaking of buddies, did you know that eating together reduces our risk of death?"

"No!" Marisol's eyes grow wide. "You mean consuming food prevents dying from starvation? I don't believe it!"

"Ha-ha, very funny." I nudge her elbow with mine. "I mean, research proves that hanging out, having social relationships, reduces the risk of death. I read about it in the latest *Stanford Medicine Magazine*."

"Hmm. How much do we need to hang out to live forever?" Marisol asks, adjusting her sweater.

"Let's find out," Jane says. "I know exactly where to start: by becoming sorority sisters. Rush week begins—"

A deep voice interrupts her: "Hey, Marisol, nice mag cover."

The three of us shift our attention to the white guy standing behind Jane. It's Stanford's top quarterback, who's currently carrying a tray piled high with multiple entrees. I don't know if he's a Star Wars fan, but the way he's ogling Marisol, it's as if he's trying to Jedi mind trick her into giving him the time of day.

Marisol doesn't reply right away. She takes her time buttoning the top of her sweater, and doubtful flickers replace the twinkling self-confidence in the quarterback's eyes. "Thanks," she replies, meeting his stare at last. She wraps her lips around the straw of her milkshake and slurps it up.

Quarterback tugs at his collar, glancing at Jane before resting his gaze again on Marisol. "Our team's co-hosting a party at the

Beta house this weekend. You both should come," he says, trying to sound nonchalant. But the yearning in his voice comes through, loud and clear.

"Maybe." Marisol winks at me, then adds, "Only if Gita's invited too."

"Sure, whatever." A dismissive shrug.

I glower at him—I don't care whether or not I'm invited. Really. I was planning on studying nonstop the entire weekend. But then, to my dismay, an embarrassing parade of memories commences in my head. . . .

High school cafeteria: Jake and Conner ask my fellow math team members Cece and Amber to the prom. Freddie's eyes dart around, landing on everything and everyone but me.

Didn't care—I didn't like Freddie. And I definitely wasn't trying to get him to notice me, much less ask me to prom.

Full Moon on the Quad: Jane receives Times-Square-like kiss after kiss. Marisol gets a bunch of offers but accepts only one. I'm stuck with nothing but vacant glances.

Again, I didn't care. I didn't want to saliva-swap just for some stupid sexist tradition.

I cross my arms and sit back, scowling. My lacrimal glands are suddenly secreting a thin layer of fluid against my will. I blink quickly, refusing to let a single tear escape.

Marisol flashes Quarterback a winning smile. "Maybe we'll see you there."

"Cool." He grins all dopey before pivoting his buff body

toward a side table of teammates. But I clock his giant melon head turning back for one last glimpse of Marisol. I shovel some mashed potatoes into my mouth, trying to force the knot in my throat back down.

"Hey Gita," Marisol says.

I glance at her, arching an eyebrow. She throws her chin up toward the football table. "Never mind him. He's a jerk."

I exhale, give her a small smile. For a second, my humiliation feels a little less humiliating.

"Why do I flirt with these clowns anyway?" Marisol mutters to herself, popping a curly fry into her mouth. In my head, I ask, *And what would Joey say about it?*

Come to think of it, what *would* Joey say about it? Or about her Full Moon on the Quad kiss? Did she even tell him about it?

"I feel that." Jane begins to inspect her hair for split ends. "Especially those guys who look at me like I'm fresh hamachi sashimi. As if I exist to lay there for their pleasure. Gross."

Which guys is she talking about? Sigma Nu boy didn't seem to think that she existed just for his pleasure. In fact, he pleasured her—*Stop thinking about that!*

I feel bad for Jane and Marisol and their boy plights, but I have absolutely nothing to contribute to this conversation.

That's when I spot another football player swaggering toward us. The next bite of my fried chicken goes down pokey, as if I swallowed the burs that always hitchhike a ride on my socks during a run.

"Hey ladies," the new arrival says. His eyes and smile drift from Jane to Marisol, skipping over me.

Don't care, don't care, don't care, I tell myself. But then I picture Sigma Nu boy's Adonis smile, and my heart stutters briefly before resuming a new rhythm *How can I get another Adonis smile? By flirting, like Marisol?* Deciding it can't hurt to give it a shot, I stick out my chest and start some Marisol inspired hair-twirling with my index finger.

To my disappointment, my beguiling ways do nothing to tempt the football player. In fact, he only stares harder at Marisol. I feel shards of me scattering like loose-leaf sheets in a strong wind. . . .

No! I'm not going out like this.

"Hey, Mr. Football Guy!" I blurt, grasping the edge of the table. "How's your day going?" I stare at him and grin, giving him no choice but to acknowledge my humanity. I wait, studying the confusion spreading over his face. Pride courses through my veins at my small yet mighty display of girl power.

Jane and Marisol snicker. Football Guy frowns, then hurries away.

Most of me is proud of myself for calling out his rudeness, but the question lingers: *What do I have to do to get another Adonis smile?* Apparently, flirtation is not the way to go. For me, at least.

"Anyway," Jane continues as if nothing happened, using her

straw to stir the ice at the bottom of her glass. "Are either of you going to rush?"

Marisol shakes her head. "No. Joey won't let me."

I scrunch my face. *Why not?* "Is he mad at you about Full Moon? Is that why he won't let you rush?"

Marisol's eyebrows cinch together. "No . . . and no; I didn't tell him about it. He wouldn't understand that it's just a stupid tradition. He'd be angry."

"I mean . . . I think *I'd* be angry," I say tentatively.

"Why?" Marisol's tone is sharp. "I'd be understanding of him if the tables were turned." But the defiance in her eyes melts into something more desperate, unsure. She clasps her hands together. "Please keep it on the down-low, okay?"

I nod. Easy enough—it's not as if I hang out with Joey or anything.

Jane puts her own hands up. "Don't worry. I don't stir pots. . . . But maybe you should tell Joey the truth."

Marisol pushes a few curly fries around on her plate, the corners of her lips turned down. As much as I think she should tell Joey, I never meant to make her sad. "Why doesn't Joey want you to rush, anyway?" I ask.

She shrugs.

"I bet he's worried about all those frat boys around," Jane says.

"Probably." Marisol shrugs again. From what she's told us,

Joey's EMT shifts keep him away from her a lot. And I'm sure it's as clear to him as Marisol's blemish-free face that guys gather around his girlfriend like ants to madhu. I wonder if he's picked up on her tendency to flirt. It must make him super jealous.

If I were him, *I'd* be super jealous.

I exhale.

I'm not him, and I'm still super jealous. But I don't want to be super jealous, or even just jealous. I want to be . . . I don't know.

"He can't just forbid you from rushing. Plus, there are guys everywhere, not just at frats," Jane says.

"Do you *want* to rush, Marisol?" I ask.

"Sort of . . . But honestly, I don't want to deal with Joey's BS."

"Just rush." Jane sips her tea. "Joey can take a hike if he doesn't like it."

"I suppose." Marisol pops another curly fry into her mouth. "On the other hand, I also don't think I have time to rush."

"But—" Jane begins. "Oh, never mind." She turns to me, her expression beseeching. "How about you, Gita? Are you going to rush?"

"I can't," I say, though I feel bad turning Jane down a few seconds after Marisol did.

"Why not?"

"The lab's increasing my hours. I don't have time either." Okay, so that's not technically true. I don't even start at the lab until Monday. But while rushing might make it possible for another Sigma Nu boy type to notice me and gift me with an

Adonis smile, the time required—from what I've heard—would be academic suicide.

Jane attempts to hide the letdown in her voice when she says, "Well, I'll miss you both."

Before I can respond, another guy's voice cuts in: "What's up, Jane? Hey Marisol."

Oh for fuck's sake . . . I slap my palms over my eyes, dragging my hands down my face.

"I'm Simon. I'm down the hall from you, Jane." His hazel eyes shift back and forth between Jane and Marisol before taking up residence on Jane. He smiles at her, an almost-Adonis smile. "You look nice today."

I blow a silent raspberry at him before propping my head on my hand to wait out the torture of Simon's presence. I glance at Jane—it occurs to me that her makeup is perfect. So is Marisol's. Maybe I should ask them to teach me how to paint my face like theirs. Maybe if I had spider lashes, burgundy lips, and pastel eyelids, then all the Simons of the world would say I look nice too, and give me almost-Adonis smiles.

I frown. *But that's not me. Since when do I want that kind of attention?*

What I really should do is call Simon out on his rudeness, right? I imagine waving my hands and shouting, "Hey jackass, I'm here too!"

Nah. I'm over it.

Am I, though?

Because if I'm honest, I wouldn't mind getting an almost-Adonis smile—it's better than no smile at all. I stab a roasted carrot with my fork.

Why do I want another Adonis smile?

It's never been a thing I've wanted before. Next thing I know, I'm imagining Sigma Nu boy's face. Again.

His blue-green eyes glow. He smiles . . . and my yoni tingles.

I quickly push the embarrassing part of the memory aside and change it to something that feels more acceptable.

His blue-green eyes glow. He smiles . . . and my heart bursts through my rib cage.

Isn't that how love starts?

I don't know. But at this moment, I convince myself it is.

Out of the corner of my eye, I see Jane staring at Simon, her expression blank. "It's extremely rare for me to hear that, so thank you," she says, her voice monotone. Then she fake-yawns.

Go Jane!

Marisol snorts. Simon stands there like a lapdog waiting to be pet by his master. Jane ignores him.

"Okay then," he finally says. "See ya, I guess." He throws up a two-finger salute and walks away, hunched over, proverbial tail tucked between his legs.

Still, he's lucky. At least he doesn't have a pitchfork impaling him in the heart, like I do.

I pick up my fork and jab at another carrot. Maybe a distraction will help—I mentally recite my hour-by-hour schedule for the rest of the day:

12:30–5:00 p.m.: O-Chem assignment. I'm giving myself extra time on this because it's difficult and I refuse to be one of *those* Stanford students weeded out of premed by the toughest freshman course on campus.

5:00–7:00 p.m.: Finish Dante paper.

7:00–7:30 p.m.: Dinner.

7:30–9:00 p.m.: Hum Bio reading.

9:00–10:30 p.m.: Geology reading.

10:30 p.m.: Bedtime.

I lay my fork down, feeling a little better. I can always count on academics to save me.

Jane taps my shoulder. "Okay—I get it, no rushing. But how about a double date tomorrow night around six? I need a wing-woman."

"Wingwoman" sounds better than the cafeteria third wheel I've been relegated to for the last half an hour. But what about my study plans? I'd decided that every Saturday and Sunday from 7:00 a.m. to 7:00 p.m. I'd hunker down in the farthest cubicle on the top floor of Cecil H. Green Library. That way, I could commit to twelve hours of uninterrupted studying, with quick breaks for bladder relief and to gobble down the snacks I snuck in.

"What about Marisol?"

Marisol shakes her head. "Can't. I've got plans with Joey."

"Gita?" Jane leans toward me, batting her mascara-curled eyelashes.

My armpits start to gush. If I veer off track on my study schedule, everything will be ruined! "I—I . . ."

"Don't make me go alone," Jane wheedles. "It'll be fun! Free food and wine . . . Plus two hot guys who live off campus and are actually *capable* of holding a conversation. Come on, Gita, please." She clasps her hands. "Pretty please?"

In the heat of the moment, my heart stands at attention in my chest, ready to accept its new mission—to not let my first-ever college friend down. If Jane needs me, I'm there. Besides, I can always wake up earlier tomorrow morning to keep my study schedule happy.

"All right. Let's wine and dine."

Marisol claps her hands. "Ooh, I can't *wait* for the 411."

Jane squeezes my arm, a broad smile stretching from ear to ear. "Thank you, Gita."

My heart revs up. *If my study schedule's happy, and Jane's happy, then I'll be happy.*

"Who are these guys anyway?" I ask.

Jane's eyes sparkle. "Todd and Angelo. I met Todd off-campus at a coffee shop last weekend. We talked for, like, *two hours* before he asked for my number."

"What do they do?" Marisol asks, twisting her rosary.

"They're in tech. Get this—the first 'office' they had for their start-up was Todd's mom's basement. Two years later, they pur-chased a house together in Palo Alto, and Todd bought his own places in San Francisco and Manhattan."

"From scrubs to self-made millionaires—I'm impressed," Marisol says.

I nod, although I'm not impressed the way she is, or probably the way I'm supposed to be. Maybe it's because Sai still lives at home and isn't a millionaire, but he's definitely not a scrub. He's practically a saint, which Mom says is one of the Sanskrit-origin meanings of his name.

"How old are they? These guys?" I ask, tracing my collarbone.

Jane shrugs. "Thirty?"

My mouth hangs open.

Jane slaps my arm playfully. "Relax. It'll be fun." She sounds calm, reassuring.

I shut my mouth. Nod. "It will be." *I think.*

And who knows? Maybe I'll get another Adonis smile. Under the table, I cross my fingers.

CHAPTER 5

The next evening, Jane and I are cruising in her red convertible Jag down a wide Palo Alto street lined with giant trees and million-dollar homes. It's surreal; the neighborhood is majority white with either old or tech money. Nothing but a highway and the San Francisquito Creek separates this place from East Palo Alto, where the majority of residents are Latino, Black, and Asian and almost 20 percent of them live below the poverty line.

Jane turns down a smaller street. A snow-white Pomeranian, sprawled out on an impeccable lawn dotted with perfect oak trees, yawns. Its just-sun-kissed owner tilts her head in adoration, then squats to stroke the dog's fluffy head. Dog and owner watch us as we roll past, and the owner's eyes land on me: They narrow in the same suspicious way as those of the suited security guard at the Gucci store an hour ago. He followed me around as I followed Jane around while she selected items to spend her daddy's money on, including her dress for tonight.

Leaving the store, I told Jane all about the security guard. "Maybe you're being paranoid," she said, unlocking the Jag.

No, I'm not! But chup-re had charley horsed my vocal cords. By the time we were out of the parking lot, I'd done a one-eighty and convinced myself that maybe she was right.

I glimpse at the dog-owner lady again. There's no question: She's definitely glaring at me.

My skin prickles. I want to point out the mean lady to Jane to show how not-paranoid I am. I want to beg Jane to turn the car around and race back to campus and the safety of racial diversity and academic overachievement. I prepare the words just as the intro guitar riff of "Sweet Child O' Mine" gushes from the Jag's speakers.

I glance at Jane. She's nodding her head to the music and grinning.

Am I making a big deal out of nothing?

Fifteen seconds of guitar, then the drums. As Jane starts a passionate sing-a-long with Axl Rose, I seal my lips, swallowing everything I want to say.

A pang of longing for Union City slices through me. My hometown is so real: Its mix of people of all races and ages and backgrounds. My family's old and small yet tidy apartment. The mixed smells of Tacos al Pastor from my favorite neighborhood restaurant, potted gardenia from the apartment next door, and Drakkar Noir on the young guys who frequented our Donutburg.

The playful squeals of neighborhood kids chasing each other outside with squirt guns and magic wands. Sai, who'd never chalk up my instincts to possible insanity. And memories of Pinky Auntie.

I hug myself, pretending Snuffles is in my arms. Union City, I decide, is like old flannel pj's. Warm, fuzzy, and comfortable. This neighborhood, on the other hand, is like new, stiff pj's with pokey side seams. Exclusive, pretentious, distressing.

Jane parallel parks between a white Benz and a blue Land Rover. She turns to me and taps my shoulder. "Let's go?"

I can feel the chill vibe oozing from her entire being drape itself over my shoulders. "Let's."

We step out of the car and Jane weaves her arm through mine, resting her head on my shoulder. The fragrance of rare blossoms and mango from her Eternity perfume is beguiling. I'm surprised when the little hairs on my arms stand erect.

"Don't worry," she says. "You look hot. You'll be fine."

I . . . wasn't worried about my appearance until then. I surreptitiously adjust my last-season, 50-percent-off, black Gap miniskirt and crop top before glancing over at Jane's designer black-and-red mini dress and stilettos. I force a happy expression onto my face. "Thanks. And you make Gucci sizzle."

Her smile is bold—I'm jealous of it.

We walk past two houses, then turn left into a driveway with a black Ferrari and a silver Bentley. We approach an ivory-colored mansion with a front door as red as a stop sign: *Enter at your own risk, into the forbidden world of Todd and Angelo,* the red door screams. The muscles in my face tighten.

Jane stops in the doorway and looks over at me. "Listen. You don't have to do anything you don't want to."

I smile, nod. That's true, and I know it, yet a not-so-small fraction of me is longing for the Adonis smile that I know Jane will get tonight. What do I have to do to snag another one? Exponentially turn up my flirt game? How do I do that?

Then again, even if I flirt, is it possible for someone like me—who isn't a Jane or a Marisol—to win an Adonis smile? Maybe the one from Sigma Nu boy was a fluke, especially since the smidgen of flirting I tried in the caf yesterday failed.

"I appreciate you being my wingwoman." Jane wraps her arm around my shoulder and squeezes. "I love you so much, Gita."

I touch her hand, feeling my cheeks flush. It's the first time someone besides my family has spoken those words to me. "I love you too," I say. While I totally mean it, I also have to tell my mind to chup-re when it whispers, *Is it really possible for her to love me already and for me to love her already? Is it really possible for me to trust her already? Because knowing the CliffsNotes of someone's life isn't knowing* them, *Gita dear.*

I grip my hands together. *Then again, is it safe to trust even the people you've loved and known all along? Or thought you knew, anyway . . .*

Jane gives my shoulder another quick squeeze, then lets go. She opens her purse and drops her keys inside. "All good?"

"All great." I crush the nagging desire to grab her keys and drive like a maniac back to campus. Jane rings the doorbell.

A tall, handsome white man wearing an artsy-print silk shirt and jeans with folded hems answers the door. His azure eyes twinkle when they land on Jane. But it's his smile that's the heavyweight champ—it KOs my straggling impulse to leave.

I tuck my hair behind my ears, wishing I'd worn the blue eye shadow and glitter Marisol had said was "so in."

Jane and hotter-than-Adonis-himself man exchange kisses on the cheek.

"This is my friend Gita," Jane says.

"Hi, Gita, I'm Todd." He holds out his hand. "Nice to meet you."

I wrench my eyes away from his chiseled jaw and shake his hand. "Nice to meet you too."

"Come in," he says, running his fingers through the dark brown hair he's upcombed like George Michael. He steps his buff body to the side, and we follow him in.

The song "Crazy" floats through the room, and Seal's powerful voice encourages me to let loose. I exhale, reminding myself it's time to do just that.

"This way," Todd says. He leads us into a kitchen filled with stainless steel appliances and slate countertops and cabinets. The aroma of sausage and fennel wafts toward us. I swallow the saliva pooling in my mouth.

Todd points to another white guy stirring something in a red Dutch oven with a long wooden spoon. "That's Angelo," he says.

Angelo glances over his shoulder and waves. He's a casual-cool kind of attractive with his denim-on-denim outfit, his black, slicked-back pompadour with faded sides, and high cheekbones.

"This is Jane and Gita," Todd says.

"Welcome." Angelo's light-brown eyes land on me. Then he smiles.

Holy moly. An Adonis smile! I turn away, touching my cheek that's on fire.

"I hope you're hungry, Gita," Angelo says. I shift my eyes back to him and nod, mesmerized.

"Good. My specialty is homemade tagliatelle with beef ragu. Learned from the best: my Italian mother." He kisses his huddled fingertips, then lets them break free.

I'm not sure how that's funny, but Jane and Todd laugh. I don't want to be all awkward, so I join in with a chuckle. Then, without meaning to, I picture the expression on my parents' faces if they were to witness a man cooking for me. "The horror, the horror," I imagine they'd whisper, like Marlon Brando in *Apocalypse Now*. . . .

My chuckle turns into a full-fledged laugh.

Todd puts his hands on the small of Jane's back and mine. "Would you ladies care for a lovely red, Italian of course?"

A lovely red *what* that's Italian of course?

Jane notices the confusion on my face. "Sure," she says quickly. "We'd love some wine."

"Duh," I mumble under my breath. *Wait.* I don't want wine.

Todd grabs a corkscrew and opens a bottle from the nearby rack. I stare at the red, blue, and gold coat of arms on the wine's off-white label. How do I say no without being a total loser? Then again, is it really that bad to try some? It's not like I'm going to become an alcoholic, like my mom's father.

Am I?

Todd pours four long-stemmed glasses. "That went fast," he says, holding up the empty bottle. He hands everyone a glass, and my fingers wrap around the thin stem.

"Cheers," Angelo says, still stirring with one hand.

A chorus of cheers, followed by sips.

I could take fake sips, then dump the wine in the sink when no one's watching.

Angelo glances at me. "How do you like it, Gita? I picked this particular wine because it'll complement the ragu."

Oh snap! Now I have to try it.

Hesitating, I take my first-ever sip of red wine, feeling everyone's eyes on me. "It's . . . good," I lie.

"Drink up then." Angelo smiles another half-Adonis smile, and I half smile back. His half smile turns whole: Another *whole* Adonis smile, just for me.

I take another sip of wine. A bigger one.

"Is this a Sangiovese?" Jane asks.

"Very good." Todd gives her an approving look.

"The full-bodied fig and fruit-forwardness gave it away," she says, swirling the wine.

Her astute analysis of the flavors astounds me. The best I can come up with is acidic, spoiled Welch's.

"A wine connoisseur, I see." Todd's eyes lower to Jane's cleavage.

She doesn't say or do anything, but a coy *Why, yes, I am a slice of fresh hamachi sashimi for your dining pleasure* expression takes hold of her face.

I get it. I mean, I have eyes too, and he's hot. Still, it's disappointing; I wish she'd give him a piece of her mind like she did with Simon. Or even just lift his chin, make him stop staring at her chest. I take another swig of wine without thinking, and end up coughing.

Angelo, who's draining the pasta in the sink, looks back at me. "Are you all right?"

I thump my chest a couple of times. "Fine," I say, getting a hold of myself. I take another sip.

"Good." He nods. "Because dinner is served."

"Thank goodness for Italian mothers," I blurt, then regret, because does that even make sense? I raise my glass nervously.

All glasses raised, everyone laughs again.

"To Italian mothers," Angelo says, gifting me with a private smile.

I grin all goofy.

Angelo dishes out the finished pasta and ragu onto four plates. He shaves some fresh Parmesan cheese on top of each, then hands the first plate to me. "For the Indian beauty," he says.

I lick my lips at the steaming plate in my hand. "Thank you," I respond automatically. Then his words register: *Wait, what?* My heart flutters. I guzzle more wine.

We go to the dining room, sit around a gray oak wood table with lit candles. The whole pasta and candlelight thing reminds me of that romantic scene in Disney's *Lady and the Tramp*. Except this isn't a cartoon. This is real life, and while Jane, Todd, and Angelo begin a lively discussion about football, I sip more wine and take yummy bites of our meal.

Next thing I know, Todd is refilling my empty wineglass from a second bottle he's opened.

"Thank you," I say, sloppy-smiling.

"You're very welcome."

I turn my attention back to the sporty conversation: Jane's knowledge of "tight ends," "sacks," "going deep," "get it to the wide receiver," and "penetrating the end zone" impresses me. And makes me giggle—I want to crack a joke as to whether they're talking about football or porn but I chup-re myself, taking big gulps of wine instead.

Everything they're saying is hilarious. I know nothing about football, but it feels like I do. It feels like I love football. My eyes bounce from Todd to Angelo to Jane. I love *them*. I long to join the conversation, but they've switched to Italian.

Kind of rude, don't you think? But I lean back in my chair, close my eyes, and let it go. There's an incredible cozy feeling inside me, like I'm wearing a fuzzy robe under my skin. I open my eyes and go straight for my wineglass. Sip, sip, sip.

Now all I want to do is smile. I touch my lips and realize I'm already smiling. Great!

A little pasta, more wine. When I realize the conversation is back to English, I wait for the right time to jump in.

"Nationalism is a myth," Jane says. "Like during war, it makes people forget all the bad things they do—or cheer on—in the name of patriotism. Save that for sports, am I right?"

I nod. "Shared amnesia," I say, pleased with myself for providing a medical perspective.

"Yes," Angelo agrees. "People stop thinking for themselves."

"And if we can't think for ourselves, are we truly free?" I ask in a philosophical voice, cupping my chin. But then I crack up.

I take another sip. The world feels like it's mine.

Another sip.

The conversation carries on, becoming more and more profound. Todd says something about compassion being the best cure for the sickness of nationalism. Sai and Anna Freud pop into my head—Sai's compassion for our family manifested as altruistic surrender, curing our parents' overwork sickness. I open my mouth to discuss said altruism when I realize that Angelo's moved from across the table and is sitting next to me now.

"How are you, Gita?"

"Really good." We clink glasses and take sips.

He asks me questions about being premed. I answer between more sips. At some point, his face gets hazy. So does my sense of time. As I hold my dizzy head, I notice Jane and Todd touching their foreheads together, whispering.

Angelo puts his hand on my arm, and the little hairs there stand up.

"You okay?" he asks.

I lift my head and inspect his expression: It's warm but worried. *Why?* Is he concerned that I'm drunk? Or something else?

It seems like too much effort to say anything, so I nod. I reach for my glass but end up knocking it over. Luckily, it's empty. "Oops," I giggle.

"I think you need to rest a little. Come with me." Angelo helps me up, wrapping his arm around my waist.

Rich Palo Alto people are nice after all.

I slide my arm around Angelo's waist. My head falls onto his shoulder. He leads me into a big room full of ancient Indian art—prints hanging on the walls and sculptures on the end tables. "My room," he says, touching the brass Nataraja statue.

I wonder for a second if he's got some weird Indian fetish, but then my eyes collide with his California king-size bed. "Wow. I've never seen a bed that big."

"Go ahead. Make yourself comfortable."

Don't mind if I do. I sit on the edge, then fling my upper body back. I close my eyes, not sure if I'm falling asleep or . . .

Someone's kissing my neck.

Someone who isn't Neil Uncle is kissing Pinky Auntie's neck.

I strain to open my eyes.

It's Bhavin Uncle!

Angelo's on top of me.

But it's okay, because I'm a queen on his Cali king bed. I stretch my arms out and clutch the satiny gold sheets. Cuddles and kisses—that's what this is, right?

But I thought my first kiss would be while watching the sunset or something.

Before I can think, his mouth is on mine—it feels like I'm choking on his tongue.

I need air! I start squirming under him, trying to push him off.

Bhavin Uncle's hand is under Pinky Auntie's skirt, and her underwear is around her ankles.

I look down. Oh shit! I'm naked.

I leave my bedroom door open, always open, and Mom walks in on me with my skirt lifted and my underwear around my ankles. I'm checking what's underneath. She rushes over and quickly pulls up my underwear and fixes my skirt. Shame-shame, *she says over and over. I touch her frizzy hair . . .*

I touch Angelo's hair. He's naked too! How did—?

He moves down, then starts licking and sucking. . . .

I close my eyes.

Sometimes he closes my bedroom door behind him. Mom never walks in then. No one does.

Shame-shame, *I whisper to myself.*

But it feels good. I push Angelo's head farther down.

He starts to follow my lead, then flips me over instead. He mumbles something that sounds like "I love your Indian . . ."

Love my Indian what?

I look back.

There's an Adonis smile on his face.

I wanted that smile. And tonight, Angelo gave me more than one.

I grin.

He's getting a condom and lube. My smile withers while my heart pounds in my rib cage.

I'm supposed to want this, right?

He gathers my hair from behind, planting feathery kisses down my back.

I do want this. Don't stop.

He wets two of his fingers and his thumb.

Maybe this is the price of Adonis smiles.

Two fingers in my yoni, then his thumb slowly in my puucha-dhi. It sort of hurts, sort of doesn't. My head is spinning: Echoes of Foxy Felicity's voice, but she's saying "shame-shame." *That's not what she's supposed to say.* She's supposed to say "Fuck me."

I hear myself correcting her out loud.

I close my eyes. "Fuck me," I say again, this time in a sexier voice.

He does, easing it in.

That's when it really hurts. My eyes water. I grab the sheets, and my mouth hangs open. A scream vaults up my throat but chup-re forces me to shove it back down.

He pulls out.

Is it over? I hope so.

CHAPTER 6

*P*anic jolts me awake, as if my entire body is a giant heart being shocked by defibrillator paddles.

My limbs flail. The first thing my eyes land on is my clock, which is tucked between my mattress and the wall. Red numbers and letters glow: 4:29 a.m., Sunday 9/20. *Ha! I beat my alarm by a minute!* I reach over and turn the buzzer off. With a drawn-in breath I sit up, ready to take on the world without tired excuses, even on a Sunday.

Immediately, I sway.

My head pounds. I touch my temple, then my fingers slip to my lips. They're cracked. I notice that my mouth is parched, like a dry Cali riverbed during the recent drought. I begin to scoot toward the ladder but then stop—*why is my* entire *nether region sore?*

That's when my head squeezes out the memory of last night.

Did Angelo know it was my first time? In either . . .

It was two first times.

I nibble on a hangnail. A quick, sharp pain in my thumb as I bite off a sliver of cuticle skin.

Why didn't he ask? Why didn't I say anything?

In the dark silence of my room, I'm acutely aware of my cardiac muscle palpitating under my sternum, echoing loudly in my skull.

I didn't want either of the first times. Did Pinky Auntie want—?

Wait a second. Why am I thinking about her right now?

My eyes bulge as I remember for the second time what I remembered for the first time last night: Bhavin Uncle kissing Pinky Auntie.

Were they having an affair? Or do I have it wrong?

Can't be! Pinky Auntie wouldn't cheat on Neil Uncle.

I convince myself that it was nothing but a drunken hallucination. *So never mind! Focus on your own shamelessness, Gita.*

I hold myself and chew on the inside of my cheek. Everything with Angelo rewinds and repeats: It started off feeling good. So good. His tongue, his fingers, not to mention that last Adonis smile. I exhale a quiet breath. That last Adonis smile in the heat of the moment felt like it could change my life. Maybe get me away from my arranged marriage dharma? Or closer to something else. What? God? Love?

Stop it!

I don't even really believe in God. As for love, I know sex

isn't love . . . but people in love have sex. Maybe all the wine tricked me into *feeling* his Adonis smile as love, and then the sex was a natural consequence? I don't know. All I know for sure is that, with him all over me, I would've done anything to get his Adonis smile just one more time, even if it was the last time.

I bite down on my lower lip, hard. I didn't just do *anything* for the Adonis smile, I did *everything.*

Actually, I let *him* do everything to me.

I retch, but nothing comes out. Embarrassing pain or not, I don't want to risk puking on my bed, so I climb down, bow-legged. I kneel with my face in the trash can that's lined with a plastic bag.

When the urge to hurl passes, I crawl on my hands and knees to my desk and pull open the drawer that has my bottle of Advil. I swallow a couple of pills with a few swigs from yesterday's cup of warm water, like Sai did that one time when he had a hangover.

I glance at the clock. Now it's 4:36 a.m. *Crap.* I have to run at 5:00 a.m. or else my schedule for the day will be thrown off. I shudder at the devastating possibility that's NEVER happened before.

I clench my fists—I'm going to run. I can't not run. If I don't run, then I will literally explode, especially when I'm stressed out like this.

So I ignore the pain, push myself off the floor, and flip on the light. I gather my tracksuit, sports bra, and socks, then strip. When I step out of my panties, I notice a dark reddish-brown crust on the inner crotch part.

The etiology is as obvious as the shingles my dad once had on his back. Still, as the future Dr. Desai, family practitioner, it's imperative to run through a thorough Doogie-Howser-M.D.-differential-diagnosis on the white board of my mind.

Menstrual blood? No, because I'm super regular and my period just ended about ten days ago.

Gastrointestinal bleed? No, I don't have any other GI symptoms.

Broken hymen blood? More likely, since a hymen can be torn by first sex. But, then again, it can also be broken before first sex by other non-sexual strenuous activities.

Shit . . . or bloody shit?

Gross!

I grab the panties and stuff them in a small plastic shopping bag.

At least he used condoms. So I didn't catch an STD or HIV. No HIV means no AIDS, which means I won't be the second Indian American person whose family originates in Gujarat to die of AIDS. Freddie Mercury, of course, being the first last year . . .

I tie the top of the bag and toss it in the trash can. Thick, unclear emotions churn like the malai my mom once used to make homemade butter.

A few tears leak out. I didn't say no after he started ramming his . . .

Foolish, foolish girl! Was it worth that price for his Adonis smiles?

I grab the phone, wanting to call Sai. Maybe he can comfort me, because this is beyond Snuffles.

I start to dial, but stop two digits short.

What would I tell him anyway? That some older guy f—

No. How could I come clean to Sai about something so dirty? I rub my eyes.

I could just tell him I miss home or something. But he'd catch the quiver in my voice and dig deeper. And what if I can't keep my mouth shut? What if chup-re doesn't work in the face of his selfless compassion?

I imagine the choppy cadence of my confession. Sai's face as he drops the phone . . .

My blood drains to my feet. It feels like a rusty shovel is scooping out my insides, which have crumbled into dry, contaminated soil.

Calling him right now is a terrible idea.

When I put the handset back on the dock, I notice the red message light blinking. I press play.

"Hey Gita, it's Sai."

Speak of the devil—well, angel. For an instant, I forget about last night and smile.

"Hopefully, you're out having a good time and not at the library. It *is* Saturday night after all. Give me a call when you get a chance." He pauses, sniffs. "Remember that girl I mentioned I was seeing? Shantel? Yeah, she broke up with me. . . ."

Silence. I think maybe he's about to hang up, but then he says, "Don't you think two people should be in love before they . . . you know. Anyway, call me."

I raise my eyebrows. It's not as if Sai and I have discussed sex before, but I know my brother well enough to know that *that's* what he's talking about.

And I guess it turns out that Sai is . . . well, he's not like Angelo. What if Angelo had been more like Sai?

I would still be a virgin.

I slide my splayed fingers into my hair, then clamp down on my scalp. Suddenly, I'm sobbing.

I can't run like this. If only I hadn't gotten drunk—then none of this would've happened. Why didn't I say no?

I draw my face back. *Did I say no?* I scoff—of course I didn't say no. I was too busy trying to chup-re myself.

Get a grip! What's there to cry about? It's not like I'm Dad when he was younger, trudging through monsoon floods to get his dying sister to the hospital. And it's not like I'm Mom when she was a kid, with a dad reeking of booze punching her in the face.

Last night was bad. But nothing in my privileged American life has been *that* bad.

So I need to get over myself and my lousy decisions. I need to get back to my schedule. First, I need to run. Then I need to *work*. That always helps.

I wipe the damp off my face and scan my CDs. I select Nirvana's *Bleach*, playing it at low volume since it's early, then skip to "Negative Creep." As soon as the hardcore guitar, drums, and lyrics burst out of the speakers, I picture an electric saw cutting my skull. I imagine shoving my fist into my cerebrum, spreading my fingers, and digging around in the cortical matter until I find the memories of Angelo. I rip them out, not caring if other, more innocent, brain matter is dangling from the edges.

I thrust my limbs into my running clothes. Put on my sports watch. Then one sock . . .

The song "Scoff" begins: The opening drums beat at my flesh. The guitar grates my soul into bits of despair, rage, and denial.

The pain I hear in Kurt's voice unleashes my tears once again. I sink to the floor, burying my face in my palms.

Sure, Angelo drove me back to the dorm. That's nice. But he didn't ask me to stay over at his place the way Todd asked Jane. Also, he didn't ask for my number.

Then there's the small detail that regular sex wasn't enough; that he fucked me in the ass without the intention of ever seeing me again. All I was to him was an asshole. Literally.

I grab Snuffles and scream into his fluffy head.

I deserved it.

I hug Snuffles. Would Sai think I deserved it?

No. Sai's got a pure heart that doesn't judge. He wouldn't like it, but he definitely wouldn't think it was my fault.

A puff of air from between my dry lips as I think about how healthy Sai's heart must be. Healthy in a way that can't be measured by EKGs or echocardiograms.

My heart, on the other hand . . .

Ugly, ugly, ugly.

I blink tears away and suck in my snot as I stand up, lay

Snuffles down on the beanbag chair, and shove my other foot into a sock. I smash the PREV button on the boom box and skip back to "Love Buzz," the song that always amps me up.

The sexy, hard guitar drops me in the middle of a Sahara ultramarathon. All the other runners around me are guys. In my mind, I'm sprinting. Soon, I'm flying past every dude, casting an arrogant *fuck you* glance at each one.

I bolt by the guy in the lead. It's Angelo! I flip him off: *I'll never make a mistake like you again.*

I lace up my Sauconys, then stretch, giving myself a pep talk that boils down to *Everything will be okay* and *I'm the master of my own universe.*

Master . . .

I'm the master of this tight pussy. This ass. Angelo said that last night, pulling my hair like reins. His hot breath is in my ear again: *Remember who was here first.*

Renewed despair, rage, and denial surge as the song's guitar goes crazy.

Why is my yoni tingling?

At the same time, my mother's voice echoes. *Shame-shame . . .*

It's too much.

I drop to my knees yet again, tears streaming, emotions stabbing, my yoni throbbing. Everything inside and out craves a sedative. But I don't have any pills like that.

If only I could shrink into myself and disappear, but I can't.

Fix it. Work hard and fix it, *Gita.*

I rub my eyes, reminding myself that someday my hard work will let me help others. And that is the best medicine for myself.

I try to chup-re the rest of what's going on in my head and body.

But how do I chup-re things that aren't words? How do I chup-re the bitter taste that's in my mouth? How do I chup-re the flames curling up from the kindling wood in my gut? How do I chup-re the wildfire that's incinerating me?

Everything goes red and burns. I'm about to scream into the air. . . .

Chup-re!

My hand flings itself onto my mouth, trapping my voice. I swallow it all, then push myself off the floor. I jog out my door . . . out of the dorm.

I run.

The cool air on my burning body. The buildings, the trees, everything is a blur.

I run, and run, and run.

I get my fastest five-mile time ever.

CHAPTER 7

*T*wo days ago, I fornicated. One day ago, I tried to forget. Today, I'm desperately attempting to persuade myself that I'm a tabula rasa, a blank slate. Or maybe the universe is keeping score, and that I've done both the dirty and the dirtiest with Angelo will be canceled out by my forthcoming contributions to the advancement of plant—specifically maize—genetics.

See, it's my first day at the lab. To my surprise, it isn't a pristine, bright white lair of quiet scientific inquiry like in the movies. Rather, machines hum in the background and laughter and lively discussions of transposons steal the foreground. The lighting is muted, not blazing like a hundred suns. Instead of the smell of bleach, it's the scent of baking bread mixed with dirty sneakers wafting from the agar plates. And none of the grad students or postdocs are wearing lab coats or safety goggles. Neither is Dr. Peters, who just finished showing me around.

"You're the only undergrad I've hired this year, so make me proud," she says as we approach her office.

My voice cracks as I reply, "I will." *I promise.*

She checks her watch, tapping its glass face. "Time for me to make a call. I'll be back in a few minutes." She goes into her office and shuts the door.

There's clapping in the small conference room to my right. I tiptoe to the doorway: Two men—one desi and one white—are applauding a young Latina woman with long, wavy brown hair as she jots a plant experiment idea on the chalkboard. I assume they're some of Dr. Peter's grad students.

"*That* is how we can significantly increase the reactivation rate of the Mutator transposable elements in the progeny kernels," she says.

"Next level Mu transposon shit," the desi replies, nodding reverently. "I like it."

I do a double take of the desi. *He's so cute!* I've never seen an Indian guy in real life who I considered to be cute. I mean, this guy is Shah Rukh Khan cute. And he's obviously smart if he's working here. . . .

A smile hovers around my lips, like a hummingbird around a nectar-rich flower.

The young woman turns around and drops the chalk as if it's a mic.

The guys start clapping again.

Goose bumps erupt up and down my arms. Inspiration grips me the same way it does—though I'll never admit this to anyone— every time I hear the guitar intro of Survivor's "Eye of the Tiger," and I want to clap for her too.

"Thanks for waiting, Gita." I jump at Dr. Peters's voice, not realizing I'd been totally entranced by the grad students to the point of losing track of everything else.

"No problem," I say, turning around.

Dr. Peters rubs her hands together. "I just spoke to an editor at *Nature*. They've accepted one of our papers."

Anyone remotely interested in biology knows that *Nature* is among the most prestigious scientific journals in the world.

"That's incredible. Congratulations!"

"Thank you. It's all because of our wonderful team, which you are now a part of."

My cheeks flush, like they're dusted with sindoor.

I could've applied to do a work study at the hospital like almost every other premed, but I chose Dr. Peters's lab because I'm not trying to be like every other premed. I'm trying to be *better*. And being well-rounded by studying plant biology with one of the preeminent scientists in the field is a good way to do that.

Dr. Peters points to a desk. "Speaking of part of the team, this is yours." Then she spreads her arms wide. "Welcome aboard. We're glad to have you."

I clasp my hands as if I'm praying. "Thank you for the tour, Dr. Peters. And for this opportunity."

"Absolutely." She tilts her head. "Any questions?"

Twenty-three to be exact, and they're all about you. Yup, I prepared a list. But this early in the game, I've earned the right to ask maybe two, tops. "How did you get interested in plant biology as opposed to animal or human biology?"

"That's an easy one. My parents immigrated to California from Germany and bought land before I was born. I grew up working the family farm." Her lips stretch into a grin. "I'd talk to the crops like they were my best friends. For my birthday or Christmas, I'd ask for plants, not puppies or ponies or dolls. When my parents would suggest going to the zoo, I'd suggest the botanical garden or a hike in the forest. The more I learned about plants, the more their elegance appealed to me. They can make new organs repeatedly, unlike animals, so it's easier to study plant development and mutations."

"Oh wow—I never thought of it that way." I pause and rub my chin. "My next question is: What drives you?"

She raises an eyebrow. "Apparently, the same thing that drives you."

My forehead wrinkles.

"Your lab application, remember? You wrote, 'There's no finish line, only the journey of helping people.' For you, helping people is healing those who are sick or hurt. For me, it's feeding those who are starving."

My mouth hangs open a little. *She remembers what I wrote.* She gets it. She gets *me.* I mean, even my own parents don't get me. . . .

I'd already told my folks what a big deal Dr. Peters was. Is. This morning, when I called them, Mom answered and I announced, "I'm starting work at *the* Dr. Eleanor Peters's lab today!"

Silence.

"Mom?"

"What?" she snapped. "Do you want me to prepare pithi?"

A part of me wanted to laugh and say, "So that my first day goes well! Good one! And thanks!"

But the rest of me went into a dejected chup-re, because her sarcasm has that power over me.

Before a traditional Indian wedding ceremony, the bride and groom let pithi—a thick paste of turmeric, chickpea flour, and rose water—soak into their skin, the yellow color considered auspicious for their new beginning together.

For Mom, when it comes to me, everything circles back to my eventual banishment to the dungeon of arranged marriage.

What would Dr. Peters think about the whole arranged marriage thing? She's single, no kids, and seems completely satisfied. Completely free.

I get the sudden urge to fling my arms around Dr. Peters for a Snuffles-sandwich-hug, even though Snuffles is in my dorm room. I hold back, only allowing myself to say, "I'm so honored to—"

A thundering clap, then a booming voice. "And who is this?"

Dr. Peters doesn't even turn to look at the person behind her. "Hello, Sora. This is Gita Desai, our new undergrad assistant."

I crane my neck to see who she's talking to.

"Gita, Gita, Gita," Sora sings, sashaying over. He keeps his steady gaze on me, then stands next to Dr. Peters with one hand on his hip. "Welcome. Are you ready to get kinky with the sex life of corn? Safe sex, of course."

Dr. Peters chuckles. "I've got a meeting, so I'll leave you in Sora's capable hands, Gita. And be sure to ask the soon-to-be Dr. Amin about his graduate research focus—it's incredible."

I nod, wondering if Sora's last name is Gujarati, Persian, or Arabic in origin, because it could be any of those. Or from some other Indian language? Punjabi? I don't know. But his first name sounds Japanese.

After Dr. Peters leaves the room, I turn to Sora. "What's your research about?"

He tsk-tsks, wagging his finger. "That can wait." He puts his hands on my shoulders and peers into my eyes. His light brown irises are sunlight shining through the Indian whiskey Neil Uncle and Bhavin Uncle used to sip. His kohl-lined eyes are striking, his strong jaw softened by a berry-pink-glossed smile. There's a tiny gold nose ring in his left nostril, which is so yellow I clock it immediately as Indian gold. Pinky Auntie would agree that he wears it well.

"There's a more pressing matter I'd like to bring to your attention," Sora says.

Dr. Peters didn't mention anything urgent. My curiosity ripens like a sweet mango. "What's that?"

"It's about the undergrad who worked here last year."

I cock my head, my face scrunched.

"One of the guys in the lab saw her as nothing but easy, tasty meat."

Right away, Jane's comment about guys looking at her like she's fresh hamachi comes to mind. Is Sora worried that whoever this guy is will look at *me* like that? If that's the case, I should set his tortured mind at ease because, generally, guys are oblivious to my presence. Besides, I've got more important things to do these days than collect Adonis smiles.

"Which guy?"

Sora tosses his head to the right. "He sits there."

My eyes shift to an empty desk with a gold name plate. *Abhijeet Sen.*

An Indian guy is a player? Is he the cute desi in the conference room? I hope not!

Slowly, I shift my eyes back to Sora.

"Everyone calls him Jeet." He pauses. "The undergrad . . . well, she and Jeet had been dating for several months before she—or any of us—discovered he already had a girlfriend. The undergrad was crushed. She quit the lab. I tried to check up on her, but she never returned my calls." The corners of Sora's mouth draw down. He shifts in place, his hands fidgeting. "Even though Jeet claims he's single now, promise me you'll be careful around him—I just don't trust him."

I feel myself nodding, but also wondering why Sora is being so straight-up with me, someone he just met.

Sora exhales, then smiles. "Okay then, Gita Desai. It's time for me to get back to work."

"Your research?"

He nods.

"What's it about?"

"How to make maize more drought resistant."

"You want to help feed the world?"

"Everyone in the lab does."

Even Jeet-the-cheater, who may or may not be the cute desi I spotted earlier? If so, do his good lab contributions make up for his previous bad behavior, the way I'm hoping my good lab contributions make up for everything with Angelo? And who knows—maybe cheating was a one-time mistake, one he doesn't plan on making again.

Sora's head falls back then, and he groans. "I'm redoing part of an experiment, though, no thanks to contaminated specimens."

"That sucks."

"It does." He shrugs. "But it's part of the process."

"Well, I'm free. Need some help?"

Sora's brows shoot up in surprise. "Gita Desai to the rescue?"

I laugh. "I don't know about rescue . . . But maybe I can help speed up your re-do process."

"Okay then—I'll take you up on it! Thanks, Gita."

"Of course."

Sora's expression grows solemn. "You know, it's still not easy for me to ask for help. . . ."

I inspect his face—I can tell that something bothersome just popped into his head. Should I ask him what's up?

Before I can speak, Sora tosses his head to the left. "This way."

I follow him, ultimately deciding to chup-re my good intentions—for now. It doesn't feel right to dig beyond what he's willingly shared. Digging for more info is an honor best saved for friends, I think.

"And lunch is on me," Sora adds, playfully batting my arm.

"Score!" I smile, hoping with all my might that Sora and I will be friends someday soon. Then it's open season on digging.

CHAPTER 8

It's a beautiful Sunday, the last in September. By the time Jane and I arrive at the upscale, open-air Stanford Mall, the sun, its hue that of saffron in water, is directly overhead in the pale blue sky.

All around us, well-dressed people saunter with shopping bags, spending their Silicon Valley money with reckless abandon. We pass by a tiny pâtisserie and the smell of butter, burnt sugar, and vanilla is a satisfying kind of torture. My stomach rumbles.

Jane gives me side-eye. "How is that even possible?"

"What can I say? I'm a sucker for chocolate croissants." I lick my lips, my thoughts drifting to the *Stanford Medicine Magazine* article on patients with tapeworm infections whose hunger felt endless.

"But I literally sat there in the caf and watched you devour a stack of pancakes drowning in syrup and whipped cream less than two hours ago."

I shrug, wondering if tapeworms have sweet tooths. "Maybe I'm eating for two."

Jane stops abruptly, her hand flying to her mouth. "What?!"

I stop as well and face her. I can see the whites of her eyes all around her blue irises.

She lets her hand drop and grabs my arm. "Did something more happen with Angelo? You said you two just talked in his room. Did you—? Are you—?"

I put my own hands up. "No, no! Don't worry, I'm not pregnant!" I know because my period started this morning, one week early.

Jane's eyebrows stitch together. She squints at me.

I pat my stomach. "I was making a premed joke about having a tapeworm."

Finally, Jane's expression relaxes. She pokes my arm. "Don't scare me like that!"

"My bad." I chuckle nervously, then swallow. How worried would Jane be if she knew about *everything* that happened with Angelo?

We keep going.

Jane glances at me, smiling. "If you were pregnant, I bet you'd out-eat those football players."

"Probably!" It comes out way more enthusiastic than I'd

intended; I'm so relieved that I'm not pregnant with Angelo's baby. My steps feel lighter, yet more controlled. *I'll never let another Adonis-smile-wearing jerk fool me again.*

Then I wonder: Will I ever actually *want* to be pregnant? I can't even consider it for another eight years at least, between undergrad and med school. Maybe even another three or four years after that for my family practice residency.

My thoughts drift back to the start of that night with Angelo. "By the way, did you and Todd *really* just make out? I mean, you spent the night." I cross my arms, high and tight.

Jane's eyes veer to the side. She rubs the back of her neck. "Absolutely. He was a gentleman." Her voice is robotic; her expression is blank.

I angle my head. *Why is she being weird all of a sudden?* But then again, I just straight up lied to her about Angelo, so I let it go.

Jane clears her throat. "Well, let's feed you and your tapeworm before it eats you from the inside out." She shudders. "Gross—I just pictured that. I'd never make it through med school."

"Sure you would."

She shakes her head. "No way! I'm too squeamish."

"That's what therapists are for, to help you work through that."

"Hmm. I guess."

I hold up a finger. "Did you know that squeamishness can be an indicator of a more caring doctor?"

"I didn't." She elbows me. "Did you read that in the *Stanford Med Magazine*?"

I pull my shoulders back. "Actually, yes. There was an article about physician empathy. Think of squeamishness as the manifestation of imagining what a patient's pain is like."

Jane doesn't say anything, but her expression disintegrates.

Did I say something wrong? "Are you okay?"

Jane lifts up the corners of her lips. "I'm fine."

"But you—" I begin.

She cuts me off. "You're hungry. Luckily, Fresh Choice is just around the corner. I can't believe you've never been—the salad bar and buffet are, like, fifty feet long and the chocolate chip muffins are to *die* for."

I know she's not telling me something, but I drop it. "Lead the way."

We pick up our pace, and I accidentally bump into a white woman in her late thirties. She's holding hands with a young girl I assume is her daughter. They've got matching blond hair and Burberry plaid dresses.

"Excuse me. I'm sorry."

The woman gives me a slight smile. "It's all right." Then she and her daughter turn and head into the Cartier store on the right.

I take a few steps forward before noticing that Jane's not beside me. I peek over my shoulder: Jane's standing perfectly still, her gaze cast downward.

I retrace my steps. "What's wrong?"

Her face goes pale. "Nothing."

"I don't buy it."

She glances at me then away, blinking slowly. "I'm going to start crying if I talk about it."

"Nothing wrong with a little lacrimation." I nudge her elbow with mine. "In fact, crying is our body's way of making us feel better."

Her mouth is clamped, but she smiles a little.

Seeing her trying so hard to hold back tears reminds me of my favorite line from *Henry VI, Part 3* that I read for high school A.P. English. "And to quote Shakespeare, 'To weep is to make less the depth of grief.'"

"Et tu, Shakespeare?"

That's when I notice the familiar distant look in her eye. In the sunlight bathing her face, a smattering of freckles seems to rise magically to the surface of her cheeks. For the first time since I've met her, she appears more like a shy, innocent little girl than royalty.

I used to be a shy, innocent little girl.

Shy, innocent girls are nice, but they aren't perfect. They're human, like everyone else. And everyone makes mistakes.

I made two big ones recently that I didn't mean to make: being a voyeur, and hooking up with Angelo. Has Jane made a mistake or two also? Was one of the mistakes with Todd? Is that why she's sad?

"Gotta release it for relief," I say, my pitch rising in an attempt to sound convincing.

Jane sighs. "True as that may be, I'm not about to ruin my makeup."

Makeup shouldn't be a chup-re. But I don't say that, because now is not the time to explain what chup-re means. "I know for a fact that you use waterproof mascara, so you'll need a better excuse than that."

She searches my face.

I give her a gentle smile. "It's okay, Jane. You can tell me anything."

She stares at me for a second, but then blinks and smiles. She touches my arm. "Maybe another time. But thanks for the heart-hug." She pauses. "I thought only my mother knew how to give those." Her smile fades.

It occurs to me that whenever Jane mentions her mom or dad, it's usually a total buzzkill for her. I consider asking her more about her mom's heart-hugs, but what if that just makes her feel worse? Instead, I toss an arm around her and squeeze her shoulders. "A real-life half hug for you."

She pats my hand on her shoulder. As we approach Fresh Choice, I notice that my friend's smile is back, and my own unfettered smile takes flight.

CHAPTER 9

*T*hat night, my geology textbook is cracked open on my desk and I'm supposed to be done reading the chapter on plate tectonics. Instead, I've been on the phone with Sai for more than an hour.

I hear him yawn. "Thanks for lending me your ear, sis."

"Anytime," I reply.

"I'm done obsessing over everything Shantel said. I think you're right."

"Of course I'm right! I still can't believe she called you 'cruel and selfish' just because you didn't go all—" I wince. Can't finish that sentence with my brother—it feels too weird. "She doesn't know what cruel and selfish is."

An image flashes in my head: Angelo pulling my hair from behind, a devilish expression on his face. I stare at the illustration of the oceanic trench on the page, wanting to disappear into it.

Sai clicks his tongue. "Gita, sorry, but Mom's over here grabbing the phone out of my hand. I'll call you tomorrow or something, okay?"

"Okay," I say, trying to forget Angelo and his good-for-nothing Adonis smile.

"Hi, beta," Mom says, warm and sweet like the gajar ka halwa she makes. "Almost a full month at Stanford already!"

I'm suspicious of her Bollywood-mom voice. It usually means some sort of arranged-shaadi pressure is waiting in the wings. My body tenses in preparation for the onslaught to bring me down.

The last time she sounded like this was a year ago, when we watched a bootleg VHS of the Bollywood film *Saajan* starring Madhuri Dixit. At the end of the film, my tearful mom had gingerly laid her hand on mine and said, "True love is sacrifice."

I tilted my head and smiled, still lost in all the post-movie goodness.

But she followed that with, "Gita beta, your arranged marriage might be a lot of sacrificing, but that is true love! You'll see."

I had pulled my hand away then, mentally rolling my eyes.

"Beta?" Mom's voice over the phone cuts through the memory. "How are you?"

My reply tiptoes out: "Fine. How are you?"

"Good. Are you eating enough?"

"Yes." I'm wondering how many momly questions she'll ask before she drops the shaadi bomb.

"Taking study breaks?"

"Yes."

"Sai said you're the only undergrad Dr. Peters hired at the lab. How was your first day there?"

She remembered Dr. Peters's name! That's got to count for something.

Still, it takes me a second to utter "Good."

"I'm so proud of you."

"Thanks, Mom." She should have mentioned something completely day-destroying by now. I drop my guard a tad. "What are you up to?"

"Sai and I are heading back to clean up the shop after my evening darshan."

I picture Mom in our Union City apartment the morning of Stanford move-in day. She was pressing her palms together in front of the heavy brass statue of Ganesh in our living room, whispering a prayer in Gujarati. *Remover of obstacles, with your guidance, let Gita gain knowledge and get good marks. Let Sai . . .*

That morning, her prayer hadn't included anything about my future arranged marriage. I remember releasing a huge pent-up breath as I listened. For an instant, it seemed possible that Mom saw me as more than an arranged-bride-to-be.

Maybe it's *that* Mom talking to me now. The Mom whose chill vibe makes up a little for the shaadi-pressuring version of her.

I glance toward my dorm room window. My expression that's reflected there is serene, like my mother's Ganesh statue. "Another day of hard work, Mom?"

"Yes—the shop was extra busy today," she says. "What about you?"

"Book darshan."

"Mmm. Dad will say hello next time—he fell asleep as soon as we got home. I'll let you get back to your studies, beta."

"Okay mom. Bye."

"Jai Shri Krishna."

"Jai Shri Krishna," I mumble. Because that's what I'm supposed to say back, and it feels wrong to leave Mom hanging. But every muscle in my body goes into rigor mortis at the nothing short of delusional echo of those three Gujarati words in my ear and out of my mouth.

"Jai Shri Krishna" is what the older generation of Gujjus say as a greeting and goodbye. Mom once told me it's supposed to loosely mean "Praise to Lord Krishna." The thing is, the phrase literally translates to "Victory to Lord Krishna," which sounds more like a battle cry than a pious phrase of devotion.

My stomach churns. Not only do my parents chup-re, ignore, or discount everything that feels important to me, they also don't bother to say what they mean or mean what they say.

Why not say "Vakhāna Shri Krishna?" From my understanding

125

of Gujarati, that phrase is closer to the praise-Krishna-non-war-mongering greeting and goodbye that I think Mom intends.

A long-forgotten memory from when I was eight materializes. Pinky Auntie had just returned home from her part-time job at a grocery store. Mom was in the kitchen; she looked up from her cup of cha and called out, "Jai Shri Krishna."

"Jai Shri Krishna," Pinky Auntie replied, stepping out of her shoes.

I followed my aunt to her room. I tugged on her uniform shirt.

She squatted in front of me and smiled. "Yes, beta?"

"Sai told me 'Jai Shri Krishna' means 'Victory to Lord Krishna.' Why do we need Krishna to be victorious? Who are we at war with?" I asked.

She chuckled. Then she gently held my chin with her index finger and thumb and peered into my eyes. "We aren't at war. The deeper meaning of the saying is 'Let the essence of Krishna that lives within me emerge victorious.'"

I nodded. I didn't exactly understand what that meant, but what a relief that it sounded beautiful and personal, and nothing like a war chant. "Then why don't you and Mom say *that* to each other?"

She laughed and hugged me, but never gave me an answer. It didn't matter though—I didn't believe in Krishna anyway. I believed in Pinky Auntie.

A year after she and Neil Uncle left, I remember Sai trying to talk to Dad about the whole "Jai Shri Krishna" thing.

"But Dad, it's right here in the paper. See?" He pointed to the bottom of the front page.

Dad kept his eyes on the TV.

"During his election speech," Sai continued, "this politician said, and I quote, 'We won't stop chanting *Jai Shri Krishna* and *Jai Shri Ram* and if the non-Hindus don't like it, let them prepare for retribution.' He said that the very same morning of the riots, when Hindus slaughtered hundreds of innocent Muslims." Sai frowned. "Dad, how can you ask me to say 'Jai Shri Krishna' now?"

I'm guessing Sai's question was mostly rhetorical; he and I both knew Dad's response would be the loathsome "chup-re." Which it was.

Years later, I learned that other bigots in the world also used the word *victory* in their daily greetings to each other and at political rallies. Like the Nazis. They adopted the phrase "Seig Heil," which translates to "Hail Victory."

No thank you to all of it!

As I hang up the phone with Mom, I make a mental note to never say "Jai Shri Krishna" again, no matter how disrespectful it might seem to my parents or any other Gujju elder.

I put the phone back in its cradle, reach for my highlighter, and knock over the birthday card from Pinky Auntie that's propped up on my desk. I let my eyes dawdle over the cover—

teal with gold floral and paisley designs—before picking it up and opening it.

> *Dear Gita,*
> *On your eighteenth birthday, you are at Stanford! One step closer to being Dr. Desai.*

My eye twitches. I read the next line.

> *I am proud of you.*

I chew on a nail as I read the rest.

> *I hope you enjoy your birthday. Every day I am thinking about and missing my kindhearted niece.*
> *Love,*
> *Pinky Auntie*

My throat aches. I want to scream, *Maybe you've said what you mean, but it doesn't feel like you mean what you've said!* If she really missed me every day, she'd call me once in a while, or give me her address so we could exchange letters and share actual stuff with each other about our current selves. . . .

A question occurs to me: Which torture is worse—bad Angelo memories, or good Pinky Auntie ones?

My lips twist. *Both suck!* Angelo was straight-up cruel. But by cutting off all contact with me—except for her one-sided annual birthday wishes—Pinky Auntie became cruel in an indirect way.

My shoulders droop.

I believed in Pinky Auntie, and she let me down.

I hang my head.

For the first time, it *really* sinks in.

I scoff and whip my head up. Every cell in my body is shouting at me to rip the card to shreds, but I quickly drop it into the bottom drawer of my desk, then slam it shut. I sit there scowling with my arms crossed and my chest heaving, wishing I could give Pinky Auntie a piece of my mind.

It takes me a good minute to calm down enough to dive back into geology.

Studying goes well for half an hour before my eyelids begin to sag . . .

. . . Against the murky dark of sleep, Krishna appears on a chariot: "I will not raise a weapon," he says, "but I will provide counsel about your righteous war."

Bright-eyed Durga rides up on a tiger. From one of her eight hands, she tosses me a trident. I catch it—it's heavy.

She points, and my eyes follow the invisible line to Angelo on the other side of a battlefield, messing around with a girl whose face I can't see, though she has my hair.

"You're ready, Gita. The shakti is in you," Durga says. "Use it for—"

A loud knock.

Startled, my upper body jerks up and my eyelids fly apart. Another knock leaves me no time to panic about falling asleep for the first time ever while studying. Rubbing my eyes, I get the door.

It's Marisol and a tall, brown-haired, brown-eyed white guy with Gandhi glasses. I assume this is Joey, since he's got his arm around Marisol's waist. Probably-Joey is a hunky-hunk, and the Gandhi glasses certainly make him appear saint-like. Though now that I think of it, the real Gandhi wasn't the saint history portrays him as. . . .

"Hi, Gita," Marisol says, her eyes sparkling like Durga's were in my dream.

"Hi," I say.

Marisol touches probably-Joey's shoulder. "This is Joey. I wanted you to finally meet him!" For-sure-Joey smiles at me and extends his hand.

I shake it. "Nice to meet you."

"You as well," he replies in a deep, intense voice.

"What are you guys up to?"

"He's got work. I'm going home for the night." Marisol touches her neck and cringes. "I have to break it to my mom that I lost my great-grandmother's rosary."

The thumb side of my fist sails to my mouth. She's worn that necklace every time I've seen her. "Oh no! What a bummer to lose it."

Marisol nods. "I didn't mean to." She pauses. Sighs. "My mom gave it to me on my sixteenth birthday. I'm—I was—the fourth generation to wear it."

Joey rolls his eyes. "Sometimes you're so careless, Marisol."

My mouth drops open. *That's kind of harsh, Joey, don't you think?*

Marisol's eyebrows draw together. I touch her arm: "I'm sure your mom will understand that it was an accident."

Our eyes meet, and a gentle smile appears on her lips. "Hey Gita—let's study together tomorrow."

My breath catches in my throat. I've never fallen asleep studying *and* I've never studied with anyone. What if I can't concentrate? It's been a month of one "I've never" after another, and I need a break!

Someone yells Marisol's name from down the hall. The three of us turn to find Matt, the guy who was blasting the AC/DC that first night—and many other nights—strutting in our direction. His hazel eyes are adhered to Marisol.

Marisol tilts her head, her lips slinking into a subtle, inviting smile. My skin prickles. Why is she doing that when Joey's standing right here?

"Hi," Marisol says to Matt. Her smile goes racy.

My eyebrows collide like bumper cars as I glance at Joey, then back at Marisol.

Matt passes by . . . and his finger grazes Marisol's arm! She's wearing a long-sleeve button-up shirt, but still . . .

Marisol doesn't flinch. Neither does she introduce Joey.

I quietly click my tongue. If I had a boyfriend, I'd introduce him to everyone. And I mean *everyone*: I'd stop random people on the street and be like, "Excuse me, but have you met so-and-so? He's my extremely handsome *boyfriend*. . . ."

Meanwhile, Joey's expression remains mild, though his eyes have narrowed slightly. He shifts in place. "This is what I get for dating someone like you," he mumbles, shaking his head.

Marisol turns to him, wraps an arm around his waist. "What's that?"

"Nothing," he responds, pecking her reticently on the cheek. *Poor Joey.*

All of a sudden, I freeze in place as Joey's words contort in my head: *This is what I get for dating someone like you. . . . This is what I get . . . This is what you get . . .*

"I'll call you tomorrow to study, Gita." Marisol's voice is innocent. Her grip tightens around Joey's waist. "See you then."

"Bye, Gita," Joey adds, his voice strained.

My hand floats up to wave goodbye, but I can't speak because it feels like I'm choking on flashes of blood. An image has resurfaced: Me crying, and Angelo, seeing my tears, yanks me by my hair, hard. *This is what you get for saying fuck me,* he says.

"Chup-re," I whisper aloud.

Of course, it doesn't work. Chup-re is to muzzle me—not my memories.

CHAPTER 10

Dinkelspiel Auditorium is at capacity for tonight's visiting professor's lecture, "It's Not Disney, or the Sinister Origins of Our Favorite Fairy Tales." The VP, Dr. Henry Herman—with his brown tweed three-piece suit and tortoiseshell glasses—reminds me of Dr. Indiana Jones in *Raiders of the Lost Ark*.

About twenty minutes into his talk, Dr. Herman steps away from the podium, jumps off the low stage, and proceeds to walk up and down the two wide aisles as he continues his oration. Every head in the audience (mine included) turns to follow him. By the end of his lecture, I'm on the edge of my seat, my pencil on fire with frenzied note-taking.

Dr. Herman hops back onto the stage, and the thunderous applause by my fellow undergrads snaps me out of my hyper concentration. I drop my pencil—the graphite tip still practically smoking—and enthusiastically join in with the clapping.

As I exit the auditorium, remnants of the lecture roil around my head. In a trance, I make my way slowly toward Tressider, the student union building, for a quick fro-yo break. Fingers crossed a little dessert before dinner will reset me for the next round of studying O-Chem. . . .

While I'm waiting in line, something Dr. Herman said throat-punches its way through my swirling thoughts: *In the original* Sleeping Beauty *tale, a king finds an unconscious girl. He tries to wake her up—she doesn't—and then he rapes her.* These two sentences loop, playing over and over again in my mind. . . .

I feel my neck cording with tension; at the same time, I don't.

My foot begins tapping in a quick rhythm against the floor; I hear it, yet I don't.

Only after I'm holding a small cup of fro-yo—chocolate with a mixed berry topping—and the coldness inside radiates to my fingertips, does my body release, my foot stilling its relentless *tap-tap-tap.*

Only after I close my eyes and take my first bite of fro-yo do the looped thoughts finally quit.

I let the first bite—a union of tart, sweet, and creamy—sit on my tongue, savoring the quiet between my ears. Keeping my eyes shut, I take a second bite. Tension I'd been holding in muscles all over my body slowly leeches out.

My eyes snap open like a toy robot with fresh batteries. Suddenly energized and ready to tackle O-Chem, I devour the rest of the cupful in no time, then head out of Tressider.

The evening is cool and pleasant, perfectly so. *Was it this nice outside after I left Dink?* Chattering students on foot, bikes, and the occasional golf cart are all around. I clasp my hands behind me and slow down, smiling a little.

Tomorrow is October 1 and one month at the school of my dreams has been—

A familiar voice up ahead chirps, "Gita!"

I blink and look to find Marisol walking her bike toward me. First thing that pops into my head: *Don't chicken out, Gita. You promised yourself that the next time you saw Marisol, you'd call her out on flirting with guys who aren't her boyfriend. Especially in front of said boyfriend . . .*

Marisol smiles and waves, while chup-re rips out half my voice box. *Bye-bye promise.* I groan inwardly as I wave back.

We walk toward each other and meet in front of CoHo, the campus coffeehouse that's also located in Tressider. "Where are you coming from?" Marisol asks.

"Tressider. I was heading toward Green." An enormous yawn swallows my face. It's irritating—the fro-yo boost wore off in less than five minutes.

"Girl, that's why I *left* Green. The library put me to sleep!" She wags a finger. "Guess we both need a study break to recharge."

I'm about to shake my head. The hour-long visiting prof lecture and the fifteen-minute fro-yo pit stop *were* my study break. Why on earth would I deprive myself of more precious O-Chem studying time?

But then Marisol flashes me another smile, and it's an unfettered one! I can't help but let my own grin unfurl.

So now we're standing here, flashing our teeth at each other the way Sai and I might do, and it feels like my heart is a fist-sized gulab jambu pumping sticky cāsanī through my veins. The thought of studying as the priority over everything and every-one—and the urgency to be honest with Marisol about her flirty ways—drowns in something sweeter.

I give her a crisp nod. "A reinvigorating study break is just what the doctor ordered. Do you have something in mind?"

"Most definitely." She puts her hands on my shoulders, her gaze hijacking mine. "The other day you said you've never done karaoke. Well, it's time you lost your karaoke virginity!"

I start to laugh, but the word *virginity* boomerangs in my skull. I clear my throat—hoping I don't get trapped in another mental loop—drop my eyes, and adjust my backpack.

Marisol's arms drift back down to her sides. "So? It'll be fun, I promise!"

I shift my eyes back to her. "Might as well," I say slowly, leav-ing out the rest of what I'm thinking: *I've already lost a couple of other kinds of virginity. What's one more?*

"Let's invite Jane."

"Nah. She's out on a hot date right now." I give Marisol an exaggerated wink and elbow-nudge.

Marisol laughs. "Go Jane." She glances down at her flannel shirt and jeans. "I need a fresh outfit for our study-break date."

Why? So you can be all sexy for the guys we run into? My lips part to ask before the thought even registers. Shocked, I tell myself to shut up.

An hour and a half later, we're in a dim, private karaoke room. Pink and blue neon strobe lights sweep the walls, and a disco ball scatters silver dots like hundreds of stars in our own little Redwood City galaxy. Two passionately performed TLC songs later—"Ain't 2 Proud 2 Beg" and "Depend on Myself"—I dare to believe that maybe someday I can feel as badass as TLC are.

Marisol had picked "Giving Him Something He Can Feel" for her first song, and, of course, her sizzling vocals and slow and sultry dance moves rivaled those of an En Vogue music video. Now it's her turn again: She sashays to the front, clad in her black mini dress, cropped black cardigan, and fishnets. She grabs the mic, her expression just as suitable for the catwalk.

"Go on girl," I shout, channeling my favorite *In Living Color* skit.

Marisol selects a new song, then points to me. "This one goes out to my homegirl, Gita. Never hold back on self-love." The emboldening guitar and drum intro of Divinyls' "I Touch Myself" penetrates our private space.

We both crack up. Then, right on cue, Marisol starts singing, slowly sinking into a wide squat and letting her free hand roam all over herself; after all, as the lyrics go, there's no shame in touching ourselves. Grinning, I wiggle my butt in the booth seat, my expression coy and arms up. I can't remember the last time I felt like this . . . like every cell in my body is smiling. I never want this song to end. I never want this feeling—this moment—to end.

All too soon the song's over, and Marisol plops down next to me. We high-five. Then she kneads her belly, which is growling. "They expect me to lose like, ten pounds before the next shoot . . . but I say we order burgers and fries."

I press my hands together in prayer. "Yes, please."

Marisol nuzzles up to me, holding out the mic. "First though . . ."

I take the mic and twirl it. "Hmm . . . 'Hat 2 da Back' or 'What About Your Friends'?"

She does a seated Cabbage Patch. "'What About Your Friends'!" she cheers. Her cardigan slips off her left shoulder. Out of the corner of my eye, I notice a large, reddish-purple patch extending from her left décolletage to just below her shoulder.

Marisol glances at me, then inhales sharply. She yanks her cardigan back onto her shoulder and pulls the little menu on the table toward her, busying herself with its contents. "Maybe I don't want a burger after all . . ." she mumbles.

She's embarrassed. It strikes me that I've never seen Marisol embarrassed before. And all because of a patch of skin?

Medically speaking, of course, it's not just some random spot. It's a birthmark known as a nevus flammeus, or a port-wine stain. It's caused by swollen blood vessels in the skin and is generally harmless. I read all about it in—yup—*Stanford Medicine Magazine*.

Nothing to be embarrassed about, but Marisol looks crestfallen. Somehow, it hadn't dawned on me that a goddess could ever suffer from any negative human emotions. Then the obvious sinks in: *Marisol isn't a goddess, she's human!* And not just because she has a birthmark, but because she, like the rest of us, feels pained about her perceived imperfections.

Should I ask her if she wants to talk about it? But *she's* not talking about it, so there's that.

I decide to pretend like nothing happened. Luckily, that's when I remember what I brought with me. "Wait," I say, exchanging the mic for my open purse. I dig around until I find a small paper bag, then pluck it out and hand it to Marisol. "A little something for you."

She sits up straighter, eyebrows arched high. "What is it?"

"Check it out." I rest my elbows on my thighs and my chin on my interlaced hands as I watch her.

Marisol unfolds the top of the bag and peeks inside. "What?" she squeals, reaching in and carefully lifting out the gift—a vintage sterling silver and wooden bead rosary. She brings her eyes to mine, her finger grazing the virgin Mary connector pendant. "Where did you get this?" she breathes.

"A secondhand store in Menlo Park." I shrug one shoulder, suddenly nervous. "It's not the same as your family's heirloom . . .

But I called around, found a place that had one similar to your great-grandmother's. I hope it's okay—"

"It's beautiful. Four generations of us approve." Marisol blinks a couple of times. "Thank you."

"You're welcome." I smile. "Looks nice," I add as Marisol slips the rosary over her head.

Marisol chuckles. "My mom told me to check my intention when I wear it. I was like, 'Don't worry, Mom, I'm not trying to be Madonna with it.'" She tucks the rosary under the neckline of her dress. "See?" Then she pulls me in for a one-armed hug. "Thanks again, Gita girl."

I pick up the mic and grip it tightly, hoping that Marisol knows I'll be there for her through thick and thin: the TLC definition of a true friend.

CHAPTER 11

Ensconced in my corner of the lab, I'm pretending to read the corn pollination handbook Dr. Peters wrote. In reality, I keep stealing glances at Jeet over the pages.

Yeah, I'll own it—Jeet is the cute desi from the conference room, and I'm blowing off Sora's warning about him. Every time the thought of Jeet hits my brain, my mental DJ cranks Heavy D's "Now That We've Found Love" and all my dopamine molecules rush to the cerebral dance floor. So far, from what I've witnessed at the lab, Jeet seems like a nice guy without any drama. I've convinced myself that he's a changed man—just like I'm a changed woman.

Hence, me over here scripting a happily-ever-after Bollywood screenplay in my head starring—no drum roll needed—Jeet and me. I'll play the daughter of a wealthy Bandra businessman; Jeet will be cast as my nerdy tutor, who's cute in an Akshay Kumar way. (If Akshay Kumar were Bengali instead of Punjabi.) Leading man Jeet is status-less and wealthless, so on-screen daddy dearest will never approve of our union. Plus, movie-Dad has already arranged my marriage to a rich and powerful bachelor who will (gasp!) turn out to be the villain. But the evil boy won't trick me. He'll never have my heart the way Jeet the tutor does. . . .

Cut to: A meadow filled with wildflowers. Dressed in a sheer pink sari, my silver jhanjar going chham-chham, I'm running through tall grasses and colorful blossoms, the sun soaking me in hope and love—not a bead of sweat in sight. Suddenly, I fall onto my back—gently, of course—cup my mouth, and laugh a shy laugh to myself.

Then . . . wait for it . . . I shoot to a stand, fling my arms out to the side, and burst into song with my high-pitched, girlish Lata Mangeshkar voice. In the middle of a Hindi verse about how my heart is quivering in my chest because Cupid is tickling it instead of shooting it with an arrow, Jeet appears by my side. He gently holds my face, smiles, then starts singing along with me—

Screeeee!—The scrape of metal against concrete.

I blink.

Jeet is pushing his chair back. He gets up and goes to the filing cabinet, which happens to be near my desk. When I bury my face in the book and turn the page—even though I haven't read a single sentence—I realize I've been holding it upside down.

Crap! Did he notice?

But Jeet doesn't even look my way as he plucks out a folder, shuts the drawer, and goes back to his desk. The book slips from my hands and tumbles to the floor. I don't bother picking it up. *Ahhhh, Jeet:* A wisp of air just shy of a sigh escapes from my parted lips and flutters away like a dime-size butterfly.

Jeet's the first Bengali Indian person I've met. And what a first Bengali Indian person he is, with his black curls, regal nose, angular jaw, and not-so-hairy arms. . . .

My lips pucker; I imagine blowing a kiss in his direction.

Is this how Pinky Auntie felt when she first spotted Neil Uncle? They had the first and only love marriage—ever—on both sides of our family.

Love marriage. The two words seem redundant. But not so when I consider the arranged marriage scheming my parents have started doing with Sai since mine is on hold. He called me from the shop this morning with an update:

"I'm in trouble, Gita," he said in a quiet voice so Mom and Dad wouldn't hear him. "The parentals are whispering and plotting about bio datas and janmakshar."

"That's what you get for giving up Caltech for the family," I teased. "Better you than me, dear bhai."

"Very funny," he chuckled. Then, somberly: "I'm not doing it. Call me selfish, but that's one sacrifice I'm not willing to make. That wouldn't be my choice."

Sai and I both know whose choice it would be—our parents'. And the weekend astrologer's, the sweet Gujarati uncle type dressed in a bright yellow dhoti kurta. Our parents would pay him to create a janmakshar—a horoscope—for Sai based on his birthdate, -time, and -place, and the alignment of the planets. Then, if his stars and planets matched those of a would-be bride, their marriage was fated to be successful and happy.

I can sort of see how this janmakshar thing can work back in India. Because if the "fated" arranged marriage turns out to be terrible, then the unhappy husband and wife, whether or not they separate, have a community of Indian relatives and friends to fall back on. But here in America, where the Indian "village" doesn't usually exist, adhering to a horoscope seems as smart as a pilot hiring a copilot who's never learned to fly.

If I'm ever a parent who entrusts my kid's future to some purchased predictions, I hope someone calls child welfare on me.

Sorry . . . Not!

Sai groaned. "Didn't the folks immigrate here so we'd have more choice? Tell me the truth, Gita, am I being selfish?"

He barely finished his question before I interjected. "Geez, Shantel really got in your head!"

"Yeah. I guess I've been doubting myself."

"Let's get something straight, Sai: She was wrong, and you're the opposite of selfish. Anyone who says otherwise will have to answer to *me*." Could he feel the passion and righteousness woven into my voice? I hoped so.

"I wish Shantel had talked to you before she dumped me."

"If she had I would've given her a piece of my mind." I didn't realize I was pulling at my hair until a few loose strands came away in my fist.

"Thanks." He sighed. "Well, at least she and I ended on a better note. She even apologized. Since no guy had ever rejected her, well . . . *advances* before, she thought I wasn't attracted to her or something. Apparently it crushed her."

"Really?" I started pacing, every step rattling my bones.

"Yeah. But even though it was a misunderstanding, we're not getting back together again."

"Why not?" I came to an abrupt stop.

"Because I need some time to think and set my mind right. Maybe we're not good for each other."

My hand began to feel clammy against the phone.

"Anyway, about the arranged marriage thing: I don't know how I'm going to get out of it."

I sunk into my beanbag chair. "Tell Mom and Dad the truth, I guess?"

"It'll break their hearts."

"But what about your heart?" I tapped my finger against my lower lip.

"Exactly." He sighed. "Also, there's no way I'm committing to forever with someone because they're 'fair and slim.' I hate when they talk about girls like they're—"

"Thinly sliced paneer?" I interrupted, adding an Indian twist to Jane's words.

"Ha! I never thought of it that way. Way to keep it real, sis."

My lungs expanded to their fullest with my next breath. It struck me that there had been no chup-re in my head during this conversation with my brother. The unusual free flow of my voice invigorated me. "Listen bhai, I'm rooting for you. Especially because you're laying the groundwork for *me* to extricate myself from this tangled web of outdated traditions."

Sai laughed. "Wow. *Someone* goes to Stanford."

I giggled. "Indeed."

It's not that I think all arranged marriages are shit. I mean, our parents' marriage doesn't seem terrible, even though there's definitely no romance between them. It's more like they're roommates + business partners for life. Roommates + business partners who happen to agree on most things.

Still, I don't want to marry a roommate *or* a business partner. If I get married, I want it to be with my best friend. I want to be in love. I want what Pinky Auntie and Neil Uncle had.

Well, before Neil Uncle started humming sad Kumar Sanu songs under his breath. Why did he seem so dejected, anyway?

Back at the lab, I exhale and rest my elbow on the desk, face in my palm. Not sure how long I stay like that before a memory pulses through my neurons:

Bhavin Uncle's beady eyes are stuck to Pinky Auntie's bottom. He sees that I see and mouths "Chup-re," with his finger pressed over his lips.

A painful lump in my throat as I look away . . .

. . . Later, Neil Uncle is yelling: "Stop lying, Pinky! Admit that you're having an affair with Bhavin!"

My face contorts. Why did Neil Uncle think Pinky Auntie was having an affair? Did something else happen between Bhavin Uncle and Pinky Auntie that I didn't see, that I'm not remembering?

I swallow.

"Gita! Oh Gita . . ."

I recognize that voice. Pushing away the past, I turn my head. Sure enough, it's Sora.

He sits down next to me, and my eyes dart back to Jeet. Sora waves his hand in front of my face, and I imagine that my cheeks are turning the color of henna with all the blood rushing there.

"Really?" Sora asks, his tone disapproving.

"It's not like that." I glance at him.

He raises an eyebrow. "What's it like, then? You're suddenly an anthropologist studying human behavior in the lab?"

I laugh. "Maybe?"

He leans forward and crosses his arms.

I tilt my upper body back and put my hands up. "I know, I know. He's a player." I shift my eyes to Jeet. "Don't worry. He doesn't know I'm alive anyway."

"Sure he does. Don't be surprised when he gets hungry for another living, breathing, tasty morsel."

"Maybe you're right." *But maybe that's what I want. . . .*

"I know I'm right."

My gaze drifts to Sora, who's inspecting his fingernails now.

"That poor undergrad . . . She was heartbroken, you know." Sora lifts his eyes to meet mine. "Have you ever been heartbroken?"

I shake my head, thinking, *Never had a boyfriend to do it. And Angelo didn't break my heart so much as my—*

I shudder.

"What?"

"N-nothing," I stutter, though my body has gone as rigid as a plank.

"Hmm. Well, consider yourself lucky then." Sora sighs, his lips curving downward.

I study his face. "Have you ever been heartbroken, Sora?"

He rests his hand on his chest. His eyes veer up and to the left. "It's a long story. . . ."

"I'm a good listener."

Sora's eyes fall back to me. "Something tells me you are," he says, with a soft smile that doesn't quite reach his eyes. "But now's isn't the time and this busy lab isn't the place. Besides, I need to finish up my work! Thanks again for all your help the other day."

"Anytime." I nod.

Sora claps once and stands. "Well, I'm off."

"See you later."

As he walks to his desk, I consider his advice about Jeet.

But how could any experience with Jeet be as terrible as with Angelo?

I take a couple deep breaths, then—before I can lose my courage—do my best nonchalant walk toward Jeet, who's immersed in data analysis.

"Hey, Jeet."

He swivels around in his chair and smiles when he sees me. "Oh, hey Gita."

"Can you help me with the autoclave? I think something's wrong with it." At this point, I can barely look at him.

"Sure." He scoots his chair back, and I follow him to the autoclave room.

Could I have asked Sora to help me with this? Sure. But what good would that do in getting the guy I like to finally notice me?

Jeet fiddles with the buttons and knobs on the autoclave's control system. In less than two minutes, he whisks around. "It should work now."

"Thanks." I want to say more. Something that'll make him laugh, or at least give me that incredible smile—my gut seizes when I think of calling it an Adonis smile—of his again. But I can't; I'm suddenly mute.

Jeet forks his fingers through his hair. "So. How are you settling in at the lab?"

All I do is nod. A beat of silence goes by.

"I uh, noticed you were reading Dr. Peters's handbook earlier.

It was a little confusing at first for me when I was an undergrad. What do you think of it?" he asks.

"It's okay."

He smiles encouragingly. "Good for you! You must be smarter than me."

"I . . . I don't know about that," I stutter. "But it's not as bad as O-Chem. Which is what I *should* be studying right now."

Jeet shudders. "Don't remind me of O-Chem. That class was a nightmare." He slides his hands into his pockets. "By the way, about Dr. Peters's handbook, you could try flipping it right side up next time—but maybe you like the challenge?"

My jaw plummets. My mind goes blank—I've forgotten how to move. The corners of Jeet's lips lift again, then he turns and walks away.

Only after he rounds the corner do I come to my senses. I blow my cheeks out, attempting to ignore the negative and focus on the positive: Jeet knows my name! He thinks I'm smart, he offered to help me again, and we even exchanged a few sentences. . . .

I whistle a little tune while finishing up a couple of things that don't include actually using the autoclave. When I'm done, I pack up and leave the lab, skipping down two flights of outdoor stairs. As I'm heading toward my locked bike, I spot Jane and Marisol—the econ building is near the lab—and I remember that they finish class on Thursdays around this time. There was something I know I wanted to ask them, but the thought escapes me now.

"Hey!" I call out, waving. We meet in the middle of the green. "How was class?"

"Marginal," Marisol says.

"Everything about this week is a drag," Jane adds. Then she holds up a finger. "Hey! You guys owe me karaoke. This weekend?"

"Sure." Marisol smiles.

"Okay," I agree, with less guilt than anticipated. I'm already mentally reconfiguring my weekend study schedule to make room for the new plan.

"Was that Redwood City place good?" Jane asks, shifting the books in her arms.

I nod. "Maybe the three of us can try to do justice to a TLC song. . . . I call Left Eye!" Oh, how I'd love to be as spunky-confident as Lisa Left Eye Lopes.

"Chilli!" Marisol trumpets.

"T-Boz it is." Jane's expression turns mischievous. "But just so you know, I've got the voice of an angel—a fallen angel."

Marisol and I groan, but we're laughing too.

"By the way, Jane, how was your date the other night?" I ask.

"I-it was fine," Jane stammers. For a second, she looks caught off guard.

"What did you do?" Marisol asks.

"Dinner and a movie."

"Which movie?" I raise an eyebrow.

"*Singles.*" Jane says. Yep, she definitely looks uncomfortable.

"Dinner and a movie—are you sure that's all?" I tease.

"Of course that's all," Jane snaps, frowning. She quickly softens her expression and adds, "I was home before midnight."

"Okay, Cinderella." Marisol nudges her elbow, and Jane chuckles nervously.

I laugh a little, remembering when Jane called me Cinderella the night of Full Moon on the Quad. Then I suddenly recall the thing I'd wanted to ask them—whether or not they're on birth control. It's not that I'm planning on another Angelo—or any casual sex—but I can't stop hoping that maybe Jeet will become my Joey. And if he does, then we might want to make love. Therefore, I should be on the pill and he should use a condom, right? The future Dr. Gita Desai concurs.

I glance at Jane and Marisol. If they're on the pill, where do they get it? Their doctor? Planned Parenthood? I open my mouth to ask, but realize it might sound out of context since I already denied anything happening with Angelo. Also, I don't want to mention Jeet and jinx our possible happily-ever-after-future. I shut my mouth.

Marisol turns to me. "By any chance, Gita, do you have a fake ID?"

I shake my head, eyebrows raised. "Do you guys?"

They both nod.

"Well then, today is your lucky day!" Marisol slings an arm over my shoulder. "I happen to know a guy who knows a guy who can make you one for a hundred bucks. The thing is, it's his last night in town for a while, so we have to go tonight."

"Ooh—I really want to . . . but a hundred bucks." I scratch my chin. "I don't know if I can swing that."

"Don't worry." Jane touches my arm. "We can help you if you don't have enough."

"For sure," Marisol chimes in. "Then we'll all be twenty-one the nights we go clubbing and drinking." She winks, giving me one of her unfettered smiles.

I don't know what to say or do with myself, so I end up pressing my lips together and staring at the ground.

Jane squeezes my arm. "And there'll be more of those nights than I thought. I decided not to rush. My mom—she used to teach econ at NYU—once told one of her students not to limit themselves by joining a sorority. So I'm not going to either. But going out won't be the same without you."

I lift my eyes to Jane, my eyebrows cinched and raised.

"We need our partner in crime," Marisol adds.

Automatically, doubt screams, *They're being pity-nice!*

But then why would they offer to spot me?

Can't argue with that. "All right. Getting a fake ID is a perfectly pragmatic study break, after all."

Jane claps. "Awesome."

Marisol holds her hand up for a high five. I oblige, letting myself savor the moment.

Jane and Marisol, the likely pair, don't seem to mind that I make us an unlikely trio. I mean, they've known me for a while now and haven't gone running for the Santa Cruz foothills. If anything, it actually seems like they're holding out their hands, asking me to run with them.

It occurs to me that TLC wouldn't be the perfect balance of classy, funky, and sensual without their feisty and funny L. I glance at Jane and Marisol, letting myself imagine that, maybe, JMG also wouldn't be the same perfect balance without their G.

CHAPTER 12

Every seat in Cubberley Auditorium is occupied for Sunday Night Flicks. Something about the rowdy vibe—a mix of cinephiles shushing rambunctious hecklers—tells me that this might be the best time with the lights out some of us Stanforders have had all week. . . . Which is fine by me!

Not that tonight's featured film, *Fried Green Tomatoes*, is fun in itself per se. And, honestly, I'm squirming at the way it's depicted Black people so far. But it feels momentous, watching a movie all about women, based on a book written by a woman and featuring an all-star cast of actresses. It's like watching Neil Armstrong land on the moon, if Mr. Armstrong were a woman, landing in the male-dominated film industry three hundred and fifty miles south of the Bay Area instead. Sort of like: *One small step over Hollywood misogyny, one giant leap for womankind.*

Well, for white womankind.

During the scene when Idgie, Julian, and Big George are

helping Ruth pack up and move out of Frank's house, I glance at my girls, who are sitting on either side of me with their eyes glued to the screen. Jane starts drumming her fingers on her thigh. Marisol pulls her bare feet up onto the scratchy upholstered seat and hugs her knees to her chest.

My eyes shift back to the screen at the exact moment that Frank unexpectedly walks through the front door. All the hecklers and cinephiles grow quiet.

Frank smacks Ruth's face.

It feels like everyone in the place leans forward and holds their breath—everyone except me, that is. I remain sitting upright, suddenly sweaty despite the air-conditioning, as if drenched in the on-screen humidity of the 1920s Deep South.

The ever-protective Idgie jumps on Frank's back. They struggle: As Idgie punches Frank's head, he slams her into the wall. She drops to the ground.

My chest rises and falls quickly with each inhale and exhale.

Frank turns his attention back to Ruth, who—by the way—is pregnant. He throws her over his shoulder like a sack of rice and heads upstairs. She doesn't fight back.

Several things happen to me at once. One of my hands ends up draped across my stomach. There's a sharp prickling all over my body that seeps through my skin and into my bones. The urge to piss and vomit is strong. I'm lightheaded. . . . Am I going to faint? What's going on with me? There aren't any blood or guts on the screen, and I've never been in a domestic abuse situation.

But maybe it's because Mom has been, with her father. Could it be that my entire body is feeling Ruth's pain the way I've imagined Mom's pain?

A second later, I'm a cold statue. *Why didn't Ruth leave Frank sooner? She should've known better. . . .*

A quiet groan escapes me. *That's not true!* I've read about other real-life domestic violence situations. Sometimes, women are afraid to leave—maybe their partners have threatened to kill them or their children if they do. Sometimes people can't afford it. Or they think they're the problem: If only they love harder. If only they strive to be better girlfriends.

Or wives.

Or daughters, like Mom when she was a kid.

I exhale. Obviously, Mom wasn't the problem. And when I really think about it, even if Mom wanted to leave, she was a child. How can a child leave her abusive father? Especially if the other parent remains silent, and there aren't any other supportive grown-ups around. Where would she have gone, besides the streets?

My heart starts pounding. I press my palm onto my chest; feels like my heart knows a secret my head doesn't. It's battering a Morse code message into my hand, but I can't decipher it.

I swallow the lump in my throat, then blink and refocus on the screen: Julian and Big George are confronting Frank. Idgie's up on her feet, blood trickling out of her left nostril. With Ruth still on his shoulder, Frank stares down Julian, Big George, and Idgie.

The auditorium is dead silent, unlike my mind. *Professor Herman would say this scene is a far cry from the romanticization of domestic violence in the original* Sleeping Beauty *tale. . . .*

On the screen, Frank puts Ruth down.

A squeak on the floor next to me, and my eyes shift to the right. Marisol is sliding her feet back into her sandals and scooting forward in her seat.

I turn my head back to the screen. Frank kicks Ruth from behind. She falls down the stairs, landing on her belly.

"No!" Marisol yells, bolting to a stand. Her seat bottom *thwaps* back up. She wraps her cashmere shawl around herself and charges down the row, pushing past all the knees like turnstiles, then disappears through the double doors at the back.

On the screen, Julian, Big George, and Idgie are helping Ruth leave the house.

Jane and I exchange glances, then get up and rush out of the auditorium.

Outside, thick clouds are a fleece comforter tucking in the dark night sky. We spot Marisol leaning against a lamppost, scowling at the ground and fiddling with her rosary.

Jane and I jog over, and Marisol drags her eyes upward. "Horror films I can handle. But that . . ." She trails off.

"It was intense," I agree.

Marisol's expression melts like butter in a hot pan. Is she about to cry? I fix the shawl that's sliding down her back. "You okay?"

"Yeah. I'm okay." Her eyes plummet. She blows out a slow breath. She shakes her head. "I've never walked out on a film before."

Jane rubs Marisol's back. "Speaking of walking out . . . I'd like to think I'd have the courage to leave a guy who was beating me. Wouldn't you two?" She's not looking at us anymore; her eyes are somewhere off in the distance.

Marisol crosses her arms under her shawl. "If Joey *ever* did, I'd be long gone."

I feel myself nodding. *Me too.*

We stand there in a silent circle, each of us lost in our own thoughts.

At least . . . I hope.

A couple of students walk their bikes past us. One of them yawns loudly, and the other one suggests stopping by CoHo to "chug double espressos for the long night ahead."

A dismayed sigh tumbles from between my lips as I remember I've got a long night ahead, with my nemesis O-Chem.

Jane slowly rocks back and forth on her heels. "I'd like to think I'd have the courage to leave a guy who was cruel in any kind of way." The light in her eyes flickers, dies. "I don't know why my mom put up with my dad for so long." She sniffs, and I spot a lone tear rolling down her face.

"What do you mean?" I ask at the same time that Marisol asks, "What did he do?"

"He didn't *do* anything except throw money at us, that's the problem!" Jane cries out. Then, softer: "I'm grateful he took care of us, of course. But it usually felt more like a gag across my mouth than a gift."

Marisol and I flash worried glances at each other—I never considered money as its own form of chup-re.

Jane wraps her arms around herself, then shivers.

"Are you cold?" I ask, and she nods. Marisol peels off her shawl and holds it out to Jane.

I glance at Marisol: Her right arm is crossed against her chest, her hand flat and firm over the portion of birthmark that peeks out from her shirt's neckline. I spot Jane peeping it too—she relaxes her muscles, then takes the shawl from Marisol.

"But what am I going on about? At least my time in high school wasn't—" Jane cuts herself off. "Is that why you ran out of the movie, Marisol?"

What's Jane talking about?

Marisol catches my expression, then shakes her head. "No, that's all in the past. That movie scene was hardcore, and I don't know why but I couldn't stop thinking about something Joey said to me the other day. I . . . I just needed some air."

"What did Joey say?" I ask.

Marisol remains silent.

Jane is glowering now. "The past may be in the past, and Joey can be a real jerk sometimes. Listen, Marisol. If anyone insults you again—"

"We'll kick their asses!" I blurt, swallowing the second nosy thing I want to ask: *Did Joey insult you?*

A laugh bursts out of Jane. "Yes, that."

Now there's a hint of a smile on Marisol's face. And though her hand stays on her chest, there are spaces between her fingers, revealing a few slivers of her birthmark to us. "Hey Jane," she says. "How about that karaoke session we promised you this weekend?"

"Now?" Jane asks.

Marisol checks her watch. "Nine p.m.—we've got three hours until the weekend is officially over. More than enough time for us to make good on our promise."

"Well, all right then—I'll drive!" Jane beams, and Marisol and I exchange smiles.

"Are you thinking what I'm thinking?" I ask her.

Marisol nods. "First song—TLC, 'What About Your Friends.'"

"Definitely."

Marisol's arm drops to her side, and the three of us walk together toward the parking lot.

CHAPTER 13

The following weekend, my girls and I are at an Alpha Sig party. It's wall-to-wall bodies that spill out onto the front porch and into the backyard. I wonder if parties are always this crowded, but never in a million years would I admit to anyone—including Jane and Marisol—that this is my first party-party.

Doesn't matter: I've got a nice buzz from an hour of what might as well have been an IV drip of cheap red wine. Naughty by Nature's "O.P.P." is blasting, and I'm in the middle of a perfect medium-tempo running man when the frat brother DJ abruptly switches the song to Nirvana's "Smells Like Teen Spirit."

My confused body freezes, my left knee hovering mid-run. Before I can even blink, I'm trampled into a mosh pit of way too many white boys. Shoving my way haphazardly out of the rowdy horde of Conners and Tanners and Bretts, I grab my red Solo cup from the mantel and search the barely lit living room for my friends. No sign of them—I teeter over to an unoccupied sofa in the corner beckoning to me, and curl up against its musty arm.

Gulping down some more wine, I remember for the third time tonight that I'd told myself I wouldn't drink at this party. I mean, I haven't exactly had the time to learn how to handle my liquor since "the Angelo," so who's to say it wouldn't happen again with some other rando?

I shrug, take another swig; Angelo isn't here. I'm not talking to any guys, and they're not talking to me. It's all good. Besides, Jane, Marisol, and I promised each other we'd stick together— my idea. I pat myself on the back, literally.

But where are they?

I go to chug the rest of my wine. Unfortunately, the cup is empty, save for one fat droplet. I tilt my head, about to throw it back like a tiny shot, when an Alpha Sig knocks my arm as he collapses onto the sofa next to me. Our thighs touch, but he doesn't acknowledge my existence, pulling a real-life Barbie onto his lap instead.

Her head falls onto his shoulder. She whispers something into his ear.

"Don't worry, I won't ravage you," he mumbles.

She giggles, droopy-eyed, and goes in for a sloppy kiss.

Marisol calls my name, and I turn my head to find her standing in front of me. She looks perfectly adorable in her miniskirt and buttoned bolero, a grin splitting her flushed face.

"I've been looking all over for you," she says.

"Here I am!" I toss my arms out. My cup slips from my grasp, sails across the room, and hits a girl in a white baby doll dress and Mary Jane platforms—so Courtney Love wannabe.

The girl inspects her dress. A few inches of its hemline is mottled now, streaked like a burgundy comet. Courtney Love wannabe scans the room for the culprit, blue-flame eyes narrowed like lasers at the ready. I whistle loudly and bend forward, fiddling with my sandals. Wannabe gives up with a loud scoff, rubbing angrily at the stain with a spit-wettened napkin.

Marisol, who saw the whole thing, snickers. She offers me her hand. "Let's go, Gita. You need a new cup."

"Why thank you, mi'lady." My words sound runny; I let Marisol pull my drunk ass off the sofa.

Holding hands, we cut through the wasted partiers—a few surrounded by dank clouds of smoke—and burst into the brightly lit kitchen. I survey the cluttered counters: Half-empty tequila, vodka, and rum bottles. Red Solo cups tipped over, lying in little puddles of partially melted ice. Smashed-up beer cans, plus a keg in the corner.

When I grab a clean cup from the top of a stack, I accidentally knock over the rest. I'm about to get on my hands and knees to gather the cups when a wine jug catches my eye. Mess forgotten, I gift myself a generous pour of the vino while Marisol fixes herself a Diet Coke and rum.

Armed and ready, we head back to the living room.

"Where's Jane?" I ask.

Marisol bends her free hand like a claw. "Prowling."

"You mean looking for love in all the wrong places?" I arch my eyebrows and chuckle, amused that I, a Gujju girl, wove an oldish country smash—Johnny Lee's "Lookin' for Love"—into our conversation.

Marisol smirks. "Aren't we all?"

We go to an empty corner near a wall of neatly hung Alpha Sig composite photos. I touch one of the gold matte frames and study the headshots of the 1990–1991 fraternity brothers in suits. Their fancy threads and subdued smiles suggest they're respectable young men. The future of America.

I glance over my shoulder. Drunk, shirtless guys yell at each other to "Stop being a pussy!" and "Drink!" A few crush beer cans on their heads; others beat their chests. One is screaming, "We're *real men*! REAL MEN!"

My face contorts. *Even at Stanford.*

"Hey Marisol." A guy's voice, soft in comparison to the roars behind him.

Though he's not calling me, I can't help but do a double take at the tall, white Alpha Sig with glimmering green eyes and long white-blond hair who's sauntering over with his beer. He stops in front of Marisol, cracking a lightning smile that could brighten the darkest night sky.

Maybe in the past I would've stood by and sulked, catapulted into the ignominy of being a nobody next to my magnificent friend who is first-name famous, like Prince or Madonna. But I'm annoyed at how these Alpha Sigs get away with being such posers. I peek over my shoulder at the real-life Barbie. Her lips are curved downward, and she's wriggling uncomfortably on I-won't-ravage-you guy's lap.

What changed? Or did I miss something earlier? Either way, she should yell at him to leave her alone!

To my dismay, Marisol twirls her hair in response to lightning-smile guy, eyeing his tall frame up and down. "Hey yourself," she murmurs.

I glug some wine.

Alpha Sig steps in front of me. "I'm—"

His back is to me, so I don't catch his name. I invent one for him: Thor. I step out of Thor's shadow, drifting back to Marisol's side.

"How's your night going?" he asks her.

"Better now." She glances down surreptitiously, making sure the top button of her bolero is solidly in place before reaching out to graze his pec.

I roll my eyes at their inane banter. I can't, however, ignore their body language: Thor puffs his chest out. Marisol's lips part while she listens to him. He touches her arm. She takes a step closer to him, her chest brushing against his.

I face-palm.

Then I picture Joey when Marisol flirted with Matt the other day. My lips flatten and compress as chup-re forbids me to even go there. But this is about my friend and her relationship, not about me. To my surprise, I manage to cleave my lips apart. I lean in and whisper to Marisol, "Hey, what about Joey?"

"What about him?" Marisol whispers back, giving me side-eye.

"He wouldn't like it if . . ." I glance at Thor.

"Joey's not the boss of me!" Marisol snaps.

True. Still, my gut drops. Chup-re lassos the rest of what I wanted to say to her and drags it back down my throat. I turn away abruptly, my head spinning, and take a stumbly step toward the sofa.

Marisol grabs my wrist. "Wait, Gita!" She cups my ear, whispering, "Speaking of Joey . . . Can you keep an eye out? He'll be here soon."

"Aye aye, captain," I drawl as sarcastically as possible. I attempt to salute but end up ramming the long edge of my thumb into the bridge of my nose. Ouch.

Marisol doesn't notice—she and Thor are back to their shameless flirting, undressing each other with their eyes. I rub my nose and scan the room, at long last spotting Jane. She's leaning her back against a wall and talking to some towering, muscular guy. Maybe another football player.

So what? I'm not impressed. Does he think that because he's a D1 athlete, he can get with my triple-threat friend just like *that*?

He says something that cracks Jane up.

I sigh and shake my head. *At least she's single, unlike* someone *we know. . . .*

Jane smooths her hair back while the guy runs his knuckle down her arm. Whatever he says next makes her bite her lip and nod. He takes her hand, leading her through the crowd and up the stairs.

I watch them until they disappear. Are they about to hook up? *You can do so much better than a hookup, Jane!*

But maybe that's all she wants tonight. . . .

I glance down, tracing one of the lines on my cup. *What if I hook up again?*

A tap on the shoulder: "Hey Gita." I pull my eyes up to find Joey standing there.

"Hi," I say. But before I can even react, Joey's brushed past me, having spotted Marisol and Thor. He squeezes himself between the two of them, bumping Thor back with his chest.

"Watch it," Thor growls.

"She's my girlfriend." Joey's voice is icy. "Now run along so I don't have to break your neck." He pushes his glasses up with a smile so feral, it raises the hair along my arms.

Thor puts his hands up, his face falling faster than the hammer he'd be carrying if he really was Thor. "I didn't know, man." He steps back, but doesn't leave.

Joey's expression is deadpan; his gaze is as sharp as a talwar.

My eyes dart back and forth between Joey and Thor. Are we in the jungle? It feels primitive, as if the guys are about to fight for alpha male dominance.

But—cue saxophone—Marisol defuses the situation in her

usual Sade-"Smooth-Operator" way. She tilts her head and goes for it with Joey, tongue-kissing him all hot and heavy. Thor and I cock our heads to the right at the same time, our wide eyes glued to the free show.

Marisol pries her lips off her boyfriend. "Let's go," she whispers.

Go? Go where? What happened to sticking together?

Joey nods. He fixes his glasses again, only now he's grinning. I sneak a peek at Thor, who's scratching his head and pouting.

Marisol winks at me, then checks the top button of her bolero once more. "I'll see you tomorrow, Gita."

I nod, conflicted. There's a three-way train wreck of thoughts in my head:

First—There isn't enough room to drop to my knees and bow down before Empress Marisol, ruler of the entire planet of men.

Second: I'm sad that Marisol still feels the need to hide her birthmark. She was telling me the other day that her agency has been encouraging her to show it off in photo shoots. Plus, Joey's got to have seen it—wouldn't he embrace it, since it's part of her?

Third: Chup-re turns up as sneakily as crooked cops, arresting my voice when I go to remind her that we're supposed to be sticking together tonight.

Joey ignores Thor but nods at me before tugging on Marisol's hand. They head to the front door. Just as they step outside, Marisol turns and tosses Thor a half smile over her shoulder.

Thor throws his hands up and groans. I elbow him. "You and me both, Thor."

He looks at me funny, then trudges away, mopey.

I sigh, wishing a *Girlfriend Rule Book* existed with a chapter on what to do when your girls abandon you. Maybe it's the good intentions that count? I should just be grateful I have friends, I guess.

I guzzle down the rest of my wine and burp.

The song changes to DJ Jazzy Jeff & the Fresh Prince's "Summertime." Everything about this song feels like freak dancing without touching. Seduction, yes; sex, no. The way I wished it'd been with Angelo.

A chorus of "Chug! Chug! Chug!" pulls my attention to the other side of the room. I spot a handful of Alpha Sigs beer bonging. Sora appears unannounced in my head: *You're suddenly an anthropologist studying human behavior. . . .*

I stagger toward them for a better view.

A dude is kneeling with the end of a tube in his mouth. His buddy is holding up the other end, attached to a large funnel. A third guy dumps a pitcher of beer into the funnel. The room erupts with pumping arms and cheers, as if beer bonging isn't merely a drinking game but a superpower that'll save humanity from total annihilation.

Maybe it's the extra wine that hits me hard. Maybe it's that I want a superpower too. "I call next!" I hear myself announce. I posture in a slight lean-back with my arms crossed, feeling suddenly emboldened.

For a second, there's pin-drop silence. Then the chanting starts again: "Girl! Girl! Girl!"

It sounds more mocking than encouraging, but still. I assume the proper beer bong position, holding the end of the tube in place and sealing my lips around it.

The beer's poured into the funnel and gushes, lukewarm, down my throat. I force myself to quickly swallow it, and keep swallowing it.

"Fish! Fish! Fish!" the crowd yells.

Out of the corner of my eye, I catch a flash of live goldfish darting around in a plastic bag. My eyes pop out of my skull. They're not going to . . . ?

The guy scoops the goldfish out with a small net, dropping it into the funnel.

I freeze. I can't get my lips off the tube—I can't even twitch a muscle. I swallow it all, beer and goldfish. The sensation is quick, a strange combination of warm, tickly, twitchy, slimy, and lumpy. I gag, turning my head and hoping that no one sees. The beer going down my throat trickles off into droplets.

Then nothing, except wriggling in my stomach. Or am I imagining it? Wouldn't the gastric acid kill the poor goldfish instantly?

After a few seconds, I realize it's finally over. I didn't throw up. I'm okay.

Maybe I'm more than okay. Unlike the Alpha Sig "Thor,"

maybe I'm the real Thor, reincarnated. In my last life—as Norse mythology goes—I couldn't drain all the mead from the giant drinking horn. In this life, I did it all in one gulp.

I yank the tube out of my mouth, rocket up to a stand, and thrust my fists in the air. Muffled hoots and hollers, then the distant chanting of "Girl! Girl! Girl!" One guy high-fives me; another claps my back. Then they turn away, forgetting about me already, and the glory fades.

The thrill of victory is gone; my arms dangle at my sides. Slowly, I bring my hands together and interlace them in front of me. My fingers begin to wrestle. *What's the opposite of having a superpower?* I lay one hand on my slightly distended belly and stare at my cherry-red toenails, peeking out of my sandals. *Where are my girls?* The corners of my lips dive-bomb toward the floor. . . .

Stop being so needy, Gita! I clench my fists. Blessedly, a wave of intoxication smothers the I'm-a-total-loser feeling.

When I finally yank my eyes up, I spot a white guy sitting on an end table, nursing a beer. We exchange curious glances. He gives me a half smile.

That's all it takes. I swear a hush and darkness falls over the entire place: There's a spotlight on the guy, and he's one of the Color Me Badd boys. He points at me, singing "I Wanna Sex You Up" . . .

I blink and the CMB fantasy vanishes, as does my better judgment. *Lighten up! Don't fight it. Besides, your girls abandoned you for boys.* I pull my shoulders back and hold my head up, walking prim and proper like Her Royal Highness Jane would. *A queen isn't ignored.*

Then I notice a rusty pedestal fan on low to the left of the guy. My eyes get lost in the blur of the spinning blades. I feel dizzy, touch my head, and sway. I remember my promise to myself: no hooking up. Do I want to break my own promise? What do I really want?

My legs get wobbly. I need to sit down or I might faint. . . .

A husky voice: "You okay?"

I blink, and he's standing in front of me. That alone sobers me up enough to nod and play along. Marisol style, I tilt my head and twirl a lock of hair.

"Having fun?" he asks, running his fingers through his own floppy, fringed hair.

I try not to stare, but it's not working. He reminds me of Johnny Depp in *21 Jump Street* with his high cheekbones, baby face, and that sexy, sexy dark hair. "Yesssirlam," I slur, wishing I could think of something more clever to say.

"Any girl who beer bongs a goldfish is a winner in my book." He grins.

My cheeks sizzle.

"Wanna see my room?" His voice is innocent, eyes lit up.

"Sure." My voice is cool, but my entire body has suddenly ignited.

"This way." He turns, and I'm already following him up the stairs.

It crosses my mind that we don't know each other's names. I should ask him . . . But then I shrug. Whatever. Knowing Angelo's name only makes it harder to forget him.

But Angelo knew my name, and he forgot me just like that.

Whatever, whatever. I'm not pretending tonight is about true love heading toward marriage or anything.

Then why am I doing this?

It's better than being left. Or ignored.

Isn't it?

Despite my doubts, my body is a giant mouth silently screaming in Foxy Felicity's voice, *Fuck me!*

I pinch my arms hard, trying to stifle my nympho-ness. When we reach his room, I stop. "Um . . . I gotta pee."

"That way." He points down the hall.

In the bathroom, I tell myself that I'll finish my business, wash my hands, then walk straight downstairs and out the front door. No looking back. But nope. The second I step out of the bathroom, I can't fight the tractor beam pulling me back to Johnny Depp's room.

I cross his threshold to find the lights dimmed and the haunting "Would?" by Alice In Chains drifting out of his boom box. If "Summertime" is seduction, then "Would?" is sex. Wicked, wicked sex. There's no other way to describe it.

I won't ravage you. . . .

I think about Jane that first night I saw her with Sigma Nu boy. She was so sure of herself naked. Did she take her own clothes off, or did he help her? I decide she did it herself: No hesitation.

I slip out of my dress, unfasten my bra, and step out of my panties. . . .

Johnny Depp Boy is sitting on his bed, watching me, his lips slightly curved up on one side.

Naked, I slink next to him.

JDB leans in, his lips barely grazing mine while his fingertips glide near my belly button. Then he gets up and strips. He and his at-attention dick stand in front of me.

"I know you can swallow," he says.

What's he talking about?

I'm about to turn away, but he reaches for the back of my head with one hand and guides his naked dick into my mouth with the other. *Oh.*

It tastes salty and sour. I bet Foxy Felicity would do this, but do *I* want to? What about a condom?

Chup-re.

JDB closes his eyes and lifts his chin.

I close my eyes too. Without warning, an old film reel plays in my mind.

"Thank you," I say between greedy licks of the Chupa Chups.

Bhavin Uncle eyes me. "You're welcome."

I avoid his gaze, staring instead at Sai, who's gone back to play-ing with his Rubik's Cube at the dining table. Bhavin Uncle puts his hand on my back.

I don't like his hand on my back. I start to frown and squirm. But I shouldn't fuss if I want him to give me more Chupa Chups, should I? I relax my face and stand perfectly still.

"Look at me," he says.

Slowly, I do.

He peels his hand off me, then twists the end of his thick mustache, eyes squinting.

A few tears push through my sealed eyelids.

I don't like it in my mouth. I start to shift in place, wanting to push JDB away. But I can't get my hands to obey. If only I were a turtle, I could retract my head and hide in my shell. . . .

His hand is still on the back of my head. He's forcing the motion.

My thoughts flip. I open my eyes and glance up at him, wondering, *Is he enjoying this?* This is my first time.

Am I even doing it right?

He shudders, and I get a mouthful of what tastes like gloopy ocean water.

"Swallow it," he commands, opening his eyes.

While it isn't a goldfish, I still gag again and turn away so he doesn't see.

He caresses my head, then lies down on his mattress, patting the space next to him.

I lie down, reluctantly, and instantly he's all over me. Kissing and rubbing. When he's hard again, he puts on a condom.

I'm not ready for that. I'm still grossed out by what just happened.

Still, I hear myself sexy-say, "Fuck me."

As soon as he's inside me, my eyes roll back.

Bhavin Uncle's voice gets softer when he says, "Pretty girls who are always good deserve special treats."

I keep quiet, but in my head I'm begging, So when can I have more?

He leans forward, resting his elbows on his thighs, and holds out another lollipop.

The initial discomfort transforms into pleasure.

I reach nirvana, soul free.

At least, for now.

CHAPTER 14

Early the next morning, I stumble—messy-haired and nauseous—out of the Alpha Sig house, squinting and shielding my eyes from the sun that pounces on me. I slog back to my dorm, counting all the ways things didn't go as planned. And as much as I want to blame it on Jane and Marisol for leaving me, they didn't make me swallow the goldfish, or the—

I cut my thoughts off with a click of my tongue and a chee expression, and accept that I deserve my head to be throbbing like a giant stubbed toe.

Back at the dorm, I climb the steps to the second floor, grateful that no one's around to behold my pathetic fall from grace . . . again. But the hallway seems double the length to my bleary eyes, my room an endless distance away. I slink onward, repeating a silent prayer to the gods I don't believe in: *Please don't let anyone come out now, please don't let anyone come out now, please—*

AC/DC-blasting Matt struts out of the bathroom, his eyes slamming into mine. For an instant, the world stops.

His lips curl up into a smirk. Then he slow-claps and, in an exaggerated British accent, says, "Bravo, bravo. Gita Desai, on a *spectacular* walk of shame."

I flip him off, my eyes both narrowing and welling up. I stare at the worn carpet as I march past him: I refuse to let him see me cry, even a little.

When I'm finally in the safe zone of my room, I slam the door shut behind me. I grab Snuffles from the top bunk and fling myself, prone, onto my beanbag. I bury my face into Snuffles's back, breathe out, and let my tears run amok.

I'm not sure how long I cry. When I finally stop and sit up, I see the red light flashing on my answering machine. I reach over and press PLAY. For a moment, I perk up: *Did Johnny Depp Boy leave me a when-can-I-see-you-again message?*

"Hi Gita."

It's not JDB. Of course it isn't; how could it be? He didn't ask for my number. It is, however, another guy's voice. An intense, deep one that pulls goose bumps from my skin.

"It's Jeet. I got your number from the list at the lab."

I inhale sharply.

"I found your O-Chem notebook in the conference room. I . . . thought you might need it to study this weekend."

My gut wrenches as I remember that my O-Chem grade

dropped to a horrific B this week. But it mellows again when it hits me that I'm listening to Jeet's voice on *my* answering machine.

"I hope you're still having an easier time with that class than I did—" He pauses.

Probably not. But who cares? You called me! I fold my hands behind my head, barely breathing as I hang on his every word.

"Anyway, I left it on your lab desk. . . . Okay then. I'll, um, I'll see you later. Bye." Another pause, then he hangs up.

I lie back on my beanbag, overcome with the sensation of floating. I close my eyes and feel myself drifting away. *He didn't have to call to tell me that, but he did. What does that mean?*

I dare to let myself consider: *Does he like me?*

Chup-re! He's just being nice. Being nice doesn't mean he like-likes you.

The phone rings and I put my Jeet thoughts on hold, lifting the handset. "Hello?"

"Hi beta. How are you?" It's Mom.

I notice a brittleness in her voice. I cock my head. *Has Mom been crying? Or is she sick?* "I'm fine. . . . Are you okay?" I smash the handset against my ear so I can catch everything in her tone.

Mom exhales a long breath. "I didn't want to tell you, but . . ." She sniffs.

I'm on pins and needles. "Tell me what?"

"There was an oven malfunction at the shop last night. It caused a fire."

My hand slaps my mouth and stays there as I imagine the worst. I force my fingers apart. "Are you okay? Sai? Dad?"

"We're all fine. Thank god no customers were there. Only part of the kitchen was damaged."

I exhale. "So nobody got hurt?"

She blows her nose. "No, beta."

Something about her tone still worries me. I spend the next five minutes trying to get more details, but she deflects every question.

"Don't worry . . . We're handling it . . . It's not that bad."

Eventually, I give up and try to problem-solve. "I'll come home."

"No, no, don't worry, beta."

"I can do the cleanup or something. I want to." I nibble nervously on a hangnail.

"No. Focus on your studies. Sai and Dad are fixing it. Glad I paid the property insurance on time, at least the damage will be covered."

"That's good."

"How was your evening, beta?" Her voice is gentle, sincere.

I melt a little at Mom being mom-ly despite the terrible situation. But then reality chokes me: While the shop burned, I spent the evening putting new things in my mouth. A strange grunt-groan noise escapes from between my lips.

"What's wrong, beta?"

"Nothing, just a cough." I fake-cough a couple of times more.

"We tried to call you last night but you were out. Where did you go?"

"The library." I wish I really had spent the evening in the library. I touch my cheek, imagining JDB's hard-on lodged inside there.

I gag. There's a stampede of bulls pounding the inside of my head.

I didn't like it. But I kept quiet and took it. Why?

My heart revs up. *I didn't like it, but when he wanted me like that, it felt . . . sort of good. Sort of automatic.*

I exhale again, suddenly picturing the pale, cold cadavers in the anatomy lab next to the Hum Bio building. *Cadavers are used for dissection, every piece of their anatomy studied. Cadavers are dead, so they don't have a choice.*

I slump over, feeling like a living cadaver. Feeling like I let myself be used for sex. Feeling like I didn't have a choice once it started even though, technically, I did.

My upper body curls in on itself like a millipede.

"With all the studying you do, make sure you're getting enough good sleep."

I freeze. Did I hear Mom correctly? To make sure, I ask, "What was that?"

"Make sure you sleep well, beta."

Yup, I heard her correctly. It's funny, she never talked to me about getting good sleep when I was growing up. In fact, she and Dad had no clue that, for a couple of years, there were many nights I didn't sleep well. My head is already playing out one of those times.

I wake up at midnight with my sheets soaked in sweat and pee. I can't fall back asleep like this—it feels so icky. What should I do? My parents will get so mad if they find out. Sai might tease me.

I tiptoe into Neil Uncle and Pinky Auntie's tiny room, crying a little, and tap her shoulder. Her eyes flutter open. She sees me and sits up quickly. "You're trembling, beta. What happened?"

"I wet my bed."

She holds my face lightly, wiping my trickling tears with her thumbs. "Poor little one. Another bad dream?"

I nod.

"So many bad dreams. Don't worry, your secret is safe with me. Let's clean up everything like we always do—together." She stands, takes my hand, and leads me to my room. "Tell me about your dream."

"I can't remember . . ." I say. But I do remember: In it, I was alone in my bedroom.

Until I wasn't.

A swoop in my stomach. I realize I'm hunched over and holding my face the way Pinky Auntie did. I straighten up and my body stiffens, a rigid plank.

How is it that my parents and Neil Uncle never found out about my bedwetting? And why didn't Pinky Auntie mention it or my bad dreams to my parents? Wasn't she worried that maybe something was wrong with my bladder or kidneys?

Mom's words cut through: "Are you still there, beta?"

"Yes." I hope she doesn't hear the quiver in my voice.

"Make sure you eat well too."

I clutch my throat. My thoughts rewind to last night, when I swallowed . . . what if I also swallowed HIV?

My eyes widen. I might have HIV! I might get AIDS!

But JDB looked clean. . . .

I knock my skull. Since when is looking clean a medical clearance for unsafe sex of any kind? That's completely ridiculous and I know it.

With the handset pressed to my ear, I begin pacing. I'm sweating as if the bulls in my head are a millisecond away from trampling me to death.

I need to get tested.

"Let's talk about something good. How are your grades?" Mom asks. Brief pause. "Don't tell me—A-pluses on everything?"

"Of course."

It slips out easily, the lie. But truth-telling is impossible when my B in O-Chem suddenly feels like an F-.

CHAPTER 15

*H*onestly, I'd much rather continue obsessing over my paper on Confucius and Socrates, but I can't put off O-Chem anymore. Not if I want that A.

I begin flipping through the pages of the most recent problem set, thinking, *Am I really going to be predicting the product of chemical reactions when I'm treating patients?* and *Will acing O-Chem really make me a more skilled, caring physician?* I doubt it.

I scoot my chair back a little, bend forward at the waist, and thump my forehead lightly on the desk. *Why do I have to do this? Why, why, why?*

A knock interrupts my internal griping. I exhale my O-Chem frustration, then get the door: It's Jane. She walks in, eyes puffy and red, mascara streaking her sallow cheeks. I've never seen her look this less-than-regal before.

She points to her face. "See? I told you crying ruins my makeup."

I quickly shut the door and turn to her. "What's the matter?"

"I . . . My . . ." Jane clams up. Shaking her head, she plops onto my beanbag. I sit cross-legged in front of her and wait.

She massages her temples. "Today is a hard day."

"Why?" I glance at my wall calendar—October 12.

She holds her head in both hands, avoiding my eyes. "My mom."

"What happened?" *Maybe her mom's finally had enough of her dad's BS,* I think. *Maybe they're getting a divorce.* Even if Jane understands and agrees with her mom's decision, it can't be easy to go through that.

"It's the ten-year anniversary of her death." Her bottom lip trembles. Her hands tumble to her lap.

"No." It comes out as a whisper.

"I kept it together the entire day. Until ten minutes ago, when I tried to call my dad. I knew calling him was a mistake. But I thought, maybe . . . maybe things would be different this year. It's been ten years . . . but I was wrong." Her face crumples. "The guy didn't even have five minutes to remember her with me. I lost it."

"Oh Jane, I had no idea. I'm so sorry." The words don't seem like enough—I take one of her hands in both of mine.

She wipes her eyes. "I wanted to tell you before, but I've never told any of my friends. It's hard for me to talk about it."

I nod. "How did she . . . ?"

"Cancer. I'm no doctor, but—" Frowning, Jane pulls her hand out of mine.

"But what?"

"Well . . . I read some things, about the link between chronic stress and cancer . . . and I swear it was her body giving up on all the stress she faced every day with my dad." Jane catches her head in both of her palms now and sobs.

"I'm sad for you." It sounds feeble, even to my own ears. I rub her back and wait.

But the silence becomes unbearable. "You were so young," I add. I'm wondering what it would've been like if my mom died when I was eight.

When I was eight, Pinky Auntie left. But that's not the same thing. Jane's feelings of pain and loss must be a thousand times worse.

Jane sucks in her snot. Seeing her as anything but perfectly composed connects my heart instantly to hers. I feel tears welling at the bottoms of my eyes, but I blink them back. "Can I do anything to help? Can I get you anything? Are you hungry? Thirsty?"

She shakes her head. "I need to ride out the night." She sighs. "That's all."

"Well, we'll ride it out together."

Jane glances at me. "That'll be a first. A good first."

"Your dad . . . ?"

She shakes her head. "He's blown me off on every single one of these anniversaries. He used to pawn me off to nannies or relatives. Not that he was around much any other time." She pauses, swiping tears away from her cheeks. "He doesn't want to know how I'm doing. My mom was the opposite. I . . . I felt so alone after she died. I still do, sometimes."

I squeeze her hand. "You're not alone."

"Thanks." She sniffles.

"What was your mom like?"

A small, watery smile tugs at the corners of Jane's lips. "She was amazing." Jane's eyes meet mine. "She was doing research on women's economic empowerment. Did I ever tell you that I'm going to finish what she started?"

I shake my head.

"My econ focus is an extension of my mom's—to 'revolutionize and improve women's economic empowerment on a global scale.'"

"Wow," I breathe. "Your mom would be so proud."

Jane nods and rubs her eyes, some of the color coming back to her cheeks. "So . . . I heard you beer bonged a goldfish." Her voice sounds a little steadier now, if not grossed out. "What else went down at the Alpha Sig party?"

Someone else's DNA. Maybe HIV.

Gross! I still have to get tested. . . .

Chup-re!

"Nothing." I hope I sound convincing. I start biting my thumb nail.

Jane wrinkles her nose. "Well, that's boring."

I laugh, relieved that she bought it.

"Did you meet anyone?"

I shake my head, eyes dipping downward. I wish I could scurry away and hide in a dark corner: like a cockroach when you flip on the lights.

Simultaneously, the plan I had for the next time I spoke with her—to ask what happened with the guy she followed upstairs at the party—goes out the window. So do the follow-up questions: *Why didn't she stick to our plan? Why did she leave me?*

How can I complain about any of that on the anniversary of her mother's death?

Jane yawns. "Time for beauty sleep." She stretches, then moves to the door. "Good night, Gita."

"Good night, Jane. Hope you feel a little better."

"I do—thanks." She opens the door.

Marisol's standing on the other side, one fist held up as if she were about to knock and the other clutching two pairs of lightning bolt earrings. "I got these for you!" she singsongs, then stops abruptly at the sight of Jane's face. "Your mascara! What happened? Do *not* tell me that's supposed to be waterproof."

"I'm going to demand a refund," Jane deadpans.

I move to stand next to Jane. "Hi, Marisol," I say quietly.

Marisol's eyes ping back and forth between Jane and me. She plants her hands onto her hips. "Okay, who died?"

I grimace. Jane's eyes fill with fresh tears. "My mother," she whispers.

189

"Oh my gosh! What?" Marisol tosses her arms around Jane, then peeks at me and mouths, *"Really?"*

I nod, laying a hand on Jane's shoulder.

Marisol tightens her embrace around Jane. "I'm a clueless jerk. I'm so sorry, Jane."

Jane rubs her eyes until they're dry. "It's okay, you didn't know. It was a long time ago."

"What happened?" Marisol asks softly.

The three of us sit down in the middle of my room, and Marisol and I hold Jane as she speaks, and cries, and laughs. Despite Jane's grief, I notice a sensation of tranquility around us, like that of a baby held safe in the womb, protected from everything that rages beyond the door.

Is Marisol sensing this too? Does Jane feel the love surrounding her, even though she's suffering? I cross my fingers and hope that it's possible.

CHAPTER 16

Whooshing wind slingshots rain against my window. In the distance, jagged lightning turns the sky violet before thunder cracks its sonic whip.

I jump at the sound—Bay Area weather isn't typically this angry in the middle of October. Is the universe foreshadowing some kind of wicked twist of fate for me?

Get over it, Gita. Your life isn't a classic, and this storm isn't a literary device.

The phone rings and I answer: "Hello?"

"Hi, Gita. It's Marisol. Listen, I can't make it to the party tonight."

This morning at breakfast, Marisol had invited Jane and me to go to the Asian American Association party with her. Jane had already committed to an econ club event, so she was out. I opened my mouth to say no too, but Marisol touched my arm: "It's the association's first party of the year. They're introducing people to the group and having students sign up for more info. Weren't you saying you wanted to build your résumé for med school?" Then she sat there, batting her eyelashes at me.

Oh snap—I paused. "Fine, but only for an hour."

"Thank you!" Marisol clapped and bounced in place. "You won't regret it. There's supposed to be a DJ *and* booze."

The DJ sounded cool, but the mention of booze made me wince. *Chup-re!* I mentally cried at the sudden invasion of Gita-the-lush memories, despite knowing that never worked. The past loved to torture me sometimes.

Now Marisol sighs over the phone. "I hate to bail on you, but it's Joey's only night off this week. He's insisting on taking me out."

Thank you, Joey! I thrust my fist into the air. Outside, another lightning bolt and thunderclap slice the sky. This time, I pretend the sky is celebrating with me—celebrating the fact that from now through Monday morning's O-Chem exam, I can cram, cram, cram. If I do well enough, I can even boost my course grade back to an A.

"I'm sorry," Marisol says.

"Wow, I see how it is," I tease. "What Joey wants, Joey gets. Or is it more, 'I'm the option and he's the priority'?"

"Dang girl, way to keep it real." Marisol laughs, then pauses. "I hope you know it's not like that."

"Nah, I know. Besides, I'm already partying with O-Chem."

"Pssh. I still think you should go to the event."

"By myself?"

"Why not?"

The solo option hadn't occurred to me. I put down my high-lighter while Marisol continues.

"Guys go alone to parties all the time. This is the nineties—women can do anything guys can do. I mean, maybe don't drink too much . . . but mingling and dancing is the perfect study break."

"Maybe." In my head, though, it's a hard no. "Have fun on your date."

"Thanks. Talk to you later."

"Bye."

I set the handset down. The next flash outside is blinding, followed by a bone-rattling boom. Suddenly, I remember the lightning bolt earrings from Marisol and smile. *I love those earrings! Why haven't I worn them yet?*

I push back my chair and go to the dresser, opening the intricately carved wood jewelry box on top—a gift for my eighth birthday from Pinky Auntie. As my fingers graze the lightning bolt earrings, tiny pearls catch my eye. I push the earrings aside and riffle through the rest of the tangled mess of mostly cheap drugstore jewelry to find an elegant red-and-gold-colored rakhi with pearly beads that Pinky Auntie gave me years ago to tie on Sai's wrist for Raksha Bandhan. I lift the rakhi out and press it against my heart.

Raksha Bandhan is the day each year when, according to

Hindu ritual, brothers and sisters renew their sibling bonds. The last Raksha Bandhan Pinky Auntie was here for, she'd tied a Kundan pearl rakhi on Dad's wrist: "Thank you for all the love, care, and support, Raj bhai. I wish you joy and prosperity always, dear brother." And yes, I know tradition required her to say that—but I also know she meant every word.

"Thank you," Dad said. He gave her a gold paisley print envelope with money and recited the traditional Raksha Bandhan reply, also words I know he felt deeply: "I'll be here for you no matter what. My love for you is eternal."

"Thank you." But Pinky Auntie's bright eyes suddenly turned dull, then flooded with tears. Her smile disappeared; her bottom lip began to tremble.

Why did her smile go away? I tried to imagine denying Sai my own unfettered smile earlier that day when I tied a rakhi on his wrist. I scrunched my face at the impossibility of it.

Why was Pinky Auntie sad on this happy day? Was she tired? Was it because Neil Uncle had smiled a kind smile at Sai and me before leaving for work, but had frowned at her?

I glanced at Dad, whose eyebrows were lifted. "Pinky, what's wrong? Tanu said you were crying earlier—is there something going on between you and Neil?"

"He . . . he thinks Bhavin and I are having an affair, and—" she started, before cutting herself off. She turned her head away. "We're not. But Bhavin . . ."

"Bhavin what?" Dad leaned forward.

Pinky Auntie opened and closed her mouth, then opened it again. "I tried to explain it to Neil but—" She withered. "I couldn't do it."

"Do what?"

"Tell Neil that—"

My heart stumbled.

She touched her neck. "Bhavin . . ." She grimaced.

I touched my own neck and grimaced, feeling her pain. In that moment, I knew *exactly* what else she wanted to say.

"Bhavin what?" Dad's eyebrows sloped down toward his nose.

Pinky Auntie blinked, then shook her head. "Nothing. I'm okay—don't worry." Then she stared at her hands in her lap.

My heart hurdled. Only one thought looped over and over again in my head: *Take away Bhavin Uncle's key!*

Outside, the wind screams. I touch my neck now, and my heart sinks. Mostly for Pinky Auntie, but a little for me as well. Dad tried to be there for his sister in her time of need. And yet, it feels like he and Mom were never there for me when—

The sky flashes and rumbles. I break into a cold sweat. A thought has struck, canceling out all other thoughts: I completely forgot about Raksha Bandhan this year!

How could I?

Probably because Raksha Bandhan was a few weeks before Stanford started, and I was preoccupied with preparations. Still, I've never forgotten before. Sai and my parents were caught up in work, so I get why they forgot. But what excuse did I have?

I examine the rakhi in my hand, rubbing the soft thread between my index finger and thumb. Then I grab the phone and punch in our shop's number.

Forget the party. The only study break I want—need—is to give Sai the rakhi tonight. It feels urgent; like if I wait until even tomorrow, then our sibling bond will be permanently, irreparably broken.

Luckily, it's Sai who answers: "Hello?"

"Hey—it's Gita. Any chance you're free for dinner tonight?" I hold my breath.

"Yup."

I exhale, relieved that our sibling bond will make it through the storm.

CHAPTER 17

An hour and a half later, Sai and I are next up for a table at Tran's Bistro. It's a hole-in-the-wall Vietnamese joint that Sora swears by, and it's packed. In the cramped entryway, the tempting aromas of mint, lemongrass, fish sauce, and sweet barbequed meat waft, making it nearly impossible to keep my hungry, are-you-done-yet-people stare to myself.

Suddenly, I get bumped, pushed from behind. I whip my head over my shoulder to find a family of four squeezing themselves into the doorway. Sai and I end up wedged between the wall and the host podium.

"Excuse you," I grumble, chup-re no match for my hunger-fueled irritation. My hostile eyes take aim first at the dad in a charcoal-gray suit, then at the mom draped in an Ann Taylor–ish white linen dress. She turns away, smoothing her blond, shoulder-length flipped hair.

Sai widens his stance and crosses his arms, but his tone is

soft and polite when he turns to them and says, "There's a sign. You have to wait outside."

They ignore Sai, just like they ignored the big sign posted on the front of the door: *PLEASE WAIT OUT HERE UNTIL A SERVER CALLS YOU IN.*

The dad chuckles. "Smells like the place farts go to die."

The mom wrinkles her nose. "I know, I know, but Mackenzie said it was good." She pats her stomach. "What it's not good for is my low-fat diet."

I move my clenched jaw from side to side, ready to say, *Then leave, you cultural heathens!*

"Nothing step aerobics can't fix, honey," the dad says.

I stare at the ceiling and exhale, wondering what *Twilight Zone* meets *Leave It to Beaver* hell I'm trapped in. Even in the vicinity of the intellectual bastion that is Stanford, there's always white people talking like white people—oblivious and loud, invading and oppressing anyone in their way.

Then one of the teenage sons, the one sporting a "Clinton/Gore" baseball hat, punches his brother's arm. "I can't believe Mom let you out of the house wearing *that*."

That is a black T-shirt with an image of a curvy woman in a bikini straddling a big bottle of whiskey, fanning herself with a deck of playing cards. The words *LIQUOR IN THE FRONT, POKER IN THE BACK* are printed in neon yellow above her head.

Clinton/Gore shakes his head. "Seriously. You're such a dick-head."

Dickhead sneers. "Everyone knows it's a joke."

"Well, for the record, no girl will ever date you if you wear shit like that."

Dickhead smirks. "Who needs dating? I take what I want." His laugh is maniacal, like a cartoon evil villain.

I'm stone-faced, staring at the gap between Dickhead's two front teeth while everything else fades away.

I take what I want.

I cock my head. My eyes widen: I remember. I *remember.* Bhavin Uncle said something just like that, only in Gujarati.

Pinky Auntie is crying.

Bhavin Uncle glides his finger over her collarbone.

Writhing, Pinky Auntie pleads, "No, stop!"

He doesn't. He kisses her neck. She pushes him away.

Bhavin Uncle chuckles. "Keep it up, and I'll have to take what I want by force." He leans in and whispers something into her ear before leaving the apartment.

Later, I ask Pinky Auntie, "What will Bhavin Uncle take by force?"

Pinky Auntie looks stricken. "Nothing. Don't worry, beta."

"Why did Bhavin Uncle kiss your neck? What about Neil Uncle?" I ask.

She laughs a nervous little laugh before her expression contorts, her eyes diving to the floor. A moment later, she sweeps her palm over her face and brings her eyes back to me with a pained smile. "It's our little secret, Gita." She winks.

My toes curl. I break eye contact, picking a scab on my knee. Bhavin Uncle winks and makes me keep secrets too—will Thakorji still love me if he knows how many secrets I'm keeping?

There are bonfires on my cheeks when I remember Pinky Auntie's wink. I didn't like it: It bound me to her secret forever. All these years, I've kept it hidden. Even from myself.

I become aware of my chest quickly rising and falling. *I've got my own secrets now, Pinky Auntie.*

Sai nudges me with his elbow. "We're almost up." He points to a nearby table, where a middle-aged couple are scooting back their chairs.

"Hey, Sai?"

He shifts his eyes to me. "Yeah?"

"I don't think Pinky Auntie liked Bhavin Uncle." I nibble on my thumb knuckle, hoping that my brother will share something—anything—that might provide another puzzle piece to our past.

Sai looks confused. Then his expression hardens. "Bhavin Uncle is an asshole," he mutters.

"Wait—what?" I touch Sai's arm, but he doesn't move. He's glaring at a crack on the linoleum floor.

I try again. "Did you ever see Bhavin Uncle act weird with Pink—?"

"No." His retort is sharp, unmoving.

He could be telling the truth. Back when Pinky Auntie and

Neil Uncle used to live with us, when Bhavin Uncle would come over, Sai was mostly out of the house, helping our parents or hanging out with best buddy Chaz. It was me who was home a lot.

Scratch that. It was me, Pinky Auntie, and Bhavin Uncle who were home a lot.

My stomach contracts into a tight ball. "What if Bhavin Uncle—"

Sai cuts me off again. "I hate that guy."

"Why?"

"I don't want to talk about him anymore."

But I want to. I gulp. *Feels like I* need *to.*

How is Sai's pissed-off-ness at Bhavin Uncle so certain, whereas mine waxes and wanes? I pick at a hangnail, feeling myself shrink.

"Table for two is ready," a server calls out, waving us over.

A quick, sharp pain on my fingertip. I lift it and see that I've ripped off a jagged sliver of skin.

Sai stuffs his hands in his pockets and heads to the table. I follow him.

Our food and drinks arrive—pork bún and sugarcane juice for me, shaking beef and a beer for Sai—when my brother heaves a breath.

"Gita . . . I'm sorry."

"For what?" I ask, concentrating on tearing apart my

flimsy wooden chopsticks without getting a splinter.

"For shutting you down back there. I hate Bhavin Uncle— I saw the way he looked at Pinky Auntie. . . . But Neil Uncle blamed Pinky Auntie for that." With his finger, he slashes through the condensation on his bottle of beer. "He said she was a home-wrecker. But I *know* she wasn't having an affair."

I set the chopsticks down. For a second, nausea suffocates my hunger pangs. "How do you know that?"

"I overheard her and Mom talking."

My eyebrows leap. "What did they say?"

"Pinky Auntie said Bhavin Uncle was being rude, getting touchy. She kept telling him to stop." Sai stares down the beer bottle in his hand. "But Neil Uncle didn't believe her."

"Why not?"

Sai shrugs. "Because we live in a world that always blames women? I don't know."

I exhale slowly. "Anything else?"

"Isn't that enough?" He gives me an odd look. "No. There isn't anything else."

I let it go—no means no, after all.

Well, no means no to people besides Bhavin Uncle, anyway.

I fiddle with one of my lightning bolt earrings, then remember what's in my purse, the whole reason Sai and I are here: the rakhi. I bring it out carefully, as if it's made of precious metal and jewels instead of thread and beads. "This is why I called you for dinner tonight." With both hands, I present it to my brother. "I'm sorry I forgot Raksha Bandhan."

Sai puts his hand on his heart. "Ah, Gita. You're the best." He extends his arm across the table. "And for the record, I don't need a piece of string to know how you feel about me. But I appreciate the gesture."

I tie the rakhi on his wrist, reciting the good wishes that Pinky Auntie taught me. "May you have all the happiness and prosperity in the world, Sai bhai."

He touches the rakhi. "Thank you . . . and hold that thought." He pulls out his wallet, plucking a crisp one-hundred-dollar bill from its depths and handing it to me. "Sorry I forgot about this too. And sorry that I don't have one of those colorful dandiya envelopes for it."

I stare at the bill in his hand. "What? You just happen to have a Benjamin in your wallet?"

"Today, yes. Just got paid: Cha-ching!" He motions for me to take the money.

I hesitate, but know he won't let me turn it away. "Thank you," I say, grasping the bill delicately between my thumb and pointer finger.

He touches the rakhi on his wrist. "I hope you know I'll always be here for you. I love you, little sis."

"You're the best, Sai." I slip the bill into my purse, deciding to use it to repay Jane and Marisol for the fake ID.

A wave of guilt. What would Sai think if he knew I had a

fake ID? That might cause our first real fight as adults. I try to picture his face during the moment of discovery—sorrow that morphs into rage? No, no. He wouldn't be pissed off about that. If anything, Sai would understand me doing normal college stuff, even if it's illegal. Maybe I should ask him if he's ever had a fake ID.

Sai takes a few bites of beef and washes it down with some beer. "So what's going on with you? Besides studying."

I could tell him about the partying and drinking. I think he'd understand that—I've seen him and Chaz drunk before, and I didn't think any less of them. But chup-re spins a partial truth into a lie instead: "I'm working extra hours at the lab."

"Okay, cool . . . But that kind of counts as studying. You're at Stanford. There's so much art and culture and, you know, other fun things."

Other fun things like drinking and screwing around? Although neither has turned out to be that much fun. . . .

I stare at the rakhi on Sai's wrist, feeling feverish despite the air-conditioning in this place. I peel away the back of my shirt, which is sticking to my suddenly clammy skin. My eyes veer to the unplugged fan in the far corner: I wish it were in front of me and on full blast.

Sai taps my hand. "Gita?"

My eyes creep to his. "Huh?"

"Fun?"

"Oh, yeah, uh . . . hanging out with some new friends."

Sai grins. "Gita Desai, hanging out just because? Tell me everything."

"Very funny," I say, fanning my face.

"Well, who are these friends?" He takes a bite of beef, swallows.

"Two girls in my dorm: Jane and Marisol."

"You three aren't getting into any shenanigans?" he asks, using a thick Gujju accent. Then he laughs, as if we both know I'd never do anything mischievous.

I laugh too, softly though. "Of course not." I make my eyes doe-like though I'm digging my nails into my palms and trying to ignore the internal battle raging between premed me and party-girl me.

"So," Sai continues. "What's up for tonight?"

"O-Chem." My eyes wander to the unplugged fan again.

"No parties you want to check out?"

I shake my head. *If you knew the things I did at the last party, you wouldn't want me to.*

The fan blades seem to spin. There's throbbing behind my eyes.

"Gita, Gita, Gita."

The pressure is building in my head, like my cerebrum is swelling inside my skull.

"All that studying will fry your brain."

I practically glare at him. "Studying isn't crack, Sai." Though I do wonder if this is how my head would feel if I really did smoke crack.

Sai's smile dampens. "True . . . But everyone needs to let loose sometimes, even you."

By now, my head is killing me; I'm convinced that I'm having my first migraine. I massage my temples, and my eyes swing back to the fan. Sai is saying something else, but the thoughts in my head are amplified, as if coming through a megaphone.

Pinky Auntie didn't like what Bhavin Uncle was doing and he didn't respect her "no," so she pushed him away. She stopped him. You didn't like what Angelo or Johnny Depp Boy were doing to you, but you didn't stop it. So it's your fault. Even if you get HIV.

I quietly click my tongue. *It's my fault.*

That *feels* true.

But if it's my fault, then maybe I can fix it. Like how I'm going to fix my O-Chem grade by acing the exam.

My migraine eases up. My hands drift to the table and interlace.

It's simple, really. Instead of wallowing or beating myself up, all I have to do is make things right for myself. Prove to myself that I can go to a party for a little while, be around guys, and leave without anything bad happening. Or stop anything I don't like. It can be like a test retake.

I think about the one time in high school when I bombed a math test. There was nothing sweeter or more satisfying than kicking butt on the retake and having that A+ replace the C.

Sai picks at the label on his beer bottle. "Seems to me that parties are part of the college experience."

I bring my eyes back to him. "You're right, bhai. And actually, there is one party that sounds interesting. . . ."

CHAPTER 18

*L*et me set the record straight about Stanford parties—the frat boys are amateurs compared to the members of the Asian American Association.

The AAA have laid out an actual dance floor that's packed with *everyone* dancing in the dark—no barbaric drinking games. The best part is they've hired a professional hip-hop DJ—a Filipino guy from Daly City—who's got the bass turned up. When he fades into the intro horns of House of Pain's "Jump Around," there's a loud, collective "aww yea!"

A smile explodes on my face. The next thing I know, I'm jumping up and down with my arm stretched high in the air, just like everyone else. This moment—dance-bonding with my fellow overachieving Asian Americans instead of studying—feels like the most beautiful thing I've ever experienced. Forget beer bonging: *This* makes me feel powerful.

I start jumping in a circle. Halfway through my mini-rotation, my eyes crash into the words *STANFORD BASKET-BALL* on a glowing white T-shirt. I tilt my head up and stumble back when I realize it's none other than 6'6" Steven Hyun. He's a starter, an NBA prospect, and the president of the Asian American Association.

I'm not jumping anymore. In fact, I feel like I'm shriveling as I stare up at the chiseled perfection of his face under his buzzed haircut. All I'm thinking is, *Steven Hyun, you are the sun and i want to orbit around you forever.*

I swallow. *Why is he smiling at* me? *I'm nothing in his universe.*

He holds out his hand for a shake. "Hi, I'm Steven!" He has to yell so I can hear him over the cranked-up music.

I wipe my hand on my jeans, then lift it to shake his. "Nice to meet you! I'm Gita."

"Want to grab a drink?" He's pointing in the direction of a table crowded with liquor bottles.

I steeple my fingers and behold his gorgeous face, thinking, *There's no way I'm trusting myself liquored up with this guy.* But sober and in full control of myself, it's pretty much a guarantee I'll ace my guy-test retake. Right?

"So? A drink?"

"Water would be good."

"Sure—hydration is key. After you."

As we weave our way through the sweaty jumping bodies, I'm wishing he was in front so I could do a quick smell-check of my armpits. Instead, I pray that I put on enough deodorant this morning. Steven grabs two chilled bottles of water and hands one to me.

I twist off the cap. "Thanks."

"You're welcome. Cheers." He tips his bottle toward mine.

I tip mine to his. "Cheers."

We stand there watching the crowd—I realize the song has changed to Eric B. & Rakim's "Don't Sweat the Technique." I can't help but to do a jazzy little move to match the song's jazzy groove. Then I glance at Steven, whose soulful eyes bore into mine.

Instant butterflies in my stomach. I stop dancing, feeling my face heat up.

He touches the small of my back. "Hey, don't stop. Your moves are good—almost as good as mine." Then he cups his chin and does a body roll.

I laugh, trying not to think too hard about his hand that was on me.

"You know what they say about people who can dance, right?"

I shake my head. "What?"

"Come to my room and I'll show you." A crooked smile blooms on his face.

I take a step back—I'm afraid he'll feel the heat suddenly radiating off me. . . . And that he'll hear every cell in my body screaming *Let's go!*

I manage to resist: This is my retake, and I'm determined to pass with flying colors. I press my palm to my chest dramatically and make a face. "What kind of girl do you think I am?"

He pokes out his lips, rubs his chin, and waits, as if he knows *exactly* what kind of girl I am.

Stay strong, Gita. This is your chance to make things right for yourself!

Steven shrugs. "We can just order pizza and chill."

My mouth begins to water. A battle commences in my head: *Don't even think about it* vs. *This retake is harder than expected . . . but I'll rise to the challenge. Just pizza, nothing else—easy peasy.*

I smile, patting my stomach. "All that dancing did work up my appetite."

An hour later, Steven and I are sitting in our underwear on the floor with an open pizza box between us. We take a second to admire the pie's pepperoni pageantry atop the browned, bubbly mozzarella.

I twist the cap off a Sprite and take a sip. "Thanks. Can I pay you back?"

He shakes his head, reaching for a slice. "My treat." He lifts the crust and half the melty cheese starts to fall off. He saves it with two fingers, then takes a bite.

I fold my slice, sinking my teeth in. The crust is crispy and chewy in just the right amounts. But it's the sauce that brings tears of joy to my eyes. It's impossible not to grin as I chew. I swallow the bite, then practically inhale the rest of the slice, eyes closed in ecstasy.

"Damn, girl!"

I open my eyes to find Steven gawking. "I know Vinny's pizza is good, but didn't I already get you there half an hour ago?" He winks.

"You did." I decide that his wink doesn't feel bad; that I got a hundred on my retake because I liked everything we did and didn't need to stop anything. This must be what Marisol meant when she said, *This is the nineties—women can do anything guys can do.*

He wipes pretend sweat off his brow. "Okay, Kama Sutra, you had me worried for a second."

I giggle. *He's so nice. And funny. Maybe he really likes me.*

He scoots over next to me.

Maybe he wants to hang out with me again.

He traces the outline of my lips.

Maybe he'll ask for my number.

"By the way," he whispers before planting a feathery kiss on my neck.

I hold my breath. *Ask, ask, ask, please!*

"Before you go . . . can you give me Marisol's number?"

A tiny yelp escapes from between my lips as I fight back tears.

CHAPTER 19

I'm arranging sterile equipment in the lab, blissfully lost in the process. Dr. Peters is in France for the International Maize Genetics Conference. Everyone else is on the fifth floor meeting the newly hired professor of Global Ecology.

Suddenly, my muscles and joints go stiff. I'm not sure what happened but, standing here alone, in the quiet, trepidation floods my senses. It's like I'm about to be pushed overboard into rough seas, and I just realized that I can't swim. Then the fear devolves into self-flagellation: *How am I even working here? What if people figure out I'm a fraud?* Strange little sounds akin to a death rattle emanate from my throat.

I glance over my shoulder at Dr. Peters's office, trying to resuscitate my breathing, to reassure myself that my boss is highly discerning—she wouldn't have hired me if she doubted my abilities. After a minute, I'm about 50 percent convinced.

My body loosens, and I try to busy my hands, to distract myself from the other 50 percent.

When I'm done, I drag myself to the conference room for our lab's weekly lunch meeting. I poke my head in and check the wall clock: I'm twenty minutes early. The rest of the crew will begin to trickle in soon and, as I've learned, the early bird gets the seat closest to the free food.

Which, to my delight, is already here—four large boxes of pizza stacked on the counter next to the sink. I perk up and take a deep inhale, only to have tragedy strike: This specific blend of baked dough, cheese, and garlic scents tell me it's Vinny's pizza. Immediately, my head is rewinding and repeating three nights ago with Steven Hyun.

I yank my eyes away from the pizza and plaster them to the four words underlined on the chalkboard: *TRANSCRIPTIONAL ACTIVATORS IN MAIZE*. I lean against the doorframe, letting the words go blurry. . . .

At least there's a smidgen of solace in that I didn't give Marisol's number to Steven. Even if I'd wanted to, I wouldn't do it without her permission. "Ask her yourself," I'd huffed, stuffing myself back into my clothes.

A tap on my shoulder. I turn my head and see that it's Jeet— he smiles.

My lips manage a goofy approximation of one.

"Let's get the good seats." He raises and lowers his eyebrows a couple of times. "That's why you're here first, right?"

"Secret's out." My heart flutters.

He extends his arm, gesturing toward the spread. "Ladies first."

"Thanks." I cross the threshold and walk around the long table that has six pushed-in chairs on either side.

Jeet strolls in behind me. We sit on the two chairs across from each other that are nearest to the pizza. He clasps his hands on the table. "How are you doing?"

I swallow. "Fine. How are you?"

"Good." Jeet pauses. "Hey, your O-Chem exam was this morning. How did it go?"

He remembered! I swoon. "It was easy. I'm pretty sure I got an A."

Jeet shakes his head. "*Easy* isn't a word I ever remember using to describe anything about that course." He leans forward. "I thought you were my academic match, Gita, but you're so much more."

Heat in my chest. Is my heart blushing? I hope my cheeks aren't! I repeat his last sentence in my head, leaving out the word *academic*.

If only.

"No, I'm just extremely efficient with studying." *Most of the time.* I drop my eyes and shove my hands under my thighs.

"Modest. I like that." He makes circles on the table with his flat palms. "I'm sure you're extremely efficient with studying, but don't underestimate your innate abilities."

I don't know what to say. I give Jeet a grateful smile.

"I get that you're a genius and all that, but even geniuses need help sometimes. Especially because you're learning the new language of maize genetics, and Dr. Peters isn't here. Let me know if I can be of assistance."

"Thanks. . . . But I think I got it for now."

"Of course you do." Jeet runs his hand through his hair. "Still, don't be a stranger if anything comes up. Plus, you're the only other full desi in the lab besides me. Since I'm older, it's my duty to look out for you. That's an unwritten Indian law, in case you're wondering." His lips tug upward.

That smile. "I appreciate that," I respond, cool as a cucumber.

I can't help but think he's right about the "unwritten Indian law." I mean, my parents are nicer to Indian customers than other customers. Jeet *has* to be nice to me, despite everything Sora said. The possibilities creep into my head: *If Jeet gets to know me, he might fall in love with me. . . . I mean, I can see myself falling in love with* him. . . .

"Anytime," Jeet says, and it takes me a second to remember that he's talking about lab stuff. He gets up and grabs a slice of pizza, even though I think we're supposed to wait until the meeting begins. "By the way: I'm having a party on November fourth. You should come."

I run through all the instances of Jeet being nice to me: fixing the autoclave when I asked, calling me about my O-Chem notebook, and offering to help with lab stuff and look out for me. Now with this invitation . . . *He's* got *to like-me like me!*

I cross my fingers behind my back, persuading myself of the possibility that "like-me like me" could someday lead to love. Unlike a hookup, which—so far—has led to nothing except regret and pain. Literally.

"Okay," I finally respond.

"Awesome." Jeet smiles, then points to the pizza boxes. "Want a slice?"

"Sure?" I quickly peek over my shoulder, as if I'm young Krishna about to steal butter and I want to make sure no one's watching.

Jeet loosens a gooey slice and eyes me. "The party's on a school night though. Are you sure you can come out to play?"

That look. My breath stalls in my chest. "H-hundred per-cent," I stutter, reminding myself that the unwritten Indian law means he won't try to hook up with me. Which means there's nothing nefarious I'll need to stop. I'm safe.

I exhale.

CHAPTER 20

Jane, Marisol, and I climb into the back of the ancient, roomy cab, and I pull the door shut. The fluffy sheepskin cover over the back seat invites us to get cozy and stay awhile. The old cabbie, with deep wrinkles carving his face like a road-map through a complicated life, glances at us in his rearview mirror; his grayish-brown eyes are dull under his bushy white eyebrows. "Where to?" he asks.

"Club Inferno Nine," Marisol replies.

One of Marisol's ex-boyfriends used to DJ there, and he gave her the 411 about tonight's visiting DJ—an eighteen-year-old girl hip-hop-phenom. It's a Thursday, and this particular 411 is quite possibly the best reason to be out on a school night—short of the guy I like inviting me to his upcoming middle-of-the-week party, of course.

"You got it." The cabbie pulls away from the curb, then adds, "Club Inferno Nine—quite a name."

I'm about to crack a joke about how we should've dressed warmer for the freezing ninth circle of hell in Dante's *Inferno*, but a sparkling, heart-shaped charm dangling from the cabbie's rearview mirror grabs my attention. Printed in the middle of it: *Wine lovers age well.*

A flash of memory from the car ride home with Angelo: He had the same charm in his Bentley. It was a gift, he said, from his mother. My upper lip curls as I imagine what I'd do if I ever saw Angelo again driving around in his fancy-ass car. *Wait until he parks and walks away, then key his precious Bentley? Louisville-Slugger the lights and windshield?*

Neither. He'd definitely call the cops on the "crazy brown girl destroying his property." Also, hardcore violence isn't my style.

A better idea: After he pulls into his driveway at night and goes inside his place, I'll slink out of the bushes—clad in black from head to toe, including a balaclava. The spray can in my hand will rattle as I shake it. When I finish, I'll stand back and admire my art—definitely art, not vandalism—a mural of giant dicks gallivanting along the sides, up and over the hood and the trunk. Inside each of the four distinctively unattractive dicks I've sprayed the words *Assholes FUCK and FORGET!*

Yeah, that's more my speed. I'm grinning as my eyes shift from the charm to the dash: There's a Buddha bobblehead on the top right, and he's smiling too. I watch the Buddha's happy face move up, down, and all around.

The cabbie reaches over with his gnarled hand and adjusts

the radio. A bebop trumpet blares. He turns it down to a nice background volume, humming along. Jane leans in toward Marisol and me and whispers, "Got your fake IDs, ladies?"

Marisol and I nod.

Jane thrusts her arm onto Marisol's lap and flips her wrist. "Like?" she asks, presenting a gold and diamond baby Rolex that gleams as bright as her eyes. "It belonged to my mom."

Marisol takes Jane's hand to examine the watch. "Your mom had good taste."

"She did."

"It's beautiful," I add.

Jane smiles. "And waterproof." She touches the watch's face. "My mom loved swimming, especially in the ocean. She said she felt the freest when she was out there."

"Do you swim?" I ask.

"I used to, with my mom."

"Maybe you should pick it up again."

"Maybe." There's a lull in the music, and the three of us rock softly with the car.

"Speaking of new bling . . ." Marisol pushes up the long sleeve of her stretchy crop top and holds up her wrist. A white gold and diamond tennis bracelet sparkles in the streetlights. "From Joey." Her voice is proud.

"Gorgeous," Jane says.

Then I feel their eyes on me.

"It's lovely," I finally say. Then I hold up both of my bare wrists. "I've got nothing for you, sorry."

Marisol elbows me gently. "Wrists bare, but heart of gold."

"A diamond in the rough." Jane nods.

"Holy dad jokes," I say, but I secretly love the cliches.

We sit in comfortable silence for a long time. Somewhere on the 101, Marisol brings up the Chinese film *The Story of Qiu Ju*.

" . . . and they're trying to get it shown on campus."

"They who?" Jane asks.

"The Asian American Association."

Instantly, before I can stop it, I'm back to that night in Steven Hyun's dorm room; I clench my teeth. Then the cab hits a pothole on the exit ramp, and my mouth fills with the taste of warm metal—I realize I've vampired my inner cheek. I poke my tongue into the wound to stop the bleeding and tell myself, *Forget all the boys who fuck and forget!*

By the time I tune back into my girls' conversation, the cab's stopped in front of the club. We split the fare three ways, thank the driver, and step out into the crisp San Fran night. Two burly bouncers in suits, with tribal neck tats that hug their hairlines and kiss their collars, guard the club's medieval-looking dark wood and iron-trimmed door. A long line stretches down the block and around the corner.

My face drops as I calculate the wait time. Shaking my head in dismay, I begin walking toward the end of the line.

"Gita!" Marisol calls.

I look at her over my shoulder.

"We don't wait."

"What do you mean we don't—" I catch Marisol's exaggeratedly beguiling expression, throw my hands up, and laugh.

Marisol weaves her arms through Jane's and mine. I realize that tonight her birthmark is a half-moon rising from under her crop top, and she isn't even attempting to cover it up. Heads turn as the three of us walk tall and proud to the door.

"Hi," she says to the bouncers.

Turns out that a single Marisol-word and a Marisol-glance is all it takes for the bouncers to fight like little boys tripping over themselves to open the door for her, Jane and me in tow. Just like that, we're in. No ID check. No paying a cover.

That is a superpower, I think, feeling small. But I remind myself that I love Marisol and I have Stanford, and that makes me big. Well, at least medium.

It's a good thing I have Stanford. I need Stanford.

The heavy door shuts behind us. In the darkness of the hall, flashing strobe lights from the main club area are a beacon, drawing us toward the dance floor.

"Damn, girl," I say, turning to Marisol. "You're the only ID we need. I should've saved my hundred bucks for the fake."

Marisol shrugs. "It doesn't always work."

"I find that hard to believe."

"You're right." Her expression turns mischievous. "It always works."

I glance at Jane, who's frowning.

"They still might card us at the bar," Marisol adds, adjusting her top.

"Ah. Money well spent then." I lean in toward Jane. "Hey, are you okay?"

She sighs. "It's irritating when guys just—just . . ."

"Just what?"

"Oh, I don't know." She shakes her head. "Maybe next time we should wait in line like everyone else."

"Girl, have fun waiting by yourself!" I flip my hair dramatically over my shoulder.

"Whatever." Jane rolls her eyes, laughing. "You know what I mean."

"Yeah. I do." I don't think she hears me, though, because the thumping hip-hop bass of Wreckx-n-Effect's "Rump Shaker" hits our chests like a battering ram. There's no denying that this song can make anyone—and I mean anyone—want to shake their rump all sexy-like. I dance-walk as we cut through the crowd—and the wafting blends of cologne—straight to the bar.

Even there, no waiting: One of the handsome bartenders shows up as if out of thin air. His voice is lathered with charm when he asks, "What can I get you ladies?" His teal eyes, their color the love child of sky and rainforest, are planted on Jane.

Her sullen expression vanishes. She blinks slowly. "Six lemon drop shots," she says in her famous Jane West smoky voice.

Still staring at her, the bartender holds up his hands. "Look . . . wait, what's your name?"

"Jane."

"Look, Jane, I really need to get to know you better. But I'm attempting to work right now, and you're very distracting. I might get fired."

I can tell Jane is trying not to give away how flattered she is. She can't do it: She blushes.

"I'll be back." The bartender knocks once on the bar, then backs up and away.

After he leaves, Marisol nods her chin up at Jane. "Go girl."

Jane smiles at her.

"Why six?" I ask.

Jane blinks, then remembers the shots she ordered. "Two rounds—got to jump-start the buzz."

"Ah. Good plan." I nod, telling myself that it's okay if I get a little buzzed. My girls won't leave me alone tonight—I mean, we're at a club in the city, not some frat house on campus. We're sharing a cab home, not walking.

I turn around, rest my elbows on the sticky bar, and scan the packed dance floor. The DJ is mixing and scratching like it's an Olympic sport—my body's feeling it. A second later, she uses the crossfader to tease the crowd with a little of Ice-T's "New Jack Hustler."

The bartender returns with the half dozen shots. He arranges them in a neat row, then scribbles ten digits on a napkin and slides it over to Jane. "I'm just giving you my number. But I really want to give you my time, so call me. I'm Lance, by the way." His finger brushes her hand. He winks, then goes to serve a group of guys that just arrived at the other end of the bar.

Jane sighs. I giggle, pleased for her. Maybe tonight, if I meet a guy, he'll give me his number too: good, clean fun.

Marisol and Jane seem happy tonight. I'm happy for them— and for me. It's everything: the hip-hop, the celebratory vibe from the pumped-up crowd, my friends, the drinks.

"To girls' night," Marisol says, lifting a glass.

We clink shot glasses, then throw our heads back and down the first round. The sweet-tart potion of good times coats my throat. We grab the second round.

"Here's to drinking, not thinking!" I cheer, then take the shot.

Jane and Marisol exchange impressed glances before knocking back theirs.

We people-watch for a bit: Hungry male eyes skip over me to get a piece of my friends. But it's all good. The alcohol has already begun to gift me with the confidence I lack in a sober state.

"Let's dance!" Marisol yells over the music. She grabs our

hands, and the three of us burrow through the packed dance floor to the middle and stand in a triangle, getting our groove on.

I feel the lemon drops taking full effect—it's a different buzz than wine. Of course, there's the euphoria that makes me Cheshire Cat grin and Jennifer Lopez *In Living Color* Fly-Girl dance. But there's something else too—a feeling of invincibility.

I don't know when, but at some point, three guys surround us. A tall Black Asian man wearing a Bulls jersey, gold chain, and baggy jeans presses up against Marisol from behind while a white guy with shaggy blond hair plants himself next to Jane.

My eyes slink to the left, and I inhale sharply.

The guy next to me is scary-hot in a Dave Navarro way, with the same black hair, sculpted beard, tattoos, and piercings. Dave Navarro doppelganger smiles, and my knees buckle.

"Dave" hands Jane, Marisol, and me drinks.

"Thanks," I say. I gulp mine down, then cough. Premed me chides, *Did you just chug a drink from a stranger? What if he pulled the whole GHB-and-alcohol trick?*

Party-girl me replies, *Oh well. Too late now. Loosen up!*

"What was that drink?" I ask Dave.

"Liquid cocaine." He pauses. "You like it?"

I nod, glancing at Marisol and Jane, who're dancing with Dave's friends. Dave touches the small of my back, and a nervous giggle escapes me.

"What's so funny?" Dave asks.

"Nothing," I say, straining to keep my cool.

"What's your name?"

"Gita. What's yours?"

"Javier."

I smile at the normal, natural exchange of information. It's kind of nice. He's nice. And nice guys don't GHB date-rape. Right?

I feel his hands snake around my waist. He pulls me closer. I'm not sure if it's the pounding music, the liquor, Javier's hard-on, or the combination, but at this moment, all good things are possible. I'm connected to the universe. It loves me, and I love it. I turn around and let Javier grind on me from behind—it feels so good. His fingers graze my neck as he moves my hair. "Come with me," he whispers into my ear.

Every thought in my head floats away. I wave to Jane and Marisol. "I'll be right back!" I hear myself yell. I think they nod.

I let Javier tow me through the crowd.

We head into a back hallway with a row of single unisex bathrooms. The one at the far end is open. The music is still loud, but muffled now. That, and time and space seem slower and thicker. In the brief moment we stand in front of the door, Javier's raised-eyebrow expression reads as, *Do we dare?*

I push him inside, slam the door shut, and lock it. I stand against the wall, not giving two shits that it's filthy. "Come here," I beckon in my best Jane West smoky voice.

"You're beautiful." Javier sinks to his knees, pushes up my mini-skirt and slides my panties down. He buries his face in my yoni.

I gasp, my eyelids drifting to a gentle close. Blurry flashes slice through the darkness of my mind: *White pedestal fan in the corner. The poke and scratch of the hairs on his face. It tickles.*

I whip open my eyes and glance around. Have I been here before? I remember wanting Snuffles . . .

Javier shoots up and spins me around. I press my palms and cheek onto the grimy wall as he kisses my neck. Part of me doesn't want him to stop, but the other part wants to scream, "Get off me!"

What comes out instead is a whispered, "I want Snuffles."

He doesn't hear me. Or maybe he's ignoring me. I look over my shoulder to see him unbuckling his pants, slipping on a condom.

My eyes well up. "I want—"

"Shut up."

My heart beats faster, my yoni tingling. The DJ is mixing a sample of Nine Inch Nails' "Head Like a Hole" into the next hip-hop song.

Javier slams his hand onto the wall next to my face.

I flinch. Then I flinch again when I feel it.

Flashing and pounding in my head.

Right away, Javier goes deep and hard. "Mmf," he grunts. Outside, Nine Inch Nails screams about getting what you deserve.

I shrink into myself. Everything sounds distant and jumbled—until it doesn't. Until there's nothing but a deep silence, penetrated by a familiar echo: *Shame-shame, shame-shame, shame-shame . . .*

"Deeper," I hear myself say. *He feels good when he gets what he wants.*

It hurts. But still I say, "Harder." *I feel good when I get what I deserve.*

Only then does my head finally go dark and silent. The pain loosens, ebbing away. . . .

I moan.

CHAPTER 21

*J*avier leaves. No look back, no nothing.

On his way out, he snatches a paper towel and wraps it around the used condom. He tosses the wad toward the trash, but it misses and comes undone. From where I'm kneeling in front of the toilet, my palms pressed onto my thighs, I stare at the full condom tip. The door slams shut.

I didn't stop it. I wanted it *and* I didn't want it. I check my wrist pulse: It's slow, steady. In my head, a different Nine Inch Nails song plays—"Kinda I Want To." My thoughts spin, and I sway to the nonexistent music.

Kinda I want to get what I deserve.

Kinda I want to—

Suddenly, my girls burst through the bathroom door. I squint, trying to keep them in focus. Marisol's hands are on her hips as she cries, "There you are! We were looking everywhere for you!"

I drop my eyes, mumbling, "Oh snap."

"We thought you'd gone home with that guy. Or he'd kidnapped you or something. Why didn't you just say you'd be gone awhile?" Jane asks.

I force my eyes up. "I said I'd be right back."

"'Right back' means, like, five minutes to go pee." Marisol crosses her arms tightly over her chest.

"You were gone for more than half an hour," Jane says, glancing at her baby Rolex.

"Call it even. You guys left me at the Alpha Sig party," I bite out.

"Seriously?" Marisol asks, then scoffs and shakes her head.

"This isn't the same thing, and you know it, Gita," Jane says.

I poke my tongue into my cheek and roll it around. I'm convinced that it *is* the same thing.

"Let's go." Jane holds out her hand. She and Marisol pull me up. My entire body feels heavy, dead weight.

"You're wasted." Jane sounds worried.

Marisol clicks her tongue. "Girls' night turns into babysitting. Thought I was done with Ginny."

Tears cloud my vision. I want to say *I'm sorry.* I want to say *I hate myself right now, for so much.*

Also, who's Ginny?

Can't get the words out, though.

We leave the club, and Jane hails a cab. The three of us get in the back with me in the middle. There's no traffic in the city this late, so when the cabbie steps on the gas, the bright lights, neon signs, and tightly packed buildings are quickly replaced by near-total darkness.

We've hit the wide, vacant stretch of I-280. Sleepy hills and thick towering trees surround us in lush silence. It's silent inside the cab too.

I sneak a peek at my girls, who are both staring out their windows. I stay facing forward, focusing on the back of the cabbie's head. His oily, graying hair gets shinier when the light from an occasional streetlamp hits it. I think maybe he's Indian or Pakistani, around my dad's age.

He forks his fingers through his hair. With my next breath, I catch the faint smell of petroleum, but it's not like a gas station. It's more subtle.

I glide a finger over my collarbone, close my eyes, and inhale. . . .

Neil Uncle finishes reading an article about African savanna hares to me. He holds out the Ranger Rick *magazine.*

Taking it, I say, "Thank you, Neil Uncle."

He pats my head. "You're welcome. I have to go to work now, Gita beta."

I nod, then slide off the sofa and head to the bathroom to pee.

But Bhavin Uncle is in there, massaging V05 into his thick black hair.

I sniff. I know that smell. It's a little like gas.

I stand there, wishing Bhavin Uncle was going to work instead of Neil Uncle. . . .

I open my eyes and start picking at a little scab on my arm. Pick, pick, pick. The scab comes off, and a few drops of blood ooze onto my skin.

Jane nudges my knee with hers. "You have to admit, Gita, you were gone awhile. What were you doing in the bathroom for that long?"

I search her face in the dark, but can't find a trace of sarcasm or judgment there. I swallow back the spit pooling in my mouth—and tonight's truth. "Felt sick. Didn't want to throw up in the middle of the dance floor, so I held my own hair and . . . you know."

I feel Jane's gaze still on me. At first, she doesn't respond. Then, maybe a quarter mile later: "But you went with that guy."

You don't know the half of it. I don't say that, or anything. But tears tumble down my cheeks.

"Are you okay? Did he—?"

"We kissed. That's it."

Jane huffs. "Be honest with me, Gita." She sounds frustrated now.

"That's it." I play with my hands. Around me, I can sense Jane and Marisol leaning forward at the same time, exchanging glances. Before they can grill me any more, I turn to Marisol:

"Who's Ginny?" I ask, throat hoarse. "Why are you done with her?"

Marisol shifts in her seat and tugs on her rosary. Finally, she sighs. "Ginny *was* my best friend in high school. She'd get wasted every time we hung out and I'd have to constantly keep an eye on her so she wouldn't do some dumb shit. When I called her out on it, she dropped me faster than a hot potato."

"She—she didn't try to talk to you about it first?"

Marisol shakes her head, her expression going blank. Her fingers slip to her birthmark, and I watch her trace its top edge. "After that, she went around school showing everyone a photo of us by her pool. Until then, the only people who knew about my birthmark were my parents, a few guys I'd dated, and Ginny. Soon, everyone at school knew about it." She twists her rosary and exhales softly. "They'd push me around and point and laugh, and the insults were terrible. 'Do your parents beat you silly? You spilled some cranberry juice on yourself! Guess you didn't outrun the fire?'" She slides down in her seat. "Marisol the walking stain," she whispers.

"Oh Marisol," I breathe, touching her arm.

Jane groans. "Fuck them. You could break barriers in the modeling industry with your birthmark, Marisol. And, really, you're already breaking barriers."

Marisol shrugs. "I guess. . . ."

"Jane's right. *You,* Marisol, could change the world," I add.

Marisol lips curve up in a tentative smile. "Thanks, you guys."

We sit quietly for a few minutes.

Marisol clears her throat. "Hey . . . I meant to ask you, Gita: What happened at the Alpha Sig party after I left?"

Every ounce of warmth leaches out of me. "Nothing."

"Okaaay." Marisol gives me an odd look. "It's just . . . I was talking to Matt yesterday, and he said he saw you—"

"I was too drunk to walk home, so I slept over. On the couch." I can't figure out why, but it feels better to lie than confess all my dirty secrets. Scratch that—*better* isn't the right word. *Easier? Automatic?*

I stare at the dried droplets of blood on my arm. I know Jane and Marisol wouldn't judge me. . . . But what if they did? What if they judged me *and* left me?

My inhales and exhales start to quicken. *I don't want to lose them! They're my first real friends—*

Breathe, Gita.

I force myself to slow my next inhale. I might not like it, but I don't judge Marisol for flirting with guys even though she has a boyfriend. And I don't judge Jane for hooking up with Sigma Nu boy, and possibly Todd and the Alpha Sig guy.

But they're not sluts. Like me.

Crap! It suddenly hits me that I still haven't gotten an HIV test after Johnny Depp Boy. What if I have HIV? What if I passed it on to Javier when he went down on me?

Crap, crap, crap!

I don't want to give HIV to anyone. I don't want to hurt people. Even if they hurt me.

The white noise buzzing between my ears ramps up, suffocating all coherent thought. My head spins and my eyes grow blurry.

"What's wrong?" Jane asks.

"I'm sorry I left you guys. I'm sorry I made you worry," I blubber.

Marisol sighs, then reaches into her purse and brings out a hankie. Gently, she dabs it under my eyes and over my cheeks as plump tears steamroll down my face.

Jane cradles my hand in hers. "It's okay, Gita, really. We're just glad you're safe."

When the tears finally slow, Marisol folds the hankie to a dry corner. "Did you know," she starts, "that women in fifteenth-century England would carry their handkerchiefs in their cleavage? Aren't you glad we're in twentieth-century America— especially after how sweaty I just got dancing?" She blots away the tears resting on my philtrum, dangling from my jaw.

A watery laugh tumbles out of me, and Jane and Marisol grin. Soon, all three of us are laughing.

By the time we reach campus, Marisol's head is on my shoulder, Jane's still holding my hand, and I'm convinced that it's possible to be a liar with secrets who truly loves her friends.

CHAPTER 22

Back at the dorm, Jane, Marisol, and I hug. Marisol heads up one floor to her room while Jane unlocks her door.

"Bedtime hygiene will have to wait until morning. I'm beat," she yawns. "Night, Gita."

"Good night, Jane," I say softly.

She shuts her door behind her. I unlock my room, grab the little bucket of toiletries hanging just inside, and trudge down the hall to the bathroom. When I reach the first sink I stand there for a minute, staring at my reflection.

Shame-shame.

I drop my eyes, pluck my toothbrush and toothpaste from the bucket, and squeeze an inch of paste onto the bristles.

Shameless whore.

My cheeks smolder.

Spit, gargle. I pump some cleanser into my wet palms, then

lather the suds onto my face. Rinse. I turn off the faucet but stay hunched over the sink, listening.

Silence, save for the *plink, plink* of water droplets diving off my chin, crashing into porcelain.

I straighten up but avoid looking in the mirror as I blot my face with a hand towel. I go to a stall to pee: My bladder feels full, but when I hover over the toilet, nothing comes out. After a few seconds I give up, go back to my room to change into pajamas, chug some water, and crawl into bed. A giant yawn stretches my face as I curl up with my blanket and Snuffles.

Shameless whore.

I hug Snuffles tighter.

Shameless whore.

Sh—

No! I kick off the blanket, climb down the ladder, and tear off my pajamas, stuffing myself into jeans and a Stanford sweatshirt. Then I hustle outside and pedal as fast as I can to the lab. The cool air rushing past my cheeks feels good.

Less soothing is the pounding in my head as I make my way down the lab's hallowed hallways of scientific inquiry. It feels like my brain is drowning in a vat of sulfuric acid—the quiet around me amplifies what I know is just the beginning of a gnarly hangover.

Doesn't matter. Suck it up, get some work done.

I pass by the sample collection room, then double back. To my surprise, Sora's sitting at the stainless steel table with a neat stack of multicolored corncobs in front of him. I stop in the doorway and watch him use a letter opener to pop off the less uniform kernels, the ones that aren't deep purple, bright yellow, or light pink in color. As I've come to learn, it's these inconspicuous, mutated kernels that hold the most important secrets to increasing and strengthening crop yield.

My thoughts drift to the busy streets of India: Pinky Auntie once told me that when she and Dad were kids back in Gujarat, they'd wait in a long line to get grilled corn from a particular vendor "with the smallest cart, but the best chaat masala." If that vendor is still doing his thing, will he ultimately benefit from Sora's research to develop corn that's more drought resistant?

Maybe. I wonder if Sora is also planning on trying to make corn more heat resistant. . . .

Sora glances up and jumps when he sees me, the letter opener he's holding crashing noisily to the table.

I giggle. "Need some help?" The lab work I was going to get ahead on can wait, I decide.

"Sure." He smiles at me.

I go to the other side of the table and pick up a cob. "Which ones?"

Sora hands me an extra letter opener. "I'm doing the spotted. You do the striped. Try to get them from the middle, if you can."

"Got it." I bring the cob I'm holding closer for more thorough examination. The stripes are faint compared to the come-hither solid colors. "In the world of transposable elements, subtle is the real sexy, huh?"

"No doubt." He dislodges a kernel. "Flashy is overrated."

My eyes and hands fall into a steady rhythm of kernel harvesting, and for a minute, the two of us go quiet. Finally, Sora breaks the silence: "So Gita, tell me. What are you doing here at this ungodly hour?"

"Couldn't sleep."

"You know, most people, when they can't sleep, count sheep or read a boring book or watch TV. But not our Gita Desai! She just starts her day at night."

A nervous laugh slips out of me before I swallow down the truth of what happened only hours ago. "Hey, you're one to talk! Starting your 'day' even earlier than me."

Sora shrugs. "You got me. Honestly, counting sheep and all doesn't really work for me. Neither do prescription sleep meds." He leans back, fixing his eyes on me. "Insomnia is just . . . part of the old me that stuck around."

"The 'old you'?"

"Oh, Gita dear. You think I just appeared in your life this perfect?" He gestures to himself with a flourish, corncob still in hand.

I laugh, genuinely this time.

Sora rests his chin in his hand. "But seriously, if you'd met me back then . . . oh boy."

"Oh boy, what?"

"Let's just say, mistakes were what I did best."

"You? No!" I gasp dramatically.

"Yes! I had to hit rock bottom before I realized I had to take a good, hard look at myself."

Sora's expression is unchanged, unbothered, like he's still talking about counting sheep. I want to ask more about his rock bottom and mistakes. Should I?

Before I can decide, Sora says, "I'm hungry. What do you say we get some food after we finish this bunch? I know a great twenty-four-hour diner."

"Sounds good." I pick up another cob. "Speaking of food, have you ever had Indian street-style corn? My aunt used to make it for me. She'd take hot cobs and slather on butter and spices, then squeeze lime juice on top. They tasted like heaven."

"Sounds divine. Was that in India?"

"No. My aunt used to live with us." I sigh. *I miss her.*

"What's she like?" Sora asks.

"Incredible." I stop harvesting kernels and hoist my eyes up to his. "I think you'd like her. She has . . . *had—*" I pause, clicking my tongue and working out a stubborn kernel. "She had a gold nose ring too."

"She must have been a queen." He winks.

I nod. "She wasn't uptight about things, like my parents were. She even used to read *erotic* Indian poems to me."

Sora stops what he's doing and lifts an eyebrow. "Do tell."

I grin. "They weren't nasty or anything. They were about thatched-roof villages, young lovers. Flowers and forests, rivers and birds and other animals." Now I'm recalling all the images that Pinky Auntie would conjure to life, and they swirl and settle around me like sweet-smelling garlands of jasmine. "I still have her little poetry book."

"You'll have to let me borrow it sometime."

I nod, tightening my grip on the letter opener. "Hey, have you ever been to India?"

He shakes his head. "Someday though."

"Ditto."

"You too? It's funny," Sora continues, "I'm half Indian on my dad's side. . . . But I *feel* less Indian than those japamala-wearing, yoga-meditation-retreat-going, namaste-bowing Palo Alto blondies who *think* they are." Sora punctuates each description with a swish of his letter opener.

"I get that," I say, mesmerized by the flash of metal through the air. A wry laugh escapes me: "I'm full Indian. But the only time I really feel like it is when I'm trying to avoid my parents marrying me off to some six-village Gujju boy who thinks patriarchy is his god-given right."

"Guess I'm lucky in that department." Sora grabs a fresh cob. "My dad is already a 'bad Indian' immigrant because he's an artist *and* he married a Japanese woman." He taps his letter opener on the still-intact kernels. "Dad pretty much left the door wide open for me to never have to stay in the closet. About anything."

"Your parents sound cool."

"They are. I always count my blessings." Sora's voice turns

dreamy. "Speaking of blessings . . . there's someone I want you to meet."

I snap my head up. "You met someone?"

He nods. "Not just someone: Hector Johnson."

I beam at Sora, setting down the half-naked cob in my hand, then reach over and pick up a new one. "I can't wait to meet him."

Sora waggles his eyebrows. But just as I think he's going to say something else about Hector, his smile drops into a scowl.

"What? What happened?" I whip my head around, as if the bogeyman might be behind me.

"Nothing, I just remembered . . . there's something else you need to know about Jeet. About him and his Machiavellian approach to ladies."

"No!" I whine, hiding my face behind my hands. "Please don't tell me he's even shadier than you thought."

Sora shrugs. "Sorry to break it to you, Gita darling, but he is. I heard through the grapevine that he has a personal bet going to get with every undergrad in the lab building. When I confronted him about it but he denied it, but . . ."

I groan. "My Bollywood hero is actually the villain?!"

Can Sora tell I'm faking my dismay?

The thing is, it's just a rumor—Jeet denied it. And the unwritten Indian law that all desi look out for each other makes it clear that Jeet won't view me as prey even if the rumor is true. I wonder if Sora's aware of that law's existence, and the impossibility of Jeet being a lawbreaker. Before I can even get the words out, though, an actual example of an Indian lawbreaker pops into my head—Bhavin Uncle.

He didn't look out for Pinky Auntie.

Was she the only one he didn't look out for?

I break out into a cold sweat, and shut my mouth.

CHAPTER 23

Sitting in the back seat of Joey's immaculate Ford Taurus, I stick my hand out the open window and watch it ride the tide of a playful breeze. *A mahogany sea star in the ocean of air.* To my left, the late afternoon sun is a tangerine slice in the blue sky. I lose myself in the vast pleated cliffs, crashing waves, and endless expanse of the Pacific. As another mile goes by, I take a deep, salty breath. "Thanks for inviting me, guys. This is exactly what I needed."

"No problem," Joey replies. "Glad you could make it. It's too bad you can't join us on Saturday though. Halloween in the city is quite a thing."

"I know," I groan, remembering the SF Halloween people-watching I vicariously enjoyed through the stories Sai and Chaz used to tell me. "Of course Professor Kenton would schedule a huge Hum Bio exam for Monday. Being premed is such a drag sometimes."

"I can imagine."

"But hanging out with chill people like you and Marisol keeps me sane." Okay, I admit that Joey isn't always chill around Marisol. But in the grand scheme of things, he seems to really care about her. Isn't that all that matters? Besides, as far as I know, Marisol isn't breaking up with him anytime soon, so he can't be *that* bad.

Joey nods. "I count on my mellow non-EMT friends to keep me grounded."

"We are simpatico in that respect." I wave my hand between the two of us. Joey gives me a small half smile in the rearview mirror.

Marisol pivots her body to face me. "Have you ever been wine tasting in Sonoma or Napa, Gita?"

I shake my head.

"It's fun! I like Sonoma better than Napa. Way more laid-back."

"Oh yeah? Day drinking does sound like something I'd enjoy."

Marisol grips the headrest, her eyes sparkling, shiny onyx. "Plus, Sonoma is where Joey and I met." She glances at him.

I peek at Joey. With the way he's smiling, it hits me who he kind of reminds me of—a brown-haired version of Brad Pitt in *Thelma & Louise.* I picture Joey in a cowboy hat, holding a blow dryer like in that scene from the movie. But, hopefully, Joey isn't wily, or all about himself underneath his handsomeness and quiet charm, the way Brad Pitt's character is.

"Spill it—the whole Marisol-Joey origin story." I clap my hands in anticipation.

Marisol grins. "It was a year ago. I used my first big paycheck to take my parents to Sonoma for the weekend. Obviously I didn't bust out my fake ID or anything, but I did sneak a few sips here and there. Anyway, our first stop was St. Francis Winery & Vineyard. Joey was there doing some wine tasting to celebrate his twenty-second birthday with his friends. He was so cute!"

I do the math in my head—a year ago, Marisol was seventeen. So Joey is five years older than her. *And* they got together before she was even legal!

I guess that's okay. My dad's five and a half years older than my mom. But they met each other when they were both in their twenties.

Does that make a difference?

Joey runs his fingers through his hair. "Marisol and her parents were standing next to us at the bar. Of course, I recognized her when she walked in. But I didn't think anything of it until I overheard what she was saying to her parents: 'Don't worry about retirement, I'll do my best to take care of you.' I turned around, knowing that I needed to meet this high-class girl." He reaches over and squeezes her hand.

"Awwww." I lay my hand over my heart and think about how Marisol really does have more in common with Sai than anyone else I know.

Marisol touches the half-moon of her birthmark rising from under her strapless top. "Here's the thing, Gita. It was hot in Sonoma that day and I'd taken off my sweater. Joey saw. He didn't stare, make a face, or turn away. He didn't flinch. That's the thing about my birthmark, it's like a kindness meter. The few times I've uncovered it in public, I've picked up *a lot* about people from their reactions."

Joey regrips the steering wheel with both hands. "The more time I spent with the inside-and-out-beautiful Marisol, the more I knew she was the only family I needed."

Marisol gazes at Joey and strokes the back of his head. "It was rough for you growing up, babe," she says in an almost-whisper.

Joey glances at her and tries to smile.

I wonder how rough it was for Joey growing up. At the same time, I feel my heart quiver and my eyes become slick—the same two things that happen when I'm listening to the SWV love song "Weak." A few miles go by with the three of us sitting in comfortable silence.

Ahead on the right, there's a quaint oceanfront café. Marisol points to it. "I'm starving. Let's stop there."

"What my baby wants, my baby gets." Joey cranks the steering wheel right, turning into the parking lot.

So sweet. A smile glides across my face. Maybe someday, someone will be Joey-sweet to me. I sigh, wanting the SWV feeling to linger . . . forever.

As we get out of the car, Marisol starts to put on her sweater but then stops. "Enough. No more," she says under her breath. She tosses her sweater onto the passenger seat, then shuts the door. There she stands in her strapless top and jeans, looking all warrior-princess.

The wind howls somewhere offshore.

Joey lays his hands on her shoulders and gives her a peck. "You okay?"

She nods. "I'm okay."

At the café entrance, Joey holds the door open. "After you, ladies."

As soon as we enter, all eyes are gawking at Marisol. There's a collective hunger in their gaze, an awe of the goddess in the midst—no judgment in sight. Still, I wonder what her kindness meter is reading from the room.

Joey's previously relaxed jaw is clenched. Is that him being sweet and protective of his hot girlfriend, or jealous and possessive? I shrug it off. Honestly, I can't help but feel a little bad for the guy.

We sit. Immediately, a server brings us three glasses of pink champagne.

"From the gentleman over there," she says, pointing to an older white guy with salt-and-pepper hair, dressed in a white golf shirt and crisp khakis. He smiles, raising his glass of bubbly to our table, his eyes glued to Marisol. He looks old enough to be one of our grandfathers.

"Do you know him?" I ask, noticing a familiar flicker in the blue of Grandpa's irises.

Marisol shakes her head. "Never met him. But hey, free drinks." Then she winks at me.

I freeze. I recognize her wink: It's Pinky Auntie's wink—the one that made my aunt's secrets *my* secrets.

My eyes plummet. Marisol doesn't know the guy, but it still feels like she's making some sort of secret about him my secret. I wish I could tell her that I, for one, would never burden her with my winks. I would never burden her with my secrets.

With my next breath, my eyes get pulled back to Grandpa. Everything falls away except the way his eyes are ambushing Marisol. Then he smiles at her, an Adonis smile.

I'm back to my first night at Stanford, thinking about cold, calculating eyes and Adonis smiles. Sigma Nu boy morphs into Angelo morphs into Johnny Depp Boy and Javier and now Grandpa.

Marisol's still got her eyes locked with Grandpa's. She raises her glass and mouths *Thank you,* leaving her lips parted in the same sexy way I've seen in one of her *Vogue* magazine spreads.

Joey touches Marisol's arm. "Babe?" It's clear he's forcing himself to stay calm.

Marisol's eyes drift back to Joey, and she seems to snap out of it. "I'm sorry." She strokes Joey's cheek, releasing a quiet breath. "I don't owe these random guys anything just because they buy me a drink or two."

Joey frowns. "Why would you owe them?"

Marisol shakes her head, her lips curving down. "I don't."

Meanwhile, I'm wondering how Marisol is oblivious to Joey's feelings when he's *right here* and she's flirting. How would she like it if Joey did that to her?

Marisol leans over and kisses Joey on the cheek. "I'm sorry. Forget about that guy." She squeezes his hand. "The only guy I want is you."

Joey mellows out, and so do I.

"I love you, Joey," Marisol says.

"I love you right back," Joey responds.

I smile.

Cold, calculating eyes and Adonis smiles—no thank you, and good riddance! What I really want is true, in-your-face love. Like Marisol and Joey.

I picture Jeet. Maybe he'll be my Joey, and I'll be his Marisol. I cross my fingers on both hands this time.

CHAPTER 24

Almost two hours into Jeet's party, his Menlo Park apartment is crowded with mostly grad students and post-docs. Sora, Hector, and I are huddled in one corner of the living room. The vibe is chill, with the lights turned down and "Tennessee" by Arrested Development oozing out the stereo. Half a case of wine and Costco-size liquor bottles and chasers are neatly arranged on a bar cart.

I glance across the room at Jeet. He's lifting the hand of the only other undergrad here besides me—Veronica, Snow White's ginger cousin, who works in Dr. Yang's lab. He leans in and whispers something into her ear. Frowning, I scoop the lime out of my mojito and suck on it. The sour taste matches exactly how I'm feeling right now.

Veronica throws her head back and laughs. I smirk. But inside, I'm secretly brushing away bits of disappointment like crumbs of Mom's nankhatai.

I wish Jeet would come over and talk to me the way he does in the lab. Nice, non-player talk. If only he'd give me a chance—maybe we could push the boundaries of the unwritten Indian law and transform it into something beautiful, just the two of us. Our own Bollywood-Hollywood romance with him singing The Police's "Every Little Thing She Does Is Magic" . . .

I release a quiet breath and turn toward Sora. He shuts his eyes—lined in forest green—and shakes his head.

"I should go warn her the way you warned me," I grumble. "Not that she seems upset or anything."

"Don't bother, Gita." Sora takes a long, slow sip of his mojito. "I talked to my trustworthy contacts in the other labs. Warnings have been issued to all the undergrads." He narrows his eyes and tilts his head slightly. "Jeet might be brilliant in the lab . . . but his lack of emotional intelligence rivals that of my ex."

Hector and I both stare at Sora, who releases a long-suffering sigh. "It's a long story," he says. Slowly nodding his head, brow furrowed, Hector squeezes Sora's arm. Sora gives Hector a grateful half smile, then looks at me. "I'm just glad it's not you, Gita."

I chug the rest of my own mojito, then smack my lips. "It'll never be me because Jeet's officially dead to me."

"No loss," Hector says, cracking his knuckles. "You can do way better."

This time, I'm the one to give Hector a grateful smile. It feels as if I've known him longer than two days; I had the pleasure of meeting him for the first time on Monday when he stopped by the lab during Sora's lunch break. I put down my glass and rest my elbow on Sora's shoulder. "Thanks for having my back, you guys."

Sora adjusts his pink linen Nehru shirt. "Of course, Gita girl. We've got a vested interest in this matter."

"Interesting," Hector comments, twisting the cap off a fresh beer. He takes a swig, then grazes Sora's arm with a fingertip. "Because I've got a vested interest in *this* matter." His deep voice and full black beard scream caveman, but his light brown eyes are playful and warm.

"Not in front of the kid," Sora fake-scolds Hector.

"As if, Dad," I whine.

"Guess the kid's all grown up," Hector laughs. He pulls his broad shoulders back, his pecs popping under his tight white tank top and baggy dungaree overalls.

Sora traces the rippling outline of Hector's dark brown bicep, then tricep. "We done good," he murmurs.

Hector pats my back. "We're proud of you, Gita, for being a Doogie Howser, MD, and all. Speaking of, I need a second opinion, Doc." He sticks out his forearm. It has a thick, raised, reddish-brown horizontal scar about two inches long. "Will this ever go away?"

I run my finger over the wound, thinking about Dr. Kenton's lectures and the above-and-beyond reading I did on chronic inflammation. "What happened?"

"A miter saw at work got hungry." He laughs it off, but

I can only imagine how much it must have hurt.

I don't chuckle. I'm in Dr. Gita mode. "How long ago?"

"Four months."

"Did it get infected?"

"Yes. Luckily, my sister's a nurse—she got me antibiotics. It's still huge though, isn't it?"

"Hmm." I tap my bottom lip with my finger. "Well, sir, I believe it's a keloid. I don't think it'll go away on its own. It's a pathological scar, meaning it 'overhealed.' Too much of a good thing isn't always good, you know?" I shake my head sympathetically.

Sora turns to Hector. "My poor man." He touches the keloid, leans in, and gives Hector a soft kiss on the lips. Hector kisses Sora back, deep and long.

"Get a room!" I cry, but I'm only pretending to be salty.

Hector sighs. "I wish. But not today." He checks his watch. "I gotta bounce. The foreman wants us on-site at sunrise." He plants another kiss on Sora's lips. "I'll call you tomorrow."

Sora nods.

When Hector turns around, Sora grabs his ass.

Hector whips his head over his shoulder, pretending to be shocked. "Now who's acting up in front of the kid?" He winks at me.

"Whatever," I say. It strikes me that this wink doesn't feel bad, maybe because it's doing what it's supposed to do—emphasize a joke.

After Hector leaves, Kelly, the grad student who was scribbling experiment ideas on the chalkboard my first day at the lab, reappears with our third round of drinks. Her brown hair is a waterfall of waves cascading to her elbows, an indigo cotton dress is draped over her tall frame. "Sorry about the drink delay!" she exclaims. "The human cost of conflict in Somalia isn't exactly a fast discussion to be had with the International Relations folks hovering near the rum."

I start to fidget in place, hoping she doesn't ask me for my thoughts on Somalia because I'm clueless. Current events have been like my less-than-part-time high school job at Donutburg—I quit for college. I groan inside, disappointed at my willful ignorance. How can I hope to be a truly compassionate physician someday if I'm oblivious to the realities of human suffering? No more! Starting tomorrow, I promise myself that I'll read the paper everyday.

Kelly hands Sora his drink. "Where's Hector? I got him another beer."

"He left. Early job tomorrow."

Kelly puts the beer on a nearby end table, then hands me a mojito. I wrap my fingers around the glass: It's sweating cold, while I'm suddenly sweating hot. "Thanks."

"You're welcome." She tucks one arm under the other that's holding her glass and takes a sip, then nods at Sora. "So, where were we?"

"The toxic societal message that only beautiful people are sexually desirable, and therefore worthy of being sexually liberated."

"A recipe for self-hate." Kelly nods sagely.

Nervous energy has me rocking back and forth on my heels. I swipe an X through the condensation on my glass, then go to stuff my free hand into my pocket . . . but I don't have pockets. So I hold my drink with both hands and gulp it.

Sora swirls his drink. "What would it look like, I wonder, to place no value on beauty or desirability?" He cups his chin. "Or sex, for that matter?"

"Maybe it would look like the end of needing other people's approval." Kelly's brown irises glow orange in the yellow lamplight. "Or maybe it would look like the end of women being largely excluded from power in society."

"Ah, the freedom of it all." Sora sighs.

Kelly keeps talking, gesturing with her free hand. But in that moment, the full effect of the three mojitos I've consumed hits me. I decide to slink away to the opposite side of the living room before I say or do something idiotic, setting my empty glass on the TV stand in the process.

Next thing I know, Jeet and another Indian guy who's like three inches taller and handsome as hell are heading my way.

"Gita!" Jeet clasps the guy's shoulder. "Have I introduced you to my older brother, Ujjwal? He lives in LA but is in town for a couple of days for a conference, hence the middle-of-the-week party."

Ujjwal holds out his hand. "Nice to meet you, Gita." His voice is more baritone than Jeet's. There's a hint of gold in his dark brown eyes, his symmetrical, angular face softened by smooth brown skin.

I almost faint. "Nice to meet you too," I reply breathlessly, shaking his hand. *How could Jeet fail to mention the existence of a demigod sibling?*

The song that was playing changes to "It Ain't Over 'Til It's Over" by Lenny Kravitz. The drums start and whisk my thoughts away to my sunny wedding. Then the violins come in, and both of my parents are walking me—in an exquisite sleek white gown, Hindu tradition be damned—down the imaginary aisle. I hand my big, bushy bouquet of white flowers to Jane; she and Marisol are my teary-eyed bridesmaids in periwinkle spaghetti strap dresses. Sai and Jeet are the groomsmen. And there's my handsome groom . . . *Ujjwal.*

I'm so happy, I want to cry.

"Oh, and everyone calls me Ujj," the divine man in question adds, while Jeet ambles away to speak with other guests.

I shake off the fantastical remnants of our marital bliss. "Cool. So, Ujj . . . are you also a grad student?"

He shakes his head. "I'm an attorney."

I cross my arms and stand in a fierce lean-back, trying not to tip over in my drunken state. "Impressive. What kind of law?"

"Criminal defense." He lifts his chin, plastering on a fake hard expression.

He's certainly got the voice of a criminal defense attorney, but I'm not intimidated. I'm intrigued. Like, is he single? I glance at his left hand. No ring.

Time for a round of Marisol-worthy flirting. . . . With the help of booze, of course. I raise an eyebrow, tilt my head, and touch his arm. "So. If you take care of the bad guys, does that make *you* a bad guy?"

"Of course," he says, quick as lightning. He sends me a self-satisfied grin over the rim of his cup before tipping it back, downing whatever was inside. "Hey." He wipes his mouth. "Can I get you another drink?"

"Sure." *Though I really don't need another one. . . .*

"What's your poison?"

"I'll take some red wine."

"What kind?"

"The redder the better?" I shrug.

Ujj cracks up. "You got it." He heads toward the kitchen, and my head starts spinning. I lean against the wall for balance.

When he returns with my wine and a couple of shots of dark brown liquor, no ice, for himself, the two of us settle on the couch. His denim-clad knee rests less than a millimeter away from my bare one. Our eyes meet, and I'm trapped by his irises, swimming in their endless gold. "So," he leans in and murmurs, "Jeet tells me you're premed. How . . . extremely *unique* for an Indian American student at Stanford. Is it possible that your parents immigrated here in the late sixties for a better life for themselves and their children?"

I nearly spit out the sip of wine I've taken. "Okay, smarty-pants,"

I laugh. "Can you also guess what my parents do for a living?"

"Most definitely." The growl in his voice burns low in my stomach. "First, what's your last name?"

"Desai."

"So you're Gujarati?"

I nod.

"Do they own a motel?"

I shake my head.

He eyes me for a second. "How about a convenience store, a 7-Eleven maybe?"

"Close." I wiggle in anticipation, nearly spilling my wine in the process.

"Gimme a hint."

"Hmm. It's . . . in the realm of fast food."

"A Subway?"

I shake my head.

"Not Donutburg?"

"It is!" I exclaim, grabbing his knee.

Time stops. We both stare at my hand. I lift my eyes to his face in what feels like slow motion. *Is he blushing?* I rip my hand away and rub the back of my neck, trying to act as nonchalant as possible.

Ujj clears his throat and takes a sip of his drink. "Now it's your turn: Can you guess what my parents do?"

I breathe out a small sigh of relief. Of course he'd let it go—he's a gentleman! Then I turn over his question in my mind.

Two things pop into my head at the same time: I haven't met any other Bengalis besides Jeet and Ujj, and Jane and Marisol's econ professor is Bengali. I end up blurting, "Professors at Harvard?"

"Ha! Close. At MIT."

More than an hour of banter like this passes quickly between Ujj and me. At some point, Sora floats over. His eyes linger on Ujj a tad longer than standard operating procedure. "Gita girl, do introduce me to your friend," he says, twisting his single dangly gold leaf earring.

I giggle. "Sora, this is Ujj, Jeet's brother. Ujj, this is Sora."

They shake hands and greetings and pleasantries. But Sora's previously hungry expression is now guarded; I read it as a what-are-your-intentions-with-my-sister-from-another-mister expression. Which I get.

Sora pokes my arm. "I'm heading out, Gita. Let me give you a ride home." His voice is casual, but I hear the underlying warning: *We need to leave before this guy tries something on you.*

"No thanks." I shake my head. I like talking with Ujj—he's not using me, and I'm not using him. We're just having fun. . . . Fun that might lead to him liking me. And asking for my number. And calling me. Taking me out on a proper date . . .

"You sure?" Sora asks, raising his eyebrows. More code: *This is me trying to look out for you.*

"Yes." I nod my head emphatically. "I'll be all right. I'm only going to hang out another half hour, then I'll catch a cab home."

Sora frowns. "I don't like it. . . . But okay. Call me tomorrow."

"Will do."

He leaves. Ujj turns to face me again, and we keep talking.

Eventually, all the guests leave. An exhausted-appearing Jeet plops on the sofa next to me. He rests his head on my shoulder, and I catch a whiff of whiskey and olives.

"Great party," I say, patting Jeet's head. "Thanks for inviting me."

"Thanks for showing up," Jeet murmurs, and shuts his eyes.

Ujj and I blab about this and that for another half hour. At some point, I yawn and stretch, realizing it feels right to leave now. I give myself a mental pat on the back for recognizing this, then push myself off the sofa.

"Well, I'd better be heading home. Got a full day of being an extremely unique Indian American Stanford premed tomorrow." I smile at Ujj: *Ask me for my number already!*

"Don't go yet," Jeet whines, at the same time that Ujj's cell phone rings. He gets up and answers: "Hi. Yes, Sheila honey, I'm heading back to the hotel now . . . I know it's late, I'm sorry . . . The baby needs what?"

Sheila? Ujj has a "Sheila"? And a baby?

My body stiffens.

Why wasn't he wearing a wedding ring? Did I read him wrong? I thought we were flirting . . . Was he just being friendly?

Ujj hangs up, then smiles at me. "I've got to get going. It was nice meeting you, Gita Desai." He sticks out his hand, and I shake it, speechless. I'm dying inside, and my vocal cords were the first to go.

Ujj drops my hand, then turns and walks away.

My hand hovers in the air, still extended, as I watch the potential love-of-my-life pull the front door shut behind him.

Jeet grabs my stuck-in-midair hand and tugs. "Please stay."

I stare at him, my eyebrows arched up. What does "stay" mean? Hang out more? Watch a movie? Talk all night? What else is there to do this late? I'm not in the mood for secret hookup number five. I glance at the front door, taking a step toward it.

Jeet tugs harder, and I tumble backward onto the sofa next to him. Immediately, he leans in and kisses me.

I tear my lips away. "Wait, I—"

He cuts me off, stroking my hair. "I'm sure you've heard this a thousand times before . . . but you're gorgeous." Jeet's eyes drop down as he slowly glides his finger over my collarbone.

My eyes dip to his finger. *Once, I saw Bhavin Uncle glide his finger over Pinky Auntie's collarbone. . . .*

My face contorts. How did we get here? I wasn't flirty with Jeet. I didn't even really talk to him all night.

Jeet starts kissing me again.

I don't want to do this. *Push him off you! Say "no!"* I tell myself. I yank my lips away from his, but I can't make myself shove him away. My arms dangle limply at my sides.

Jeet reclaims my mouth, then pulls me onto his lap. He's strong, and efficient. In what seems like two seconds, he tosses my blouse and bra onto the coffee table, then kisses my neck. "You're so fuckin' hot," he mumbles.

Who cares?! Say "no!" Put a stop to this right NOW!

I try to say it—I do. But in between hot and heavy breaths, all that comes out is: "But . . . you like . . . that other girl."

"Shhh." Jeet tightens his hold on me. He kisses my neck again, then lower.

The smell of his hair product . . . *I know that smell.*

Then my panties are off, and all Jeet is wearing is a condom. "Ready?"

I close my eyes, and imagine that I'm a turtle.

CHAPTER 25

By the time I'm gripping the handrail in the dorm stairwell and slowly hauling my deadweight up each step, it's 3:00 a.m. My lips are pressed together in a grim line, my eyes empty holes. I pause on the landing, my brain flickering like lights from passing trains in the BART station.

I stand there and listen to my breath go in and out, in and out.

A few seconds—or is it minutes?—later, my robot hand opens the door to the hallway that stretches out before me like the Via Dolorosa in Jerusalem. But I'm not Jesus, and what heavy cross do I have to bear? None.

Are you sure you can come out to play?

An image of him on top of me . . .

I grimace. *I didn't mean like that!* I wasn't planning *that.*

I lift my hands up. I inspect the backs, the palms.

Why couldn't I use these to push him off me?

I glance at Jane's door, then drop my eyes and creep toward my room.

Why is it that I don't see guys as pieces of meat but they see me that way? What's wrong with guys?

What's wrong with *me* for letting it happen? I ball my fists up and decide, right here and now, to go back to what always worked for me in high school: no guys.

I make it official: *It's Wednesday, November 4—I mean, early morning on Thursday, November 5—and I, Gita Desai, promise that from now on until med school, no more guys.*

Resigned to be a single cat lady without the cat, I stick my room key in the lock.

The creak of Jane's door behind me. A sleepy voice: "Gita?"

Oh no. I plaster on a fake smile and turn around. "Hiiii," I say, as if it's totally normal for me to be coming home at 3:00 a.m.

Jane rubs her eyes and yawns. "Where were you?"

"A lab party." Not a total lie, right? I adjust my blouse and skirt as Jane stares me down.

"Marisol and I were looking for you."

"Oh. What'd you guys do?"

"Dinner in Palo Alto."

"Fun."

"It was. But we missed you." Jane takes a step closer, and I take one back. Her eyebrows furrow.

"Have you been crying?"

"No. Why?" I make my voice light, innocent.

She points. "Your face is all puffy and red."

"Oh this." I force a sniffle. "Seasonal allergies." I sniffle again, swallowing the truth that was me weeping softly the entire cab ride home.

Jane looks fully alert and awake now. "Was Sora at the party?"

I nod. Though Jane and Marisol haven't met him yet, I've told them all about him, and vice versa.

"Did he give you a ride home?"

I shake my head. "Took a cab."

"Hmm." She touches my arm. "What's going on with you?"

"Nothing." I avert her gaze. "Just a little hungover."

A beat of silence. Jane raises an eyebrow, then sighs. "All right, hold on." She disappears into her room, then comes back with a bottle of Gatorade. "Take two Advil and drink this entire bottle before you go to sleep. The *entire bottle,* Gita."

For the first time in hours, I smile. "See, I told you—you'd be a good doctor."

The corner of Jane's mouth twitches up. She hands me the bottle, turns back to her room, then stops and looks over her shoulder: "Gita . . . you know I won't judge you, right? No matter what."

"I'm fine." But even I can hear the edge in my voice. "Really," I add.

Jane studies my face for a few more seconds. " . . . Okay." She pauses. "Breakfast tomorrow?"

"Definitely."

"All right," she yawns. "I'll see you then."

As Jane returns to her room, I unlock my own and flip on the light, then catch my reflection in the full-length mirror on the back of the door. There's a giant dark spot the left side of my neck.

A hickey! Did Jane see it?

I trace the outline in a clockwise motion, then shudder.

Jeet doesn't love me. He used me, then branded me like a cow.

I trace the hickey counterclockwise.

I let him use me.

Outside the window there's a brilliant flash, followed by a loud thunderclap. For a second, I imagine that the lightning has struck me and I'm standing there in the rain: charred and smoking, jolted to my senses.

CHAPTER 26

*P*ounding on my door and yelling: "Party tonight!"

I bolt up in bed, check the clock: 8:20 a.m. "Fuck!" I scramble down from my bunk. I'm late for an 8:00 a.m. lab meeting—I must have forgotten to set my alarm last night. I stuff my feet into sneakers, fling my door open, and dash down the hallway, bumping into AC/DC Matt as he pounds on another door. It isn't the first time he's being annoying and rude way too early in the morning; but every other time, I'd already been awake and a few hours into studying before his BS even began.

"Thanks, man! I owe you one!" I yell over my shoulder, waving at him before speeding past. He stops, fist raised by the door in midair, a confused expression on his face. For the first time ever, I think I've rendered him speechless.

Outside, I jump on my bike and push hard on the pedals, reaching the Quad in no time. The unexpected early morning storm left a shiny lake in the middle of the courtyard, but I don't have time to bike around. My wheels slice through the reflection of Mem Chu and wash small waves over my sneakers, soaking my feet.

Splat. A plump drop from above lands on my cheek, then another on my hand. I squeeze the handlebars tighter, silently pleading: *Don't rain, don't rain, don't rain . . .*

It pours. I hunch over, wet bullets piercing my flesh, and begin pedaling as if my admission to med school depends on it. Everything around me—students walking their bikes, colorful open umbrellas, yellow and orange leaves littering the ground—becomes a misty blur.

The lab building, shrouded in a menace of clouds spitting rageful tears, looms up ahead. I don't slow down as I approach but, thankfully, braking hard at the last minute doesn't eject me onto the slick pavement. I hop off my bike, lock it to the rack, and pound up the steps, skipping one or two in between and tripping a few times.

I haul ass the rest of the way into the lab. *The hickey!* Quickly, I sweep all my hair forward on the left to cover that side of my neck, then burst into the conference room, breathing hard and completely soaked.

Plink, plink. Water drips off my hair onto the floor tiles. Everyone's eyes are plastered on me, expressions carved and stuck like a new Mount Rushmore for scientists. Jeet snickers, and I glance down at myself. *No, no, no . . .*

If this was high school spirit week, I might have an excuse for wearing flannel teddy bear pajamas to the lab. But it isn't, and I don't. Now *I'm* the one slowly turning to stone.

I glance at Dr. Peters. The mixture of confusion and disappointment that shines in her eyes is worse than any of the punishing words I'll be flogging myself with later . . . and for eternity.

"Gita," Sora says, pushing his chair back. "Come with me. There's . . . something that needs your attention." He ushers me back into the empty hallway, then stops and pinches my wet pajama sleeve. "Well, this is a first at the lab," he mumbles. Then his gaze turns sharp. "What time did you leave last night?"

"An hour after you left," I lie, rolling onto the outer edges of my sneakers and tugging on my ear.

"Are you hungover?"

"No." Relieved to be telling the truth, I send a mental thanks to Jane for the Advil and Gatorade. We stand there, Sora trying to catch my eye and me avoiding his.

"Something's up. What is it?"

"I-I . . ." I stutter, smashing my hair over the hickey on my neck. *I can't say it.*

"I'm . . ."

I tuck my chin and drop my eyes, my cheeks burning.

Sora comes closer. "What is it, Gita?' He reaches for my shoulder.

Mom's voice shatters the fragile silence in my head: *Shameshame.*

My jaw clamps. I ball my fists. *I'm not six!*

I whip my head up. "It's not like I ruined someone's experiment," I snap.

Sora's arm falls to his side. "True." He pauses. "But this isn't like you."

I don't respond.

Sora shakes his head. He turns and walks back to the conference room. "Go home, Gita. I'll call you later."

I hang my head, sniffle.

Just as I'm about to leave, I hear clapping behind me. Then: "Gita, Gita, Gita."

Oh god. I recognize that voice. Slowly, I pivot on my heels.

Jeet smirks when his eyes meet mine. "How was your night?"

I try to pry my lips apart, but it feels as if they're sutured shut. Jeet struts toward me. He passes by and his hand brushes mine. He opens the lab's heavy front door, then laughs. "Good luck getting back into Dr. Peters's good graces."

A sharp pain slices through me, and I picture my intestines dangling to the floor. *Eviscerated, like a hunted rabbit.* I swallow hard, grabbing my stomach.

"Don't worry though. You're still in *my* good graces." Jeet lifts his finger, presses it against his lips, and winks.

CHAPTER 27

*T*he pale yellow-green agar plates in front of me blur, kind of like how the last couple of days have blurred behind me.

How long have I been standing here? My head goes fuzzy. *Standing where?*

I blink a few times and turn, waiting until the lab clears in my field of vision. The clock on the opposite wall reads 9:00 p.m. I finished pouring the agar at 8:45. . . .

Fifteen minutes, lost as easily as the backs of my fake-gold hoop earrings.

It's Friday, November 6, and I'm here late because I won't stop trying to make things up to Dr. Peters. After apologizing profusely to her this afternoon, I begged her for extra tasks to do.

She sighed. "All right, Gita. Everyone deserves a second chance. . . . But there won't be a third, understood?"

"Yes!" I nodded my head furiously. "Yes, I understand."

That was seven hours ago. I turn back to the plates, feeling hollow under paper-thin skin. There's a bulletin board to my left, and the thumbtacked close-up photos of dark red and purple maize kernels remind me of ecchymosis. I slip my fingers under my scarf, grazing the fading bruise on my neck.

To my right is Jeet's desk. I glare at it, punching my palm with my fist. The urge to destroy his computer, his knickknacks, and everything that's his surges through me like a tsunami.

But I don't want to be arrested. I don't want anyone like Ujj to have to defend me in court. I let my body go slack, then march over to my own desk and sit on my hands. I shut my eyes and rock back and forth, back and forth.

Why, why, *why* didn't I just leave the party with Sora? I scrub my face with my palms. "I'm so stupid," I whisper.

I wish Sai were here. If he knew what happened, he'd want to kick Jeet's ass.

If he knew what happened, he might call it rape.

My breath catches. My stomach rolls.

Did Jeet . . . *rape* me?

No . . . right? I mean, I didn't say no. Though I didn't say yes either. . . .

I know no one else is in the lab, but I check over my shoulder anyway. The silence feels cold and heavy. I hug myself and start rocking again.

Just get over *yourself, Gita!*

This time, I can't stop the tears from erupting. I cry and cry and cry. I sob into my hands, my whole body shaking.

Then I feel a hand on my back. Though gentle, it still startles me.

"Oh, Gita." Sora pulls up a chair. "What's going on?"

"I . . . I didn't know anyone else was here this late." I swipe roughly at my face.

"Chronic insomnia, remember?" He holds up his bag. "Plus, I forgot this."

I suck in my snot. Sora doesn't bat an eye—his gaze is unwavering, a lighthouse beacon through the storm.

"Tell me what happened, Gita."

"I . . . I . . ."

Sora waits.

If he knew the truth, it would change the way he saw me forever.

I shake my head, holding my stomach. I give him a quick, forced smile. "It's just . . . bad PMS." Honestly, I wish it was—my period is five days late. I'm giving myself two more days before I buy a pregnancy test. As I twist the toe of my sneaker into the floor, my mind jumps to the time Pinky Auntie used that same excuse with Neil Uncle.

Neil Uncle paced in the living room. "We're done, Pinky. As soon as we land in Gujarat, we're done."

I slowly peeked out from my hiding place behind the sofa.

Pinky Auntie's eyes hit the floor, her body withering. "Yes . . . I understand," she breathed.

I nearly rocketed up, but forced myself to remain hidden, watching. A few tears dangled from my jaw.

Neil Uncle stopped pacing and stood in front of Pinky Auntie, glaring at her stomach. "I heard you throwing up this morning. And you and I haven't even tried—How can we, when I'm always working to support us?" He shoved his splayed fingers into his hair and resumed pacing.

Pinky Auntie works too! *I wanted to scream. Then the questions started spinning around me:* Is Pinky Auntie sick? What haven't they tried?

"It was just bad PMS. You know I appreciate all your hard work. . . ."

The front door opened—Mom and Dad arriving home from Donutburg. Mom started removing her shoes, but Dad stopped, surveying the scene in front of him. "What's going on here?"

Neil Uncle grunted, pointing an accusatory finger at Pinky Auntie. "Your sister is a shameless whore," he growled.

Dad startled, then pressed his fists into his hips. "Don't talk about Pinky like that!" He turned to his sister. "Pinky, what's going on?"

A crash shook the room. All of us jumped as Neil Uncle pulled his fist back from the new hole now in the wall, pieces of plaster scattering to the floor beneath him. "Your precious sister is sleeping with Bhavin! And now—I can't even say it . . ." he spat.

Tears barreled down Pinky Auntie's cheeks. "No. No, it's not like that," she cried, shaking her head.

276

I bit my knuckle. I knew what it was like. I knew exactly what she was trying to say.

"Where's Bhavin?" Dad asked, clutching Pinky Auntie's arm.

Pinky Auntie shrugged, one trembling hand landing to rest on her stomach.

I know! I know where he is! He's going back to India—he told me yesterday.

He told me he was going back to India, and I was to be a good girl and chup-re. . . .

Sora rests his elbows on his thighs, and the movement dissolves the cloud of memories around me. "Sometimes human biology is cruel, isn't it?"

PMS. He's talking about PMS. I nod. "Yeah—I mean, to you and me both. I'm sorry about your insomnia."

The two of us sit quietly for a second. I can feel Sora's eyes on me as I count the divots in the floor.

"But that's not what's happening right now, is it Gita?"

I freeze.

When I don't reply, he continues: "Can I tell you a story?"

I nod. I've lost my voice more times than I can count this past week.

Sora clears his throat. "Now, I know it's hard to imagine anyone ever wanting to break *my* heart. . . ."

A weird cry-laugh-snort noise bursts out of me, and my eyes move back to his face.

"Seriously. It was one of the worst times in my life. Even Hector doesn't know about this yet." Sora pauses, the skin bunching up around his eyes. He takes a few deep breaths, and I try to breathe with him: In and out. In and out.

"The relationship was great. I thought we were in love. . . . And then I found out that he was secretly married. When I confronted him, he laughed in my face: 'Who do you think I am?' he said. 'I was just fucking you because I was bored with my wife.'"

My jaw drops. "Oh my god, Sora—I'm so sorry."

Sora nods. "I felt so ashamed. I couldn't talk about it. I couldn't ask for help. I sunk below sad. Below hopeless even. I . . . I took a bunch of pills."

I grab his hand, my eyes slick with fresh tears.

"My parents found me in time, thankfully. But I ended up in the psych ward for almost a month." He sniffs. "The point is, I think if I'd confided in my friends—or anyone—then maybe things wouldn't have gotten so . . . *extreme* in my head."

I squeeze his hand. "Was that your rock bottom?"

"Yes. . . . But things are better now, Gita, and the first step was opening up to the people who cared about me." Gently extracting his hand from mine, Sora sits up straight and takes another slow, deep breath. "So. Will you please, *please* tell me what's really going on? As your friend?"

Despite the invitation, my brain immediately shuts down. "Nothing," I say, trying to compose my expression. Sora frowns, and I add the only excuse chup-re allows: "But I really appreci-ate the TLC. At least PMS is only once a month."

That's it, I decide. I'm not going to obsess or wallow anymore. Five hookups later, I've *really* learned my lesson. There won't be a sixth. Now it's time to forget the past and be grateful for what I have in the present—my family and friends.

"Thanks for caring, Sora." I reach over to hug him. "I know you've got your shit together now, but if you ever need a shoul-der, I'm here for you." I hold on to him the way I used to with Sai: tightly, like a Snuffles sandwich.

CHAPTER 28

A couple of days later, on my way back to the dorm from Green after a solid ten hours of studying, I decide to take a detour through the Inner Quad.

The courtyard is quiet. I pedal slower, enjoying the chilly but sunny weather and counting the sandstone arches. I weave my bike between the islands of greenery, imagining the flame trees suddenly blooming brilliant red again, just for me. My heart beats as steady as Ustad Zakir Hussain's soft tabla warm-up.

When I arrive at the dorm, I hop off my bike and lock it to the rack. Eyes on the ground, I mosey toward the entrance, remembering and relieved all over again that I got my period this morning, exactly one week late. It occurs to me that if it had started on November 1 like it was supposed to, then perhaps saying no to Jeet on the fourth would've been a no-brainer for me. I mean, I doubt there's anything dangerous about period sex, but—

I crash into a pair of strong hands: "Whoa! Easy now, little lady," says their owner.

Immediately, I recognize the voice.

I lift my eyes to find that, yup, it's Sigma Nu boy. And he's smiling at me—an Adonis smile.

"You . . ." he starts, tilting his head and squinting his blue-green eyes. He shakes his head. "Naughty, naughty little voyeur."

I stand there, nothing but putty all over again.

Adonis is taller than I remember . . .

"What's your name?" he asks with a slight Southern accent that I hadn't caught the first night in Jane's room.

"Gita."

"Hey Gita. I'm Adam." He holds out his hand for a shake.

My hand rises to meet his. He wraps his fingers around mine, then pulls me forward, his soft lips grazing my cheek as he whispers, "We could finish what you started, you know."

Is he joking?

A group of students dart past us. One of them bumps into me, and I wriggle my hand out of his. "Gotta go," I mumble, hustling toward the dorm entrance like an avalanche gaining speed. *Don't look back, Gita,* I tell myself. *Don't you dare look back.*

I turn.

Adam waves, a gorgeous smile slung across his face. Against my will, I find myself waving back.

Groaning, I face forward, marching into the building and up

the stairs. *Why was he here anyway? Was he with Jane? Was he serious about "we could finish what you started"?*

Heat crawls up my neck, and Mom's voice rings loud in my head: *shame-shame*.

I slap the sides of my face, keeping my hands there the rest of the way.

Back in my room, I lock the door and go to my desk, taking comfort in my neatly stacked books and papers. I exhale, ready to work. Then there's a knock at the door.

I stop, stand still, and hold my breath. Maybe whoever it is will go away.

A louder knock, followed by Jane's muffled voice: "Gita, we know you're in there."

"Let us in!" Marisol calls.

I hesitate, then scold myself for hesitating. It's my girls—I love my girls! I fling open the door and they waltz in, all smiles.

"Where have you been?" Marisol asks, plopping onto my beanbag and flinging her arms out.

"Grinding at the lab and library. Taking breaks for class."

Jane stands beside me, her hands on her hips. The crisp floral scent of her new perfume is inviting. "You bailed on breakfast the other morning. What's up with that?"

I smack my forehead with my palm. "Shoot! I'm so sorry. I overslept and ended up being late for a lab meeting, can you believe it?" I laugh. Jane and Marisol exchange glances.

"Okay . . ." Jane hesitates. "But I left a message on your machine and a note on your door. Why didn't you respond?"

"I . . . forgot?" I wince—it's a weak excuse, even to my own ears.

"You didn't return my calls either," Marisol adds, rising from the beanbag.

Jane frowns. "Just admit it—you've been ignoring us. What's really going on?"

"Because I missed a few calls?" My voice rises. Heat creeps up my neck, my cheeks. "There's nothing going on. Not the other night, and not now."

"Cut the BS, Gita." Marisol steps forward. "Jane told me about the hickey."

"What?" Before I can stop it, my hand flies to my turtleneck. I turn to Jane. "Why didn't you say anything?" My heart is galloping in my chest now.

Jane avoids my eyes, a guilty expression on her face. "I wanted to! But you wouldn't even admit to crying." She rubs her arm, then raises her eyes to mine. "Anyway, I'm saying something now—I'm worried about you."

Both Jane's and Marisol's expressions are sincere: I know they care about me. I know I should just tell them why I've been avoiding them. But even as I open my mouth, chup-re claws at my throat, hurling that ever-present word around and around my mind: *shame-shame, shame-shame, shame-shame.*

My eyes dart between the two of them like a trapped animal,

my vision blurring. Who do they even think they are, backing me into a corner like this? *Finish them,* something inside me hisses.

"Fine!" I snarl. "So you saw my hickey. Well, I just saw Adam outside. Did you two hook up again? I saw you two going at it our first night here. Bet you didn't know that you left the door open, huh?" I smirk, even as my mouth runs dry.

Jane gasps. Marisol's eyes grow wide.

"That is so . . . so . . . *wrong,* Gita. Like, on so many levels," Jane sputters, her face splotchy red. "And no, I didn't hook up with Adam again, not that it matters. . . . After all this time, were you ever going to tell me?"

No no no no no. What have I just said? What have I just done?

"I . . . I didn't think it was my business and I . . . I didn't want to embarrass you." Tears slip from my eyes as I frantically grasp at an excuse, any excuse, that will fix this.

"It became your business when we started hanging out." Marisol's voice is even, but I can hear the storm rumbling underneath it. "Jane didn't say anything about your hickey for less than a week, and we're bringing it up now because we're worried about you. What excuse do you have?"

My face goes slack, my gaze tumbling to the floor. I lick my lips and taste the salt of tears there. "Well, I worry about you guys too!" I cry, swiping at my nose. I raise my chin and point to Marisol. "What about you and Joey? Why would you be with a guy—*flirt* in front of a guy—who's that possessive? And don't you think it's weird how young you were when he hit on you—"

"No." Marisol shakes her head so emphatically, I almost miss the sheen of tears coating her eyes. "No. What we're *not* going to do right now, Gita, is go there." Marisol takes a step back and crosses her arms over her chest, covering the half-moon of her birthmark.

"Well, *fine* then!" I screech, banshee-like. "You're right— clearly I'm ignoring you! Clearly I don't care! It's all my fault, always my fault. Why don't you two just leave me, like you were always going to?!" I suck in my snot and point to the door. "GET OUT!"

Jane shakes her head. "That wasn't necessary," she says, quietly. Then she turns around. "Let's go, Marisol."

Marisol's face crumples. "Whatever." Her voice is flat, lifeless. She follows Jane to the door, then stops. "Don't forget, Gita. *You* asked for this, not us."

"Yeah, yeah, tell me something I don't know!" I yell, throwing my arms into the air.

The second Marisol slams the door shut, I fall to my knees and bury my face in my palms.

CHAPTER 29

*L*ater that night, as I stare at an O-Chem problem set, pencil poised in hand, my thoughts jostle around my mind like the wheels of a bike hitting potholes: *Will Jane and Marisol ever speak to me again? Can I fix it with them? I didn't mean to scream at them, much less kick them out of my room. . . .*

I lower my forehead to the edge of my desk and thump it gently, thinking and thinking. That's when I catch sight of the bottommost drawer of my desk, open slightly, and Pinky Auntie's teal-and-gold birthday card resting in its depths. I reach down, pluck the card out, and stare at it. I can *feel* the yearning to see my aunt again festering inside me, like an oozing wound that hasn't healed.

I lost her. Now I might've lost Jane and Marisol too.

I wilt. My pencil slides out from between my fingers and thumb as another memory washes over me. . . .

It's the day before Pinky Auntie and Neil Uncle are moving back to India. They've been fighting every night for the past week, Neil Uncle's shouts a broken record: Once we're in Gujarat, we're done!

Hours have gone by, and Pinky Auntie hasn't moved from a slumped position on the floor, next to the ficus. Her hands are draped over her belly. Her head droops, her unkempt hair falling over her face like a thick, frayed curtain.

I wonder if she's eaten yet. Or peed. Doesn't it hurt to sit so stiff all day?

My little eight-year-old body tingles. I sit on the sofa and hug my bent knees to my chest, shutting my eyes and squeezing every muscle as tightly as I can. I'm trying to lock away all the yucky, secret things I've seen Bhavin Uncle do to Pinky Auntie, and how mean Neil Uncle has been to her recently.

I open my eyes and stare at Pinky Auntie. I want to lift her chin and fix her hair, the way she does for me when I'm sad. I'm scared for her—Bhavin Uncle should be apologizing to her. So should Neil Uncle.

Why am I the only one on Pinky Auntie's side?

I shut my eyes again, keeping my worries to myself. Maybe, if I stay strong, I can help Pinky Auntie snap out of whatever this is. She has to get better. Who else will help me when I have bad dreams, when I wet my bed? Who else will be on my side?

I rock back and forth, crying softly. Is Pinky Auntie on my side? Is anyone?

I shudder, coming back into my body. My chin is tucked and I'm staring through my O-Chem problem set. My pencil, which had been teetering on the edge of my desk, drops to the floor.

A frustrated scream tries to catapult itself up my throat. I swallow it.

I bend to pick up my pencil and notice that it's lying on top of Pinky Auntie's book of Indian poems, which I'd been reading last night. I push the pencil aside and flip the book open to my favorite title-less poem, its page dog-eared. I smile to myself; I used to love when Pinky Auntie read it aloud to me, even though she had hesitated that first time.

"Maybe when you're older." Pinky Auntie shook her head. "Besides, your parents wouldn't like me reading these to you."

I nuzzled up closer to her on the sofa. "Please, Pinky Auntie, please?! I love when you read to me!"

Pinky Auntie exhaled, stroking my cheek with the tips of her fingers. "All right," she breathed. "Only one though." She thumbed through the book, stopping about halfway through. "Ah—this one is about strong women, Gita. Listen." Then she cleared her throat:

The sun rose
painting the river gold.
Saraswati on a white lotus.
Glowing goddess
offers gifts
to quench the mind

with the cool nectar of wisdom.

Quiet days of truth

melt into

nights of crushed petals

and flattened grass.

Voluptuous Rati appears

in dreams,

guides hands to dewy places, hard places.

Breath caught.

Bangles shift.

Love-play on moonlit nights

until the sweet perfume of raat rani surrenders

to fresh dawn rain

and once again

four hands purify.

Eternal rebirth

sunlight,

starlight,

swan,

parrot,

book,

sword.

A fortuitous life

of learned days

and bandit nights.

My finger glides over my collarbone as I contemplate the words and the Hindu deities Saraswati and Rati. I picture Saraswati, the champion of learning, knowledge, and wisdom, then Rati, the expert on love, carnal desire, sexual pleasure, and lust.

I close my eyes and the images sharpen, glow.

Saraswati is radiant in her white sari. She speaks to me, lilting words like the notes of an Indian flute: *Gita—drink the cool nectar of wisdom by day, to quench your thirst for learning.* She hands me a book and a pencil. Her lips part, her next words as soft as a mother's kiss: *Your love of learning is beyond anything worldly.*

Rati appears under a rising moon, dripping in golden sensuality and smelling of raat rani. She purrs: *Gita—all those boys were your secret love-play by night.* She strokes my cheek, then whispers, *Your beautiful body is a gift. Use it for your pleasure.*

Saraswati and Rati, barefoot in the cool grass, hold hands. Together, their voices are a cooing dove. *Follow in our footsteps. Own both learning and pleasure.*

My ancient roots don't care if I'm a believer, agnostic, or atheist. My roots are telling me to work hard, play hard. That in this duality is my true survival.

Or am I reading too much into it? I open my eyes. Is this just me coming up with some culturally sanctioned excuse for sleeping around?

I sigh, set the book down, and walk to my mirror. Gazing at my reflection, I trace my lips. I touch my right eyelid, nudging it down into a wink. Then I stop it halfway.

What am I doing?

I stare at my reflection with both eyes wide-open. For a second, it's not me in the mirror. It's Pinky Auntie—I see her clearly now.

This isn't about Saraswati, Rati, or any duality. This is about Pinky Auntie. She loved me, and I loved her.

But she had secrets. She made me keep her secrets, and then she left. She cut me off from everything except the annual birthday card.

Pinky Auntie loved me. But she hurt me.

I don't understand. I want to understand. There must be reasons.

I rub my eyes. When I look again, it's just me in the mirror.

I glare at myself for a few seconds. Then I glance over my shoulder at the book of poems. *What good is learning and wisdom if you hurt people with it? What good is pleasure if it brings someone pain?*

Eyes back at myself in the mirror.

What good are my good intentions if I end up hurting others?

The realization hits me: *The more pain I lock up, the more I hurt the people I love with it.*

I startle, eyes flashing wide in the mirror. That's it, isn't it? If I can't be honest with the people I love, I'm going to hurt them. I'm going to lose them, like Pinky Auntie lost me and my family.

I cross my fingers, hoping that Jane and Marisol will let me try to make things right with them again.

CHAPTER 30

CoHo's heavy door takes some muscle to pull open. I poke my head into the café, and the collegiate vibe that feels at once well-known and foreign lures me in. My senses are overwhelmed by the colorful, eclectic art on the walls; the chattering, over-caffeinated students; and the sounds of grinding, banging, gurgling, and whistling from behind the counter.

I take a deep inhale of the nutty coffee aroma. The line to the counter is long, probably because it's Veterans Day and no one has classes. My eyes roam around slowly until they meet those of a Black girl with shoulder-length box braids who's taken a pause from writing. She gives me a quick, wide grin before jotting down another note.

My unfettered smile unravels. I glance at the book on her table: *The Eyes on the Prize Civil Rights Reader.* It takes me a second to notice that the line has moved ahead of me, lost as I am in the rhythm of the girl's pencil dancing across her notebook.

I take a step forward and turn my attention to the tatted guy working the espresso machine as he talks to someone waiting for their coffee.

"Gita!"

I whisk around—Sora and Hector are waving from a corner table.

I wave back.

"Come join us!" Hector calls out.

"Will do! Lemme just get my coffee." I order and pay, then wait on the side, intrigued by the way the guy's hands—one bearing a skull tattoo and the other a phoenix rising from flames—flit about as he crafts my beverage. He stops for a moment and scratches his chin, studying my face. Then he grabs the squeeze bottle of chocolate drizzle, finishing my mocha with a perfect chocolate butterfly on top of the foam.

"Yours." He sets my drink on the counter and smiles.

I wrap both hands around the ceramic mug, its warmth seeping into my palms. "Thanks," I say, leaving him with a tip in the jar and another unfettered smile. Then I weave through the packed tables to Sora and Hector and sink into the empty chair across from them.

"Hey! What are you guys up to today?" I take a sip, then wipe the chocolate foam that gathers on my lip.

"Hopefully finishing the 'results' and 'discussion' sections of another article I'm coauthoring with Dr. Peters," Sora says. "Fingers crossed for *Nature* again!"

I hold up crossed fingers, then turn to Hector. "How about you?"

"I'm off today—so maxing and relaxing. You?"

"Some studying, then a follow-up appointment at Planned Parenthood later. Woman stuff." I roll my eyes but, truth be told, I'm proud of myself for being at least 50 percent honest. The 50 percent that I leave out are the details of the "woman stuff"—getting the results of the STD and HIV tests I had done there last week. It's not a lie of omission or a chup-re secret, though—it's not something that's hurting me or someone I love. It's me keeping some things private, which I'm allowed to do.

"Which Planned Parenthood? The one in Mountain View or Redwood City?" Hector asks.

My eyebrows lift. "Mountain View. You know it?"

Hector grins. "My sister's the head nurse there."

"Oh wow! What does she look like? I wonder if I saw her the last time I was there."

"She's a little shorter than I am. Shaved head—"

"Does she rock combat boots under her scrubs? Her name is Rosario?"

"That's her all right." Hector nods.

"She took care of me when I went for the first time. She's so on it!"

"That she is." There's a tender, brotherly look in Hector's eyes now. "Hey, let me give you a ride to the clinic—I haven't seen Ro in a while. What time?"

"Four thirty. You sure? I was going to bus it."

"I insist." Hector smiles at me, and Sora's eyes glisten in the morning light coming through the window beside him. I smile back at the two of them, then take a sip of my mocha.

Back in my room, I put the *Boomerang* soundtrack on at low volume, bopping my head to the first upbeat track. Then I settle in at my desk, flip open my O-Chem notebook, and dive into a problem set.

Three complicated questions later, I hear laughter in the hallway.

I stop writing and listen closely. The muffled sound of Marisol's voice: "I was like 'my bad.'"

Someone else laughs in response—Jane.

At that exact moment, the first soulful beats of Boyz II Men's "End of the Road" ooze out of my boom box speakers. The little hairs on my arms stand up, and my eyes grow moist.

I hope this isn't the end of the road for our friendship. But what if it's too late? What if—

Get out of your head, Gita! Do something!

I stop thinking, stand, and march toward the door, determined to right my wrongs face-to-face.

"I was totally lost in econ today," Jane says now.

Before my nerves can drain away, I open the door. All the way.

Jane and Marisol stop talking and the three of us stand there, eyes darting from one person to the other. It's so quiet, I swear I can hear their hearts beating. Meanwhile, mine turns slow somersaults in my chest.

The LaFace Cartel's "Reversal of a Dog" starts playing from my boom box behind me. The chipper *Bow wow wow, yippie yo, yippie yay*'s of the intro only add to the awkwardness of the moment. I roll onto the outer edges of my feet, chewing my lower lip.

Do something, *Gita!*

The only thing that comes to mind is the joke Sora told us at the lab the other day: "How does an economist divide relatives?!" I blurt.

Jane and Marisol stare at me, blank-faced.

"Into two columns . . . assets and liabilities," I mumble.

It was a lot funnier when Sora delivered the punchline.

Jane raises an eyebrow, and Marisol crosses her arms. I swallow, forcing myself to maintain eye contact with them. "Listen . . . I'm sorry for being an asshole. Really. I didn't mean to scream at you . . . And I want you to know that I'd never judge either of you, or ignore you on purpose. I love you guys." I pause. "Want to grab some dinner tonight, off campus? My treat!"

Jane's expression turns quizzical.

I read it as, *Gita, Gita, Gita. After the way you treated us, why would we ever want to?*

Marisol blinks. "I don't know . . ."

I hold my breath, preparing myself for a double rejection.

" . . . which restaurant you should take us to," she finishes with a small smile.

I exhale, glancing back and forth between them.

"And, hey, I'm sorry if I pushed too hard to make you tell us stuff," Marisol says.

"Me too," Jane adds. "I mean, the thing about you not closing my door our first night here was kind of fucked up . . ."

I cringe. Jane gives me a look, then presses on. "Even so, Gita dear . . . I forgive you. I know it's something you wouldn't do again."

"Yes, of course!" I say earnestly. Point taken.

Jane finally smiles. "So dinner. How about Vinny's?"

I wince.

"What?" Marisol asks, squinting at me.

My first instinct is to lie, to say "Nothing." But I'm not a liar anymore. This is my chance to be real with them, and I'm not about to blow it.

I pry my lips apart. "It's . . . it's a long story. But I promise to tell it over a slice and soda."

"Sounds good to me!" Jane claps.

"Pizza, soda, and a story: The simple pleasures are always the best," Marisol agrees.

"Absolutely." My eyes land on one of the tiny white flowers on Marisol's navy blouse. It resembles a poppy—I can't help but picture the broken limb grasping a chipped sword and a little flower in *Guernica*. In my analysis paper, I'd written that the flower represents "ever-present hope, even when there is tremendous pain and tragedy."

For a second, I wonder if I was writing that line for past, present, or future Gita—or maybe all three?

That's when I remember what Dr. Peters said after I apologized to her, and add: "Thank you both for giving me a second chance. I promise you that I won't need a third."

CHAPTER 31

*T*hat afternoon at Planned Parenthood, I'm in a tiny gray room watching Dr. Young flip through my chart. The doctor closes the metal clipboard holder, hugs it to her chest, and settles her eyes on me: "Good news first, Gita."

"Great!" I say, trying to ignore the implication of bad news.

"Your tests showed no signs of HIV—which I know you were worried about. And your pregnancy test was negative."

"Good news? That's the *best* news, doc!" I find myself clamping down on the edge of my seat, so I don't jump up and take victory laps around the office.

Dr. Young chuckles. "Great. Now let's talk more about HIV transmission—you were right that HIV is passed through bodily fluids like semen and blood. The risk of transmission through oral sex is low—though not zero. Condoms are highly effective at preventing transmission, but there is still a risk, so it's important to test frequently."

I try my best to listen, but my body's vibrating with excitement—no HIV! No eating for two! (Though I did already know this last one, since my period just ended.)

"Any questions?" Dr. Young eventually asks.

I shake my head.

"Good. Now for the bad news—"

"Do we have to?" I grimace.

"We do," Dr. Young says, though not unkindly.

"All right," I sigh. "Hit me with it."

Dr. Young nods. "Your oral swab was negative for STDs, but your vaginal swab revealed trichomoniasis."

Sharp inhale—I've got flagellated protozoan parasites swimming around my yoni?! *Gross!* A chee expression bursts over my face. My thoughts come in rapid-fire now: *But all the guys used condoms during sex! Well, except for Johnny Depp Boy, but that was during oral . . . So how is genital trich possible?*

Dr. Young is still speaking: " . . . and condoms don't offer full protection from trichomoniasis. It's good you got tested even though you were symptomless, like most people with it are. That's why it's easily passed on. But it's completely curable with a course of antibiotics."

My eyes go misty, and the questions swirling around my head still. "Really? What a relief." My voice catches in my throat.

Dr. Young's forehead creases. "Are you all right, Gita?"

"Yes. Just . . . grateful." I shut my mouth, afraid I might start crying if I say anything else.

Dr. Young gives me a small smile, then pats my hand. "You'll be just fine." A few seconds later, she whisks around and opens the door: "Rosario will be in shortly to wrap up," she calls over her shoulder.

"Thank you, Dr. Young!"

Dr. Young nods. A minute after she closes the door there's a knock, and then it swings back open. Rosario comes in, proffering a brown paper sack: "Your doggie bag, m'lady."

I slap a palm to my forehead: *Shame-shame, Gita! Two and a half months at Stanford, and you already need a doggie bag's worth of meds?*

"It's not that bad," Rosario says, still holding the bag out to me. "The antibiotics—take them twice a day for seven days. Plus a three-month supply of birth control pills, and a handful of condoms."

I muster up a weak smile. "Thank you—I'll definitely take the antibiotics. But I don't really need the other stuff. I'm not having sex again for a *looong* time."

Rosario shrugs. "That's your choice. So is using these. But I want you to have them so you never feel caught off guard."

I pause, exhale a silent breath, then take the bag from her. "You're right—thanks, Rosario."

"No problem." She turns to go, and another, more uncomfortable question jumps to the forefront of my brain.

"Hey Rosario?"

"Yes, Gita?" She turns back around, arches an eyebrow.

"Um . . . Do you think I should warn all the guys about the trich?" My gaze drifts down to the brown paper bag in my hands.

"There's no law that says you have to." Rosario crosses her arms. "It's your choice—it would only be illegal if you knew you had it and still went around transmitting it."

I meet Rosario's eyes again, shaking my head. "I'd never."

Rosario smiles. "Then whatever you decide is okay."

After getting dressed, I meet Hector in the waiting room and give him a thumbs-up. He grins, stands up, and holds the door open for me. I practically sprint through the exit.

Outside, the chilly November air meets me with a celebratory gust. I take a cleansing breath, then turn to Hector. "Thanks again for the ride. And for waiting."

"You're welcome." He squeezes my shoulder, the cool breeze lifting the curls on his head. "And it was great seeing Ro."

Sunshine emerges from behind a crowd of heavy clouds as the two of us cross the parking lot to Hector's pickup truck. Unfortunately, the bright moment is quickly overshadowed by the dozen or so anti-abortion protestors who've gathered at the edge of the property. They're singing hymns, praying with crucifixes, and waving huge signs: *PRO-LIFE! STOP MURDERING CHILDREN!* The worst sign has no words but, rather, a picture of an aborted fetus.

I turn my head back to the clinic and—thankfully—spot a couple of vigilant security guards monitoring the situation.

As I open the door to Hector's truck, one of the protestors catches my eye and shouts, "How does it feel to be a murderer?! You'll regret your abortion!"

I hop into Hector's truck and slam the door shut behind me. My body shakes as I stare through the windshield.

"You okay?" Hector asks quietly.

"Yeah," I mumble. "I didn't even get one. . . ."

He gives me an understanding nod. "Our mother raised Rosario and me to be Catholic." He tosses his chin toward the protestors. "But it was never like this with her. Maybe because she's a doctor, and pro-choice."

"I didn't know your mom's a doctor." I try to ignore the protestors' muffled shouts. "What kind?"

"Pediatrician, specializing in allergies. She's got a private practice in Daly City."

"Good to know." I smile, dreams of a summer internship in Daly City dancing in my head. . . .

Hector sighs and rests an arm on the steering wheel, popping my dream bubble. "If she was walking with us, know what she'd do?"

I shake my head.

"She'd go over to them, smile, and start a conversation. She'd try to understand their perspective, while also trying to get them to understand hers. That's just how she is."

"Wow—she sounds amazing." Still, I can't help but wonder what good it would do to talk with these protestors; I'm pretty sure that no matter what anyone says, they won't change their minds. And if it were me talking with them, nothing they could say would change mine.

Also, what if they got violent? I've read about some of the ways these protestors have threatened, bullied, harassed, and harmed clinic doctors and staff, not to mention women seeking abortions. Some have even vandalized or destroyed clinics.

"That's my mom," Hector replies. "She'd turn this situation into a lesson for me. Something like, 'we have to be the light so they can find theirs.'"

"How noble. All *I* want to do is flip them off!" I click my tongue, and Hector laughs.

"Yeah, I argue with her about it. I personally don't think it's worth giving them the time of day."

Hector's words turn over and over in my mind. It strikes me that giving people who disagree with you the time of day feels a little like giving them a second chance to make their case. The question is, do these protestors deserve that chance? What about other people in my life who I've hurt—and who have hurt me?

"All good?" Hector asks now, turning on the ignition.

"All good," I say. But as we drive out of the parking lot, I catch myself peeking at the protestors in the rearview mirror and wondering, *Is it wrong of me to think that some people deserve second chances, while others don't?*

CHAPTER 32

*T*hat evening, Jane, Marisol, and I are halfway through a huge fried calamari pizza and icy Cokes at Vinny's when the rowdy group of Stanford students at the table next to us push their chairs back, doubling over with laughter. "Way to write your own story!" cackles a flannel-shirted girl in baggy jeans, complete with a chain wallet.

As the group traipses out, Marisol eyes me from across the table. "Speaking of 'your own story'—you said you've got one for us?"

"Ready when you are," Jane adds with a golf clap, the kind where only the fingers of one hand gently tap the center of the other palm.

"Okay . . ." My body stills though my heart goes berserk in my chest, throwing itself against my rib cage again and again. I can feel the snakelike tendrils of chup-re winding themselves around me, my neck, my mouth.

I pinch my thigh, hard, and start talking. "So . . . Remember when I got weird about the Vinny's suggestion?"

Jane and Marisol nod.

"Well, the first time I had Vinny's was with a certain Steven Hyun after the Asian American Association party. . . . In his room."

Marisol crosses her arms and leans back in her chair. "Something tells me you two did more than just eat pizza?"

Jane giggles.

I drop my eyes for a second, blushing.

"Yup." One of Marisol's eyebrows shoots up. "You guys definitely banged. Was it good?"

Wide-eyed, I nod. Then I pluck a calamari off the half-eaten slice on my plate, pop it into my mouth, and chew.

"Damn you, Joey, for making me miss that party! I would've loved to see my girl Gita in action," Marisol cheers.

"Plus his 'lil' Steven. . . ." Jane cracks up.

My mouth hangs open. I was *not* prepared for Her Royal Highness Jane to make a dick joke.

Marisol elbows her.

"Sorry." Jane clears her throat and wipes the laughter off her face. "Proceed," she continues.

"Okay, well . . . there *was* action. But it turns out he was just using me to try to get your number, Marisol." I grab the napkin from next to my plate, folding it into smaller and smaller halves. "But I didn't give it to him." I nearly whisper this last part.

A beat of silence goes by. Then: "What a prick!" Marisol barks, scowling.

I stop folding the napkin.

"If I see him, I'll tell him as much too."

I raise my eyes back to Marisol. "Really?"

Jane frowns. "He doesn't deserve you, Gita." She reaches over and pats my hand. "Are you all right?"

I nod. "I think so." But then my heart sinks—story time isn't over.

I mean, it could be. I could pretend that the connection between Vinny's and Steven Hyun was the entire story.

Thoughts gust through my head like the winds of change: *Saraswati on a white lotus. Voluptuous Rati appears. "What good is learning, wisdom, and pleasure if you hurt people?" they say. "The more pain you lock up, the more you hurt yourself, and those you love."*

I massage my temples. Jane is sipping her Coke. Marisol grabs another slice of pizza.

"Also . . ." I begin.

Jane sets her glass down. Marisol drops the new slice onto her plate without taking a bite.

I rub my sweaty palms on my jeans, trying to figure out how to tell them the rest of my secrets. *The gory details aren't important, Gita. All that matters is that they know.*

I take a deep breath, release it, and focus my gaze on the pizza in the center of the table. Then I hold up a fist and shut my eyes, raising one finger at a time as I say, "Angelo, a guy from the Alpha Sig party whose name I don't even know, Steven, Javier from Club Inferno, and Jeet from the lab."

Silence. I crack my eyelids open, peering at my girls.

Jane's eyebrows are pinched. Marisol's wearing a sad smile as she fiddles with her rosary.

They look worried, empathetic. Not shocked or disgusted. Not like they're judging me.

Jane's expression tenses as she holds up her fist. She keeps her eyes fixed on mine as she raises each finger: "Adam, Todd, Mike, Henry." She sticks out her thumb. "The bartender, Lance, the week after we met him."

My mouth hangs open once again. My hand falls to my lap.

"I'm sorry I lied about Todd. I was too embarrassed to tell you the truth," Jane says.

"Y-you were embarrassed?" I stutter. "But you didn't do anything wrong!"

Jane sighs. "I thought he was interested in more than a one-night stand with me. He wasn't. I felt so stupid. . . ."

"I'm sorry, Jane," Marisol says.

"He doesn't deserve you." This time, I'm the one to lean forward and pat her hand. "And you're not stupid—I thought the exact same thing with Jeet."

"Fuck them. Fuck all of them." Marisol clears her throat and, defiantly, raises both her fists. She puts up seven fingers at once. "Before I met Joey." She shifts her eyes to me. "I used to be proud of it, and then I was embarrassed for a while. Now I'm more neutral—it doesn't matter how many girls a guy sleeps with, and it shouldn't matter for us either."

My throat has gone as dry as a desert. I'm speechless, and not because I thought my girls never slept with guys before. The opposite, actually—I had assumed that they were completely confident in their choices, impervious to feelings of confusion or shame. But they're just human beings making their way in the world . . . like me.

As simple as the realization is, it steals the air from my lungs.

Marisol rests her head in her hand. "Speaking of Joey . . . I've been feeling more and more unsure of our relationship lately. Especially when he's so . . ."

"Controlling?" Jane asks. I look over at her in surprise—her expression is sympathetic but stoic. It's then that I remember the time we walked out of *Fried Green Tomatoes* and she was so sure when she called Joey a jerk, the same way Sai was so sure when he called Bhavin Uncle an asshole that night at Tran's Bistro. And today, Jane is certain about Joey being controlling. Why am I so wishy-washy about people sometimes?

"Yes," Marisol concedes. "*Controlling* is probably the right word."

Suddenly, in my mind's eye, Joey is Frank in *Fried Green Tomatoes* and he's kicking Marisol down the stairs. "Does Joey hit you?" I blurt.

"No! No, nothing like that." Marisol releases a soft breath.

"It's just . . . I don't know. Lately, it feels like he's trying to lock me away from the world. Like I'm Rapunzel or something."

"Marisol," I start. "I'm no relationship expert, but if things with Joey aren't great . . . maybe you two should break up."

"Yeah . . ." Marisol exhales.

"I agree with Gita," Jane adds. "And you don't have to do it right away, if you're not ready. You're allowed to take some time to figure things out."

Marisol clutches her rosary, but she looks more reassured now. "Thanks, you guys." She gives us each a small smile. "What would I do without the two of you?"

The three of us eventually get back to sipping our Cokes, devouring the rest of the pizza. It all tastes the same, but I know that what just happened was major for me and my girls.

Like we may have entered this pizza parlor as friends, but we'll be leaving it as sisters.

CHAPTER 33

The next day, Sora and I mount the steps of the lab building in sync. We're both feeling warm and sleepy from the bliss only lunchtime lasagna can provide.

As we climb, a late autumn breeze tangos with my hair. I tilt my head back and gather all the flyaways. The sky crowns my eyes with a stretch of pearl-flecked aquamarine as my fingers do some quick ponytail acrobatics.

When we reach the landing, Sora groans: "I wish the data would crunch itself."

"Need some help?" We turn the corner, starting up the second flight.

He shakes his head. "This is solitary suffering."

"You sure? I'm ahead on everything, I can't get my grades higher than the A's they already are—" I stop mid-sentence, all good intentions dangling from the tip of my tongue.

My eyes have collided with the side profile of Jeet, who's

standing at the end of the outdoor corridor. It would have been bad enough if he was alone. . . . But there he is, brushing copper-red strands of hair off Veronica's snow-white cheek.

Jeet leans in and whispers something into her ear. Veronica covers her mouth with her French-manicured hand and laughs.

I fling my own hand over my mouth. I suddenly want to puke—I lean forward slightly at the waist, saliva coagulating in my mouth like blood in a wound. But no matter how hard I try, I can't stop staring.

Sora, a few steps behind me and completely oblivious to the disaster playing out in front of us, comes up behind me and tsks. "Come now. Gita the overachiever, wasting precious time?" He chuckles.

I don't respond—the neurons that had been smoothly firing in my brain have now descended into a cyclone of icy regret and fiery wrath.

Sora shifts his eyes from me to where I'm committing ocular homicide. His expression darkens. "I *knew* it wasn't just PMS."

Jeet's voice in my head: *Ready?*

Someone else's muffled words: *Take it by force . . .*

Mom: *Shame-shame . . .*

Me, a tiny voice cutting through the gale: *I hate myself.*

Suddenly, I can't get enough air. There's a prickle in my fingers—I lift my hands, inspecting them front and back. Then I touch my lips: cold. I touch my neck: clammy.

Sora moves so he's standing directly in front of me. His voice is gentle but firm when he says, "Don't you dare tell me every-thing is fine."

I open my mouth. I want to tell him the truth, I do.

Chup-re! Secrets aren't meant to be told!

My mouth shuts.

"Gita, what did Jeet do?" Sora asks.

Chup-re!

But wouldn't my family *want* me to tell Sora if Jeet hurt me? *Sai would.*

I blink, and a tear drips down my cheek.

Sora looks distressed. "Now I'm assuming the worst, Gita. *Please* tell me everything before I lose it on him. . . . You can trust me," he adds.

Can I? In this moment, it feels like I can't. I don't know how to explain it.

Maybe, when—deep down—you hate yourself, anyone who tries to show you otherwise becomes the enemy.

Maybe I don't trust myself to trust the right people anymore.

But then Sora takes my hand, as delicately as if it's a plucked flower whose petals could scatter to the wind, and I know it's time.

I wrap my other hand around his as well, holding on to him as I take yet another step out of rock bottom. "Jeet asked if I was ready," I whisper.

Sora's face crumples. "Ready for what?"

Tears roll down my cheeks. "It's my fault. I didn't say—didn't say no," I blubber.

"Oh honey." Sora pulls me into a tight embrace. "So that's why you've been acting off. It was after I left the party, wasn't it?"

I nod into Sora's shoulder. He holds me as the sobs wrack my body—I've long stopped caring about the students moving around us as I cry.

A minute goes by. Two. Then, without warning, Sora lets go of me and grabs my hand. "That's it—let's give that asshole a piece of your mind."

"Sora, no!" I rip my hand out of his. "I can't."

"Why not?"

My heart's in my throat. My eyes dart around like a caged animal. "N-not right now. Not like this. It took me this long to tell *you*. I just . . . need to clear some things up in my head first."

Sora crosses his arms. "It sounds pretty clear to me. Crystal, in fact." His eyes search my face, and then his voice turns pleading. "At least let me help, Gita—I can talk to him for you."

I shake my head. "What would you even say?"

Sora drops his arms and balls his fists. "That he's a disgusting predator for taking advantage of the situation. And you." Indignation paints his face bloodred.

He's so sure. I wish *I* was that sure.

My head slumps, chin grazing my chest. My brain surges with hazy snippets of memory, but of what? As the chaos ramps up in my brain, my body stills. I don't move, don't blink.

Sad doll.

"Gita?" Sora touches my arm.

I snap out of it. "Yes?"

Sora sighs. "Should we get out of here, then? Take a break from the lab?"

"No." Once again, I shake my head. "You've got a ton of work to do. And like you said, 'Gita the overachiever' can't waste any more precious time."

After a long moment, Sora finally says, "Okay."

Slowly, the two of us turn and begin walking the outdoor corridor toward the lab entrance. In my periphery, I see that Sora's moving with his shoulders back, chin lifted—a proud, regal posture.

Even though it feels totally unnatural to me right now, I copy his body language, pulling my shoulders back and lifting my chin. I make my face stoic, the same expression I've seen on Jane. "Fake it 'til you make it," I whisper to myself.

When we near Jeet and Veronica, Sora takes my hand.

As we pass them, Sora throws Jeet the dirtiest look I've ever seen.

I don't let myself steal even a glimpse of them. But I feel Jeet's eyes shift to me for a second, then away again.

Flashes: *My legs over Jeet's shoulders. The way his upper lip curled as he . . .*

My nose remembers too: *The smell of his hair product when he . . .*

I don't want it to, but my yoni tingles.

CHAPTER 34

*P*etit Boucher is one of those fancy Michelin star restaurants that most people have to book six months in advance to get a table. Especially on a Saturday night.

But not Jane's dad. He's a fancy man with a fancy job. He flies first class to SF last minute on fancy business. He's got a fancy chauffeured car to pick up his daughter and her friend for a fancy dinner.

I mean, this place has a live pianist in the corner and servers in stiff black waistcoats and bow ties who anticipate his every wish. Need I say more?

But fanciness doesn't compensate for Mr. West's absence, which I'm experiencing firsthand tonight. The guy can't even get through this dinner without excusing himself to take calls. Seriously—he's been away for two out of the four extravagant courses we've completed so far.

Why did he even bother taking Jane out? I'm starting to suspect that's why he told her to invite me along: Since she's an adult now, he can pawn her off to a friend instead of a nanny. . . .

Jane clicks her tongue when he excuses himself for the third time, cell phone pressed against his ear. "How did my mom put up with this?" she mumbles—more to herself than me—and fiddles with the new gold bracelet her dad gave her before dinner.

I don't know what to say, so I give Jane a smile I invent just for this occasion—a lighthouse smile. Unlike my unfettered smile, my lips don't part. It's all in my eyes—I make them clear and bright, like flashlights in a blackout. I steady my gaze on Jane the way Sora has done for me countless times now—like she may be a lost ship, but I am the lighthouse in the storm, calling her home.

Jane blinks, then returns my lighthouse smile with a wilted version of her own. I reach across the table and squeeze her hand. It takes everything in me not to get up, march over to Jane's dad, and yell him out of the fancy restaurant.

Jane squeezes back, then rolls her eyes. "Being with my dad for more than one hour, and I've got to spend like twenty-four decompressing." She lets go of my hand, throws her napkin down on her plate. "No, you know what? Not this time—let's go check out that new club after dinner, Gita. It's just down the block—we can walk." Her eyes are beseeching as they peer into my own. "You in?"

"Definitely." It barely takes me a second to respond. *This is for her.*

Jane comes back to life. "Great! And if you need a bathroom break, we'll go together this time." She winks.

I writhe a little at the memory of Javier. But I know Jane didn't mean anything hurtful with her wink. The opposite, in fact—she was telling me that she has my back.

Jane and I exchange matching lighthouse smiles.

Then my eyes shift to the middle of the table, to a white flower in a small crystal vase. I stretch my arm and brush one of its petals with my fingertips.

Jane starts humming "Edelweiss."

"Aww—I love *The Sound of Music!*"

"Me too. It was my mom's favorite." She pauses, then adds: "We used to watch it together. I remember envying the dad in it." She throws a wistful glance toward her own father now, who's still on the phone.

I pluck the flower from the vase, wipe the water off the stem with my napkin, and slide it over Jane's ear. "There."

She strikes a pose.

"Gorgeous!" I giggle.

Mr. West returns to the table then, snapping his cell phone shut. A server magically appears at his side, handing him a new glass of whiskey.

I excuse myself to the restroom—I want to give Jane a chance to say whatever she might want to say to her dad in private.

Unhurried, I stroll down the narrow hallway to the ladies' room, hands clasped behind my back. Romantic black-and-white photographs of the Parisian cityscape line both walls. I stop in front of a photo of a couple kissing at an outdoor café.

A tap on the shoulder.

I turn my head and jump.

It's Jeet.

My lips flatten. My arms flop to my sides.

"Well, well, well. If it isn't Gita Desai." Jeet's voice drips with canned astonishment, as if he's just run into a long-lost friend.

My body tenses. I force air back into my lungs, smile through gritted teeth: "Oh, hey Jeet. What are you doing here?"

"Dinner with a friend."

"Cool." My pits and palms are suddenly moist, while my mouth is bone-dry. I inch back. "Um, nice to see you, I guess, but . . . nature calls!" I chirp before turning away.

Jeet grabs my shoulder. "Wait!"

I slowly face him again, staring pointedly at his hand on me.

He gets the hint and lets go. "Listen, I feel bad about what I said to you at the lab the other day. Let me make it up to you. Do you want to hang out tomorrow? I'll cook."

The last time a guy cooked for me was the first time . . .

Jeet runs his finger down my arm. "Or we could skip dinner."

I jerk my arm back and glare at him. There's an odd flicker in his eyes—his expression reminds me of the tiger Shere Khan, when he cornered Mowgli in the Disney movie version of *The Jungle Book*.

I squint. I've seen this flicker somewhere else before too . . .

Sigma Nu boy—aka Adam.

Jeet winks. "So. Tomorrow?"

My traitorous yoni starts tingling.

Damn you, yoni!

I open my mouth to tell him off. All that comes out is a boiled down "Can't."

I back away slowly, then whip around and practically sprint to the bathroom.

In the safe zone of one of the luxurious stalls—which has thicker, softer toilet paper than I've ever unrolled before—I shakily do my business. Then I go to the sink, pump some lavender soap onto my palm, and wash my hands. *It's okay.* I breathe in and out, slowly. *You're okay now.* Between deep breaths, I hum a few notes of "Edelweiss."

The ladies' room door opens, and in walks Veronica. "Edelweiss" dies in my throat as quickly as a flower in the Alps under heavy snow.

Veronica goes straight into a stall, not even glancing my way. That's when it hits me: Jeet's here with a "friend" all right.

My heart sinks; she gets a world-class dinner before sex. All I got were some drinks that we didn't even drink together.

Or maybe they won't even have sex tonight. Maybe he'll be a "gentleman" with her, the way Sai *actually* was with his ex. My mom would probably justify it with something messed up, like it's because Veronica is a fair-skinned girl, and therefore more prized than a desi girl like me who's let herself "go dark" in the sun.

Forget all of that! I scrub my hands harder, faster. *Who cares? Jeet's a bad guy!*

But then an image of Jeet whispering into Veronica's ear pops into my head, and my mind goes up in flames.

How could Jeet do that to me? Was it my fault?

Shere Khan eyes. Take it by force. Fan blades spinning.

How could Pinky Auntie do that?

Do *what?*

Wiping my hands on my pants, I kick the ladies' room door open and hustle back to our table.

I come back to Jane guzzling the rest of her father's whiskey, Daddy dearest nowhere in sight. But she stops mid-sip when she catches sight of my face. I sit, slowly.

"Gita! You look like you saw a ghost." Jane sets the glass of whiskey down. "Actually, you look like you saw something that *scared* a ghost."

I feel myself nodding, laying my palms on the tablecloth.

Jane tilts her head. "What happened?"

Chup-re starts a war in my head. I glance at her, then bury my gaze in the cold sweat on my glass of water. *Don't tell her, don't tell her, don't—*

Jane touches my arm, and the thoughts subside. Her fingertips are soft against my skin.

I exhale a quiet breath, and Jane squeezes my arm. "What's going on?" she asks again.

I examine her face—nothing there but worried eyes.

321

Jane won't judge me. She's shown me that already. And Sora didn't judge me when I told him about Jeet. These thoughts help me chup-re my chup-re. I swallow, imagining a crowbar prying my lips apart. "I just ran into that guy—Jeet—from my lab." I pause.

Jane's brow furrows. "Go on. . . ."

"Well, I mean, he's here on a date with a girl from a different lab. Taking her out for a nice dinner, treating her like a human. But with me . . ." I can't even finish the rest. I try to relax the sneer on my face.

Jane scoffs. "Forget her. And fuck him." She cracks her knuckles as she adds, "Want me to go kick his ass?"

My heart slams against my sternum in surprise. This was not the reaction I expected from Jane. I just witnessed my girl go from upper crust to down and dirty in 0.2 seconds.

Jane's on my side figuratively and by my side literally. Right now, that's enough to make me feel Hulk-strong.

Stronger than the Hulk, actually; I don't need violence, destruction, or excessive rage to stand up to Jeet. All I need, at this moment, is to know I'm not alone.

"No," I say, shoving my chair back and grabbing my purse. "Let's get outta here." I reach my hand out to Jane, who takes it with a lighthouse smile.

CHAPTER 35

At 3:oo p.m. exactly two days before Thanksgiving, most people are probably still in class or at work, not here at this bar that's more a futuristic chemistry lab—including a centrifuge, rotary evaporator, and super chiller—than a place to get drunk. But Marisol and I are done with classes for the day, and Grandpa, aka salt-and-pepper man, who we saw a month ago at the oceanfront café, is retired. Guess that's why the three of us are the only ones here, perched on barstools and sipping neon-pink science-experiment-looking cocktails in beakers.

Marisol and Grandpa are in the middle of sharing laughs about his "back when I was at UCLA . . ." stories, all of which make me want to upchuck. I can't get it out of my head that Marisol and I weren't even *born* when he was an undergrad.

Grandpa takes a long sip, and Marisol goes to adjust her blouse so that it covers the half moon of her birthmark peeking out, but then leaves it.

That's right! Fuck what he thinks!

I swirl my drink and study the resulting whirlpool in the beaker as Grandpa leans in and whispers something into Marisol's ear.

She giggles.

I scoff silently, then take a couple of sips of my drink.

I'm only here because Marisol begged me to be. With the three of us, this is clearly a "business meeting," not a date. Just in case a certain boyfriend were to find out about it . . .

Another sip of my drink as I peek at Grandpa's left ring finger. His skin is tanned except for a white horizontal stripe near the knuckle.

I roll my eyes. But who am I to judge? Just weeks ago I had flirted with Ujj. Although, to be fair, that was before I knew that he'd left his partner and baby at a hotel while he went out to party at Jeet's.

I sigh, then down the last of the potent concoction.

Grandpa waves at the bartender. "We're ready for the next round," he says authoritatively. "Three 'deviant desires.'"

I bet you've got more than three, you old geezer. I snort.

The bartender—donned in a crisp white lab coat and safety goggles—nods at Grandpa.

I exchange glances with Dr. Bartender, whose expression remains unmoved. What does he think about Grandpa hitting on a barely adult hottie? I mean, I bet he's seen it all, but still. And he didn't even check our fake IDs!

Not two minutes later, the bartender places three amber

drinks in big beakers—fog billowing off the top of each—in front of us.

Grandpa and Marisol don't acknowledge the bartender, but I do: "Thank you," I say, then offer a smile.

The bartender's expression doesn't change, but he lifts his goggles and gives me an it's-our-little-secret wink.

I hate it. It reminds me that, I, Gita Desai, am not only Marisol's cover but Grandpa's silent accomplice in this . . . whatever this is.

My skin prickles.

I side-eye Grandpa, then hunch over and slice the fog off my drink with the knife edge of my hand.

"This drink is smoky yet youthful." Grandpa holds up his glass, then takes a sip and smacks his lips. "Appropriate for the situation, it seems." He ogles Marisol for a second, then reaches over and taps a finger on her thigh.

Marisol raises an eyebrow, but she doesn't push his hand away. Instead, she tilts her head, twirls a curl, and says, "Why sir, we hardly know each other." Although her words are critical, her tone is flirtatious, her expression inviting.

"Girl, you just said the truest thing I've heard today." The words slip out before I can stop them. Marisol and Grandpa turn their heads, staring blankly at me. I clear my throat and take a sip of my drink—which, for the record, tastes like a stronger version of what I imagine rubbing alcohol does—and the two of them immediately go back to talking.

Grandpa smiles at Marisol, then raises his beaker in her direction. "To the most beautiful woman on the planet," he says.

They clink beakers, take a sip. At the last second—remembering that I'm there too—they both give me afterthought clinks.

Whatever. I gulp down half of my drink, then gag a little.

Marisol sips. Her nose scrunches. "I . . . I like it," she says unconvincingly.

"Excellent," Grandpa—whose real name is Jack McCarthy, though I refuse to call him by it—nods at her. Marisol told me that he recognized her that day in the café. Later that evening, he tracked down her agent's contact information. The next day, he called the agent and managed to finagle Marisol's number. Now here we all are.

"So, Marisol," Grandpa says, "about your nonprofit for underprivileged children . . ."

Marisol straightens up. "Yes?" she asks, crossing her legs.

Grandpa's eyes drift down to where her miniskirt has hiked up a few inches, then back to her face. "Well, I'm in the habit of funding three new nonprofits a year. Yours sounds like a great investment—all you have to do is let me know where to sign."

So that's it.

Marisol's eyes light up. She puts her hand on Grandpa's knee and leans in. "Really?"

Marisol's flowy top slips down, and Grandpa's eyes lose themselves in her cleavage. "Of course."

I tap Marisol's shoulder.

"What?" she asks, without so much as a backward glance.

"You can get your own funding," I say, my voice firm.

"I know I can. . . ." She explains slowly, as if spelling it out for a child. "But why bother when this nice gentleman can just give it to me without all the paperwork?" She gestures back to Grandpa, who flashes his too-bright teeth at us.

I chug the rest of my drink—taste buds be damned—and open my mouth to call her out, when the café door slams open.

The three of us turn to look: It's Joey. His chest is heaving, fire raging in his eyes.

I shake my head—I don't know what else to do at this point. Joey has either the best or worst timing that I know of.

Why oh why is he still with Marisol? Obviously she's just going to keep flirting with guys, no matter how upset Joey gets, how much he tries to stop her—to control her. *But maybe Joey's controlling* because *Marisol is such a flirt,* whispers a little voice in my head.

I frown and push that last thought away. I can't put my finger on why, but it sounds like something my parents would say.

Still standing in the entrance, breathing hard, Joey snarls. Should I try to talk him down? That seems about as smart as running into a burning building. . . .

I pluck an ice cube from the beaker and toss it in my mouth, contemplating what I'd even say or do if I stepped in now. The ice crunches loudly as I chew.

Before I can make a move, Joey charges at Grandpa.

CHAPTER 36

*L*ate the next morning, soft sunbeams angle themselves through my dorm window as I hunch over my desk. I tap, tap, tap my pencil against the blank notebook page in front of me, where I had intended to start my next Integrated Humanities paper on the philosopher Albert Camus. Instead, all my thoughts are consumed with Marisol.

Yesterday, Marisol managed to stop Joey just short of punching Grandpa's lights out, then packed up her stuff and stormed out of the bar. Joey and I followed her out to the parking lot. I was allowed into her car. Joey was not—Marisol said she needed some time to think about things. After a terse ride back to the dorm, Marisol dropped me off, then sped away into the bright afternoon sunlight.

Since then, she's been unreachable: I knocked on her door.

I called her and left a couple of messages. Nothing. Jane hasn't been able to reach her either.

The phone rings now, making me jump, and I answer quickly: "Hello?"

"Gita? It's Joey."

I wrinkle my nose. "Hey."

"Hey, do you know what's going on with Marisol? I can't get ahold of her." The desperation in his voice is palpable.

"No idea, sorry." I set my pencil down. "You haven't talked to her?"

"No—she's not responding to any of my messages. I'm so worried, Gita. Do you have time to meet up? I can buy you lunch at Vinny's."

My mind whiplashes at the request. I frown. "What? Why?"

"I don't know, I just . . . I can't think straight right now. I need to talk to someone. Will you come?"

"Okaaaay," I say slowly. I have no idea how I can help him, but the poor guy's clearly in agony—the least I can do is keep him company, right? "What time?"

"An hour? I'll meet you there." He pauses. "Don't tell Marisol we're meeting, okay?"

"Wait, wha—" But the line's already dead. I stare at the phone in my hand for a moment, then slowly set it back in the cradle.

It hasn't escaped my attention that, in the span of two days, I've somehow gone from Marisol's cover and Grandpa's accomplice to Joey's confidential informant. I am deeply, *deeply* entrenched in what should just be an issue between the three of them.

Crap. I hold my head in my hands and groan.

An hour later, I'm standing on my tiptoes, scanning Vinny's for Joey as the tantalizing smells of cheese, pepperoni, and crust swirl around me.

Through the bustle of people and the din of chatter and cutlery, someone from a back table lets loose one of those loud, gross burps. My eyes home in on the source—it's Joey. The guy thumps his chest, then picks up his mug of beer and guzzles the rest. Some of the amber liquid dribbles down his chin.

My face scrunches. *Ew.* Then I remind myself that I'm not here to judge. I don't know *why* Joey has asked to meet up, but I'm determined to sit, listen, eat some pizza, and leave. Nothing more, nothing less. I pull my shoulders back and weave my way through the crowded dining area.

"Hi Joey," I say, taking a seat across from him. There's a full pitcher of beer and an empty one on the table. I rest my hands on the plastic gingham tablecloth, a layer of cleaning product residue sticking to my palms.

"Hey," Joey mumbles, staring into his beer. His eyes are red and puffy.

A server appears with an anchovy and garlic pizza. The pungent smell—like that of a Caesar salad on steroids—makes my mouth water. After the server grabs the empty pitcher and leaves, Joey points to the pizza: "Go ahead."

"Don't mind if I do." I lift a slice, and gooey cheese stretches into strings that I break with my index finger. I take a bite, then: "Wow," I murmur, mid-chew.

"No other word for it, is there?" Joey lifts the full pitcher and reaches for my clean mug. "Want?"

"No thanks." I slide my mug toward me. "I have a bunch of lab work to do after this, so I shouldn't."

Joey shrugs. "More for me." He grabs his now-empty mug and refills it, then helps himself to a slice. Awkward silence descends over us as we eat our pizza.

I glance over at the table next to us, where a white girl in a gray Stanford sweatshirt says, "Compared to high school, my memory is *so* bad now." She chomps down on a slice of cheese pizza.

A white guy in a San Francisco Giants hat sitting across from her takes a sip of beer, then leans in. "Well, you probably weren't, you know," he says, holding up his frosty mug.

"I guess," she laughs. "It's weird though."

"Yeah, I know what you mean." The guy takes a sip, then sets his beer back down. "Not only is my short-term memory terrible . . . but my short-term memory is too."

The pair crack up, and I can't help but wish I was sitting with them and their normal college good times.

Across from me, Joey pushes his glasses up his nose, then clasps his hands on the table. "S-so," he slurs. "Tell me the truth."

Here it comes. "About?" I grab another slice.

He rolls his head side to side, cracking his neck, then stills. "Is Marisol fucking that dinosaur?"

There it is. Even though I expected the anger, I almost choke on my bite of pizza. *How can he talk about his girlfriend like that?*

Coughing, I bang on my chest, convinced that my airway is blocked. A thin layer of perspiration seeps onto my forehead. "No." I finally gasp. "She isn't."

Joey scoffs. "I don't believe it."

My eyes water as I cough a few more times. I take another steadying gulp of air, then reply, "It's true, Joey. The guy's rich— he wants to help fund her nonprofit."

"Oh please." Joey rolls his eyes. "You and I both know that's not all he wants. Let's face it, she's probably already given it up."

I freeze. My heartbeat pounds in my ears. I jut my chin out and clench my fists under the table. "She's not cheating on you, Joey."

Joey chugs the rest of the beer in his mug. "She is. Bitch," he growls.

"No." My voice is strained. I push my chair back to stand. "This was a bad idea. I'll see you later."

"Wait!" Joey nearly drops his mug onto the table, and small streams of beer spill over the tablecloth. "Gita, wait."

I cross my arms. He's got less than a second to say something that will convince me to stay.

"Can you drive me home?" He reaches into his pocket, then pulls out his keys. I raise an eyebrow but don't respond.

Joey's expression softens. "Please, Gita. The last thing I need is a DUI. My job, you know."

I huff air out of my lungs. There's a moment of silence as the two us stare each other down. Finally, I throw my hands up. "Fine! Fine . . . But only because it's a safety issue."

Joey grins, then scoots his chair back. "Yes! Thank you, Gita." He wobbles a little as he stands.

Joey throws some bills down onto the table, then staggers out of Vinny's behind me. It takes him a minute to remember where he parked his Taurus.

The drive back to his place is a series of last-minute directions, with him telling me to turn just a beat too late. Each time, we have to double back around.

Ten minutes later, I pull into Joey's driveway and park. I notice that his house, and the Redwood City neighborhood where he lives, is nicer than my family's apartment in Union City, but not as posh as where Angelo lives. I shiver at the memory of Angelo, quickly brushing it off as we step out of the car.

"I'll catch a cab back to campus," I say, handing Joey his keys. I'm already scanning the street for a pay phone.

"Thanks for driving me." Joey slides his hands into his pockets and begins to turn around, then stops. "Actually, can you come inside for a minute? There's something I want to show you."

My brow furrows. "I . . . I don't know about that." I search Joey's face for anything out of the ordinary, but his expression is neutral.

"Please, Gita?" Joey presses his palms together in prayer. "I'd love your opinion on something I got Marisol. . . . And you can use my phone to call a cab!" Joey's cheeks are flushed, his words garbled slightly—whether from the beer or excitement, I'm not entirely sure.

The frustrated breath I'm about to release gets sucked back down into my lungs. Is he giving Marisol an engagement ring? *Holy . . .*

I force a smile. "Okay, fine. But let's keep it quick—I need to be at the lab soon."

Joey bobs his head. "Sure—no problem." He moves to unlock the front door, then beckons me in. "After you," he says, his voice just a little too innocent. There's something familiar about the smile that spreads across his face, something that raises goose bumps along my arms.

Gita, stop—it's just Joey. I hesitate, then take a step inside. . . .

The thud of a door shutting. The click of a lock.

I whip around and Joey's facing me, chin down, eyes narrowed. If wicked was a colored powder for Holi, it'd be the shade of his face right now—devil red.

I take a few steps back, and my spine hits the corner of the entryway. A cold draft from the ceiling fan settles over me. I look up, losing myself in the spinning blades for just a second, then slowly bring my eyes back down to Joey and raise my hands.

CHAPTER 37

Joey lunges and pins me against the wall. He clamps down on the sides of my head like a steel-jaw trap. A desperate cry starts to escape my lips, but his kiss is a forceful chup-re. He thrusts his tongue so far back into my throat that I'm scared I'll swallow it.

Everything is happening at rapid-fire speed. It feels like my heart is beyond tachycardia, beating out of my chest. I can't breathe.

Somehow, I manage to free an arm, and I slap and punch Joey's back. But the thrusting of his lips and tongue only become more forceful. My liberated arm flails and knocks a picture off the wall behind me. A second later, the sound of glass breaking shatters the air.

Joey pins my arm to the wall. The more I struggle, the angrier and stronger he becomes.

With one hand, he grips both of mine behind my back.

Then his other hand is in my pants. He shuts his eyes.

Mine are wide-open, glued to the wall directly behind him and to the right of us. It's a Marisol wall, with three of her magazine covers framed and hung in a neat row. Three Marisols smile sultrily at me while Joey sticks his fingers up my yoni.

Maybe it's the dread. Maybe it's the acceptance of things beyond my control. Either way, I stop fighting and make a wish: *Please let me be a turtle, so I can hide in my shell. Please let me be a turtle, so I can hide in my shell. Please let me—*

Joey grunts. . . .

Suddenly, the front door swings open. Marisol saunters in, wearing a black coat and high-heeled boots. "Oh Joe—" she starts to sing, swinging a six-pack of beer—what I can only assume was meant to be a peace offering. Then she sees us; her jaw drops.

Marisol goes catatonic. The six-pack lands with a loud thump on the jute braided rug at the front door. Her gaze pounces onto mine.

I can feel my eyes bulging in terror, pleading: *It's not what you think! It's not what you think, even though your boyfriend's tongue is in my mouth and his fingers are in my . . .*

Marisol's nostrils flare, and her upper lip curls. In my mind's eye, she transforms into the goddess Kali—dark blue skin, wild long black hair, bloodred eyes, four arms. All the eyeballs on the garland of human heads around her neck are glaring at me. Kali's tongue lolls. . . .

"What the fuck, Joey?" Marisol screams.

Joey freezes, unsuctions his mouth from mine, and turns his head.

I realize his body isn't crushing mine anymore. *Here's my chance!* I knee him in the balls. Joey groans, then drops to the floor, mute, holding his crotch. His face is contorted and red.

I swipe at my mouth with my sleeve and immediately start blubbering. "I-I didn't—"

"Shut UP!" Marisol shouts, her expression fiery. But a moment later, the flames in her eyes die down. "How could you?" she whimpers.

"Marisol, I didn't, I swear! He—"

"No! It's you!" she yells, the sparks rekindling. She rips the tennis bracelet off her wrist and flings it onto Joey, who's still writhing in pain. "Asshole!" She shifts her focus to me, and I scurry backward.

Marisol yanks my arm and drags me to the door. She's saying something else, but I don't hear it. All the sound has disappeared. My body goes limp, the way it's done before. An echo in the back of my mind . . .

Tame kavi rite kari sako?

Marisol pushes the lump of me out of the house, then slams the door shut behind her.

Out on the stoop, I feel myself wilting. The image of the arm holding the little white poppy in Picasso's *Guernica* comes to mind. Only this time, I am the poppy, and the bull is stomping all over me. One by one, my petals fall away. . . .

All of a sudden, I'm watching a black-and-white film behind my eyes. A little girl is lying on a bed. She can't be older than six. Zoom in: The girl is me.

A white pedestal fan in the corner, circulating hot air.

"*I want Snuffles,*" *I whimper.*

"*Chup-re,*" *Bhavin Uncle says, a sinister flicker in his eyes. He's Shere Khan and I am Mowgli, cornered in the jungle.*

I shut my mouth. He slides my underwear down.

But Mommy said that's shame-shame!.

I recoil. Bhavin Uncle holds me in place.

I want to shrink my body into itself. But I can't—I stare at the fan's blades, spinning so fast, they blur. I become a turtle. I hide in my shell.

Then, I'm not a turtle. I'm Silly Putty—pliable, yielding.

Bhavin Uncle kisses the inside of my little thigh. His mustache tickles.

But I thought kissing was only on the face!

Bhavin Uncle's mouth moves to my shame-shame.

Mom's voice echoes in my head: Shame-shame, shame-shame.

My hands tingle. I touch his oily hair, then sniff my finger. It smells faintly like gasoline.

Everything tingles, but I'm scared. I want to hug Snuffles. The spinning blades are a blur. . . .

Time jumps almost two years—I'm eight now. Once again, Bhavin Uncle has me pinned to the bed.

This time, the door opens and I turn my head to look: It's Pinky Auntie.

She shrieks: "Tame kavi rite kari sako?" How could you? *Then she charges at Bhavin Uncle.*

She pushes him off me and starts slapping him, shouting in both English and Gujarati.

Bhavin Uncle's crouched on the floor now, arms covering his head.

Pinky Auntie stops, then lays her palm on her tummy. Suddenly, she starts punching herself there. "You can't force this!" she yells, before running out of the room.

Pinky Auntie, wait! Take me with you!

But she doesn't hear me. I'm only screaming in my head.

Bhavin Uncle slowly lowers his arms. Then he turns his head to look at me, and presses his index finger to his lips.

My mind goes blank.

Then, and now.

CHAPTER 38

An outcast nomad wandering through Redwood City—that's me.

Shame-shame.

Shameless whore.

Tame kavi rite kari sako?

How could you?

Outcast.

Cast out.

But I didn't mean to—

I stop, my eyes glued to the sidewalk. My legs get wobbly; it feels like I'm melting Jell-O under the hot sun. Soon, I'll be reduced to nothing but a puddle. . . .

My eyes ascend, and I see that I'm rooted before an immense tree. My legs feel like I've walked to another state, but when I glance over my shoulder, I see that I'm only a couple houses down from Joey's.

I focus on the tree. Its gnarled branches are twisted and pointing at me—accusing me—while my arms are like vines dangling by my sides. A chilly breeze jostles my hair and carries the stink of fatty lamb cooking somewhere down the block.

Another breeze, this one bolder: A jury of a thousand leaves murmurs in deliberation. My chest gets tighter, pressure building in my forehead. I press my thumbs into my temples, massaging them in circular motions.

A car drives by, windows down, blaring the Bob Marley song "Three Little Birds." I close my eyes the way I always do when I hear this song. In my mind, forest critters lay giant fuchsia flowers redolent of jasmine at my feet. Birds tweet and sing.

I start to smile. *Maybe things will be okay. . . .*

Wait a second—why is there a tiger slinking in the background? He's not supposed to be there. . . .

My eyelids can't open fast enough. When they do, everything appears hazy.

A woman who's walking her dog on the opposite sidewalk glares at me. Her head swells and her eyes pop out.

But she's not a cartoon.

Shame-shame.

Did *she* say that?

I blink. Now she's two-dimensional. So is her dog.

This can't be real. Am I going crazy?

I lift my hands. Whose hands are these?

Not mine.

Whose body is this?

Not mine.

Who am I? Not Gita, because I'm standing behind and to the right of her. Her wingwoman. She's in danger, but the threat is inconspicuous. Can I save her?

Her heart is twitching. She's terrified. She opens her mouth to scream, but no sound comes out. She pulls her hair. Her body crumples.

I think she's trying to tell me something. I listen.

Her thoughts come to me in the voice of a frightened child: *Can I tell you a secret?*

I hesitate, then nod.

My body is a bad body that hurts people, little Gita whispers.

My face contorts. The Gita in front of me rocks back and forth, her breaths heaving in and out of her, the same heavy way she was breathing this morning after her run. *My body is bad, but I'm worse,* Gita whispers.

My eyes go wide. I shake my head. Blurry memories cut loose from their chains.

Why else would he stop giving me Chupa Chups? Gita knocks her skull with her knuckles. *I let him do those things. I didn't stop it. Pinky Auntie ran out without me. Did she think I wanted it? I did want it—that's how bad I am.* Gita pinches the back of her hand and I copy her, trying to feel her pain.

Then Gita puts her hands up—as if in surrender—and takes slow, deep breaths.

I do the same, and close my eyes.

Minutes or hours later—I've lost all track of time—I finally let my eyelids flutter open.

I'm curled into a tight ball on the sidewalk. My entire body is sore, heavy. I slowly release my knees, then shakily push myself to a stand, dust a couple of pebbles off my butt.

Everything in my line of sight is clear—a peaceful neighborhood with cute houses and neat lawns.

Everything sounds clear too—chirping birds perched in old, towering trees. A car honking faintly in the distance.

I inspect myself, pat down my body, then glance behind me. No one there. It's only me, one me. I hold my hands up in front of my eyes—they're familiar, my own. Though my head pounds, waves of relief pump through me.

But the short-lasting peace is shattered by the image of Marisol, flames of anger and betrayal flashing in her eyes.

Marisol! She trusted me, and I met Joey behind her back.

My face falls. *It was only as a friend! I was only trying to help. . . .*

What if Marisol hadn't walked in? I hope she's okay. . . .

Marisol. Poor Marisol.

Has she told Jane? My heart starts pounding in my chest again. I can't stay in the dorm tonight—I just can't.

What should I do?

Miraculously, I spot a pay phone across the street and jog over to it.

After staring at it for a second, I start digging around in my pocket for coins.

How many dirty quarters, dimes, and nickels has this pay phone collected? How many dirty, whispered secrets?

I lift the oily handset, press it to my ear, and insert a couple of coins.

I call Marisol's cell phone first—no answer. I try her dorm. No answer.

I don't leave a message. A message can't fix this.

I rest my head on the pay phone unit, not caring how gross it is. I close my eyes. Maybe I'll turn molten, my skin melding with the metal.

But that doesn't happen. I thump my forehead against the cold edge, then open my eyes and reinsert the coins, pressing the digits I know the best.

"Hi," I say when the line clicks.

"Hey, Gita," Sai says cheerfully.

My voice fractures like a clavicle when I ask, "Can you come pick me up?"

CHAPTER 39

*T*he sidewalk curb I'm sitting on becomes a boulder in my imagination. With my chin resting on one hand, I'm *The Thinker* sculpture, contemplating my own damned-to-hell fate.

The sound of a car engine roars through the still air, and I lift my head.

A rusty green Toyota pulls up—it's Sai. His brow is furrowed. He sees me and gives me an uncertain smile.

Would his smile flip if he knew what just happened?

A hollowness expands in my gut as I stand and take snail steps to the car. I lift the handle on the passenger side and the door opens, making the same old grating sound as always. I get in and slam it shut.

"Sorry to bug you on your day off," I mumble. "And for asking you to pick me up earlier than planned."

"It's okay." Sai waves off my apology. "We'll get your stuff from the dorm, then go home."

My stomach growls.

Sai chuckles. "You're in luck! Mom's making dal-bhaat-shaak-rotli for dinner tonight."

Pressure builds behind my eyes, but my lacrimal glands have suddenly run dry. I can't cry like I want to. Like I need to. All I can do is force a feeble smile.

"Why are you in Redwood City anyway?" Sai asks, with the naive nonchalance of someone who'd never consider the kind of stuff that could go down between a girl and her best friend's boyfriend.

Or between a child and the man she looked up to as an uncle . . .

"Visiting a friend," I say.

"Who?"

"Marisol." I stab at my palm with my nails.

Sai goes to shift the gear to drive, then freezes, his hand hovering over the stick shift. He glances at me: "You okay?"

I nod, but avoid his eyes. I glance at my reflection in the side mirror—I look different, even to myself.

Sai touches my shoulder. "What happened?" His voice is as delicate as the opening notes of an Indian flute.

I shift my gaze back to him for a second. His eyes are soft, beseeching.

"Gita?"

"Chup-re," I whisper, mostly to myself.

"No." Sai shakes his head. "Fuck chup-re." His tone is tight as a sitar string, his forehead crinkled with worry. He reaches out

346

again, but stops just short of my shoulder. His hand falls onto his thigh. Then, gentle as a meditation raga, he says, "Gita, it's okay. It's just me."

I chew on my lower lip. It *is* my brother. My bhai. But where do I even begin?

"Later, okay? Please." The words wheeze out of me. All of a sudden, I feel exhausted—like I could sleep for a week straight.

Sai's eyes search my face. Then he regrips the steering wheel and exhales. "Okay. Later," he agrees, and we drive away.

The next morning, it's 10:00 a.m. by the time I rouse from a fitful sleep, cracking apart my crusted-over eyelashes.

Was I crying?

A huge yawn swallows my face, spits me back out. When I go to roll over, I realize I slept on the floor—I couldn't stand to sleep in my childhood bed. Not after everything that happened there so many years ago. . . .

Did it really happen? I close my eyes, but only the image of Marisol's rage-filled face bursts forth.

Everything with Joey yesterday—*that* really happened.

I force myself to reach up for the phone on my desk, and pound out Marisol's number with my index finger. No answer. This time, I leave a message.

"Um, hi, Marisol." Pause. "I'm sorry I—" Longer pause. " . . . please call me back." I recite my home phone number for her, then hang up.

Unease roils through my body now. I get dressed and go to the kitchen, where I sit at the dining table with my head in my hands. I feel hungover from the nightmare that was yesterday.

Mom comes out of the bathroom. She hovers behind me, then strokes my hair. "Did you sleep okay, Gita?"

I shrug, avoiding her eyes.

"Are you hungry?"

Staring at the table, I nod.

"Lunch will be ready soon." Mom moves to the stove and, minutes later, the fermented aroma of dhokla floats through our apartment. My mouth waters and my stomach rumbles.

I play with my hands.

If my body responds automatically, does that mean that deep down I want it? But how can a little kid want . . . *it*? There's no way—

Crackling of mustard seeds when Mom adds them to the hot oil. Curry leaves and asafoetida next . . .

Sai sits down across from me, his expression worried. My eyes drop down to my thighs, and I slide my hands under them.

Sai exhales a heavy, minty breath. He still uses the same mouthwash as always.

Neither of us speaks, but the silence is familiar. Like we could be kids again, him doing homework while I read a book or color. Those times sitting with him were safe.

"Dad's on his way home from grocery shopping," Sai says after a while. He shifts to pull something out of his jeans pocket, then lays a blue aerogram with Indian stamps on the table in front of me. "This arrived for you yesterday morning."

I run my finger over my typed name and our address. Then I glance back at Sai, who lowers his voice.

"I think it might be from Pinky Auntie—I'm not sure. I didn't tell Mom or Dad about it." Sai props his elbows on the table and rests his chin on his interlaced fingers. He peers at me: "Aren't you going to open it?"

"I . . . I have to pee." I avoid his eyes as I get up and drag myself to the bathroom, taking the aerogram with me.

"Gita!" Sai calls out, his voice quivering this time. "What's going on?"

To my surprise, he sounds choked up. But I don't stop—I can't.

What kind of sister makes her older brother cry?

There's a bookshelf halfway down the short hall to the bathroom. I stand in front of it now, my eyes glued to the stack of old Hindu mythology comic books that I'd spent hours poring over as a kid. I stuff the aerogram in my pocket and flip through the comic book on top—*Stories of Hindu Gods & Goddesses*—and wait for the same excitement and awe to flood my senses, like when I was younger.

Nothing. I lay the comic book back down.

When I turn, the hallway in front of me transforms into a long pit of burning coal and sandalwood. In this vision, our apartment becomes the large courtyard of a Hindu temple. Heat rises from the pit—I could be Sita in the *Ramayana* or Draupadi in the *Mahabharata*. If I'm pure, I'll cross the glowing embers and come out unscathed, fresh as the Saugandhika lotus.

I take one tentative step into the fire, and ignite. Pure intentions—it seems—don't make up for actions deemed vile. Deemed vile, of course, by men with bad intentions who have done much, much worse. I imagine the ancient voices of Indian priests chanting, "*Women aren't to be trusted . . . shameless whores, all of them!*"

My imagination crosses time, space, cultures, and continents: *Angelo, Johnny Depp Boy, Steven, Javier, Jeet, Joey, Bhavin Uncle, all of them are glaring at me. In unison, they wag their fingers and declare, "Gita, the burden is on you to atone. . . ."*

A minute later, I'm in the bathroom with the door shut behind me, breathing hard. I lay the aerogram on the edge of the sink, then lift my eyes to the medicine cabinet mirror.

No fire. No burned flesh. No scene from an epic Sanskrit poem; just me in Union City. Staring at my reflection, I raise a weightless hand to my cheek—to the dark circle under my right eye, and the one under my left. I blink a few times, and the color drains from my face as a scene unfurls itself in my mind. . . .

Bhavin Uncle unlocks the front door with his key. Six-year-old me is standing in the living room, holding Snuffles. "Where is everyone?" Bhavin Uncle asks.

"At work. Pinky Auntie's sleeping," I reply.

350

A glint in his eyes. "Do you want to play a game?"

I look down to Snuffles, then back at Bhavin Uncle. I nod.

"Let's play in your room." His voice is casual.

I follow Bhavin Uncle, and he closes the door quietly behind us.

I fly Snuffles above my head as I run around the room. "Do you want to play Candy Land, Bhavin Uncle?"

Bhavin Uncle rubs his chin, as if considering. Then: "How about doctor?"

I hug Snuffles to my chest and smile. "Can I be the doctor?"

"Yes, yes." Bhavin Uncle lies down and grabs his chest, wriggling his whole body on the floor. "Doctor! My heart has stopped and I can't breathe. I need CPR!"

I giggle, staring down at my silly-looking uncle. "What's CPR?"

Bhavin Uncle stops wriggling. "You have to blow air into my mouth to save my life."

Into his mouth? Yuck! *But Mommy says I always have to listen to my aunties and uncles. . . . "Okay," I finally respond, setting Snuffles down on the bed.*

"And doctor," he whispers as I approach him, wrapping his hand around mine. "You can't tell anyone about this treatment. If you do, they'll hate you—and then they'll die. Do you promise to keep it a secret?" He winks at me.

My eyes grow wide. He and Pinky Auntie both wink at me, and make me keep their secrets.

But I nod—I don't want anyone to hate me. I don't want anyone to die. I'm a doctor: I save people. That's my job.

I sit on my knees near his head. Slowly, hesitantly, I bring my lips to Bhavin Uncle's mouth. His mustache tickles.

Then his hand is gripping the back of my head, his mouth swallowing my face. His tongue wraps itself around mine.

Is this CPR? Why is he unbuckling his pants?

Everything goes blank.

Then, and now.

CHAPTER 40

I blink, and my horrified reflection stares back at me. I grab the medicine cabinet door and throw it open: I can't stand seeing my face anymore.

My focus zeroes in on the first thing in my line of sight—a big bottle of Dad's pills. *Alprazolam 1 mg tablets. Take 1 tablet by mouth at bedtime as needed for insomnia.*

The pills rattle when I pluck the bottle off the shelf.

But for a fleeting moment, Dad's name on the worn label makes me nostalgic. My mind races through sensory-filled memories of my family: The brilliant colors of Pinky Auntie's saris and Thakorji's shelf-mandir. The smells of the masala dosa and sambar Mom always makes from scratch, no matter how many hours she just worked at Donutburg. The sound of Dad's and Neil Uncle's blended laughter over a rare joke (usually a bad one). And Sai . . . So many shared bhai and ben moments of joy, I can't even recount them all.

My eyes well up. I knead them, swallowing down the lump in my throat, then shut the medicine cabinet and lower myself onto the tub's outer ledge. I twist off the childproof cap of the bottle clenched in my hand, staring at the nest of tiny white tablets inside. It's nearly full—I guess Dad never took more than a couple.

A breeze sneaks in through the crack of the bathroom window, lifting the aerogram and gently dropping it at my feet. My brow furrows. *Who else would write to me from India besides Pinky Auntie? But it's not even my birthday. . . .*

I pause, slowly replacing the cap on the bottle. I set the bottle on the tub ledge beside me. Then I stab my fingernail into the aerogram's seam, tearing it open.

Inside the aerogram, I recognize Pinky Auntie's handwriting immediately. Even though I suspected it was from her, breath still catches in my throat. But my eyes stay sharp in their careful reading. Every one of her painstakingly etched English words reverberates through my head in a thick Gujarati accent:

Bhavin's dead. Please call me 224-9813324. Now it is safe. I'm sorry so long. Pinky Auntie.

I gasp. My fingers release the aerogram, and it floats down like a blue feather, landing on my right foot.

Dead . . . safe . . . sorry . . .

My next breath stays trapped in my chest. I force my near-paralyzed lungs to move air in and out, in and out.

A knock at the door: "Gita?" comes Sai's voice. "It's Marisol on the phone. . . ."

I wrap one hand back around the pill bottle.

Sai knocks again. "Gita?"

Like a zombie, I move from the tub to the door, opening it just a few inches and sticking my empty hand out.

I can't bear to see Sai's face right now. I can't bear for him to see mine.

Sai lays the cordless handset in my open palm, and I quickly pull my arm back and close the door.

"Hello?" I whisper, then hold my breath.

"Hey, Gita." Marisol's voice is untroubled, as if she's calling to ask about dinner plans.

Time stops for an instant.

"Gita?"

Heat blooms across my cheeks, like red marigolds in the spring. I want to say *I'm sorry for what happened with Joey.* I also want to say *You have no idea what I just found out.* But I'm silent.

"Are you there, Gita?" Marisol asks, her voice suspicious now.

I pin the phone between my shoulder and ear, setting the bottle on the edge of the sink. My fingers fall away from it like four untied ribbons at a grand reveal.

"Gita!" Marisol cries.

I clear my throat. "Yeah," I finally grunt.

"Oh my god. Sai said you were in the bathroom—are you seriously taking a shit right now?"

Her question shatters the air around me: It's gross. And blunt. And funny. And so . . . weirdly normal.

Everything is okay. I'm not in danger. I can relax. My mouth breaks into a grin, and a laugh that sounds more like a donkey bray escapes me.

"So you *are* taking a shit." I can practically hear Marisol rolling her eyes on the other end. "I'll call you ba—"

"No!" I blurt, my heart suddenly racing. I can't let her hang up the phone.

"Are you okay?"

The aerogram catches my eye from the floor. I've waited nearly a decade for some real information—any information—about how to get in touch with Pinky Auntie. Now I have it, and I don't know what to do with it.

"Gita?"

"Yeah?" I squeak.

"Joey's an asshole," Marisol mutters.

I freeze.

"Did you call the cops yet?"

I remind myself to breathe. *In, and out. In . . . and out.* "No." My voice wavers like leaves in a strong wind.

A pause. "It's not your fault," Marisol whispers.

Blinking back tears, I press my lips together and grab the bottle of pills.

It's not your fault. It's not your fault. It's not . . .

It takes everything in me, but I relax my lips and focus

on breathing slowly and steadily, while Marisol's words swirl around and around in my head.

A couple breaths later, my lips part slightly: "Marisol?"

"I'm here."

Two words. Three more unspoken, but there nonetheless: *No matter what.*

Marisol's voice is a thin veneer of superglue, holding together the jagged pieces of me.

"Jane and I get back to campus on Sunday," Marisol continues, after a quick pause. "We were thinking of ordering some Vinny's that night. You in?"

Am I?

"We've got an important agenda for our pizza meeting."

I raise an eyebrow. "Oh yeah?"

I can hear Marisol take a deep inhale on the other end. Then: "Joey hurt you. Jane and I need your help figuring out how to make his death look like an accident."

Another jagged laugh escapes me. I can picture Marisol's face on the other end—deadpan except for the right corner of her lips tugging upward.

"And as your best friends," she continues, "you know we'll help you get rid of the body."

I laugh again, louder this time. "Thanks Marisol—you have no idea how much that means to me." With a jerk, I realize I'm still holding Dad's pill bottle. I quickly return it to its rightful place back in the medicine cabinet.

I don't need what's inside that bottle. I'm not alone with any of this—not the way I was as a child.

I clear my throat. "Marisol . . ." I begin. "I have things to tell you and Jane."

CHAPTER 41

*D*ays later, my girls and I lumber out of the library, finally done with seven straight hours of studying for finals. The sunshine belies a cold December gust that lashes at us. But the three of us are unfazed—I don't even bother zipping up my jacket.

We stop and sit on the stone bench surrounding the circular fountain out front, beckoned by the rainbow lights flashing off the sunlight-kissed cascading water. I remember similar rainbow lights once flashing from Pinky Auntie's dangling diamond earrings as she stood outside our Union City apartment. . . .

I touch my ear, wondering if my aunt still has those earrings. *What will Pinky Auntie say when I finally call her?* After ten years, I figured I wouldn't wait a single second to get ahold of her if I knew how. But here I am, still thinking it over.

Sunbeams are stretching their gilded arms and draping themselves over our shoulders, like sheer gold shawls.

Marisol sighs, and Jane and I glance at her.

"I swear I spent most of the time in there zoning out," she says.

"Bummer." I frown. "I'm sorry."

"Are you extra tired or something?" Jane asks.

"It's not that." Marisol squints at a pebble near her foot. "I was so wrong," she mumbles.

"About what?" A second, biting gust of wind blows hair into my face, and I push strands of it out of my eyes.

"Blaming you when I walked into Joey's place . . ." Marisol's voice falters for a second, and something in my stomach lurches.

"Don't worry, Marisol," I say automatically, then stop to think it through.

Sunday night, when the three of us got back to the dorm and split a Vinny's pie, neither Marisol nor I brought up Joey, or anything else serious, for that matter. Maybe we both felt too raw after everything that went down. But now Marisol's bringing it up. And if she's brave enough to talk about it, then—I decide—the least I can do is meet her halfway. "We're past that already," I finally add.

"I kept flirting with other guys," Marisol continues, as if she didn't hear me. "Even though I knew Joey didn't like it. I took things too far at the bar. . . . You tried to tell me, Gita, but I didn't listen. I hurt Joey . . . and then he turned around and hurt you." Marisol's voice breaks.

I'm shaking my head vehemently before she can even finish

her sentence. "Only Joey is to blame for his actions. It's not your fault, Marisol."

Marisol sniffs, then closes her eyes. "You're so fast to forgive, Gita," she whispers. After a long moment, she opens her eyes again, and the tears are gone. She kicks the pebble, watching as it bounces away from us. "Even when I wasn't."

I rest my elbow on her shoulder and try to catch her eye. "It's okay, Marisol, really. We're good."

"Well, I hope Joey's *not* good." Jane crosses her arms. "Why does he get to be invisible after all of this?"

Marisol pivots her body to face me. Her voice is no-nonsense when she asks, "Speaking of which—are you ready to report him yet, Gita?"

"No . . ." I say sheepishly.

"Why n—?" Marisol stops herself. She inhales, holding her breath for a moment. "Okay." She exhales, wraps her arms around herself, and nods. "Only when you're ready, Gita." She bumps my knee gently with hers. "There were things you wanted to tell us first, right?"

I freeze, then force a nod.

"What kind of things?" Jane asks.

Hot panic sizzles my brain like an egg in a frying pan. I feel myself chickening out: "It can wait until after finals. I don't want to bug you guys about it now. . . ."

"Bug me! Please bug me, put me out of my finals misery!" Jane begs, clasping her hands.

I chuckle, but there's an old, familiar swirl in my head: *Shame-shame . . . How could I? . . .*

No, I say firmly to the thoughts in my head. *We're not doing that again.*

What if, instead of being told to chup-re, to listen to my elders, I had been taught how to speak up? What if Pinky Auntie had told my parents about what she'd seen Bhavin Uncle doing to me? Or—even before it reached that point—what if she had told someone what Bhavin Uncle was doing to *her?*

I feel Jane's and Marisol's warm gaze on me, and let myself bask in it. Something tells me my girls would say that *none* of what happened to me back then was my fault—so maybe I should start believing it.

Tears spill from my eyes, and I pry my lips apart: "When I was a kid, my uncle's friend . . ."

My girls exchange concerned glances, then scoot closer to me.

Jane takes my hand, and Marisol wraps an arm around my back.

"It's okay, Gita. Take your time," Marisol says quietly.

The three of us huddle together on the bench, listening to the sweet sound of falling water while tears dribble down my cheeks.

When it finally feels like I'm done crying, I sweep my hand over my face and take a deep inhale. *I will tell my girls. And later today, when I see Sora and Hector, I'll tell them too.*

It's time to kick chup-re to the curb, once and for all.

"My . . . my uncle's friend did things to me. He . . . *made* me do things to him. He died recently." I exhale shakily.

"Oh, Gita," Jane says, giving my hand a good squeeze. "He hurt you."

I tuck my chin into my chest.

"He can't hurt you anymore," Marisol replies, tightening her arm around me.

I squeeze Jane's hand, lay my head on Marisol's shoulder. "He . . . made me promise to keep it a secret. He said if I told anyone that they'd hate me and . . . and they'd die," I whimper.

After a long, drawn-out beat of silence, Jane finally speaks: "I'm so glad you told us, Gita. He was wrong. We don't hate you. Nothing bad is going to happen to us just because you told the truth."

I rub my nose, nodding. Tears start rolling down my face again, but I force the words out: "But back then . . . I mean, I was only six. How was I supposed to know he was bluffing?"

"You weren't. You were a *child*." Fury lines Marisol's face, but I know it's on my behalf—on little Gita's behalf.

I lift my gaze, staring at the sharp, bright rays diving off the sun.

My girls hug me, and after a moment, I hug them back.

CHAPTER 42

In the quiet of my family's apartment, I remain curled in a tight ball on the sofa. It's late on a Friday afternoon, and no one else is home yet. I should be back at the dorm studying—finals begin on Monday. But instead, I hopped on a bus to Union City, and now here I am.

After recounting everything to my girls—and Sora and Hector—I've barely been able to grip my pencil or flip a page in my notebook. Angry waves keep battering the shores of my cranium. This time, though, the waves are less *shame-shame* and *I hate myself,* and more *shame on you* and *I hate everyone.*

Except for my friends, of course—and Sai.

I stab at Pinky Auntie's aerogram on the cushion next to me with my finger. It's so much more than a thin sheet of folded blue paper, isn't it?

A piercing pain lashes inside my chest: I still haven't called

Pinky Auntie. But do I even want to? What could she possibly say after all this time that would make me want to forgive her, let alone give her a second chance?

The groan of the front door opening—I grab the aerogram and dart to the bathroom before anyone sees me. When laughter from the outer hallway reaches my ears, I peek out.

Dad enters the apartment first. His uniform has an oil stain on the front and lower center like a big belly button. He waves his hand, punctuating every word he says in Gujarati. "But of course India is the greatest country in the world. And Hinduism is the best religion, bhus."

I click my tongue. Sai and I have heard Dad spout the same old nationalist rhetoric time and again. In the past, I'd chup-re my retort—*If India is so great, then why did you move here?*—and tune him out.

Sai tips his head side to side like a bobblehead doll, steeping his English in a thick Gujju accent. "Yes, and let's not forget that Jesus and the Buddha were Hindus originally."

I quietly snicker—Dad did actually say that once. Come to think of it, it's like my parents have shared amnesia when it comes to their unwavering belief in Hinduism and India—it makes them forget that Hindus, like anyone else in the world, are capable of doing bad things too.

"Yaar," Mom says, her tone frustrated, motioning for them to take their shoes off. Then Mom and Dad collapse on the sofa while Sai goes to the kitchen. Mom massages her knee and Dad makes circles with his shoulder. They appear to be more skin and bones than usual. There's also more gray in Mom's frizzy hair and Dad's chin stubble.

My eyes get watery at the thought of their long hours, day in and day out. I start to tell myself to suck it up and knock it off with my defiance.

No! I'm trying to change my life for the better. Their struggles don't negate my own.

I rub my eyes dry, reassuring myself that I don't always have to put their troubles before mine. In the living room, Sai returns with a tray of limbu nu paani and leftover patra. He sets the tray down on the coffee table.

I used to do that. I think about the first time I served them the refreshments, when I was six. I'd waited up for Mom and Dad because I wanted to know why Bhavin Uncle's finger was so naughty with Pinky Auntie. Why did it graze her bare midriff under her pretty gold sari, the one with intricate paisley designs? Red roses had bloomed on Pinky Auntie's cheeks, her eyes nearly popping out of her head like Bugs Bunny.

I remember wanting to protect my aunt, to yell at Bhavin Uncle. But all I could do was chup-re myself: Even if I did protect Pinky Auntie, who would protect me? Because Bhavin Uncle's naughty finger touched *me* sometimes too.

Shame-shame had reverberated around my head like a death knell.

366

Later that night, after my parents had had a few sips of the cool lemon water, I tried again. I'd opened my mouth. "Why did Bhavin Uncle—"

"Not now, Gita," Dad sighed.

"Go to bed," Mom said.

"But—" I began.

"Chup-re," they responded, voices weary.

Twelve years later, and Mom's winding her hair into a bun. She pours herself some lemon water and sips it loudly. Dad takes a patra, chews it violently, and swallows.

I gulp down a breath that feels like broken glass.

The phone rings, and Sai answers. "Hello?" Pause. "Hi, Shilpa Auntie. How are you?"

Another pause. "I'm fine. Here's Mom."

Mom takes the handset. "Jai Shri Krishna. Bhol." Long pause, interspersed with many "Huh-uhs" from Mom. "Chaal, saras. Okay. Jai Shri Krishna." Mom clicks the off button and sets the handset on the coffee table.

Jai Shri Krishna–Jai Shri Krishna echoes in my head, only it's in Mom's *shame-shame* voice. Something inside me snaps. I want to scream: *How can you hide behind your war chant while Bhavin Uncle—*

Before I can think about it, my feet are marching me into the living room. Sai spots me first. "Gita!" He's startled, but an unfettered grin quickly soars across his face. He moves in for a hug.

"Hi, Sai bhai." I force calm into my tone as he wraps his arms around me.

"It's nice to see you, beta." Mom downs the rest of her lemon water.

"How are your studies?" Dad asks without looking at me, popping the last bite of patra into his mouth and reaching for the TV remote. Neither he nor Mom seem particularly surprised to see me—I assume they're too exhausted to care.

"Good," I say.

Dad turns on the TV. *Is he even listening?*

"How was the shop?" I ask, doing my best to keep the frustration at bay.

"Busy," Dad says. He takes a quick sip of the lemon water, then holds out the stainless steel cup. He turns to me and wags his finger. "You were home but you didn't prepare the limbu nu paani? You made your elder brother prepare?" He turns back to the TV and changes the channel.

"Don't forget, you'll have to do this for your husband when *he* comes home from work," Mom adds.

You don't know what I've had to do. What I've done. And he wasn't my husband—none of them were.

The image of a big rig about to career off a cliff comes to mind.

It's now or never, Gita.

I clear my throat, then hold the aerogram out in front of me. "This is from—"

"Pinky!" Mom exclaims. She gets up, lunging for the aerogram.

I pull my arm back, quickly stuffing it into my pocket. "She sent it to me."

Mom holds out her hand "Give it to me, Gita!" she barks.

I jump back.

"Listen to your mother, Gita!" Dad commands, shooting up to a stand and taking a step toward me.

"Leave her al—" Sai starts, at the same time that I say "No. I—"

"Chup—" Dad snaps, but I get in his face and cut him off.

"Why are you always *so fast* to shut me up?!" My voice shakes. My eyes burn. "And not just about Pinky Auntie. About everything!"

Dad thrusts his jaw out, moving it side to side. His knuckles are turning white with how hard he's clenching his fists, but he doesn't respond.

Did my words chup-re *him*?

In the silence that blankets us, I swear I can hear his heart pounding furiously. But this time, I'm not afraid of him. I've been through worse.

Mom punches her thigh, muttering, "Ah, chokri. So long we've waited to hear from Pinky and now you won't share? Selfish chokri . . ."

I ignore her, pluck the aerogram out again, and wave it around. "'Chup-re, chup-re, chup-re!' That's all you'd ever say! Do you know just how much I've put up with because of that?!"

Dad stares open-mouthed at me. Mom grips his arm, as if trying to stop herself from charging at me.

"Do you?!" I yell.

Neither of them says anything. Of course they don't—they can't. They're clueless.

I unfold the aerogram and jab at its contents. "Pinky Auntie says Bhavin Unc—" I catch myself, then start again. "Bhavin is dead. You wouldn't give me the full story of why Pinky Auntie and Neil Uncle left; I've had to piece it together from random memories. And she didn't try to talk to me—to us—until now. Just another way to shut me up." I crumple the aerogram between my hands, then throw it to the floor.

"Well, I'm *done* shutting up! Bhavin hurt Pinky Auntie—I saw it. You know what else? Bhavin hurt *me,* and Pinky Auntie knew about it. I just shut up and let Bhavin do bad things to me. Not just once—many, *many* times."

The ticking hand of the living room clock slows down.

Sai's hand floats to his mouth to catch a gasp.

Mom's eyes widen as she bites her knuckles.

Dad backs away, lowering himself onto the sofa.

Seconds go by before the sound of the clock finally breaks through the white noise in my head.

I burst into tears and run to my bedroom.

Minutes later, I'm lying face down on my stomach as far away from my bed as possible. My tears have eased up, and I'm listening to plump raindrops splat against my window. A cleanse for Union City. *But Union City isn't the dirty one. . . .*

I used to think I was the dirty one. But no—it's Bhavin. He knew exactly what he was doing. He knew it was wrong—which is why he needed to keep it a secret. Why he needed *me* to keep it a secret.

He knew it was wrong, but he did it anyway. In his eyes, I wasn't a child. I wasn't even a human. I was his . . . his . . .

I was his.

I learned how to always be "his," no matter the guy.

"Gita?"

Dad's voice. Only it's calm, like the eye of the hurricane.

I roll onto my side and face the wall with the window. A sunbeam slices through the drizzle.

"Gita . . ."

Sai's voice this time.

Slowly, I flip to my other side, and see my family standing in the doorway—Sai, Dad, and Mom.

Mom walks over and squats next to me, her eyes shiny. She reaches out with trembling hands to lift one of mine, then bows her head so her forehead rests on my knuckles. Her tears drip down my fingers.

Dad positions himself near my feet. "Tell us everything that happened, Gita. We want to know." His voice shakes.

Sai kneels on the floor between Mom and Dad. The three of them stay like that and wait.

I exhale a soft breath. "I . . . I don't know where to begin." I stare at the particles floating in the air. "I needed you like this, back then. . . . How could you not see what was happening? In your own home, right in front of you." I stop as Mom grabs on to Sai's shoulder and thumps her head against it, sobbing.

"We should've seen it," Dad says, wiping his eyes.

"Why didn't you?" I ask.

Dad can't look at me as he shakes his head.

After a minute, Mom finally lets go of Sai's shoulder and rubs her eyes. She bends forward, kisses my head, and whimpers, "It's my fault. What kind of mother—?" But she can't finish. She breaks down again, this time pressing her face into my arm, the long sleeve of my shirt soaking up her fresh tears.

My first instinct is to comfort her, but something stops me. While seeing her pain like this is torturous, it strikes me that maybe—just maybe—she's beginning to understand how awful things were for me back then.

Dad reaches over slowly and squeezes my foot. "Tell us what happened, Gita beta—please." This last word comes out of him in a whisper.

I look at Sai. He scrubs his face with his palms, then gives me a tiny, encouraging smile. I sit up and drop my eyes to the floor. Then I open my mouth, and the truth trickles out.

As I talk, Sai begins to pace, his previously tender expression turning to rage. "If Bhavin wasn't already dead, I'd kill him," Sai mumbles. He paces faster, wringing his hands.

"Why oh why didn't Pinky tell us?" Mom strokes my cheek, her face contorted with shock.

Dad opens his mouth to say something, then chokes up. It takes him two more tries before he finally manages to utter "I'm sorry, beta."

Three small words—just three. Yet they pack the same amount of weight that *chup-re, Gita* used to.

I shed a few unearthed tears, tears that little Gita buried years ago.

Sai stops pacing and plops down next to me. He puts his hand on my shoulder and says, "He broke you. . . . That's why you want to fix people, isn't it?"

I stare at Sai's hand on my shoulder for a second, then at him. I'd never thought of it so simply, but that feels exactly right. I nod.

Crying quietly, I remain motionless, letting my family protect me and love me the way they can. The way I wish they would've a long time ago.

CHAPTER 43

It's the Sunday after finals are over, and I'm home for winter break. Shortly after I wake up, Mom invites me into the kitchen. I find myself standing sullen in the corner, arms crossed, the way I often did as a kid the first few months after Pinky Auntie left.

Back then, Mom would sometimes caress my cheek in an understanding way. More often, she'd click her tongue and mutter, "Ah suu che? Modhu uthreli kadhi ni gem." Translation: "What's this? Your face is like spoiled yogurt and gram gravy."

Today, she does neither. Today, she gives me a consoling smile and a gentle arm squeeze. Then she squats, opens the cabinet, and brings out one of her shiny, stainless steel masala dabbas. She places it on the counter and removes the lid to reveal seven small stainless steel containers inside. Six in a circle and one in the center, each holding a different colored spice and miniature spoon: cloves, ginger, cinnamon, cardamom, nutmeg, black pepper, and brown pepper.

"This cha recipe was passed down from your great-grandmother to Ba to me, and now to you. It's the blend of all these spices that makes the cha incredible." She wags a finger at me. "Don't leave any of them out," she warns, but there's a playful lilt to her voice.

I stare at her. Mom used to make cha for Sai. Never for me. And now she wants to teach me how to make it? Still, it's sweet. . . . My emotions seesaw.

Mom points to the basket on my right. "Pass me the ginger." She takes the gnarled stem from me and starts peeling it. "Don't use the ginger powder, only fresh. The healing properties are similar, but fresh is always better." She grates the fresh ginger straight into a pot, then tosses her chin toward the canister on the counter. "Measure out five tablespoons of those tea leaves."

Mom pours milk into the pot as I measure, then spoons in the rest of the spices. I throw in the tea leaves, and Mom sets the burner on low to get a slow boil going.

I drop my arms and stand there, fidgeting and watching the milk turn a deep caramel color. As I lean in to sniff the warm scents of my heritage, it occurs to me that Pinky Auntie would have loved to be here with us right now, telling us stories as we prepare tea.

Mom stirs the cha with a wooden spoon, before closing

her eyes and deeply inhaling. "Ahhh." She opens her eyes and looks at me. "This smell takes me back to my childhood—our little place. My mom stirring, my aunties squatting next to her around the single burner." Her face grows somber. "Me hiding in the corner. My father—when he wasn't drunk—waiting for teatime outside."

Before I can respond, Mom shakes her head, as if freeing herself from the bad parts of the memory. She turns off the stove, then strains the cha into two mugs. The sound of the thick liquid pouring rolls into my ears like a tranquil waterfall. I blink.

"Here," Mom says, offering me a mug.

"Thank you." I wrap my hands around the warm ceramic, and we sit together at the dining table.

On the wall calender behind Mom's head, there's a painting of Devaki staring lovingly at her child Krishna. My gaze drops to Mom, who has a similar look in her eyes as she watches me. I smile at her, and she smiles back.

The cha's complex masala fragrance dances up between us in warm wisps. We breathe it in, the steam kissing our faces with a million tiny lips.

"Drink up, beta," Mom says.

I blow on the cha and take a loud, drawn-out sip.

Mom does the same. Then: "Cha swadist che?"

I cradle the mug to my chest, nodding. "It's delicious. I love it."

But even more than that, I love that Mom's with me in this moment. Really with me.

That night, Mom, Dad, Sai, and I sit around the coffee table in peaceful silence. It's a silence that's a choice, though, not the aftermath of chup-re. A silence that feels like a promise.

We haven't sat like this since my sixth birthday. That night, I got two gifts: First, the new Star Wars LEGO set I'd been begging for ever since I saw the movie. Second, Pinky Auntie and Neil Uncle moving in with us.

That night, we enjoyed slices of my Baskin-Robbins chocolate ice cream cake as they told us about their trip. It took almost two full days and four plane rides to get from Gujarat to Union City. I'd run to my room to get my folded *National Geographic* world map, so I could trace the route they took from Ahmedabad to Bombay, London, New York, and San Francisco.

Today isn't my birthday. Pinky Auntie and Neil Uncle are no longer here. But the vibe is just as relaxed, our bellies just as full after one of Mom's Gujju feasts—fafda, oondhiya, rotli, dhal, and bhaat. The four of us go for occasional pinches of the after-dinner mukhwas in a stainless steel bowl on the coffee table. Sai hunches over the bowl of colorful seeds and nuts, carefully picking out the pink sugar-coated fennel, the same way he did that night twelve years ago.

Some things never change.

But my parents closed the shop today to be with me.

Some things do change.

My eyes drill into the crinkled aerogram on the coffee table, which one of my family members must have picked up off the floor and smoothed out. It's finally time, I decide, to make the call.

Some things are about to change.

Mom's sitting next to me on the sofa. She lifts her bony hand to tuck a lock of hair behind my ear. Her calloused fingers graze my neck and linger there.

Something shifts in my heart, like soft clouds on the dawn horizon. The sun peeks out. . . .

I tilt my head. Mom's face, drained of desperate Gujju parental duty, is tender.

"You know, Gita, Donutburg has been doing well lately. We've been saving up for you."

Oh no. Here it comes: dowry BS. My shoulders pull up all the way to my ears as I cringe. I turn my body toward the door, the hope that had just hung suspended in the air now floating away from me like a balloon.

"Gita!" Mom yells. "Wh—" But this time she stops herself, raises her hands, and exhales. Then, gently, she grasps my chin. "Beta, look at me."

I don't want to, but I do.

"The money is for your medical school," Mom says, smiling.

My mouth makes a small O, one that grows larger and larger.

Then my arms flail up. I fling them around Mom and hug her. "Not for shaadi?" I ask excitedly.

Mom hugs me back. "No, not for shaadi."

Dad sighs. "All those years ago, Pinky was right. Your studies come first." He shifts in his seat, clearing his throat. "You wanted to know the truth about why she and Neil left. Pinky will tell you herself now." He pauses, pressing the tips of his fingers and thumbs together. "All these years, Mom and I didn't tell you or Sai because we . . . we thought we were protecting you."

"But you didn't," I say simply.

"Chup—" Dad starts, then cuts himself off. He takes a deep breath and releases it slowly, his expression softening. "I'm sorry, beta. I regret the day we gave Bhavin a key to come and go as he pleased."

I'm tempted to leave it at that, to let silence take over the room again. But if Dad's not going to tell me to chup-re, then neither will I. "Didn't you think it was weird that he even wanted a key?" I persist.

Dad stares at the floor. "Bhavin was Neil's friend, and Neil said he was between apartments, then having a hard time living alone. We trusted him. . . . But we shouldn't have." He forks his fingers through his thinning hair. "We made mistakes, Gita. Big ones."

Will Pinky Auntie admit that she made some too?

A flash in my mind: Pinky Auntie pulling me in for a hug, the sound of her bangles tinkling together as sweet as her laughter.

379

"I miss her so much," I whisper.

Dad finally meets my eyes. "I know," he says, glancing at Mom. "I miss her too."

Sai frowns. "Why didn't she tell you guys what that asshole did to Gita?"

"I don't know," Mom murmurs, shaking her head. "I just . . . don't know."

In the brief silence that ensues, Dad reaches across Mom's lap to touch my arm. Then he gets up, goes to the kitchen, and comes back with the cordless phone.

"It's time, no?" He hands it to me. "Now Pinky can tell you everything herself."

I take a deep breath, grip the phone tightly, and nod. Mom squeezes my other hand.

Sai picks up the aerogram and opens it. "Ready?" He asks.

For just a second, my fingers trace the buttons to 9-1-1. Then I stop myself, exhale, and dial the US exit code, followed by the Indian country code. I look over at Sai. "Ready," I say.

Sai reads Pinky Auntie's number aloud while I tap the corresponding digits. I bring the phone to my ear: "It's ringing."

My parents and Sai lean in, and the four of us grasp each other's hands.

"Hello?" Pinky Auntie answers.

CHAPTER 44

Four days before Christmas, my girls are walking me to my gate at San Francisco International Airport. The midday light, amplified by the multitude of windows, warms and energizes my spirit, as if I'm in a greenhouse for my soul.

Halfway down the concourse, I do a double take at a large foam board panel on the wall beside us. It's a *Vogue* ad with Marisol in a black strapless gown, the half-moon of her birthmark front and center.

"Oh my gosh, Marisol!" I point to it. "You didn't tell us you did that!"

"Wow—it's beautiful," Jane says, reaching out to touch the bottom corner of the panel.

"Thanks." Marisol beams. "Believe it or not, it was my idea."

"I believe it!" I blurt, and Marisol giggles.

"I'm so proud of you, Marisol," Jane adds, a triumphant glint in her eyes. "That was a huge step forward."

"For you, *and* for the industry." I nod and grin at Marisol.

"It's a start." Marisol shrugs nonchalantly, but her face is lit up in a way I've never seen from her before.

After another minute, the three of us turn, link arms, and make our way to my gate. It's packed, full of other groups of family and friends talking and laughing, crying and hugging. After squeezing through the crowd, my girls and I finally find a spot in front of a large window overlooking the tarmac.

"Got your passport?" Jane asks.

I nod, wondering if I'll get a passport stamp at each layover. It turns out that my first-ever plane ride—paid for by Pinky Auntie!—consists of not one, not two, but *four* flights: San Francisco to Seoul, Seoul to Bombay, Bombay to New Delhi, and New Delhi to Bagdogra, West Bengal.

Just then, Jane's cell phone rings. She plucks it out of her purse. "Hello?" she answers, followed by a long pause with eye-rolling and head-shaking. Her voice is monotone when she eventually says, "Tell him I can't."

Jane ends the call and stares at the phone in her hand for a second before dropping it back into her purse. "That was my dad's secretary. Apparently, he flew into San Francisco this morning and wants to take me to lunch in half an hour." She shakes her head. "It's not happening. Until he learns how to respect my time, he's not getting any of it."

"That's what I'm talking about!" Marisol high-fives Jane, who smiles.

While Jane seems fine, I still decide to ask, "Are you okay?"

"Better than ever," she replies immediately, with a lighthouse smile.

The three of us turn our gaze out the window and study the long baggage cart on the ground below us. One of the ground crew wiggles it toward the plane, like a centipede toward a huge metal bird.

Marisol sighs. "I'm jealous. Never been to India."

"Jealous, ha!" Jane exclaims. "Says the girl who's flown first class to Paris, Rome, London, Tokyo . . . plus wherever else I'm forgetting."

"Job hazard, huh?" I laugh.

Marisol smiles, and then her eyes go shiny. My girls move a little closer to me, so that our shoulders almost touch, while the workers below continue to load baggage into the plane's underbelly. The midday light outside is picture-perfect: I imagine standing at the edge of a flower-filled valley with a few dirt paths stretching out before me. The brilliant sun overhead shines down on the trail directly in front of me. . . .

The gate attendant announces that we're about to start boarding.

I dig out my headphones and Walkman—which already has TLC's *Ooooooohhh . . . On the TLC Tip* CD in it—from my backpack, then turn to my friends.

"The *second* you get back, Jane and I are driving your ass straight to Vinny's. We want to hear about *everything*," Marisol says.

"Perfect." I shoot them a lighthouse smile.

We hug it out, and then I get in the line to board. As I watch the two of them walk away, disappearing into the sea of people behind me, I flip my hat to the back, put on my headphones, and skip to the song "Hat 2 da Back." There's a new depth to me, I decide, one that just *gets* these empowering TLC lyrics about being a hat-2-da-back kind of girl.

Because that's the kind of girl I am.

CHAPTER 45

As we bump along the narrow, winding West Bengal road in an old SUV, Mr. Das—the driver I hired on Pinky Auntie's recommendation—adjusts his grip on the steering wheel. Though Pinky Auntie assured me of Mr. Das's trustworthiness, I keep peeking at him from the back seat, my left hand hovering over the door handle. This is my first time in India, and I'm riding alone with a stranger. A stranger who's a man.

Am I just being paranoid? I ask myself.

I take a second to listen to my gut: It's quiet.

Not paranoid, I decide. Just . . . careful. As long as my gut isn't screaming at me to leap out of the car, I should be all right.

The next time I glance at Mr. Das, there's a peaceful smile creasing his wizened face. I inspect the grass hat on his head—it looks handmade.

So far, everything feels *okay.*

I let myself look away for a longer moment this time, indulging my eyes with the gorgeous view outside.

We pass occasional cars and small trucks, but otherwise, the road is empty. Ahead of us, thick morning fog slowly lifts like a heavy curtain, unveiling lush green hillsides.

When we round the next curve, tall grasses lining the steep roadside slope sway in the breeze. I catch Mr. Das's eyes in the rearview mirror: "Sir, would you mind turning off the AC for some fresh air instead?" I ask it in English, because he doesn't speak Gujarati and I don't speak Bengali or Hindi.

"Yes, ma'am." Mr. Das turns the knob to off.

"Thank you." I roll down my window, and so does he. The cool air and smell of pine bathing in fresh sunlight is rejuvenating after my long trip across oceans and continents.

Finally, I begin to relax.

The minutes and miles pass. At some point, Mr. Das slows down to let a wild dog cross the road. Birdsong flutters in from the lower branches of a towering cypress to my right. I'm about to ask if we can make a pit stop so I can stretch my legs, but Mr. Das is already stepping on the gas.

As we trundle along, my thoughts rewind to the start of my freshman year at Stanford. It was only three and a half months ago that chup-re sanctioned both terrible secrets I didn't know I had, and new ones I created.

Re-created?

The colossal hills in the distance snag my attention again. I picture a dirty, sweaty Sisyphus pushing a boulder up the tallest one, keeping on despite his grim fate.

The SUV's wheels hit a stretch of potholes. My heart thumps, my bones rattle, and the hills outside my window appear to vibrate. Mr. Das steers the SUV to hug a set of curves, and I stick my hand out of the window in an attempt to distract myself.

I cross my fingers out the window, watching the sunlight paint them gold. Here's hoping that the next four months, four years, four decades will be different—starting with this four-week winter break in Kalimpong.

I already feel worlds apart from all the studying that ended less than a week ago, with the last of my finals. I touch my collarbone—I also feel worlds apart from the drinking. From the fucking.

My eyelids dip. My shoulders sag.

How could I?

The cows grazing on the next slope morph into monstrous meat eaters before my eyes, munching away at my heart.

How could I?

I sit up straight, frowning. *It wasn't my fault. Bhavin should've only been playing Candy Land with me.*

I think about my phone calls with Pinky Auntie: The first from our living room, when my parents, Sai, and I all spoke to her. The second from my bedroom, just her and me.

Pinky Auntie's words from that second call float through my head.

Balātkāra. Rape.

She confirmed my memories: It wasn't an affair like Neil Uncle thought. Bhavin raped her. She didn't tell Neil Uncle, or anyone else. A few weeks before they all moved back to India, she discovered she was carrying Bhavin's child. And Neil Uncle, just like he said he would, left her as soon as they landed in Ahmedabad.

"But why didn't you tell anyone what Bhavin did to you . . . or to me? Why did you go live with him?" I asked over the phone.

Dhamakī. Threaten.

"I didn't have a choice, Gita. He didn't give me a choice." Pinky Auntie's voice is softer than I remember it being, raspier. "He was waiting for me at the Ahmedabad airport. I had no money on me, no access to my bank accounts, nothing except the clothes in my suitcase. We boarded the next train headed east." Pinky Auntie paused, sniffed. Then: "Gita beta . . . I was going to tell your parents everything, I promise. But Bhavin . . . he vowed to kill you if I did. And later, after Asha was born . . . Well, then he vowed to kill her. I believed him—you have no idea what he was like, Gita."

A tendril of anger rose, serpent-like, within me. How could Pinky Auntie—of all people—tell *me* I had no idea what Bhavin was like? Then, another flash of memory: *Bhavin choking Pinky Auntie . . . She's wheezing, her eyes are bulging . . . A warm trickle down my legs.*

Mr. Das swerves to avoid a pack of dogs. My fingers freeze, my mind goes blank, and my throat begins to close. . . .

I blink rapidly, squeeze the seat belt across my chest. *Bhavin died a month ago in a car accident,* I remind myself. *Pinky Auntie and I are safe.* I have to repeat this at least ten times over and over again, slowly, before I can breathe easily.

Pinky Auntie wanted to come to me to explain everything face-to-face, but that was impossible.

Pathārīvaśa. Bedridden.

When Pinky Auntie had Asha, I learned, serious delivery complications left her paralyzed from the waist down.

Ēkalā. Alone.

She and I still feel like that sometimes, we admitted, even though she has Asha now, and I've got my friends and family. Maybe Pinky Auntie and I will have each other again too. . . . But there's still a part of me that's mad at her, even now that I know her side of the story.

Forgive, not forget.

Will I be able to give her a second chance?

My eyes go slick, and I rub at them.

Mr. Das glances at me in the rearview mirror.

"Miss," he says kindly. "You must go to Deolo Hill on a clear day. The view of Mount Kanchenjunga from there is first class."

"I will," I say through the tears, with a tentative smile. "Thank you," I add.

We pass by the fourth Gorkhaland protest sign in half an

hour. My hand balls up: I imagine pumping my raised fist out the window in solidarity with the Nepali-speaking Gorkha people's resistance. But just as quickly as I think it, my fingers fall away from my palm.

Why didn't I resist Bhavin?

Because he had said "Chup-re."

Because he'd made me promise to keep it a secret.

Because I was a child, and my parents had taught me to obey elders.

Bhavin taught me I was nothing but his . . . No, scratch that.

Bhavin taught me I was nothing, *period.*

This is how it is for me now, no matter how hard I try otherwise: A constant rewind and replay of what Bhavin did and how it all turned out, sometimes with a bit more understanding. But understanding doesn't always make me feel better. Not yet, anyway.

I gaze at the terraced cottages and cacti growing out of the sleepy hillside. Jane's voice echoes inside my skull: *I need to ride out the night.*

Maybe I have no choice but to ride out this torturous process of rewind and replay. If I was doomed to the same fate as Sisyphus, I ponder, maybe this—the remembering, over and over again—would be my boulder.

But boulders wear down, I remind myself. They don't loom large forever—and neither will this.

By the time we arrive at Pinky Auntie's address, it's late afternoon.

I pay and tip Mr. Das, thanking him again. He turns the SUV around and drives away. I'm alone now.

I stand still, attempting to absorb all the beauty around me: The wide river below and the hills on the opposite side of the valley stretch for miles. Wildflowers blanket the slopes behind me. A breeze whispers; I pretend it's uttering a resounding *Om*.

I'm alone, but not lonely.

When it feels right, I head down the narrow dirt road that's too narrow for SUVs. The wheels of my suitcase bump over pebbles. I count the dense trees on both sides, finally stopping at fifteen. I let my mind be still.

At the dead end, there's a small A-frame house with one pink wall and one orange one. Pastel flowers in identical clay pots line the four steps to the door. Tattered prayer flags strung between two pine trees flap in a sudden gust.

I reach the front door—maroon with an iron handle and metalwork—and knock.

A young girl with two jet-black, folded Indian schoolgirl braids answers. Breath catches in my throat. Her eyes: Pinky Auntie's.

A beat of silence. Finally, in Gujarati, I say, "Hi Asha, I'm Gita."

Asha nods. "Come in," she says. Her voice is small, fragile, her eyes serious.

I start to follow her, then stop and hold up a finger. "Wait—"
I swing my backpack around, unzip it, and reach into its depths.
"I've got something for you." I bring out Snuffles. For a second,
I hold the worn teddy bear in my hands, gazing into his shiny
plastic eyes. I smooth down the hairs on his head as I say a silent
goodbye to him, then hand him over to Asha. "Sai bhai gave
this to me when I was even younger than you. I thought . . . I
thought maybe you could take care of him now."

Asha's eyes light up as she takes the teddy bear from me, her
lips parting. "What's his name?"

"Snuffles. Do you like him?"

She nods, then hugs him to her chest, burying her face in his
fur. "Thank you," she murmurs.

After a moment, Asha turns with Snuffles, and I follow her
inside, marveling at just how much she resembles Pinky Auntie. . . . And relieved there's no part of Bhavin I can see in her. I
send up a mental *thank you* to merciful genetics.

Asha leads me past a tiny kitchen and living room. I exchange
smiles with Pinky Auntie's hired help—a full-time caretaker,
Yogini, and part-time housekeeper and cook, Bharti. Personal
service is way cheaper in India, and Pinky Auntie said she can
afford to give them good salaries from her savings and inheri-
tance. Especially now that Dad wired his half to her.

Big brothers rule.

We get to a small bedroom in the back, where Pinky Auntie

is napping. Her face appears thinner, paler, more weathered. A blue-and-red chorso covers her legs.

I stop in the doorway, my feet frozen to the floor. *What hasn't my dear Pinky Auntie been through?* It takes everything in me not to back away. But Pinky Auntie and I have both been through a lot—maybe now, we can help each other on our healing journeys.

I swallow. "Pinky Auntie," I whisper, finally forcing myself into the room. I sink slowly into the chair next to her. I want to fling my arms around her, but I'm afraid it'll hurt her.

Pinky Auntie's eyes drift open. "Gita beta—I've missed you."

"I've missed you too," I squeak. My eyes fill with tears. "I-I . . . How—" I stop; if I say another word, I'll break.

"What is it, beta?"

I mash my lips together and shake my head.

"Come closer." She beckons to me.

I lean in, and Pinky Auntie holds my face, wiping away errant tears with her thumbs.

"No more chup-re," she says.

I blink a couple of times, then meet her gaze with my own. The love and understanding in her eyes softens everything in me.

"No more chup-re," I agree. I take a deep breath, exhale it slowly, and let the words pour out.

Dear Reader,

So much of this book is autobiographical to my own story, and, as I've witnessed in my work as a psychiatrist, similar to what many teens today still experience. If you've gone through—or are experiencing—anything similar to Gita, please know that you're not alone. Here are some free and confidential resources that you can reach out to at any time:

For anyone who has experienced or is experiencing sexual assault, or who knows someone who has or is, **RAINN** (Rape, Abuse & Incest National Network, rainn.org/resources) focuses on programs that prevent sexual violence, help survivors, and ensure that perpetrators are brought to justice. They have a National Sexual Assault Hotline with free and confidential 24/7 support. Call 800-656-4673 or chat online at hotline.rainn.org/online.

For anyone who is, or knows someone who is, experiencing suicidal thoughts, the **National Suicide and Crisis Lifeline** provides prevention and crisis resources and free and confidential 24/7 support for people in distress. Call 988 to reach them.

For anyone seeking information on sexual health (STD/HIV testing, birth control, emergency contraception, abortion, pregnancy, healthy relationships, identity, and more), **Planned Parenthood** (plannedparenthood.org) provides information, appointment scheduling and treatment, and free and confidential 24/7 online chat support for sexual health issues at roo.plannedparenthood.org/unifiedonboarding/intro.

You don't have to struggle or suffer alone. Please reach out for help. You're worth it, whether or not you believe it yet—I promise.

All my best,

Sonia Patel

ACKNOWLEDGMENTS

I wasn't alone in the process of transforming shadow, heat, light, pain, and love into Gita's words. My eternal gratitude goes out to the following people:

Victoria Wells Arms—my fantastic agent and muse—for falling in love with, and fearlessly championing, this book from the jump. For our laughs over F-bombs and spiders, and for her patient guidance in everything from the title to the big picture.

Rosie Ahmed, my brilliant editor, for her thoughtful vision and inspiring feedback that left me "charred and smoking"—like Gita during times of insight—and constantly including the term *next-level* in my email replies to her.

Stacey Barney, for profoundly shaping the initial manuscript with generous and astute insights, and Nancy Paulsen for steering it.

Regina Castillo, Jason Henry, Tabitha Dulla, Jayne Ziemba, Nicole Kiser, Sierra Pregosin, Nancy Mercado, Jen Klonsky, and the entire team at Dial Books and Penguin Young Readers, for their enthusiasm and tireless advocacy of this book.

Fatima Baig for this jaw-dropping, iconic cover, and Kristin Boyle for designing it.

J. L. Powers for her care and wise comments that allowed me to layer flesh onto the bones of draft zero.

Komal Patel, Payal Cudia, Priya Parmar, M.D., and Jose Manaligod, M.D., for their kindness and encouragement as they read an early version.

James, my husband, who's loved me all the while I've learned how to fully love myself and others.

Maya and Joaquin, my grown-up children—I'm awestruck by the two of you, period.

Hansa, my mother, for her strength. She taught me how to dig deep, how to survive. Your sacrifices gave me the privilege to thrive, Mom—thank you.